IDA AND MARTHA
A MONTANA STORY

Sara Fretz-Goering

 FriesenPress

Suite 300 - 990 Fort St
Victoria, BC, V8V 3K2
Canada

www.friesenpress.com

Copyright © 2018 by Sara Fretz-Goering
First Edition — 2018

ISBN
978-1-5255-2389-2 (Hardcover)
978-1-5255-2390-8 (Paperback)
978-1-5255-2391-5 (eBook)

1. FICTION

Distributed to the trade by The Ingram Book Company

To the real Martha Joy, who was the inspirational spark for this writing.

And to friends who think they see themselves in this book—please forgive me.

I am in love with Montana.
For other states I have admiration,
respect, recognition, even some affection,
but with Montana, it is love, and it's difficult
to analyze love when you're in it.
- John Steinbeck (*Travels with Charley*)

NOVEMBER

Of one thing Ida was certain: If she wanted to, she could wear blue jeans and flannel shirts the rest of her days. If she wanted to. It had taken seventy-two years to get to this place, and it sure was something not needing to please anyone. Not needing.

Even before looking at the clock Ida knew what time it was. Six a.m. The front door opened and closed and she heard Martha's boots shuffle across the porch floor. The slam of the screen door punctuated the sequel of morning sounds. Martha would be making her way through the blue-winter November darkness to tend to her horses. She'd be muttering on the current state of affairs as she hoisted buckets of water and throwing hay.

This was Ida's favorite time of day. In the sliver between dark and light, snuggled beneath the down comforter, she willed the physics of time and space to contract and suspend her there. Darkness was still a permeable essence hovering above the cottage, seeping in through the rafters into her bedroom. She listened to the silence but there was no such thing. *Her breathing. The humming of air. The sighing of the furnace. A heaving wind working up to some mischief outside.*

Burrowing deeper into the warmth of her blanketed cocoon, a childhood story rose up about miniature creatures living amidst roots and wormholes just beneath the earth's surface. Tiny souls amused themselves nurturing the soil (*much like microbes!*) so that beautiful plants sprouted and bloomed all year round, wreaking havoc in the human world by causing the unexpected to happen. Human beings were quick to believe these were miracles. Look! Colorful sprouts – even in snow – happening just for us!

Ida thought that memories were like these plants, rising up from the depths to surprise us at any given time. Everyone carried around this repository, a resource always at one's disposal. The narratives accumulated, waiting for self-expression and editing. With *age, more stories got collected and recollected. If only there was a way to organize and catalog the memories instead of our gray matter releasing them so quixotically.* She wished sometimes there really was a miniature benevolent world. If there was such an alternative community – intent on working for the common good of humans – life would be less burdensome. She wished she could even believe in an omniscient presence juggling life on this planet towards some goodness. Too often now any rosy thought was clouded by the recognition of potential harm. Toxins infiltrated our waterways, trickling through dark earth and into the foods we eat. Cancer cells hid in secret bunkers, hanging out sometimes decades, only to emerge one ordinary day in deathly attire. Even nibbling thoughts lay deceptively beneath the surface, and like weeds in certain conditions could one day rise up and overtake the rational garden.

IDA AND MARTHA
A Montana Story

How had her early morning reverie turned dour so quickly?
Tossing onto her side she again checked the clock: 6:42.
How did time do that? Time like an ever-rolling stream. She
was well aware in her seventy-second year that time was carrying her along that stream with entirely too much force.

What day is it? Saturday?. She'd consented to help Annie
with guest breakfasts on weekends until they hired more
help. *"Time to be up and doing/with a heart for any fate,"*
as her father had so often quoted. Longfellow? *Still pursuing,*
still something. *How did the rest of it go? Still achieving?*
Still pursuing?

Novels about cold, brusque Montana were full of gritty
characters toughened by nature's adversities. She'd known
cold. She'd lived *in Colorado for God's sake,* but she was still
a softy. She made her move, throwing the comforter back
and hot-footing it to the bathroom where an electric heater
provided her a warm dressing room.

The mirror reflected her pixie-like face framed by a tow-
headed mop of short, shaggy hair. Honestly, there were
days when she'd just forget to comb it. Now the ends were
proceeding to lengthen and explore their own direction of
growth. She'd have to ask Martha for a trusty person to cut
her hair, as well as a doctor and dentist who at least gave
the appearance of being personable and attentive. Moving
geographically required more than a new mindset. A dab of
tinted moisturizer helped camouflage a sprinkling of freck-
les and dark spots around her eyes. A quick brush of her
teeth and she was off for the day.

"Let us then be up and doing with a heart for any fate/
Still achieving, still pursuing/Learn to labor and to wait."

Longfellow. That's it. Henry Wadsworth Longfellow. Don't get too smug, Ida, just for recalling some tidbit of a poem. Where was Peabody? Out with Martha no doubt. She bundled up in her coat and gloves and stepped onto the porch,into the morning chill.. *Cold yes, but not brutish.* The snow layers were light and powdery this early in the season. Peabody, her steady companion, came running full speed toward her, wiggling his old bottom in pure joy, and then was off sniffing his favorite spots, tenaciously on the prowl.

Ida paused midway in her walk as she so often did these days. A gibbous moon hung low in the sky, balancing atop a mountain peak. Rustlings in the woods behind her were either white tailed deer or ubiquitous nomadic elk making their way to somewhere else. No moose sightings this morning. Earlier in the fall after she'd just arrived, she'd seen a mama moose with her baby drinking from the buckets they used for rain water. Observing the maternal bond from the safety of the porch, she'd been cautiously respectful of the solid distance between herself and the thousand pound creature. Martha said there was nothing meaner than a mama moose protecting her young. She'd best keep Peabody by her side. While a horse might kick a dog for being a nusiance, a moose wouldn't think twice about stomping it to death.

The ranch nestled between two mountain ranges in Big Sky country – the Gallatins to the east and the Madisons on the west. In the distance, a curtain of Douglas firs edged the perimeter of the ranch, indicating where the foothills began their ascent. Pasture land stretched to the north and west geometrically marked by fence boundaries. Aspens with their ghostly trunks cozied up to Ida and Martha's cottage and the two cabin bunkhouses nextdoor. The barn, recently repainted a dark green, lay to the north with the garden and a chicken coop between it and the old garage. Completing the panoramic circle was the original farmhouse with an appendage of guest rooms attached, like a long tail bent to the northwest. A painted wooden sign flapped in the morning wind: *The Dusky Grouse Guest House & Ranch.*

Ida crossed a paved driveway to reach the guest house. Through the kitchen windows she could see Martha's daughter setting plates and silverware out on the buffet. Annie, in her late forties, was full of kinetic energy and one who thrived on challenges. This morning she appeared flustered, fluttering at full throttle between the buffet and the counter..

Ida stopped her dawdling and hustled to the back door. "Good morning Annie. Sorry I'm running late." She hung up her coat and grabbed a pull-over apron from another wooden hook. "What's the rush?"

"I just want to get this group out the door by nine. They were very insistent about that last night."

"Are they all together?"

"Yes, skiers and snowboarders." Annie stopped laying out the dinnerware and turned towards Ida. "I'm sorry. I've forgotten my manners. Good morning. And thank you for coming in this morning."

"Goodness, Annie. Don't you worry about me. I'm family now and family sometimes just takes one another for granted, isn't that right? I said I'd help you Saturday and

Sunday mornings." Ida tied the apron and opened the oven to check the muffins.

"You're definitely family now. I just get preoccupied with things running right since we opened and I think I forget to be civil."

"Annie, you're one of the sweetest persons I know, and I seriously doubt you'd know how to be *uncivil.*" Ida had come to know Martha's daughter in the past few months as earnest and self-confident, but even those who appeared strong and assertive sometimes needed reassurance . "You're off to a bang-up start in this business. And keeping it simple with only a breakfast for guests is pure genius. Guests can take care of themselves for their other meals with all the touristy places around here."

Just then a young man with a sprouted goatee emerged from the hall to the guest rooms, all cheer and good will. "Hey, good morning. Anything I can do to help?"

"Help yourself to coffee or juice," Annie replied. She swiveled around to address other guests bee-lining toward the coffeemaker. "Good morning! Looks like you know the drill. Please make yourselves at home!"

A young woman tugged her fleece jacket snugly around her as she sipped her black coffee. "I have to say I really like this place. It's so cozy tucked back in the woods."

Her friend nodded. "So serene. And much quieter than the big resorts." She turned to Annie standing at the head of the extended wood table. "How do you keep this place running?"

"Mainly on caffeine," said Annie holding up her mug. "It's a new venture for us, but we're learning daily."

"And the name? How did you come up with the name – the Dusky Grouse ranch?"

Ida leaped in. "I love this story. Martha – that's Annie's mother – told me about a grouse that kept thumping his desires when they were building this place. Pretty noisy, and he was doing his mating call night and day. She said it sounded like a tractor starting up – three slow thumps, then whap, whap, whap – and it drove her crazy for weeks. One morning she got up at three a.m. to get a drink of water and heard the grouse outside her kitchen window thumping away. She said to him, 'Go get yourself a girlfriend. I'm not the one you want.' Next morning, he was gone."

"Was he gone for good?" chuckled the young man with the goatee.

"Only for about three weeks," Ida replied, "but Martha reported he was much more subdued when he returned."

"Like some boyfriends I've had," cracked one of the women.

"And the bird was a dusky grouse?"

"I think the breed is also called the blue grouse."

"I like the name," said a young woman with a ponytail. She pointed to the walls and windows around her. "I love all this wood and the natural light."

"It has a European feel to it – clean and simple lines," added another. "It's really unusual to have single beds in the U.S."

"We decided on single beds because we cater to older travelers in groups and many of them are singles who don't mind roommates. We do have a couple of rooms with queen beds."

"Can I be nosy and ask how you got started?" asked a guest.

Annie took a sip of coffee. "My mom encouraged the building of the guesthouse after my dad died. We built ten bedrooms and bathrooms in the back wing so we could host up to twenty guests. We made sure it was on one floor with at least four rooms wheelchair accessible. Then we renovated this part – the country kitchen and gathering space."

"And you all live and work here?" asked the ponytailed woman.

"I live upstairs with my daughter, Elsa, but she's away at college now. Mom and Ida live in the cottage."

"And I'm Ida." Ida sat down beside the ponytailed woman who responded with a smile and a wave of her hand.

"I'm Lily," she said, then pointed outside. "And you raise horses?"

"Martha – Annie's mom – rules the kingdom of the stables."

"Are guests allowed to ride them?"

"The ones here are draft horses, working horses. They'll use them for trail rides when it's warmer," Ida explained. As if she knew what she was talking about. She was just rattling off what Martha had told her.

"And sleigh rides too," added Annie. "We're starting those in December."

"Would it be possible so see them? The horses?" asked Lily.

"Sure. You can wander out there on your own or I could take you. I wouldn't want Martha to scare you."

"I took lessons when I was twelve. I've just always had a thing for horses."

The others finished up and left to get ready for their day on the slopes. Lily hung back, helping to clear plates and scrape leftovers into the compost bucket.

"You don't need to help. Go get ready," Annie said as she loaded the dishwasher.

"I wondered. Will you be taking on extra help?" Lily asked.

"I hadn't thought about it." Annie responded slowly. "We definitely will in the summer. But aren't you in college?"

A clamoring from the back door indicated Martha was making her entrance, a basket of eggs held high in one hand. She was as petite as Ida, but her strong, muscled body gave the impression of a large determined presence blowing in. Long, dark hair, graying in wavy strands, framed a stoical and weathered face. She had it pulled back to stay out of the way. Hazel eyes twinkled as she stomped the snow off her boots. "Damn it, you mean I missed the guests again?"

"Your timing is impeccable," Ida remarked, "but Annie and I haven't eaten, so yes please, scrambled if you would."

Martha nodded at her with just a hint of a smile and pointed to the egg basket on the counter. "There they are."

"Mom," Annie nodded in the direction of the young guest, "this is Lily. She's interested in coming to work here."

Martha took her time removing and hanging her coat by the back door before turning towards the guest. "Do you know anything about horses?"

Lily shrugged. "I took riding lessons when I was twelve. That doesn't mean much but I've always wanted to learn more."

"Well, learning's always a good thing." Martha loosened her work boots and kicked them off. "And how do you feel about shoveling horse shit?"

"It's just a job," Lily responded. She pulled her long hair from the ponytail forward where she playfully curled it around her fingers. "That's kind of like asking a mother how she feels about diapers."

"You've might have a point there." Martha abruptly dropped her arms and disappeared into the pantry, emerging shortly with a hefty bag of dog food, which she dropped ceremoniously by the back door, flicking dust off her two hands. "If you do come here to work, you know you might have to clean toilets and do other things that are none too appealing."

Lily nodded. "I'm not afraid of working hard."

"We don't have an application form yet. It's one more thing on my *to do* list," said Annie. "Maybe after we create our website."

"I know a little about that too," said Lily, drying her hands on a dish towel.

"Too bad you can't start today," Annie smiled. "Let's talk about this summer as a possibility. Maybe this evening?"

"I'd like that." Lily folded the towel meticulously and laid it on the counter. "Well I did come here to ski. I'm sorry to have to rush off."

"We'll see you this evening." Annie waved in her direction and began loading the dishwasher without looking at her mother.

Ida finished chopping an onion and tossed the pieces into the frying pan where they sizzled and splattered. She turned away from the silent engagement of mother and daughter to crack some eggs into a bowl. Bits of spinach were tossed in with the onion. Whisking the eggs suddenly required a concentrated effort. She added shredded cheese before flipping the rest of the mixture into the skillet.

Martha poured coffee into three mugs and sat down at the rustic table. "We don't need to hire rich college kids."

"She's a guest. You could be friendlier," Annie admonished. "We may not need the help right now but we will."

"What happened to just hiring locals?"

Annie jabbed the dirty silverware into the dishwasher cutlery slots, piece by piece. "I know your feelings about that, and I agree in principle, but it's just not practical. We never had a ten-room guest house before."

"Well I don't want anybody else messing with the horses. Moses is all I need and I pay him enough." Martha leaned back waiting for the next charge.

Annie threw her hands up in the air. "Moses is over eighty years old! You can't keep relying on him for all the heavy work!"

"Really?" asked Ida. "He's over eighty?"

"We celebrated his eightieth birthday last summer," Martha said, setting her cup firmly on the table.

Annie rolled her eyes. "It was his eighty-*fourth birthday!*"

"Eighty or eighty-four, what's the difference?" said Martha. "You can stop worrying about me."

"What's the expression – you're no spring chicken?" asked Annie. "Even with the tractor, you and Moses are both doing more lifting than you should."

Three plates of eggs and toast were laid on the table, and Martha settled into eating.

"The housekeeping help is good right now," Annie continued, "but we need to hire someone for the horses. You can't keep ignoring that. We've got to figure out trail rides – maybe with another ranch."

Martha got up to retrieve the salt and pepper. "Sure feels like snow is coming."

Ida and Annie exchanged looks. Martha was done with the discussion.

"I heard five or six inches by the end of the day. Enough to make the skiers happy," Ida responded.

"I'm kind of worried about old Molly. She's not eating the mash I give her."

"Is she pretty old?" Ida had no idea how long horses lived.

"She's old at thirty with lots of wear and tear on her knees."

"Like us, eh?"

"Just like us. I hate to shoot her but her teeth are whittled down to nothing and she's in pain just hobbling around."

"Shoot her? Really?" asked Ida. "Then what?"

"We get a backhoe and bury her in a hole between us and the farm next door. It's that or get a rendering truck to come take her."

Annie shook her head as she stood up. "Mom, you sound so tough but I know it gets to you every single time an animal has to be put down."

"I don't like to think about horses dying, that's for sure."

Ida was curious now. "Don't they do cremation of large animals? I read about that somewhere."

"That's way too expensive out here. We couldn't afford that every time one of the horses died."

"I guess I have moved to the Wild West. Have you ever had to shoot one of your horses?"

"I have to confess – I let Moses do that."

"With a shotgun?" asked Ida.

"Well, a rifle. I could do it. I just don't want to. Horses get hurt all sorts of ways out here and have to be put down."

"Like by what? Bears?"

"Well, yes, there could be bears, although we haven't spotted them for some time now. Around here, mountain lions attack horses and cattle. Even wolves have been known to ham-string a horse and start eating it before it's dead. It's pretty gruesome."

"It's awful." Ida said, pushing her chair back and abruptly standing up. The grisliness of the stories disturbed her morning equilibrium. She didn't like to think about such violence in the natural world around her. She didn't like to think about violence—period. She took her time at the sink rinsing plates and silverware.

"But horses get hurt by running into branches, impaling themselves." Martha was going full steam now. "I had one horse came back from the pasture one day with a two-inch gash that was actually a hole in its side. I sprayed water on it and felt around but couldn't find anything. Remember that, Annie? I took her to the vet in the truck and he dug around inside and found two pieces of a branch."

Annie was too busy tidying up to bother acknowledging her mother's ramblings. But Ida, shaking her head in disbelief and disgust, sat down again ready to engage in what had become their daily morning ritual: a heart-to-heart conversation over coffee at the old kitchen table. Martha scrutinized Ida's face and continued, "It's something none of us like. Does that kind of bother you? Killing animals with our guns?"

"I know in my head I should be able to reconcile this use of guns, but not in my heart."

"Nobody likes shooting their own animals."

"I just don't care for guns."

"What about hunting? Is it okay to use rifles for hunting?" Martha enjoyed pushing the argument.

"Of course, for hunting. And I understand how you need to use one to put down an animal. I just don't like guns."

"Well, there's a different attitude out here." Martha tapped her fingers on the table. "If you drive by a high school in town, nine times out of ten, there will be pick-up trucks with rifles in the back windows. 'Course they're supposed to park across the street – not on school property."

"You're telling me kids might be hunting on their way home from school?"

"Yep, that's what I'm telling you. Or before school. They're not being reckless with their rifles."

"No one starts out being reckless. But accidents happen all of the time. And I just don't get folks shooting for fun

– target practice – when the ultimate purpose of a gun is to maim or kill. That's what I can't get past."

"Target practice is necessary to be accurate when you do shoot for hunting. Otherwise, you might have a mess," clarified Martha. "You'd have an injured animal bleeding to death."

Ida looked at her hands. "So, you're trying to put the animal out of its misery."

"Well, you're trying to prevent the misery."

"With an accurate shot?"

"Exactly. That's why we do target practice."

"Okay. That makes sense with rifles. But handguns are not used for hunting."

"You never know when a gun could save your life."

Ida looked skeptically at her old friend. "Or when a gun could..." She left it hanging. "Is there one in our cottage that I don't know about?"

"There's a handgun locked up in the office there," Martha nodded behind her, "and a rifle in the barn."

"Are they both locked up?"

"It's not the law out here, but I prefer it that way."

"Okay then." Ida was done.

Martha had to add her two cents. "Okay then."

Annie scurried back through the kitchen and out the back door to talk to the van driver. The guests followed, geared up for hitting the slopes for the day.

The two women sat in silence, regarding the fluttering of activity out the window. The thought again came to Ida that she needed to wake up. Here in Montana at this stage of life, healthy, content, being useful, not used up. With a best friend she'd met over forty years ago. How had this happened so effortlessly? *Over forty years.*

Just three years ago she'd read in their college news that Dan had died from cancer. She'd sought Martha's address and sent her a note of condolence.

"Why don't you come for a visit?" was Martha's response.

Ida drove out to visit her old friend. She stayed a few days, then a few more, then another week. Martha threw out the "what if?" scenarios. What if Ida pulled up stakes and moved to windy, cold Montana? What if they built a cottage to grow old in? What if they helped Annie and Elsa with the guest house?

Ida considered her connection with Martha. Certain people fell into one's life, fitting snugly into the puzzle: into the self-map. She claimed she could hear the click. When they left, the space opened into a sacred fractal. Where did they go? Why? The pondering went on for years. Were they still connected by invisible bread crumbs, ethereal threads across miles, decades, death? When she'd heard a lecture by a cosmologist on "entangled particles," she suspected her theory was correct. Actions performed on one particle can affect another, though separated by distance and time. To Ida, it was just a notion, a feeling. She regarded it more as a belongingness, to something or someone outside herself. Invisible threads. Things not easily seen. She'd had her friend in her thoughts many times over the years.

On a visit she'd made to Mesa Verde National Park in southern Colorado, a ranger had elicited responses from the guided tour group to his question, "Why do people move?" Jobs. Boredom. Retirement. Climate. Family. War. Political persecution. Love. No one had called out, *To live with an old friend into old age.*

"What are you thinking?" Martha awakened Ida from her meandering thoughts. "Something deep?"

"I was thinking about you, me, friendships."

"Martha's eyes held apprehension. "Having second thoughts about this move?"

"Nope. I was thinking it's all pretty remarkable really. Think back to when we were in our twenties. You, me, a commune in Kansas?"

"A *collective*," Martha corrected her, "not a commune. Seems like we've had this conversation before."

"Yes, and every time I remember it with you, it seems like we recall something else!"

"Like how we drifted apart?"

"In my memory you left so impulsively – throwing your belongings haphazardly into the back of a truck. You and Dan traveling around the country, looking for a place to live."

"We were in love. We were romantic vagabonds out on the road! It was just our luck we ended up in Montana in September. Talk about summer suckers. We froze in our tepee that winter, barely getting by waiting tables and dishwashing."

"That's when we lost touch. You wrote about that winter and looking for wrangler jobs and then, no more letters."

"We kept moving around the state so I didn't have an address. I look back and think how naive we were. And I left you. I'm sorry now. I was pretty self-centered."

"We were in our twenties," Ida stated wryly.

"That excuse again."

"And anyway, we had to leave each other. We were headed in different directions."

"Like the country mouse and the city mouse." Martha smiled.

"I got serious about doing something with my life. Destiny and all that." Ida could be flip.

"And all I've done is play with horses," Martha stated.

"But you've always loved them."

Martha nodded. "I can't deny that. One of my first memories was riding the ponies around in a circle at a rodeo side show. The cowboy running the event winked at my dad and said, 'We need someone who's willing to test ride each of these little ponies. Do you think your girl here is up for that?' Talk about destiny."

"I think that's how most of us get going on a path in life. A happenchance encounter of some sort that wakes us up or makes us think about our lives differently."

"So, did your Boulder friends think you were crazy for moving here?"

"Are you kidding? They staged interventions for me."

"Like group confrontations?" Martha was laughing now.

"One friend brought over a map of the United States and pointed to Montana. She said, 'See, it's almost Canada.' And I said, well, good, maybe there's universal health care."

"Don't get me started on that!. Damn federal government can't get it right."

"Canada got it done right a long time ago." Ida had opinions too. "It wouldn't be that hard if our political parties weren't so divisive…and self-righteous!"

"Should turn it over to the states," replied Martha.

"Okay," Ida sighed, "We'll never agree on this, so let's move on." She picked at a crumb of toast on the table.

"You have to admit most folks our age move south to a retirement community."

"We'll make community here. We've got a start with three generations of women and a revolving door of guests."

"And Moses, don't forget my old friend, Moses."

"One of my friends talked about creating a compound with her friends. That was pretty funny. A compound."

Martha smiled at this but she had something else on her mind. She twirled a spoon in her two hands, spinning it, and thinking. "I want you to be able to tell me if this move here to Montana doesn't feel right for you. I know it took a lot of gumption to leave the home you created in Boulder."

Ida responded slowly. "This was a leap of faith for me really, but I was ready. I think a lot about threads of love; the way lives stitch together over time. And I needed to change my landscape, my community, my life, but probably wouldn't have if you hadn't reached out. Change is hard, and we don't often make necessary changes until something cataclysmic happens to nudge us. I often can't find words but I feel there is such a mystery to it all."

"Like some grand plan?"

"Not quite. More like threads spinning in one's life."

"It can't have been easy to pull up and move here. Giving up lots of security with what you'd known."

"Well, it's not the usual expected move, but your friendship means a lot – and the concept of the guest house bringing in folks of all ages from all over the world meant I wasn't just moving to an isolated ranch."

"Still, I know you had a good life in Boulder."

Ida thought how moving across the country, selling her old car, eliminating material things had been relatively easy, like shedding old weight. Leaving relationships – not so much. Yet after only a few months, those friendships were memories; memories that had a habit of springing up to be noticed when she was doing some innocuous chore – say, making a bed, raking leaves, washing a coffee mug. In this day and age, one could stay in touch and connect online at any time. It was the intention and the continued effort that required work – like any friendship near or far away. "Thank you letting me bring my good old dog, Peabody."

"Peabody's a human in dog form. Anyway, you'd never give him up."

"You know we're the lucky ones to have made it this far. Alive. Semi-cognizant."

"Only a few aches and pains." Martha grimaced. "So far."

"And more importantly, now we can look back and see the narrow escapes, the choices we could have made."

"God no, I don't want to think about it. The choices I made were bad enough." Martha ran her hands through her hair.

"I think as we age we live with our choices better, not blaming or regretting. Accepting the givens."

"If Dan hadn't played the fiddle in that band, I wouldn't have fallen for him. How's that for a simple twist of fate?"

Ida pondered. "See, but maybe music is one of those intangible influences we don't think about. Music, popular fiction, cultural trends, our parents' voices…those unconscious things that move and sway us."

"Joni Mitchell?" laughed Martha. "We lived and breathed her lyrics for a time."

"Absolutely," agreed Ida. "Joni was our archetype."

"But I caved and did the conventional thing. Marriage. Family."

"You were never conventional. You tried to fit the mold, but sorry, nope, didn't quite work," Ida said.

"You were the one who made me question things. After we parted, I didn't have your compass badgering me."

"Badgering?"

"You know what I mean," said Martha.

"I still think it's kind of amazing how our lives forty years ago still affect us today. Who I was in my twenties is kind of parallel to who I feel I'm becoming now – in my seventies!" Ida was testing out this newfound theory.

"I think I've changed a lot," said Martha.

"We both have changed, but there are still so many parallels to who we were," responded Ida. "Our essence is the same."

"I'm glad there wasn't more damage done."

"This morning I'm reveling in the here and now – feeling something quite profound." Ida's index finger traced the grain of the planks on the table, suddenly aware of the lines in the wood itself.

"You are profound. How can you be *feeling* profound?" asked Martha.

"I've been thinking about a poem where happiness arrives as the unexpected guest. We can keep inviting it to come in, but happiness seems to arrive in its own time and place."

"Or unhappiness," said Martha.

"Unhappiness. Yes, that too. For sure. How do we get the two to meet?" asked Ida. "Unhappiness. Happiness. On a line that meets in the middle somewhere."

"How Buddhist of you," observed Martha.

"The Middle Way?"

"The Middle Path." Martha let out a sigh. "Ok, enough of this." Pushing back her chair, she stood up and padded over to her work boots by the door. She forced her feet into each one, flung her arms into a well-worn plaid coat and strode out into the cold, her silk kerchief flying in the wind.

Ida would get up soon and go about her business, but a few minutes of quiet contemplation never hurt anyone. In fact, she knew, a few moments of solitary silence was sometimes the only balm that could heal.

WINTERING

DECEMBER

ONE

The first week of December brought more snow and twelve elder travelers to the Dusky Grouse. A tour company called *Verdant Pathways (VP),* catered to the actively retired, mixing education with adventure and social engagement with group activities. Annie was giddy to have these regular guests booked every Tuesday, Wednesday, and Thursday for eleven months of the year. The VP guests ranged in age from sixty to ninety, travelers from countries all over the world. Day excursions took them to Yellowstone, parts of the Lewis and Clark trail, Big Sky, and the surrounding Madison and Gallatin mountains. In the spring and summer, the tour would include Glacier Park, but it closed in fall and winter.

Ida suggested a social hour in the late afternoon for the Verdant Pathway travelers. She envisioned having hot drinks and wine in the cozy living room for guests to unwind together before getting picked up for dinner.

"They're dropped off by four-thirty every day and picked up at six again. Some might want to nap but I think having a place to unwind and gather would be lovely," explained Ida.

"Are you volunteering to staff this hour?" asked Annie.

"Sure. I think three afternoons a week would be doable."

"Then you need to give up the breakfast time," said Martha. "The afternoon hour could be your responsibility."

Ida looked at Annie tentatively. "If Annie can manage the breakfasts without me."

"Yep, I can do breakfasts. I will hire help in the spring and summer, but I can manage for a few months. I also suggest having a tip jar to help defer costs of tea and wine, and appetizers if you start that."

"Tips? Seriously?" asked Ida. "I'd feel funny about that."

"You're serving them like a wait staff," replied Annie. "We need to figure out something to help with those expenses because they'll add up fast. And I don't want to deal with a liquor license. Not for something like this."

"I'll try it with a jar with single dollars on the wine buffet, but no sign. Let's see what happens this week."

Truth be told, she looked forward to these social interaction with the older guests. Of the things she missed most from her previous life, it was simply having coffee and lunches with friends. The social hour might prove to be mutually beneficial.

On this particular afternoon, the second week of December, Ida stacked sticks and newspaper in the massive fireplace and struck a match. Red and ochre flames kicked up. She placed two logs at angles over the excited sparks. She'd become an excellent fire-maker.

Pine garlands with mini-lights were strung on the smaller trees, illuminating the front yard. Battery candles in all the windows of the farmhouse and cottage cast that ambience of good cheer and welcome in the winter season. An eight-foot Douglas fir tree with lights and home-made ornaments was making itself at home in the corner of the living room, sending out a sense that the world was all right, if not always peaceful.

A rosy-cheeked older gentleman approached Ida from the wing with the guest rooms. "Well, what have we here? A delightful spread of cheese and crackers *and drinks?*" He beamed.

"Well good afternoon sir," Ida replied playfully. "Would you like some wine or a hot beverage?"

"I'd really like an Irish whiskey, but I think I might settle for a glass of that red stuff." He pointed to the Malbec. He pulled out his wallet, fumbled with a couple of bills and stuffed them into the jar with a "Thank-you!" beside it.

"Ah, Mort, always the first one in the bar," called another white-bearded man.

"You know me Stephen, the official taster," responded Mort as he took a few sips. "Yes, Yes, I pronounce this a very fine wine indeed."

"How many glasses have you downed?" asked his friend on his way to the buffet.

"I'm not keeling over yet."

"Very well, then that's what I am having," Stephen filled his glass, then pivoted around to evaluate the room. "What a lovely fire!"

Other guests entered and congregated around the buffet to select drinks and nibbles. Soon their phones and cameras were passed around for photo sharing.

Ida approached a petite woman with short, gray hair and black-rimmed glasses standing off to the side. "How was your tour of Yellowstone? See any wildlife?"

"Yes, we did. The bison were out and about. Probably just for our benefit."

"That was kind of them to show up!" Ida chuckled.

"Let's see, we also saw bighorn sheep. And then on the ride back this afternoon we spotted wolves. Our guide told us they're repopulating the park."

"Yes, they've been moving northward. The ranchers are not enamored with them since they kill a lot of the farm animals." *Here I am sounding like Martha.* "Wolves are known to ham-string their prey and start eating before it's dead. Gruesome yes, and none of us want to see wolves come into this area. It's a bit controversial but wolves are deadly killers around here."

"Oh my," was all the older guest could utter.

"I apologize for telling you this." She held out her hand in greeting. "I'm Ida."

"It's nice to meet you. My name is Gretel."

Was that a European accent? "Gretel…as in Hansel and…?"

"Yes, yes, and also like the little Von Trapp girl in *The Sound of Music!*"

"Oh that's right…the youngest girl?"

"Yes, but the spelling of her name was G-r-e-t-l. Mine is Gret-e-l."

"A bit of trivia to know," responded Ida. "Are you Swiss or Austrian by chance?"

"I was born in Holland but I've lived in the States all of my life."

"So you probably don't remember the tulip fields?" asked Ida.

"No, not really," Gretel shifted her footing and placed her hand on the back of a chair. "This trip was a gift from my son for my eightieth birthday!" she announced proudly.

"Oh my goodness! Happy Birthday!"

"Thank you," Gretel nodded shyly. "It's been a good trip and quite special for me."

Mort called to them from his comfy chair where he held court with the others. "Gretel, Ida, come join us here by this ferocious fire."

Ida's hand directed Gretel over to the group. "Tell me about the snow coach. That's something I'd like to do some time."

"Oh that was wonderful! Like riding in a warm bubble across the snow!" said Gretel.

"A very noisy bubble!" interjected a woman named Florence.

"Well, what *was* really noisy were all those skimobiles whizzing around us!" exclaimed Stephen.

"But we were humbled by those hardy souls on snow bikes," said Mort. "I didn't know there were such things until today."

"Old Faithful was old faithful being right on time," said Florence.

"And not too many people at this time of year," remarked another guest. "I loved eating in the dining hall of the Old Faithful lodge, but..." He lowered his voice..." I'm personally glad we're not staying there."

"The lodge had its rustic charm." said another.

"I, for one, appreciated hearing about the diversity in the animal population," remarked John, one of the retired scientists.

"Diversity? What do you mean?" grumbled a white-haired man called Al.

"I meant that it's a healthy thing for the national parks to have a wide variety of wildlife. It gets tricky when one species becomes prey and gets wiped out," explained John.

Al grunted, "What about the grizzly bears? What would you do if one of them charged you?"

John wasn't about to get trapped into an argument. "Well, you heard the guide. He said some folks believe bear spray works better than a pistol. People have their agendas on either side of this debate."

"The grizzly has his agenda too!" snapped Al. "When a grizzly's coming toward you, I bet you he won't be thinking about the *diversity* of the species."

Ida tactfully changed the subject. "Were there any favorite things?"

"I liked the mud pots!" exclaimed one lady. "They just seemed like some kind of soup simmering on the earth's surface."

"Primordial soup!" remarked John.

Mort held up his index finger. "I think I'll always remember the anecdote about the baby bison falling into a hot springs, boiling to death, and the place smelling like beef stew for days. "

"Oh that's just awful, Mort," responded Florence. "Personally, I was spooked by those hot springs."

"It was like what I imagine walking on the moon to be," said Stephen.

Gretel nodded. "I had no idea Yellowstone was a volcano."

"*Is a* volcano! A super volcano!" John jumped to his feet in his excited state. "I read where scientists are calculating when it might be active again, and when it does, mass destruction could occur."

"Thanks John, for bringing that warm glow to this happy hour here," teased Mort. "Nothing like talk of mass destruction to spread some cheer."

"Oh, I do apologize. I get carried away sometimes."

"I'd like to come back and see Glacier Park in the summertime," remarked Stephen.

There was a sigh from Gretel. "I wish I would see the glaciers while they're still here."

Mort chuckled. "Hell, I wish I could see them while *I'm* still here!"

"I thought we'd agreed not to talk about climate change," retorted Al sharply.

His wife intervened. "Nobody said anything about climate change except you. They're just making observations."

"Yeah well, I know they'll work it in sometime."

Florence raised her glass as if to make a toast. "How about that old-fashioned sleigh ride we're going to get? Nothing like that where I come from in Mississippi!"

"Is that Thursday?" asked Mort. He looked around for confirmation.

"Yes," nodded Gretel. "It's on the last evening here. Florence and I were talking about it last night before bed."

"That was our girl talk," giggled Florence. She smiled happily at Gretel and turned around towards Ida. "Say, is that stud of a cowboy going to be one of the drivers?"

Ida was amused. "You mean Moses?"

"If that's the-fine looking man I saw outside, then that's who I'm talking about," Florence said.

"I think Moses is the designated driver for the sleigh ride."

"Well then I want to make sure I get on if Moses is at the reins!" declared Florence. "Gretel, you're on your own."

Gretel smiled. "Moses will have his hands full with the horses and Florence. Will there be one or two horses?"

"Definitely two with the big wooden sleigh," stated Ida.

"A TWO-horse sleigh, you say?" Stephen asked in a teasing manner. He began singing enthusiastically, "Dashing through the snow/ on a TWO-horse open sleigh/ O'er the fields we go/ laughing all the way. Ha Ha Ha." Several others in the group moaned, now familiar with Stephen's corny humor.

A rapping on the front door indicated their tour guide had arrived, and he stepped in. "Looks to me like you're all warmed up for a great evening."

The guests hurriedly bundled into coats and scarves, humming "Jingle Bells" as they headed out the door for their dinner at a local restaurant.

"Have a lovely time!" Ida called as the last guest filed out. She cleaned up the glasses and cups of tea. Noting bills overflowing in the jar she stopped to do a quick count. Over thirty dollars! She couldn't expect the cash help every day and with every group, but it was nice to know folks were willing to help out with these extra expenses.

Christmas music? A little atmosphere might be nice in the next few weeks. She'd talk to Annie about that. She clicked off the lamps and stepped back to appraise the twinkling reflections on the fragrant Christmas tree. What was it about this ritual that still elicited childhood happiness? Ida poured herself a glass of the red and sat down by the fire. Peace, perfect peace. Martha was probably heating up leftovers in the cottage, waiting for Ida and the seven o'clock news. That was fine. She would head over soon. But for now, peace, perfect peace.

TWO

Ida could hardly contain her excitement about the Thursday night sleigh ride with her newly made friends from the Verdant Pathways group. Old fashioned bells twisted around the harnesses and clusters of miniature lights circled the rigging around the heavy wooden sled. The largest draft horses, Grayson and Black Hawk, were partnered up as old working buddies. They chafed at their bits, eager to get out on this cold winter night to do their appointed jobs.

Ida walked out with Florence to wait for Moses and the horses at the front door. As the sleigh pulled up, Florence called out merrily to Moses, "Hey there, handsome. Going my way?"

Moses jumped down off the sleigh and tipped his hat toward the two women. There was a softness in his handsome cragged features and a dignity in the way he carried the image of the legendary old black cowboy. "Good evening. I assume you're talking to one of my horses? Would you like some assistance?"

"I would like some assistance from you!" Florence exclaimed, "Good manners and good looks! My kind of man!"

Moses looked toward the house and then the ground. He put out his hand to Florence and quickly lifted her onto the sled. He turned again towards the house and stepped towards Ida, who was carrying a bundle of blankets.

"Can I help you with those?" he asked, quick to get out of Florence's range of vision.

"Oh Moses," Florence called out. "I'm just joshing you. I just like to tease."

"It's okay ma'am, but if it's all the same to you, I'd rather just do my job here," said Moses. Gretel appeared then and he bustled over to help her into the sleigh, wanting no displays of favoritism.

"Thank you, Moses," Gretel said as she held onto his arm. "Bless your heart."

He glanced at her, "I haven't heard that expression in years!"

"Bless your heart? It's one of those old sayings that seems to cover everything." Gretel explained simply.

Moses gave her a second look. "I just haven't heard it in a long time."

Ida tucked blankets around Florence and Gretel and whispered, "He's a bit shy. He's not one for easy conversation."

Ida tossed comforters around the others who snuggled together on the large sled, then jumped up to sit between Martha and Moses. They were off then into the cold darkness. A quarter-moon appeared front and center amidst the stars splattered above on the massive canvas. The miniature lights bundled to the sleigh appeared as swarms of fireflies moving in mass migrations through the darkness. The horses kept a steady pace over an open meadow, through a grove of aspens, and into a deeper trail through part of the woods.

Martha whispered to Ida. "Wait till we stop. Bet you ten bucks someone points out Orion in the sky and the others go nuts."

Ida was mesmerized by the artwork of shadows and light on the snowy ground. And the smell. She could not describe it. Hints of pine and earth and air. Why weren't there more words for air, for oxygen, this breath, this voidness?

Moses slowed his horses to a stop where they could see the open sky. There were myriad stars scattered above them. They sat in the stillness, present to the moment that they'd been informed would happen. To be alive and to witness the natural world – at night – far from artificial light – in winter – was an awesome thing.

"There's Orion!" John pointed to the constellation above them. All the others oohed and aahed and pointed skyward too. Martha gave Ida a nudge.

They returned to the guest house a little colder but with a fuller appreciation of the vast western night sky. Hot drinks and cookies awaited them. Annie helped gather the blankets and comforters while Moses attended to those in his command, helping them down one by one. Ida waited to lend an arm if needed. As Moses assisted Gretel he said, "I've been thinking about that expression you used. I'm kind of wondering what you meant by 'it covers everything'?"

Once down on firm ground, Gretel took Ida's arm for stability as she watched Florence descend. "Well we say it when someone is good and when someone is not so good. I could say, That Florence, she just takes care of everybody – bless her heart. Or I might say, That Florence, she's just into everybody's business – bless her heart."

Florence exclaimed, "I like that! So I could say – that good for nothin' man done me wrong again – bless his heart!"

Gretel laughed. "Yes, that's it!" She glanced shyly at Moses. "Or maybe – that man's just doing the best he can – bless his heart."

"Gretel, girl, you are such a sweetie," said Florence. "Bless your heart. But I'm cold as the dickens out here! Thank you again, Moses!" She headed into the house, waving her hand in farewell.

Gretel stood firm, one hand on Ida, one hand on the sleigh. "It says a lot and not much at all." Her Dutch accent was barely perceptible.

Moses began backing away, reaching for the lines. "It's kind of forgiving somebody without having to say it."

"Yes," she nodded, pushing her glasses up on her nose. She looked as if she wanted to say more, but he was already up on the sleigh, lifting the lines for the horses to go. Ida let Gretel take her elbow as they shuffled into the warm kitchen. After removing her gloves and coat, Gretel took her glasses off and wiped condensation from the lenses. She motioned to a chair opposite her at the kitchen table. "Could you sit down with me for a spell?"

Seeing distress on the older woman's face Ida asked, "Gretel, what's wrong?"

"Moses, the man who works here, did he come up here from Kansas do you know?"

Ida nodded. "I believe that's right. He worked for Martha's dad back in Kansas and she asked him to come here to work on the ranch. It was a long time ago."

"Over fifty years ago," Gretel responded.

"Yes, that's probably right." Ida eyed Gretel intently. "Do you think you know him?"

The eighty-year old sighed softly. "Yes, I knew him back when we were both young and foolish, although Moses was never foolish, not really. It's a long story." She looked down at her hands folded on the table. "I fell in love with him and never fell out of love with him...that was the problem. My husband didn't love me. For years I wanted a divorce and he refused. He was the sort of man who liked to control everybody. "

Gretel shook her head and stared at the table, seemingly lost in a memory. "And it wasn't just because I loved another man. It was because I loved a black man. I didn't care if he hurt me anymore, but I knew he would find ways to hurt Moses. It was such a painful time and I don't wish to bring that up with Moses now." Gretel looked towards the window only to catch her own reflection. "This thing we call time, what a strange thing. It just helps us understand our days here. But time is rather unimportant when you get to my age."

"Do you think Moses knew who you were tonight?"

Gretel shook her head. "I don't think he recognized me. We look so different. And he would never expect to see me here. Not now. I had to search to find him. And I thought coming on this tour – at my age – would be the best way to find him."

"I believe Moses would very much like to see you and know you were here," Ida said kindly.

"Perhaps he would," Gretel sighed. "But how do we get the old moments back? We don't. Memories are always getting stuck."

Ida reached out and took the aged hands in her own.

Gretel went on, "I'm very tired tonight. Please don't share this with anyone, least of all Moses."

"I can respect this, but you've come all this way."

"We left each other a long time ago. Over fifty years. I don't want to bother him. What's that saying – it's all water under the bridge. We all...this life...we just keep flowing along like water."

"But sometimes the water returns to where it came from," smiled Ida.

"Oh dearie, thank you for listening to an old woman ramble on." She patted Ida's hand and pushed herself up from the chair using the armrests for support. "I'm very tired, and I think you are too. Let's just sleep on it tonight. I may feel differently in the morning."

How very strange. Strange for a love story. Ida had also been under the impression Moses was gay. Martha had told her Moses attended gay rodeos when he was younger.

Ida had long ago discarded easy definitions of love, even sexual love, but she knew there were many things she'd never understand about the ways of the human heart. *What was love really?* Gretel had waited a long time and had traveled a long way to see her old friend. Whatever they had meant to each other, it was a relationship long buried in the heart's attic.

THREE

At six the next morning Ida was wide awake, replaying the conversation with Gretel over and over, trying to discern a clue to the mystery. It was baffling how someone could travel this far in distance and in years, but be timid then about revealing her identify. Ida wanted to understand. Maybe it wasn't fear or shyness, but respect for Moses' life and not wishing to intrude into it. From her few encounters with Gretel so far, that intention would make sense. And both Moses and Gretel appeared to be quiet, private people.

Moses routinely arrived later in the morning, and Ida would keep an eye out for him. She got up and began scurrying about the guest house kitchen, doing all her tasks routinely now: the apron, the stove, the coffeemaker, the setting out of the drinks.

Annie fumbled with opening the office door, her hands full of papers for last minute signatures from the tour guide. She placed them on the kitchen counter with Mort following behind her.

"Didn't we just say goodnight to you?" he asked.

"We never sleep – as you can see." Annie's arm swept out to acknowledge Ida's domesticity in the kitchen.

Mort bowed with an exaggerated flourish. "We are indebted to you for running such a fine establishment." He began helping himself to the buffet, apparently wanting to get a head start on the other guests, now trickling into the room. Each one greeted Annie and Ida and continued to express gratitude. Was it generational to show gratefulness and good manners? Even Al, the sourpuss, muttered a thank-you to Ida on the side.

It was after everyone was seated and eating that Ida noticed Gretel's absence. "Florence, aren't you Gretel's roommate? Was she okay this morning?"

"She didn't say anything when I said I was leaving for breakfast, but she often gets up after I do. Should I go check on her?"

"Would you mind if I toasted some bread to go with these hard-boiled eggs?" asked Stephen. "I'd love to eat my eggs with toast."

Ida pointed to the toaster on the counter. "Please help yourself." It pleased her that they felt at home here. She whispered to Florence, "You enjoy your breakfast. I'll go check on Gretel. What's your room number?"

"Number 3." Florence's attention was on a warm blueberry muffin.

At the door of Number 3 Ida heard no sounds coming from behind the door. She knocked twice and called out, "Gretel, it's Ida. Are you okay?"

She rapped harder one more time. *Nothing.* Now she was alarmed. After testing the handle, she took out the set of manager's keys. She was a little rattled. *Which key? Why won't it turn?* Finally, after several attempts, the key flipped and the door handle turned.

A crumpled comforter covered a lumpy shape on the bed. Gently Ida lifted the top duvet. Gretel's kind eyes were closed and her silver-grey hair sprawled over the pillow, her forehead cold. Ida gave her a nudge. "Gretel? Gretel?" She moved to lift a stiff wrist. No pulse. She sat down on the bed beside the still presence. No breath.

Gretel was dead. She was no longer here. Ida needed a few minutes to comprehend, to acknowledge it. *She is here, but not here. Gone into the drift.*

A paperback book of poems and a National Parks pamphlet lay on the bedside table. Ida picked up the poetry book and quickly laid it back down. It just seemed disrespectful, an intrusion, to look further. There were multiple bookmarks stuck in its pages. A plastic prescription bottle lay behind the book. Without her reading glasses, she couldn't make out any of the other words. They were a blur.

Ida hadn't thought about dying for several years now. *Death is so strangely miraculous really. How it comes on its own terms.* She placed her hand upon Gretel's. *Maybe you did come here to die. Maybe the reason is beyond our understanding.*

Florence entered behind her. Ida stood up motioning to the still presence on the bed. "Gretel died the way most of us would like to – in a deep, peaceful sleep."

Florence stopped, looking from the body back to Ida. "She's dead?"

"Yes, I'm sorry." Ida said.

"Last night as we were getting ready for bed, she said she felt so awfully tired. I didn't pay her much attention. I said I was too. I'm…I don't know…"

Ida moved to put her arms around the older woman.

"I'm so sorry," Florence mumbled.

"Yes, it's a shock. But she died peacefully." Ida softly turned Florence toward the door. "Let's go back to the kitchen. We'll sort it out."

Florence took a step back. "She seemed so alive! Healthier than I am!"

"Yes, she was vibrant." Ida pulled the comforter over Gretel's head and they left the room together. The door locked automatically behind them.

First things first, Ida thought. *I'll call 911.* She headed for the office while Florence informed the group and Annie about Gretel's death. They listened through the open door as Ida explained the situation to the dispatcher, repeating things several times to clarify. After hanging up, she stood silently for a few solitary minutes to breathe and comprehend what had just happened.

Annie stuck her head into the office, "You okay?"

"Yes, yes, fine. I just need a moment, thanks."

"I radioed Mom. She'll be over soon."

Ida stood up. *Numbness.* This she recalled. This coldness was often regarded as stoicism in the grieving, but it was a tourniquet for the emotions, a natural procedure to buy time to just keep going. She walked into the kitchen where the others were attempting to sort out the event.

"Gretel was a very sweet lady," said one of the women. "She was always so kind."

"Did she have children?" asked Mort.

"She had one son, but she never wanted to talk about him," remarked Florence.

Another woman added, "I was complaining about being cold the other morning and she said to me, 'A little chill is good for you…lets you know you're alive!'" The woman blushed as the irony of her statement took hold.

Florence said thoughtfully, "Yes, she had an innocence about her. She hadn't traveled much."

"I hate to say it but none of us are getting younger. It could have been any one of us," said Al.

"There but for the grace of God go you or I?" puzzled Mort.

There were murmurs of agreement; others shook their heads despondently.

"Not to be insensitive, but are we going to continue the tour on schedule?" asked Stephen.

"I would think so," said Ida. "You may have to delay leaving for a couple of hours till the police are done. But we have guests arriving tonight, so we need to get the rooms cleaned and ready this afternoon."

Annie hung up the phone and approached the group. "The sheriff is on his way. The coroner and rescue-medics will be here too as they have to pronounce her...Gretel... dead. They may want to talk to you, but don't worry. It's just to get a full report. They'll take the body and notify her family."

"Are we allowed to go back to our rooms?" asked one of the guests.

"I think everyone except Florence can pack up and bring your bags to the living room. You won't be leaving until later this morning. Florence, you'd better wait here."

"Yes, I believe I'll do that," Florence replied sadly. The other women in the group clustered around her, patting her hand, giving her hugs. One by one they left to pack up their things in an attempt at normalcy in what was a very unusual beginning to the day.

Martha burst into the room seemingly propelled by cold air. She looked at Ida and motioned her to a corner of the living room. Ida explained in whispers what had happened. "Are you okay?" asked Martha.

"Strangely, yes." Ida replied. "I'm fine. It's not the same, if that's what you're thinking."

"Still…it shouldn't have been you having to walk into that room."

"Death and shock and grief," said Ida. "Every death is different. We will get through this. I just have to fix on the things that need doing right now."

"Yeah, okay, that's what we can do. Focus on now." Martha turned and walked over to Florence to say something, then turned to Annie. "Can you call around to get more help to clean this afternoon before the next guests arrive?"

"Already taken care of," Annie responded.

The sheriff arrived first, followed by the paramedics and the coroner. Annie directed them to Room 3 and returned quickly to sit with Ida and Martha. The sheriff had a few questions for them. What about Gretel's next of kin? What information could the tour company provide? Annie signed papers without reading the fine print. It was death by natural causes. This was not considered a crime scene. Nevertheless, the sheriff rifled through Gretel's suitcase and took the bottle of prescription pills for analysis. Relatives of the deceased would be contacted to claim the personal stuff so Annie agreed to store Gretel's personal belongings in her office till notified.

The body was carried away under a white sheet on a padded gurney. Florence quickly went to pack up her things as the others huddled together in the living room, ill at ease, making idle comments. Ida built a fire for want of something to do. Martha and Moses came in from doing chores, perhaps with intentions of showing respect but their unease pervaded the room. Moses pulled out a chair to sit, decided against it, and stood near the window facing the front yard. Martha's attention was focused on one thumbnail.

Annie carried Gretel's book of poems out to where people were gathered. "Would it be fitting to read a poem or two from this book – since it was by her bed?"

"I'd like that," Florence answered.

"Absolutely fitting," muttered Mort.

Annie held out the book to Ida. "You choose one."

Ida fingered through the faded pages and found several sticky notes indicating poems Gretel may have read more than once. She stopped at a page where specific phrases had been underlined in blue ink and beside the title was the word "Yes" with numerous exclamation marks.

"I'm going to read this one. It must have been a favorite." Ida cleared her throat:

A New Thing is Creating
by Janet Umble Reedy

The bleak landscape holds me
like a womb.
I never loved the winter fields,
brown and dead they stretch to the horizon as I pass,
dry stubble, sad vestiges of life and hope.
Bare branches like the gnarled hands

of ancient crones
beseech the brooding sky,
are met with icy silence.

In this season of my life
the fields of winter suit my state of mind.
The past is gone.

Within this space
where sunlight is not seen day after day,
as I once grew to life within a womb,
a new thing is creating.
Ink drawing on gray paper sky,
the naked trees and fields in muted shades
of beige, gold, brown,
mauve, lavender, and rose,
gaudy green leaves like excess finery discarded,
buds will emerge soon enough.

Stripped of distraction
in this winter season, the roots and branches of my life
endure,
sustain the waiting.

A few seconds had ticked by when Mort broke the silence. "What a beautiful poem, even if it wrenches the heart."

"It's very fitting for this winter tour," commented Florence. "I like that – something about the fields of winter suiting my mind."

Ida searched for the line and reread, "In this season of my life, the fields of winter suit my state of mind. The past is gone."

"And what were those last lines about roots and branches of my life?" asked John.

"Stripped of distraction in this winter season, the roots and branches of my life endure, sustain the waiting," Ida read clearly.

"Yes." John nodded. "Roots and branches of my life endure."

Moses coughed slightly and spoke up. "Last evening after the sleigh ride she shared a favorite expression of hers. I've been thinking on it this morning and would just like to say, well, bless her heart."

Florence looked up. "That's right. She used that expression a lot. I said it last night and I'll say it again – she was a real sweetie, bless her heart."

Several others repeated the lines like an invocation. "Bless her heart." "Bless her heart."

"Could you print that poem for us?" asked Florence. "I'd like that."

Annie said she'd make a copy and send it through the company email. Soon they were standing and shuffling about, gathering coats and daypacks. Moses left unobtrusively by the back door. Luggage was packed into the van; it was time to say good-bye. Bundled in their padded vests and coats the guests waddled out to the tour bus.

Ida and Martha quickly tossed on coats to follow them outside. They wouldn't make a habit of getting this familiar with guests. When the van was a speck at the end of the snow-packed lane, Martha turned to her old friend. "Should I ask?"

Ida took a deep breath and stared at the ground. "I know what you're thinking, but it's not the same. My baby was stillborn. That was different," she swallowed. "I've sat with many through death since then."

"Still – the very deepest of sorrows," Martha replied.

"I don't think about her every day anymore, but when I do, my God it hurts." Something inside her, a vise between the throat and her heart, clenched tight. She couldn't speak.

Martha was not given to physical acts of comfort. She couldn't reach out to Ida because it was not in her nature to be consoling. She didn't know how.

Ida took off her mitten and rubbed her eyes. "I'm sorry."

Martha patted her softly on the shoulder. "It's a mess, this life."

"Yes, but you! Here I am slobbering away, and you've lost Dan, and it's just, oh it's just with us all the time, this death stuff."

Martha nodded. "It hurts bad some days, and other days I want it to hurt more."

They both looked out to the mountains as if for a sign, a holy condolence. Finally, Martha spoke, "We come into this world, we live, we die. That's it…but yep, it's painful shit sometimes along the way." She tugged on her gloves as if to make them more secure.

Ida grabbed those gloved hands and turned them upwards, open palmed. "Thank you, Martha, for being here for me."

"Don't start with that thank you stuff. You know I don't like it."

"Did you hear the poem I just read? And the last lines; "the roots and branches of my life endure, sustain the waiting – as a new thing is creating? Like the title?"

"I heard it and I get it and I'm here for you in this – what – winter of our lives? But sometimes I think all that gratefulness crap is just a way of saying, well lucky me, I lucked out, hit or miss, too bad for everyone else."

"Oh for pity's sake! Here we are with open hands wondering what next? It's okay to be grateful," exclaimed Ida.

"I'm grateful for farmers who get food to my table."

"Well, there you go!"

"I'm thankful for vets who treat my horses."

"And scientists who discover medical cures?"

"Yeah, maybe."

"See…you can be grateful."

"I'm not grateful for luck in life…as if I was especially blessed."

"But look at your life. You have a wonderful daughter and a granddaughter and Moses and me! You have your horses and a warm home!"

"So who am I thanking for all this? A God, a spirit, who has granted me these things?"

"Probably not the material things, but possibly the healthy heart and mind to be able to be conscientiously thankful?"

Martha shook her head. "Okay, so I'm grateful you're here. There. Leave it at that. Now I'm onto being practical."

"You have a practical heart," said Ida. "A practical, grateful heart."

"What's the point of this?"

I'm still thankful for what is. My palms are open. And before you say you have work to do, *I* have work to do.

Martha pulled back, squinting with a playful glint in her eyes. "What needs doing?"

"Bedsheets, laundry, cleaning toilets," said Ida. "The real poetry of life."

"Mucking horse shit," added Martha.

"And where there's horse shit, there's a pony!" reminded Ida.

"And with that I'm out of here," Martha announced as she secured the hat on her head and pulled up her neck scarf. She spun towards the barn.

"It's meaningful if I *choose* to do it, right?" called Ida. "Maybe I should come out and shovel manure."

"Maybe you should."

Peabody loped happily towards Martha and ran circles around her. He did his wild dog dance running frantically, giddily in large figure eights as Martha made her way across the frozen snow. He sidled up to Ida then, checking for treats before scooting off to roll in the snow. Later that afternoon, she'd likely find him curled up on the rug like a canine Buddha. Dogs.

"Okay, let me get on with this day – stripped of distraction, with my roots and branches intact." *Yes, let me accept these things and move on, grateful, grateful, grateful, despite what old practical Martha says.* Ida shut the door by leaning back into it, her fanny pushing hard to close it completely, securely, tightly. In this winter state of mind she did indeed contemplate the roots and branches of her life and how they sustained her as she faced the uncertainty of the years ahead. Was there a new thing creating?

FOUR

Monday morning, Ida took her "Things to Do" stack of stickies and hefted herself up into the cab of Martha's rusty old Dodge Ram. Across the dashboard she stuck up the rainbow papers in a chronological flow-chart. Fitting the key into the ignition was her first challenge. Though accustomed to the truck's sensitivity, she nevertheless felt impatient with it. Martha and Dan had named it Ornery Gus for a reason. She gunned the motor and shifted into gear. A revving noise indicated otherwise. *Come on you old cuss. Move into gear. Good, there it was: a satisfying clunk.* She'd have to buy a car of her own, a dependable new one. She fumbled for her sunglasses as a glare reflected off the snowpack. It felt too warm for December, certainly too warm for a Montana Christmas. She hoped the forecast of a cold front from the Canadian Rockies was accurate.

In the village she followed the "To Do" stickies in order: Bank. Yoga. Library. Haircut. Groceries. She found a parking spot behind the bank and hunted through her backpack bag to find the paper-clipped checks and deposit slip. She hustled around the brick building, entering the front door. A young woman behind the plastic window smiled sweetly and asked if she knew she could make her deposits at the Drive-Thru ATM.

"Yes, I do know, but I prefer to see my money taken by a breathing human being, thank you." She bit back the urge to ask, "And you are a human being aren't you? "She was rarely catty but she knew she could be.

"There's a real live person at one of the windows of the Drive-Thru ATM," responded the young woman. Her tone indicated she'd been trained to deal with difficult customers.

"Really? That's something new." Ida turned away, and then thinking she'd been a tad impolite added, "Thank you for your help." She peered into the ATM window as she passed. *Where is the person now?*

Her "old woman's yoga" class was led by Madeleine, an instructor in her early eighties, who was far more flexible than her students in their sixties and seventies. She guided them through stretches that were gentle to bodies prone to arthritis and osteoporosis. CDs of humming voices, harpsichord melodies, and sometimes YoYo Ma's Bach concertos played in the geriatric boombox.

Today Josephine was waiting for her, sitting upright with her legs twisted beneath her. Tall, gaunt, with high cheek bones, she had an aura of self-importance that seemed to dismiss the idea that she herself could age. In another era, she might have been labeled a busybody socialite, with gossip being her drug of choice. "Hi Ida. We heard about the death at the ranch! It's so tragic!"

"I was sorry to hear about this," added Madeleine. "It must have been devastating for you and the guests."

Ida stood on a mat weighing how much to share. "She was a lovely person. The whole tour group was very upset. We're still processing it all." She lay down on her back and shut her eyes, attempting to segue into a meditative state.

Someone shuffled beside her and there was a gentle kick on her leg. Josephine whispered, "Hey Ida, was there foul play involved?"

Ida refused to open her eyes. She sighed and said, "No Josephine, no foul play."

Madeleine calmly instructed everyone to breathe deeply, imagine their bodies sinking into the mats, and let the day fade slowly away. "Remember to keep palms up if you have osteoporosis. Palms outward for maximum stretch. Remember don't push your body to do anything that feels painful. Stretch. Flex. Breathe."

Ida escaped from all of her swirling thoughts. Where she went during this hour she wasn't sure, but she always left feeling calmed. Transfixed.

After the final chimes and "namaste" Josephine turned to Ida again. "Hey I just noticed your second toe is longer than your big toe. Did you know that?"

"I guess I hadn't noticed," said Ida. "I think it's called a 'hammer toe' but I never really took notice of the length."

"It also means you can curl your tongue, which is a sign you're good with languages. Are you a linguist? Do you speak more than one language?"

"I'm actually lousy with languages but I do love words." Ida managed to spout as she stood and stretched. "I had no idea our toes could tell us so much about ourselves."

"Oh yes," said Josephine, "our appendages indicate a lot about who we are."

Ida chuckled. "Well now that I know that, I might take up learning Spanish again." She hurriedly packed up her things and headed for the bulletin board. "Thanks for that tidbit!"

"There's more where that came from," called Josephine, tapping her head.

Ida scanned the community board for the announcement she'd posted the previous week. It was printed on bright, neon-green paper. She noted three of the contact tabs were torn off the bottom. She re-read the announcement she had penned:

> **Women of a Certain Age (WoCA)** - Women who are close to sixty or over. I'm looking to gather a group of strong-minded woman together for monthly discussions on issues of pertinent interest as we "age."
>
> (This is not a book group although we can be open to that once in a while.) We'll brainstorm topics that relate to who we are, eat a little, drink a little, and share our stories. If interested, contact me at the email below.

Ida wondered why she hadn't seen any emails from these interested parties. She'd check when she got home. She suspected Josephine might be one of the early responders.

At the gas station she filled the tank before heading into the "library" at the back of the store. Five book shelves in a corner, fiction and non-fiction, met the literacy needs of the community. Western thrillers and mysteries were the favorites but she'd often found a classic or a current best seller on the Most Read shelves. She quickly browsed the covers. A snappy title was worth something.

On a side street she located the 411 address of Martha's hair-cutter friend who lived above a boutique. She double checked the address, trudged up the outside stairs and lifted the knocker, which appeared to be a painted woodpecker. She released the spring and heard it tap three times. The door opened to reveal a large woman with hair twisted wildly in a nest of curls; her face a darkened weathered brown.

"Hi, I'm Ida? Are you Carol?"

"You Martha's friend?" The woman had not even the hint of a smile.

"Yes, that's me. Martha said you were the best haircutter around for miles," Ida said, pointing to her head. "I was hoping you could do something with this mop."

Carol's eyes examined the unruly chopped hair and nodded. "Yep, best get started on that." She opened the door and gestured toward a chair on wheels by a mirror on the wall. "I'll get a pillow, since you're kind of short."

Ida removed her outerwear and placed it and her bag on a small couch in the corner. The "kitchen" appeared to be a multi-purpose room: laundry, living, cooking, dining, and haircutting. Carol pulled the chair to a deep sink and indicated that Ida should sit to get her hair washed. Ida leaned back on a soft towel. It didn't strain her neck as she had imagined it might.

Carol wrapped a towel around Ida's head and swiveled the chair slightly to face the mirror. She combed out the tangles and regarded Ida's hair. "Looks like you have layers all over the place. Do you want it as short as here?" She pointed to the Ida's ear lobe.

Ida nodded. "Yes, I like to keep it simple."

"Well, I'm going to cut along these same lines and edges and you should end up with what you want. You scream if I start cutting somewhere I shouldn't." Like a surgeon preparing for a major operation Carol laid out various sizes of clippers, an electric razor, and several combs. Wasting no time she held up a swath of hair and snipped away. "So you're the one who knew Martha way back when she was a young rabble-rouser."

"As opposed to an *old* rabble-rouser?"

"I'll tell you, that woman likes to come across as a crusty old broad but she's a little pussycat with a heart of gold." Carol leaned over Ida's shoulder and squinted her eyes into the mirror.

"She sets me straight whenever she can."

Carol kept her eyes on Ida's hair. "You came to a mighty cold place and a long distance just to live with an old friend."

Ida respond cautiously. "Martha and I were good friends at an important time in our lives. After I came to visit after Dan died, it was clear our friendship was still pretty much intact."

Carol squinted at Ida in the mirror. "You're just friends."

It took a moment for Ida to realize this was a question. "Neither one of us had a sister. I think we're like sisters to each other. But she's so much stronger than I am. Lifting fifty-pound saddles every day. Running a ranch for years. I look up to her as if she were my older sister."

Carol finally let herself smile. "Back in the day, she took on the big developers when they first started excavating land in Big Sky. She started organizing some of us to get off our butts to take on Turner and the rest of them big landowners."

"I didn't know that."

"There's still a lot of big money coming in from outside the state. Your little guest ranch up there closer to Bozeman, well, that's the kind of family-run place these fat cats would like to squelch. But the locals will support you all."

"Annie runs the place. Martha and I just help on the side."

Carol stopped snipping and bent to look at Ida's reflection. She put down the shears to finger both sides of Ida's hair length, pulling it down to eye whether it was even on both sides. She fussed with the hair at the back. "Martha was around when I needed a safe place to hide from my ex-husband. He got kind of wacko before the divorce was final. Threatening me, even stalking me.. Martha let me stay in one of the bunkhouses for about a year. She never charged me a cent. I guess I owe her some."

"Was this when Dan was still living?"

"It was the last year he was really sick, in and out of the hospital. She didn't need to help me on top of all that, but she did." Carol picked up a hairdryer in her right hand and blew warm air through the short tresses. With her left hand she fluffed up the layers. "How does this look to you? I think it looks great."

Ida felt free of the weight of several inches of hair. She felt her neck. "I think I like it. I can let it grow and not worry about a cut for a couple of months."

Carol appraised her work. "I think I did a damn good job. I cut it more bluntly so you shouldn't need a cut for a while. Let it grow."

Ida got up and dug around in her bag for her wallet. "How much do I owe you?"

"Tell you what. I'll give this one free if you tell Martha she's due for a haircut too. Between the two of you letting your hair get all shaggy, it doesn't pay for me to charge."

Ida pulled out a couple of twenties. "Really, I want to pay."

Carol pushed the hand away. "I said no. Just come back, okay?"

Ida nodded. "I'll definitely do that."

Carol opened the door. "Ida. You're all right." Somehow Ida had passed muster.

Back to Old Gus for one final errand. She parked front-first at the grocery market in order to pull out easily. As she jumped down from the high seat she spotted Moses shuffling towards the front door limping from an old rodeo injury.

Ida called out, "Hey Moses."

He turned in his stilted way to see who was yelling. "Hi there, young lady," he grinned, tipping his cowboy hat. "Martha finally drive you away?"

"Somebody has to take care of the real business of running the place," she said. "This way I can also buy my contraband on the side."

"You came to the right place." He held the door as they entered. "I know you came to buy more than just groceries. Wine is that direction." He pointed down an aisle.

"Is it written on my face?" Ida laughed.

"I figure any friend of Martha's has got to drink something harder than water," Moses said with a devilish grin. "That woman could drive Jesus to drink."

"Oh now, Moses, we don't need to blame Martha for our vices. I take full responsibility."

He waved as he sauntered away.

Gretel's last words came to her. Ida hadn't mentioned that conversation to anyone else. She watched him from a distance as he picked up frozen items for his solo dinners. *We've got to have him for meals more often. We can do that.* She bustled around the store tossing this and that in the cart and caught him as he was going through the self-service checking line. "Moses," she called to get his attention. "Can you come for Christmas dinner – if you don't have other plans already."

Moses scratched his chin and nodded. "That would be nice to do. Thank you, Miss Ida. I'd like that."

"Ok, great. It'll just be us women and you."

"That's fine by me." He concentrated on his last item and got out his credit card, fumbling with his wallet a long time. He looked up and caught her eye. "I wanted to tell you I liked the poem you read for the lady who died. My sympathies to her family – and to you. "

Ida's lips felt dry. "It was a poem from a book of hers that was marked up pretty well."

"Something about it made me think I heard it before," Moses said as he picked up his bag, "but I'm not big on poetry."

Ida deliberated. Gretel had asked her not to say anything to Moses, but now she was gone, and if there was an old connection between them, was it up to her to bring it up? Indecision.

Moses stood at the cashier counter as Ida unloaded her cart. He cleared his throat and spoke, "I've got a buddy who would appreciate a home-made Christmas dinner. We were going to go to a restaurant together. You think it'd be okay to bring him along?"

"Of course. Yes. Please invite him. Anyone Martha knows?"

"Oh sure she knows him. He plays guitar in Dan's old band – and a mean ukulele."

" A mean ukulele?" she laughed, "How can that be?"

"Oh it be. You'll have to come hear the band when they play up at Jack's next weekend. So anyway, it's okay to bring him on Christmas?"

"It's fine. Please bring him."

"Ok, thanks. I'll do that. Be seeing you." He waved his hand and was gone.

Too late. She hadn't said anything about Gretel's disclosure. What would she have said? So many years had passed. If you're not expecting to see someone, it's easy not to recognize them after so many years. Maybe Gretel was right about letting the water run under the bridge and flow to wherever it's going, out to the everlasting sea. Well, maybe that's not what Gretel said.

Gretel had said to leave it be, she'd sleep on it. Perhaps Ida should do the same.

FIVE

A week to the day after they'd discovered Gretel's body, an officer from the Bozeman police department phoned the farmhouse as they finished breakfast. The guests had departed. Martha picked up the phone in the office. "Yep… Sure thing… Okay…Fine and dandy… See you then."

Annie and Ida looked at her expectantly. Martha helped herself to another cup of coffee and sat down. "An officer named Elaine somebody is on her way out to talk to us."

"About Gretel?" asked Ida.

"She didn't say. Just that she had some stuff to talk to us about."

"Sounds serious," said Annie.

"I assume they've been in touch with the morgue," said Ida. "I wonder about Gretel's last wishes. Which reminds me – Annie, you know about the lock box in my bedroom, right? If something should happen to me, my will and last wishes are there. DNR."

"What?" asked Martha. "What are you talking about?"

"My will, a legal will, to take care of my prized possessions, you know, like my books!" said Ida.

"Yeah, but DNR…"

"Do NOT Resuscitate!" Ida enunciated.

"In any instance? No grey areas?" asked Martha.

"Oh come on, do you want to be resuscitated? Seriously? If I can make a quick go of it, please let me go. And cremation for sure. Or maybe that new thing called regeneration – like composting the body. Just don't let my body hang around taking up space."

Martha eyed the ceiling. She heaved a sigh.

"Stop it, Martha. I just want you both to know what would make me happy if I die and you don't know what to do. It helps to have it all in writing," responded Ida.

"I agree," said Annie. "Mom, we should both make out wills."

Martha poured out the cold coffee in the sink and put on her coat and boots. "Radio me in the barn when the officer shows up."

Annie looked at Ida after Martha shut the door. She threw up her hands. "What does she think?"

"She doesn't. You know she's one for just letting life throw at us what it will."

"But after Dad's death, you'd think she'd want to get stuff in order. We had to second guess what he'd want. It's like they never talked. Horses die, the rendering truck comes or we use the neighbor's backhoe and bury them. Chickens die, we give them to our carnivore neighbors. Dogs die, we bury them in our little gravesite up the hill. Dad died and we scrambled. What would he want? He never talked. None of us could bring the subject up if he didn't. We guessed…cremation."

"Did you scatter his ashes?"

"I found a wooden box online. Mom was okay with that. We buried the box at the community church cemetery. Mom wanted a marker, so that was important."

"Maybe I'll ask her if we could visit the cemetery sometime. Do you think she'd go?"

Annie thought about it. "She might. I really don't know if she goes there on her own. She doesn't talk about it. Surprise, surprise."

They heard the sound of a car pulling up to the house. "We'll talk more. We will." Ida said reassuringly. She opened the door for the officer. "You must be Elaine."

"Are there others who live here?" asked the officer. "I need all of you to hear this latest information."

"I'll ring my mom in the barn." Annie hurried to the office.

"Coffee?" asked Ida, holding out the pot.

"Yes, thank you, I never turn down coffee," replied Elaine. She sat down at the table and opened up her computer "Wifi password?"

"Let me get the Wifi card." Ida returned with the information and placed it next to the cup of coffee. She took a seat across from the officer. Within minutes Martha and Annie were there.

"First things first," said the officer. "The story is that this woman called herself Gretel but was not really Gretel. Her legal name was Miriam Mailer. Six months ago, she inherited a significant amount of money from her husband who apparently, she separated from, like years and years ago. Never divorced. There are lots of missing pieces. She was also homeless for some of that time, living on the streets."

"Homeless?" exclaimed Annie. "Really?"

"Wait a minute," Ida interjected, "She wasn't from the Netherlands?"

"Here's the thing. She was born in Amsterdam and moved to the States, to Kansas, with her mother when she was a child. It may have been an arranged marriage or something like a mail-order bride situation. Her mother was single with this child. The name changed to Miriam when she began school. Maybe the kids teased her about the name Gretel. She grew up in Kansas and then married some guy, let's see, yeah his name was A.J. Mailer. So, another name change – Miriam Mailer. When he died six months ago, she inherited his money and kept her married name for financial accounts. She's been using her maiden name socially."

"So the Dutch accent was a ruse?" Ida was incredulous.

"Remember her mother was Dutch so she grew up hearing that accent and language," reasoned Elaine.

"Why the story about her son paying for this trip for her eightieth birthday?" Annie questioned.

"Well this is where it gets interesting. This *Miriam* had a baby which she gave up for adoption.. Once adopted there are no legal connections, so he's not considered next of kin. However, it appears he was in contact with her before she took this trip."

"So she didn't just make up the son as something to talk about with the others? Children and grandchildren are a prevailing topic for older folks," said Ida.

"And folks our age." Martha glanced at Ida.

"Was she actually eighty or was that made-up too?" Ida inquired.

"According to the records she was eighty," declared Elaine. "And here's another puzzler. She had medication with her – Benezonatate, which is commonly used to alleviate breathing problems. But the analysis revealed a mixture of pills." She skimmed the notes. "Benzodiazepines…which can be harmful and even lethal, especially in older folks."

"What are you saying? That she may have been poisoned?" asked Annie.

"I can't say for sure. I don't want to conjecture."

"Are you thinking it might have been one of the other guests?" Annie leaned in. "A cozy murder mystery here at the old inn?"

Elaine shook her head. "It may have been an overdose on her part. It happens when older folks forget if they've taken their meds or not. You wouldn't believe how many folks overdose on aspirin.

"And what's our part in all this?" asked Annie.

"The attorney for the bank should be contacting you. Sorry I can't give you a time frame. I've never had anything quite like this to deal with."

"Just so weird," muttered Annie.

"She had that slight accent. And then with the name – Gretel – I thought for sure she was from Austria when I first met her." Ida shook her head. "She had me fooled."

"Maybe she was just having some fun being someone else," said Martha. "You know, just acting and playing a character?"

"She certainly had it down," Ida replied. *What about Moses? Maybe by taking the pseudonym, Gretel was trying to disguise her identity. Should I say something? Maybe I should speak to Moses before anyone else. Even before Martha.*

"People are just not who we think they are," said Martha. "I think it happens more than we think."

"What now?" asked Annie "We have a suitcase full of belongings and her body in a morgue in Bozeman. Any directives?"

Elaine continued. "She's not exactly a Jane Doe."

"What happens then? Will she be cremated?" asked Ida.

"In cases where the body is not identified or where no one claims responsibility, the state turns the body over to medical facilities for research. If the facilities can't take the corpse for some reason, the state pays for a cremation."

The women had nothing more to say. It was a lot of information to absorb.

"Keep her belongings for now. You might want to go through them quickly just to check for other possible clues. We really can't treat it like a crime." Elaine rose to leave.

Annie walked her to the door. "Please keep us informed if you find out anything else,"

Ida went to the office to retrieve Miriam's suitcase, which she dragged into the great room and opened. The book of poetry was on top. With her reading glasses on her head, she put them on and skimmed through the book. There were a few dog-eared pages.

Ida took a few more minutes to sort through the clothes, holding up each item for closer inspection: a buttoned-up flowered blouse, a pair of elastic-waist, black stretchy pants, a heavy knit beige cardigan, white cotton panties. She quickly folded the clothing in a tidy pile and shut the suitcase. Unwinding her legs stiffly, Ida stood to get her balance, then limped to the office lugging the suitcase. An image of a homeless Miriam came to mind, pulling this bag behind her on a crowded street, not unlike a hermit crab Ida had once seen on a beach, scuttling along the sand, his backend tucked into a cola can.

Many people live quiet private lives, secluded in homes, apartments, farms, huts. Perhaps they find solace in their solitariness, their aloneness, their privacy. They are found the world over. It's not fair to judge them. It was hard to understand how a life could come to that illusiveness, the utter lack of a family or a community or a tribe. Perhaps it happened over time, that settling into the comfort of a space, a pattern of existence, until it just seemed natural. The *everydayness* of it.

But she just couldn't get over how one could live without a sense of belonging to something or someone beyond the self. Truthfully, how does one live with oneself without a connection to the world, a frame of reference for the self – to the world of something, a belief system, a purpose, a neighbor, a friend. Maybe a memory could keep one tethered to a place in the world, a memory of someone, or a memory of a time, a memory that held the roots of who one was – or who they thought they were.

SIX

Thick, billowy snowflakes fell throughout Saturday night to create a heavy white icing geo-scape the following morning. Ida got up once during the night to peer out the window. *So beautiful when one is safe and warm inside. What happens to all the life underground, buried beneath comforters of snow?* She quickly climbed back under her fluffy duvet and felt a soulfulness, a heartfullness that bordered on giddiness. *I'm such a child really.*

Ida had planned to attend the small congregational church in town but there was no going anywhere this morning. What would the guests stranded at the ranch do? How deep would the snow be? How soon would the plows come? The contract was for them to plow early and often to keep the lane to the highway open. Would they be able to get through?

When she heard Martha rattling the wood stove, she rose quickly out of bed, slipped on her fleece robe and slippers, and padded into the kitchen. Peabody rose from his bed to greet her, stretching and nonchalantly wagging his tail.

Martha turned from running water at the sink. "You're up early!" she exclaimed. "This is a surprise."

"Nothing like some snow to get me hyped up. It looks like a blizzard out there."

"Yep, it's pretty major. I'm making extra coffee since we may be here for a while this morning."

"What will the guests do?" asked Ida.

"They'll stay put till the plows come. I'm sure Annie's on top of things." She looked out the front window and flipped on the porch light. "The animals need to be fed."

"Can you make it okay?" She looked out to the darkness. "Can you see the barn?"

"It's not blowing as much as it seems. And anyway, I could find my way in my sleep." Martha pulled on her work boots, threw on her coat and scarf, and topped them off with a furry cap. "If I'm not back in an hour, call Annie. Save some coffee for me."

Ida closed the door tightly before any more snow could blow in. She stepped to the window putting her face to the pane, hoping to catch a glimpse of Martha's shape in the yard. There was nothing but bluish-white fluffy flakes. She checked the thermostat, determined not to bump it up. An extra log in the wood stove stoked the red-hot coals.

She wanted to be dressed and ready for whatever needed to be done. *Lots of layers today.* Where had she put her long underwear? Flannel shirt, sweater, jeans, wool socks.

This is an oatmeal morning. Maybe baked oatmeal - if there's fruit. She rummaged in the fridge and found a couple of apples. *Yes.* The milk was low but she could substitute orange juice. Sometimes it tasted better that way. Ida poured herself a cup of coffee before getting down to business. She looked at the clock. *Good to keep busy and not worry. Chop a couple of apples, add nuts and raisins.* She placed the large casserole pan in the oven and set the timer: fifty minutes.

The phone rang. Annie was checking on them. Plows should be there in another hour after they'd finished the resort's lots. The county had its plows on the highways so the roads were keeping up with the snowfall, not letting it get ahead of them. Annie had plenty of food for the guests. As long as they knew they could get out sometime, they were fine. Some might have to re-schedule flights.

Peabody lay in front of his bowl watching her expectantly. "What's wrong with me? I'm sorry!" Ida scooped the dry dog food into his bowl. He didn't give her a second look.

A stomping of boots on the front porch signaled Martha's return. She breezed in with a declaration; "It's fifteen below. I have to say – it's cold out there." Tugging off her boots she lifted her nose sniffing. "What's that? Cinnamon? Apples?"

"Baked oatmeal. I haven't made it in years but it just feels right on a snowy day."

"Smells delicious." Martha put on another layer of wool socks and padded over to the coffee pot. She leaned against the counter. "I had a bit of a scare out there."

Ida looked up. "What happened?"

Martha gazed intently at the floor. "I was grabbing hay bales from the top of the stack. The third bale bounced back onto me, hit me in the chest, and knocked me back against the wall. I hit my head pretty hard."

"Oh Martha," began Ida. "May I feel? Is there a lump?" She reached out to touch the back of Martha's head but Martha tilted away.

"The bale pinned me against the beam. It was pretty heavy, but I finally pushed it off. When I turned to look behind me at the beam my head had hit, I saw a row of nails sticking out. Those skinny nails. My head must've missed hitting them by three inches."

Ida shivered. She was reluctant to admonish her friend. Still, Martha had no business lifting those heavy things. "I'm glad you didn't hit the nails, but are you okay? Really? Sounds like you gave yourself a major bump on the head."

"I'll probably have a headache. I do feel a little funny, but mostly astounded I escaped a near fatal accident. Guess we all come close to things like this more often than we might think."

"This was a serious scare. I know Annie is worried too about you – and Moses – when something could happen."

"You are *not* to tell Annie about this. I know she'll worry, and what's done is done."

"I won't tell her if you promise to be more careful, more cautious."

Martha stood upright and stretched her arms out. She bent left and then right and twisted her head this way and that. "See, I'm fine."

"Are you?" Skeptical sarcasm.

Martha stopped her stretching and faced Ida.

"It's just amazing more things don't happen – so close to the borderline of death."

"I often feel that too. It's a wonder how we stumble through our lives."

"Anyway, the pregnant mares are okay, but I wanted to throw in some extra hay today. I'll go back a little later to make sure the snow is not blowing in. Had to break up some ice and give the horses some water. I didn't get to the chicken house."

"Ah, such a good mom," Ida said.

"Well, yeah, to my animals I am."

"Oh come on. Do you need me to say what a great mom you are to Annie and a spectacular grandmom to Elsa? Do you need me to validate your mothering expertise?"

"Not *all* of us are mothering types."

"Seriously?" Ida asked. "You're doubting your mommy creds?"

"Ask Annie. She'll tell you straight away Dan was more of a mother than I was." Martha opened the oven door. "How much longer?"

Ida did the toothpick test. "It's good. I'll turn it off and open the oven doors to let out the heat."

Martha flipped on the faucet and held her hands beneath the running water till it warmed her hands. She scrubbed her fingers like a surgeon, shaking them over the sink to dry.

"Let's eat in the living room," Ida suggested. "I'll put some nappies out for our coffee."

"Nappies?" laughed Martha, "Aren't those diapers?"

"Probably. It's what Brits might say on a day like today. So let's do have a bit of a chinwag."

Martha laughed again. "A chinwag? Is that what it sounds like?"

"Exactly. A proper chinwag. A good conversation."

They pulled their soft chairs to face the bay window and nestled in with bowls of warm oatmeal and cups of fresh coffee.

"So…explain yourself. What makes you say you're not the mothering type? What is the mothering kind?"

Martha put her feet up on a stool in front of her chair. She leaned back and settled into the cushions. "I don't think there's a mothering gene or anything, but don't you think some women – and some men – are just more inclined to be mothers – just more emotionally there?"

"Sure, but there are all kinds of parents...all kinds of relationships. It's those qualifiers that get us into trouble; a *good* mom, a *bad* mom, the *best* dad, the *worst, etc.*"

"Well okay, maybe not a bad mom, but I definitely was the one in the picture who was way in the background," Martha said. "Dan was the one who went to all the school events, the games, the back-to-school nights, the 4-H Club stuff. I only went to the county fair the year Annie raised a couple of lambs. But other than that I just had no interest. I never really liked kids, though I love Annie and Elsa."

"You know what? I don't think that's so uncommon. And anyway, lots of us were never mothers or grandmothers – though it seems those expectations are everywhere."

Martha looked slightly chagrined. "Me and my mouth. I'm sorry. I forget."

Ida shrugged. "Being a loner is not the same as lonely, and being single did not make me any more lonely than some of my married friends. You and I were never keen on social events. It's not a reflection on mothering – or not."

"Okay, I'll give you that."

"I think sometimes how difficult it must be for a woman to give up her child for adoption. There are so many reasons why it might happen, but that moment of relinquishing must be so painful."

"When horses give birth, the baby attempts to stand up within five minutes after coming into the world. The mother nudges it a few times and that's that. What if human babies came into the world ready to stand up and get on with things?"

"But isn't the foal dependent on the mother for several months?" Ida asked. "Don't they have to be nurtured for a time?"

"Domesticated horses are different than those in the wild. I've seen foals try to suckle at six months and mom kicks them away. She's saying 'Git on out there and fend for yourself.' If the foal is really clingy, we have to separate the two. But with horses out in the wild, the foal needs protection from predators so there's a survival reason to stay close."

"I'd like to see a horse give birth sometime," Ida mused.

"I think Rhiannon will foal in May so you might get your wish."

They contemplated their thoughts in silence, gazing outside their bay window at the powdery flakes flittering in random freefall. The snowfall brought on a meditative quietude about the place, an early afternoon weather vespers.

Eventually Ida spoke, "I thought I never wanted to get married because I liked my independence, but it may have had more to do with not wanting children...not after Marguerite was born."

"That's the name you gave her?" asked Martha.

Ida responded slowly. "Mom's name was Marguerite, but she explicitly told me 'don't name your child Marguerite because it's too long of a name to write.' I thought morosely, she'll never get to write it anyhow."

"Do you remember anything?"

"Not much. There's an emptiness in my memory. I call it the shock mode...no voices, nothing. I felt like I couldn't breathe either. I don't remember anyone ever saying any-thing – I just knew – there weren't any sounds. A vacuum of air sucked out of the universe in that room."

Martha rocked in her chair. She listened with a full heart as Ida continued. "I was so tired. But they brought her to me. A tiny, lifeless thing wrapped tightly in a blanket. She had the tiniest fingers…the softest tuft of hair." Ida's voice cracked. "I don't like to remember but that much I do. And holding her, touching her, just for that time meant so much."

"Cathartic?" asked Martha.

Ida paused, trying to get the memory right. "In my mind there is only silence. They gave me a sedative, I'm sure. Later, hours maybe, a social worker or therapist came and just sat with me. I kept thinking about the baby – poor little one, you're not to blame. Poor little thing." She wiped away a tear. She hadn't meant to get to this place.

"I have to ask. Was he there?"

Ida reached for the box of tissues on a table. "He missed it. And that's part of the grief too. He missed it all. Nothing of the birth was shared, just the death. We had to pick out a coffin together. That's what we shared. Selecting a pine box big enough for a large doll."

Martha looked around the room, then reached out to place her hand on Ida's shoulder. Finally she spoke. "This is tearing me up. Nothing like this should happen on earth. It's not right at all."

Ida wiped her face. "It was only after they took her away that a heap of emotions flooded in. I felt I must have done something. I hadn't been paying attention. I was responsible. I hadn't been paying attention."

"You didn't make it happen!" Martha leaned back, her voice louder now.

"I know that but at the time I kept looking for reasons. Why did it happen? The baby had been okay, no signs of fetal distress. Nothing out of the ordinary. Then…the birth." Ida took a breath and shrugged. "We reacted differently, he and I. He got all withdrawn and wouldn't talk. Days. Weeks. I think back and neither one of us could speak. Seems like hurt is often in what is not said."

"He was always moody, always into himself," Martha snapped. "I never did like him, you know."

"I'm not sure I did either. But at the time I thought I loved him." The anguish of remembering was releasing its grip. "We need to have someone or something to blame. Doctors. God."

"Hell yes!" Martha agreed. "Or lovers."

"Monitoring equipment."

"Technology for sure!"

"Politicians."

"Pollution."

"Our national health care system – or lack of."

"Uh oh," Martha grinned. "Next you'll be blaming guns."

"Absolutely. Blame them!"

"It does seem like we need to blame something. We have to have reasons, don't we?"

"Yes," Ida agreed, "but in the end it was just a natural breakdown of a relationship. A *dismantling*. The love of a baby was no longer there to keep us together. No love, no fusion."

"So it wasn't you who broke up the relationship? Was it mutual?"

"Is it ever mutual? One person always seems more invested. Or maybe it seesaws." Ida shifted around in the chair and leaned forward on her knees. "It just got more and more painful to be together. Arguing. Withholding. Demanding. That's just not love. But what do I know about love?"

"But the grief is still there, even now, isn't it?" Martha asked.

"You know how grief is. Finds a place to settle down deep in your soul and then saunters back at inauspicious times. And the grief for the loss of my baby got all mixed up with the grief for the loss of our love for one another. When there was no Marguerite, there was no me anymore." She sighed, picked up her empty bowl, and reached for Martha's to carry back to the kitchen. In a few minutes, she was back with the coffee pot.

"Yes please," replied Martha, holding her cup out with both hands.

Ida filled her mug and returned the pot. She hunted in the closet for extra throw blankets, threw one on Martha, and then curled up in her chair, swathed and comforted. "I've thought sometimes the stillbirth was karma for my getting an abortion when I was twenty. I know it's not rational. It's like something some anti-abortion preacher, evangelical in his zeal, might tell me." Ida looked at Martha.

"And I would say he was a judgmental, narrow-minded prick. But I'm allowed to still think it about myself."

Martha shook her head. "Some kind of cosmic retribution for your sins? Seriously?"

"I said I didn't think it was rational. The Old-Testament God out to get me personally, while wars and rumors of wars go on infinitum."

"But you were alone. You had few choices."

"It was bad time for me. No job. Drifting around. And single mothers at that time were still scorned women. Abortion seemed the only option but it was by far one of the toughest decisions I've ever made in my life."

"But it was your decision and not some politician's! Martha shifted around in her chair.

"It was my decision and I live with that. But it's a human thing to think about cause and effect in our lives."

"And what about karma that got you to this place and time now? Did you do something extraordinarily good?" Martha teased.

"Fair enough," smiled Ida.

"I remember taking you to that clinic and seeing all the protesters outside shaming women as they sought help."

"You took them on face to face," Ida recollected. "I recall you even being quite calm and rational with them."

"Wasted breath," Martha admitted. "We don't change minds that way. But what really bugged me was the way they used their Christianity to be hurtful.

When it comes down to it, I guess none of us really change till something happens to force us to change. Or someone happens. But our Mennonite upbringing, with the emphasis on turning the other cheek, always had this implication – to me anyway – that we need to clean the gunk out of our own hearts before doing anything else."

"Once a Mennonite, always one? At least in one's heart? You don't think you might be idealizing that Mennonite thing, do you?" prodded Martha.

"There are many good things about the faith –especially given the perspective of distance and years. But I appreciated being taught that Jesus was about being truthful with himself and others, not blaming or shaming."

I've done a lot of things I regret. I judge myself pretty harshly too," said Martha. "But you know, I'm a lot easier on myself as I get older. I'm a nicer person, don't you think?"

"I don't even know who you are any more." Ida's eyes twinkled. "Compassionate. Non-judgmental."

"Don't push it," Martha warned.

"There's a good side to this aging business. Feelings pass fairly quickly. If I feel like being kind of bitchy today, it's okay. I know it will pass and I'll get to that feeling of kindness again. If I become melancholy and kind of blue, I know it will pass and some sort of hope will appear." Ida suddenly rocked forward and got up to look out the window. "Hey, look, I think it stopped snowing!"

Martha threw off her blanket and hobbled to gaze out through the clear pane. Peabody was by her side, alert for signs of life, some rodent perhaps, or even the barn cats. "Good. The plows will be here soon."

"Moses isn't coming out today, is he?" asked Ida.

"If he shows up on a Sunday I won't pay him for his weekdays."

"Did I tell you I invited him for Christmas dinner?" asked Ida.

"When did this happen?" Martha paused on her way to the kitchen. "We haven't even talked about Christmas dinner."

"I saw him at the grocery store last week buying those frozen single meals and I thought, we need to have him over more often. So, I asked him for Christmas dinner!" Ida was quite pleased with herself. "Oh, and he asked if he could bring a friend. Someone who played in Dan's bluegrass band?"

"Hmm, That's probably Landis. They're A.A. buddies." Martha considered this. "Yeah, that's good. Landis needs to get out and socialize too."

"Wait a minute…Alcoholics Anonymous? Moses?"

"About twenty years sober, I'd say. Landis not so long. His marriage fell apart years ago, but he drank in the early years with the band. He and Moses are good buddies and look after each other now."

"I have to tell you something else about Moses."

Martha was puttering about in the kitchen but called out,, "Okay, what? I'm listening."

This would take a longer explanation. Ida remained seated and when Martha returned, gestured for her to sit.

"Before Gretel…Miriam went to bed that final night, she spoke to me privately in the kitchen. She asked if Moses had come from Kansas, and then proceeded to tell me she knew him from over fifty years ago – and more than that, they'd been in love. She didn't say much about that except it happened when she was still married. Her husband wouldn't give her a divorce – out of spite – not because she had fallen in love with someone else, but because he couldn't stand that she had fallen in love with Moses. Miriam claimed he couldn't abide that a white woman and a black man could be in love."

"So there's that about not getting divorced for thirty years but inheriting money from an estranged rich husband," said Martha. "How did she find Moses after fifty years?"

"She said she hired somebody to help her find if Moses was still living and where he was. Then she found the VP group and thought it would be the best way to travel here to find him."

"A good cover while checking him out?" asked Martha. "Hence the slight Dutch accent and the name change to disguise herself until she was sure."

"That's my theory," responded Ida. "She was a bit scared to meet him really. She didn't know whether she wanted him to know it was her."

"You think it was a great romance, don't you?"

"A strong bond of some sort for sure," replied Ida.

"And you know he's gay, right? It's not something we talk about around here, but he told me a long time ago."

"Well you said he attended gay rodeos in his younger days. But gay people – what's the word – pass for straight in different circumstances," said Ida. "And love is love in its many expressions."

"I think you need to tell Moses. He'll set you straight on the story, even if it takes him a couple of days to think about it."

Peabody was whining and pacing the floor inbetween the two women. Martha opened the front door to let him out. She stood on the porch looking toward the guest house.

"Please close the door, you're letting cold in," said Ida shivering. "What are you doing?"

"I think I see Rusty's truck again," Martha commented. "He must have driven out last night."

"That's Annie's business, isn't it?" asked Ida. "Who she invites to stay over?"

"Yes, but Rusty?" asked Martha incredulously.

Ida laughed. "Annie likes him."

"Yes, but Rusty?" repeated Martha.

"And what were you saying about yourself just a few minutes ago? Kinder? Less judgmental?"

"I said I'm easier on myself."

"Say one thing, do another," Ida teased.

"I don't claim to be consistent," Martha retorted. She pulled on her boots. "I think I'll go over to the guest house, see how I can help."

"That's a first," remarked Ida, "but do what you gotta do. I'll clean up here. I think I'll snuggle in with a good book today."

As Martha headed out onto the porch, Ida heard Peabody come inside, nails scratching on the tile floor. She closed the door to the mudroom where the smell of wet fur over-powered any cinnamon aromas. "Hello old boy, welcome back," she said, attempting to dry his snowy back with an old brown towel. He panted happily.

Restlessness settled in as soon as she picked up one of the books stacked by her chair. She concentrated on one sentence, then another, plodding through one line at a time.

"Enough of this. Let's go get nosy," she said out loud, putting on her coat and snow boots. She followed the deep prints Martha had sunk in the snow. A middle-aged man with curly red hair was heading out the backdoor.

"Hi there," she said. "You must be Rusty."

"Yep. You must be Ida!" He gave a nod towards the barn. "I'm headed out to check on the horses and the chickens. Care to join me?"

"How can I refuse an invitation to do chores?"

He handed her a shovel and pointed to the first stall. "Shovel what you can into the bucket and then dump it on the pile out back. I'll slide the back door open. There's a bin out there and we reuse it in the gardens. I'll take the horses out to the overhang once I break a path through the snow. The snow's too deep in the corral right now."

Ida did as she'd been instructed, mucking out the stalls one at a time. She had managed to complete three in the time Rusty had done all the rest. "'Excellent work!" he said. "Martha may have to worry about you taking over."

"That will never happen." Ida had to ask. "Did you drive out here in the blizzard?"

"That's just what Martha asked!" Rusty smiled at her. "I drove out last evening, spent the night with Annie. "It seems like I'm a topic of curiosity around here."

"It's not my business."

"Oh, you can make it your business. Annie and I've known each other for years. My dad owns one of the resorts, but I won't work for him. I think you might know my stepmother,

Josephine?" Rusty nodded towards the stalls. "Let's finish brushing these horses down before Martha comes out to supervise."

Ida took the brush and entered the first stall. *Josephine? The quirky Josephine from yoga and WoCA? Will wonders never cease? That explains Martha's animosity.* Martha and Josephine barely tolerated one other. Just very different people. *And why won't Rusty work for his dad? And is it your business Ida? Hardly. Still, it feels good to be part of a community,* she thought, with the gossiping of friends and the tight, little inter-personal tensions and watching the sparking of romance with the younger folk.

SEVEN

By Tuesday, the landscape was rearranged. Canyons walls of snow appeared on both sides of the road. The branches of aspens appeared like frosted filaments against the sky. Temperatures dropped further. The white ground cover was just a reminder that winter was fully present. The last tour group of the season would be here, and then the guest house would close for two days over Christmas. It was prime time for tourists to get away to the mountains.

Elsa came home for a month-long break after her first semester at the University of Montana in Missoula, bursting with hyperkinetic energy, more self-confident and worldly. As a responsible young adult now, she got herself up to help with the household chores and volunteered to help Ida with the afternoon social hour for the Verdant Pathways group.

This week's VP tour consisted of four German men, four Canadian men, and six Australian women. They were in their sixties and seventies and opted for skiing in lieu of a day touring Big Sky country. They were all single as well – or assumed to be by Ida – and flirted with one another with insuppressible delight during the social hour. This group would fit nicely in the one sleigh for the night ride. She speculated on what switch-ups might be occurring in the guest rooms.

Meanwhile WoCA , the Women of a Certain Age group, was planning its first gathering. Six women had responded to the announcement she'd tacked up at the community center. Ida sent out email invitations to meet at nine on Saturday at the Elk House coffee shop, and reiterated how she looked forward to meeting everyone and working together to tackle some discussion issues they faced as they aged.

On Saturday, Ida gathered up her things and drove into town. She staked territory pushing two tables together in the café. Josephine and Madeleine appeared, and two other hardy women she'd seen around the village. After placing their orders and sitting down a fifth woman approached and asked if this was the WoCA group. Heads nodded and a chair was pulled out for her to join them. Ida suggested they go around the table to say a few words about themselves; perhaps their ages, and why they were at the meeting.

"How about the oldest going first? I'm Madeleine. You all know me. I teach the yoga class on Mondays and Fridays. I've lived here a long time. I'm eighty years old. But I'm always open for something new, and this sounded right up my alley. I'm facing a few health challenges, and I thought maybe this group could help me sort some things out."

A woman with long white hair pulled back under a hat sat to Madeleine's right. "I'll go next. I'm Millie. Sadie here is my partner and life-long love. We used to run a sheep farm up by Ellis, but we got a little old for that. I have a brother here in Big Sky so we thought we'd move closer to family. Sadie and I get tired of each other's voices so we thought this group might be a door to open to others."

She looked to Sadie who jumped right in. "I'm seventy-five and Millie is seventy-six. Can't say we've ever been in a group like this, but hell, we've known Martha for years and we figured any friend of hers had to be all right." She nodded approvingly at Ida. "I like to read a lot. Millie doesn't. I like to keep up on politics. Millie doesn't." She chuckled. "Maybe we need to jump start our relationship… kind of stuck in our old ways."

"Speak for yourself," said Millie. "I'm happy just how I am."

Before an affectionate spat could start, Josephine spoke up, "I'm Josephine, as you all know. I'm married to that handsome rancher you may have seen on a billboard around here. I got to know Ida at yoga and then I read this blurb on the bulletin board, and I thought this sounds great! Get together with other women and talk about what's on our minds. So that's why I'm here."

"And Josephine, you don't have to say your age, but are you over sixty?" asked Ida.

"Oh my, that's a compliment! Thank you! I'm actually close to seventy, give or take a year," Josephine smiled slyly. She wore her hair stylishly coiffed with crimson colored manicured nails.. "I do try to take care of myself."

The others nodded, not having words, and looked to the sedate, quiet woman sitting at Josephine's side..

"My name is Karen. I'm actually the pastor at the congregational church in town. I hope that doesn't disqualify me for this group. I'm planning to retire in a couple of years. I really liked the way the announcement was worded. I don't want a book group or a therapy group. I just would like to hang out with women over the age of sixty. We just have different perspectives than younger folks. So that's why I'm here." She smiled at the circle of women. "Oh, and I'm sixty-five."

"I'm so glad to meet you all. I'm Ida. I'm seventy-two, but with each year I get older, my age seems irrelevant. You all know Martha as my old friend – and she may come to our gatherings once we get started. I wanted to form this group with other women at this stage of life because I think of myself in many ways like I thought of myself in my twenties. I feel like this age is just as open and new."

She looked around the circle for affirmation. They were all listening intently.

"Like the *reminiscence bump*?" asked Karen.

"Sorry, I'm not familiar with that," said Ida. "What's that?"

"It's a term that refers to our tendency to remember events more clearly about our early twenties because that's when we were figuring out our identities. But I like your observation that these later years might be just as invigorating."

Ida nodded and plunged ahead. "Yes, we are still creating ourselves. And I've found that women sharing personal stories with one another is very meaningful. It's easier than a book club because there's no book having to get read. And in discussing topics, we share about ourselves on our own terms."

"So what kind of topics are you thinking about?" asked Josephine.

Ida pulled out her journal. "I started jotting down some ideas. Let's see. *Best Friends. Our Grandmother's Trunks.* What we might find genetically and metaphorically. *Women's Altars* – What do we collect? *Responding to Sorrow* – like deaths or even stuff in the news. These are just a few; you all must have some ideas too."

"Those are wonderful topics!" exclaimed Madeleine. I can see us talking about any one of these for hours."

"I think the one you mentioned first might be a good starting point. *Best Friends.* We can all get out of the gate with that one," said Sadie. "Best friends can be more than one friend in our lives."

"What do you mean?" Millie asked mischievously. "You have more than one best friend?"

"You'll have to wait to find out," Sadie quipped.

Millie smiled. "Best Friends. That could mean someone we knew a long time ago."

Ida tried to remain neutral. "It can mean anything you want. I think we should feel free to share only what we want to with one another."

"I'm for beginning with that topic too," said Josephine. "Best Friends, now, or at another time in our lives."

"How about if we each come to the next meeting with something to share, like a memory or a story about someone who we considered a best friend at one time. Does that sound okay?" Ida felt it was important to focus on something specific. They concurred that they liked meeting in the morning and not having to drive at night. They agreed to meet the second Saturday of each month at nine at the Elk House coffee shop.

EIGHT

That same night, Elsa and Annie planned to take Martha out for her birthday. Rusty offered to cover the guest house so the four women could go out on the town. Dan's old bluegrass-country band was playing at Jack's Bar and Grill in Bozeman. It was a social gathering Martha tolerated and even enjoyed if she'd be honest. The four women trundled into Annie's Subaru and headed north thirty miles along the Gallatin River with the ice-blue mountains as a backdrop. Hand-made wooden roadside crosses with scratched-in names bordered this particular stretch of highway. Signs warning of the dangers of drinking and driving were placed intermittently between these crosses, while plastic flowers - bouquets of remembrances - littered the ditches. They were gratified to have Elsa as their designated driver home.

Live entertainment at Jack's on a Saturday night meant an overflowing crowd. Annie had reserved a table weeks before. "I requested one near the stage!" Anne called to the others as the hostess guided them through the maze of patrons.

Two younger men were setting up sound equipment while four others, definitely older, were unpacking their instruments. The one without a cowboy hat looked up and pointed to Martha and said something to the others. He was distinctive with his full beard and not much on top. They waved and headed over to the table single file. "Hey lady, you made it," one teased as he hugged her tight. "Good to see you again."

"It's been too long," said another waiting to embrace her. Elsa and Annie made the rounds of the older men and waved to the younger musicians on the stage.

"Ida, these are the guys who kept Dan in line all those years." Martha pointed, "Tipp, Jon, Hank, Landis. Gentlemen, this is my dearest friend, Ida, who moved across the country to live with me."

Ida stood up to shake their hands, say hello, happy to meet you, how much she was looking forward to the music. When she came to Landis motioned him off to the side, "I think you're coming for Christmas dinner. Did Moses tell you you're invited?"

"He did. I hope it's not an imposition," he replied. "Moses is my mother hen."

"No, absolutely not. We're expecting you."

"He told me you moved up here to live with Martha." Landis had that way of looking up even when towering over Ida's five-foot two frame.

He's sort of attractive with his dark eyes and receding hairline, well, balding head.

"You two kind of like Norwegian bachelor farmers?" he asked.

"Kind of…" she hesitated, her mind skipping around to what he might mean.

"I was thinking about an obscure reference there, not really fitting." he said.

"Kind of funny though. Maybe hermits with limited social skills?"

He appeared amused. "It was a lousy thing for me to say. Bad joke."

She pointed to the stage. "How did you come up with the name for the band?"

"*Unbroken Firebrands*? Ah Mark Twain – Tom Sawyer. Twain calls him a firebrand."

"Trouble maker?"

"You got it. Renegade rabble rousers but mainly just in our musical fantasies. Unbroken is a horse term."

"So you guys are literate – and musical?" Ida complimented.

"Well we just have a little fun playing together." Landis grinned. "And you moved here from Colorado, is that right?"

"Yes, from Boulder." Ida was aware of how small she felt. He really was a tall, sturdy man with dark eyes. *Quite dark. And a very long beard. Maybe just balding a bit.*

"Ah Boulder!" he said as if it was an inside joke. "A true Boulderite?"

"What's that mean? Stereotype liberal? Non-conventional? Quirky?"

He held up both hands. "No offense intended. Boulder does have a reputation. I actually taught there one summer. We'll have to compare notes." He nodded toward the stage. "I have to get set up, but maybe later."

Why was she even looking if he had a ring? Why? "Yep, sure." Ida fumbled back to her seat at the table where beers had been ordered. "Cheers everyone!" she said as they raised the glasses. The fiddle and banjo players began as fans clapped along, well acquainted with the music.

Moses wandered in during the set, sitting down between Elsa and Annie. He nodded to the others. When the waitress returned, he ordered food, pointing to the menu item. Such an unobtrusive soul. It seemed tragic that Miriam hadn't been given the time to talk with him. Why had death come that night? It wasn't fair. How well did Moses know Landis? Moses was such a good man, just a very kind and humble man.

A consciousness of the restaurant's lighting and ambience formed a protective haze over Ida. Talking was minimized with the upbeat music. She looked around the room nonchalantly but her eyes returned to Landis. He didn't quite look the country and western type but he could play. *And that full salt 'n pepper beard. Really a bit long but it works on him. And the receding hairline, well, just sort of endearing.* He reminded her of someone. She knew she hadn't even fleetingly thought about a man in this way for a very long time. She recognized the feeling. She wanted to get up and drive away – as fast and far as possible.. She really just didn't want to have to do this anymore. Maybe it was just the second beer. It would pass.

At the break, the four men joined them at the table. Ida got up to go to the bathroom and then returned by way of the postcards and candy rack, which she perused longer than necessary. Whether it was shyness or introversion, she sought out detours to certain social interactions. When she finally returned to the table, they were sharing stories about Dan.

"Hey Ida," said Moses, "you knew Dan. Got any stories on him?"

"Oh yeah, I knew Dan." She sat down and looked at Martha for encouragement. "All three of us lived together back in the day. Martha and I were strict vegetarians, obnoxiously so, but Dan didn't help. He claimed he was hypoglycemic and had to eat organ meats. He'd fry up hearts and livers daily while Martha extolled the moral virtues of only consuming veggies."

"So your hate-love passion began over food?" asked Landis as he glanced at Martha. "You're no longer vegetarian, right? Did he break you down?"

"For the sake of world peace, I had to consume meat, but I've since returned to my sanity. Ida is helping me get back on the right path," Martha retorted with a grin.

"Any other stories from your commune days?" Landis asked.

Ida again looked to Martha. "Remember the time a bunch of us went swimming in that pond at night? It was a full moon and god-awful hot. All of us jumped in with our clothes on except for Dan who, of course, said skinny dipping was the only way to go. Well our clothes turned yellow, but none of us got a rash like Dan did. Turns out it was a cow pond."

The others hooted. "A cow pond! What were you thinking?" asked Hank.

"We all did stupid things when we were young," said Landis, "even you Hank."

"That story's a keeper," said Tipp. "I'd feel sorry for anyone else, but not Dan."

"His skinny dipping was probably another ploy to get my clothes off," Martha said, shaking her head. "He had no shame."

Landis leaned over her as he got up. "Great stories, Ida. If you have more on Dan I'd like to hear them."

"I'll try and think of a few," she smiled reflexively. "And I want to hear about your escapades in Colorado!" *What was that? Escapades?*

The second set was mellower than the first. The crowd thinned out, dinners were finished, miscellaneous noise was muted. Landis played his ukulele for a solo, something familiar but with more of a reggae lilt. When the applause died down, he held his hand over his eyes looking at their table. "Elsa? Are you ready to join us?"

Elsa reached beneath the table and brought out her flute case. "Absolutely," she stated and headed to the stage. "Happy Birthday to my fabulous grandmother – Martha. Please help us sing her a happy birthday."

Martha was suitably embarrassed but managed to mouth a "thank-you" around the room. Elsa joined the band with her flute for the final number that left folks humming and singing as they dispersed.

Ida approached Landis as he packed up his gear. "We'll see you on Christmas then?"

"I accept and I promise to keep Moses under control," he said as he caught his friend walking by. Moses looked surprised, then gave him a pat on the back. *Good friends, though Landis must be ten years younger.*

She turned away but Landis called, "Hey Ida, it was nice meeting you tonight."

"You too!" she responded over her shoulder waving good-bye.

Somehow she made it out of the restaurant and into the backseat of the car. She collapsed and feigned sleep on the long ride back to the Dusky Grouse. She knew sleep would evade her on this night when a certain kind of emotion had come slinking in, catching her unaware. *Silly silly infatuation at your age,* she scolded herself. *Foolishness. Silly, silly old girl.*

NINE

The day before Christmas, Ida decided she must find Moses and tell him about Miriam. No more procrastinations. The other women had gone to town for last minute dinner items. In the barn she heard noises near the back door. "Moses," she called, "It's me, Ida."

"Well good morning! I didn't expect to see you out here this morning." He looked up from flaking the bales of hay, mixing the new in with the old. "Something I can help you with?"

"Yes Moses, there is." She sighed, not sure of where to begin. "Do you remember a woman named Miriam from your past?"

He stood up, leaning on the pitchfork. "Why do you ask?"

"Because I have to share some things about her with you...some things which are very difficult."

He leaned the fork against the barn stall, turned around and folded his arms in front of him. "I'm listening."

"Do you remember the woman who passed away here several weeks ago? She went by the name of Gretel?" He nodded and she continued, "The night before she died, she sat down with me and asked some specific questions about you. She told me, ever so briefly, that she had loved you, and that you had loved her – but it happened over fifty years ago. That woman, Gretel, was Miriam Mailer."

Moses looked around for a place to sit down. He settled on the edge of a wooden chest and put his head into his hands. "Why didn't she speak to me? Why didn't she say something?"

"I suspect she was a little afraid of how you seeing her, after all this time, might affect you. She didn't want to upset you. She just wanted to know you were okay. When you didn't recognize her, she was relieved, but I also think she was seriously thinking of telling you, of talking with you the next morning. It just didn't work out that way."

Ida scooted in to sit beside the man and put her hand on his shoulder. "I'm sorry I didn't tell you sooner. I was trying to figure out how to tell you. And then we were still trying to figure out who she was – as Gretel - with the Dutch accent – but the police confirmed a lot this past week. She was known as Miriam Mailer. She was separated from her husband for years and years, but he wouldn't give her a divorce. He died last year and all of his money went to her. So she decided to use some of that money to find you, if you were still living. Gretel...Miriam just didn't know what to do when or if she found you."

"Where has she been living?" He shook his head. "What took her this long to get here?"

"I don't know, Moses. There are lots of gaps in the story. The police told us she'd been homeless for some of that time, living in Kansas City. Maybe she was ill, maybe she didn't have the resources to do it."

"Bless her heart," Moses whispered, shaking his head. "She was trying to tell me, trying to get me to recognize her and I didn't. I'd lost her and the memory of her a long time ago. Bless her heart." He got up and lifted the pitchfork to commence working. "Thank you for telling me, Ida. You've given me something to think about, that's for sure."

"We're still waiting for more information from an attorney in Kansas City. Maybe there will be more information about her. I'm so sorry, Moses."

He stopped and suddenly turned toward her. "What will they do with the body? Where is she now?"

"Her body is in a morgue in Bozeman. They told us the state gives an unidentified body to medical facilities for research – unless someone claims it and takes responsibility."

"Can you find out about that for me please? I think I owe her this respect in death. I'll be responsible for her."

"Yes sure, Moses. I'll see what I can find out. I'll drive up to Bozeman with you if that'd help. Let me call around today if any place is open. Again, I am so sorry."

"Well, we do what we do. I guess we may know more about it by and by," replied Moses. "I think I'd best get back to work here."

"Yes, I'll leave you to it. I'll be in the cottage if you do want to talk more," Ida walked away feeling clumsy and awkward in this situation talking of love and loss and grief. *What part had chance played in their lives? Chance. Luck. Fate. Invisible threads. Things Unseen.*

***

Later that afternoon Moses wandered down to their cottage. Ida welcomed him into the warm room where he pulled off his boots before stepping onto the rug. Martha was wrapping a present for Elsa on the kitchen table.

"I've got some things on my mind I feel I should share with you both. A little history. Some of it may explain why Miriam was up here looking for me after all this time." Moses limped slowly to the sofa and sat on one end, with his hat in his hand. "You may know some of this, Martha, but I'll start at the beginning anyway."

"And apparently there's lots I don't know." Martha entered the room and plopped in her favorite cushy chair. "Please tell."

"I came to work for your dad as kind of a lucky fluke. You remember I used to work on the railroad, the Santa Fe line. And Newton, Kansas was one of the turn-around towns, one of the places where any of us working the train could spend a couple of days before the next shift."

"Yep, I remember the trains. I have my own memories of the Santa Fe."

"Well, there used to be a little restaurant on Main Street in Newton. I'd walk down there for lunch because it was one of the few that wasn't segregated. They had good food and the best homemade pies. Lots of times farmers came in for lunch because of the cheap buffet. *Take all you want but eat all you take* was the motto. Now, how did I remember that after all this time?" Moses shook his head and stared at the floor.

"I remember it too," said Martha. "Dad took us for Sunday dinners. I loved the lemon meringue pie the cooks made."

Ida let out an exasperated sigh. "And then…?"

"So, one day Martha's dad got to talking with me and found out I grew up on a farm. He asked if I knew anything about horses. I said mostly mules. Then he asked if I'd ever thought about working on a farm again, and I said I had not, but I liked the idea. Well, he said he was looking for a hired hand, 'a dependable hired hand' were his words; someone who'd be willing to live on the farm, work with him. He had about a hundred head of dairy cows and he did some wheat farming. Mostly though, he wondered if I'd help his daughter learn how to care for a couple horses and teach her how to ride."

"Yes!" Martha exuded. "After Mom died he bought my first two horses – Snowball and Riley. But they were feisty youngsters and I was scared of them. You came in and worked your magic. They just didn't seem scary after you came."

"I don't know about that," Moses said. "But your dad was a good man. He must have had a sense about it."

"Dad was good at reading people. He either trusted you or he didn't."

"You were only – what twelve, thirteen years old? I was living in the upstairs room over the garage, remember that? I was working for your father and it was a good life…your dad- a lot of the folks around there – Mennonite folks, were good people. But Miriam's step-father – no he wasn't really part of that community; he was a mean son of a gun. They lived on a farm south of us, so we ran into them from time to time. Anyone could tell he was a hateful man. Miriam and her mother looked like scared rabbits out in public. She lived at home a few years after high school, working in town, trying to save some on the side. Her stepfather always demanded her money but she saved enough on the side to finally leave, get a place in town. A few years later Miriam ran away with this fellow by the name of Mailer, which probably seemed like a good idea at the time to get distance from her stepfather."

"Social services weren't equipped to deal with abuse back then," said Ida. "I imagine folks just looked the other way."

"That's the way it was," Moses nodded his head. "Everybody just walked around him; Miriam's mom, poor soul, I don't know what happened to her. Anyway, Miriam escaped her stepfather but walked right into a bad marriage. There are lots of ways of being a bully. He came from a family with money and had that air about him; could say and do what he wanted. They lived on the edge of town in a newer development."

"Where was I? How come I don't remember any of this?" asked Martha.

"You were a kid, then a teenager. You'd lost your mother." Moses was consoling. "It was a difficult time in your life."

"So what happened with Miriam and this guy?" asked Ida.

"I lost touch with her until one night I was driving home from town and saw her standing by her car with a flat tire. I stopped to help and it was clear she was a little out of her head, scared and shaking. She said she was on her way to her mother's – that she needed to see her mother and she definitely knew she did not want to go back to the house where her husband was."

Martha interjected, "But why would she go back to that house where her stepfather lived?"

"That's what I said to her. Seems those were the only choices she had: her stepfather's or her husband's house. Anyway, I convinced her to come with me to your dad's place, so he listened to her too. She talked to both of us. Her husband was a bully, that's for sure. She told us things that made me ashamed to be a man. Your dad felt he needed to call the police. She finally agreed. Apparently, it wasn't the first time they'd been notified. The police came for her but she refused to file a report. She became kind of defiant with us saying we didn't understand. She ended up going back to her husband that night."

"She went on living with her abusive husband?" Ida asked.

"Yep, and every so often there'd be a flare-up. She'd leave and go back. So a few years later, I'm doing the late afternoon milking and who do I see but Miriam come walking into the barn. Her face bruised and her hand all mangled. This time the abuse was physical. I asked her how she'd gotten there and she couldn't even answer. She was in a state. Right or wrong, I made a decision to hide Miriam in my place above the garage. She stayed there in hiding, just getting to a place of feeling safe. It wasn't what you might think. I was just hiding her and she felt safe for once in her life."

"That was pretty dangerous," said Martha.

"And pretty stupid. But she needed help. After a couple of weeks of hiding up there we had to do something. She couldn't stay there. I was feeling pretty mixed up. I went to your father and told him about her and about the whole situation. I asked if there was a way I could get her some distance from Mailer."

"Why didn't I ever hear any of this from Dad? It's strange he never told me."

"Your dad wasn't one to talk about people. You'd left for college by that time anyway. Long story short, your dad had an old friend in Kansas City who could find her a place to live and help her get a job. I drove her to K.C. one afternoon, helped get her set up."

"And then Dad sent you up here, ostensibly to help me, but really to get out of that community?" asked Martha.

"To get out of the line of fire from Mailer." Moses spoke slower now. "Guess I need to back up a little bit. You know what 'gay-dar' is, right?"

They were mum, quizzical, trying to follow his story.

"I had my suspicions about Mailer. See I used to go down to Wichita to a little gay bar on the north side. Lo and behold Mailer was there one night. He saw me. I saw him."

"Wait a minute, I knew you were gay but I didn't figure you for the gay bar scene," Martha said.

"Just remember I was quite a bit younger then. I did some stupid things and I took more risks. No offense, but it's not something I need to talk about – with you or anyone. But it's important to this story." Moses sighed and continued, "So Mailer and I see each other in this bar; there's only one reason anyone's in a bar like that in Wichita. He threatened me, told me he knew it was me who'd taken his wife away. He said if I ever told a soul about him in that bar, he would make sure everyone knew about me. And you know in that community, at that time, being gay was considered something immoral, a sin of one's character. It just wasn't talked about, and if it wasn't talked about, then it didn't happen. He had me. Neither one of us could speak of it."

"Ah the tangled webs of Mennonite communities," said Ida. "I could see how this would be ostracizing."

Moses regarded her comment. "Things likely haven't changed that much. Still a lot of folks would call it…me… an abomination."

"Even some of those good Mennonite folk you talked about?"

"Easy to hate what you don't understand," he replied solemnly.

"What about Dad? Did you ever tell him?" asked Martha.

"Well I'm getting to that. After he helped me get Miriam away from there, I told him what I just shared with you. I told him about myself, that he could fire me if he wanted. I had this feeling Mailer was not only abusive toward Miriam, but had married her as a cover-up – not just for being gay. He was into a lot of shady stuff and she made him appear more legitimate. Now that she was safely away from that rat of a husband, I told your dad I'd better move on too. Mailer would make trouble eventually."

"So Dad sent you up here to us."

"Your father didn't want me to leave. He didn't like to think that this stuff would bother me, but I left soon after that. I had to go by way of Kansas City first to check on Miriam. Your dad's friends helped her rent a room and get a job within walking distance."

"What did she end up doing there?" Martha asked.

"When I left her, she was working as a waitress in a diner. She preferred working the night shift – in case Mailer came looking for her."

Ida interrupted, "But Gretel...Miriam told me she loved you."

"She may have been in love with me, and I loved her too, but not in the way she may have wanted...or deserved to be loved. I think because I was kind to her, she made that out to be romantic love."

"And so her husband refused to divorce her – for spite – as well as a cover for him?" asked Martha.

"That's the way I figure it," he replied. "And to keep me quiet."

"Fifty some years go by and then she shows up in Montana to find you," remarked Ida. "She told me her husband wouldn't grant a divorce because she was white and you were black. She believed it was the racial thing."

"I never told her I was gay. I never led her to think my love was anything but concern for her well-being. She may have dreamed it as larger than it was. So..." Moses took a deep breath and exhaled. "So I'm confessing it now – I slept with her that weekend in Kansas City. I felt she needed some comfort."

"That's a kind of comfort that happens more often than we think," reflected Ida. Sexual interaction was one of those befuddling things in life that had to be coupled with intention. Shallow or deep, lustful or loving, tawdry or hateful – it was a strange sort of communication that was not easily confined to a label. She could see how tenderness toward another human being in a vulnerable state could be misconstrued and imagined as more than it was. Wasn't it a peculiar and mystifying exchange if it was consensual?

"You're right about that. I did care for her, but again —
not the way she would've liked. Me being black and her
white, well, that was another way to look at it. Our society
still has trouble with that too."

"That's the truth," said Martha. "It's just a sad
story, Moses."

"Everybody has some sad story in their life. Everyone has
sorrow. Everyone has disappointments," he said philosophically. "I know I didn't handle it too well. I started drinking too much, way too much, and you know the rest." He
looked at Martha for confirmation.

"That was a long time ago," she said.

"But now I feel mighty blessed." His tone shifted. He
was preaching now. "Good friends. Good job. I couldn't be
happier — being with the horses every day, knowing they
need me and I need them. I'm getting older, a little slower,
but the horses don't seem to notice."

"I don't notice either," said Martha.

"Thank you for sharing this," Ida replied. "Keeping
silent is helpful at times but it can also deepen wounds. I'm
grateful that you trust us."

Martha lips tightened. "Is that your social worker voice?"

"I'm sorry. Do my words sound canned or something?"
Ida asked with a tinge of irritation.

"Yeah, they do," Martha replied. "You don't have to do
therapy here."

Ida shook her head and smiled. "Moses, Martha doesn't
like the word 'grateful' so I'm not allowed to say it or think
it. At any rate, I appreciate you being able to tell us."

"It's good to have friends, all kinds of friends," Moses reflected. "And Martha, I'm damn *grateful* to you and Dan for being my family all those years. So, how'd you like them *grateful* apples?"

"Well hell," Martha said, standing up, and hobbling out of the room. "I've been sitting too damn long."

"I think we got to her," Moses laughed.

"Yep," Ida grinned, "Nothing like seeing Martha squirm."

TEN

Christmas morning, the four women gathered in the farm-house living room around the Douglas fir to open presents. Elsa set up her laptop to play Christmas music. The year before, the three generations of women had taken a trip to Belize since it was the first Christmas without Dan; the spouse, the father, the grandfather. This year they hoped to embrace new traditions and live into the good memories of him.

They gathered in the kitchen in the afternoon to prepare the dinner. Martha whipped up a marinade for the fish. Root vegetables were scoured, peeled, oiled, and salted for roasting. Ida chopped fruit for a colorful salad while Annie and Elsa created appetizers.

"So I have to ask, how long have you known Landis?" asked Ida.

Annie nudged her mother. "Yeah Mom, how long have you known Landis?"

"I'm asking all of you," said Ida, "not just Martha. Unless there's something special about you two."

"We are both special," responded Martha. "But I think the first time I met him was when he was traipsing around in the woods off that South Cottonwood Trail near Bozeman. Old Landis scared me a little with his long, bushy beard. He came out from behind some trees, off trail. I thought he might be living out there. There's lots of folks living kind of secluded in the mountains."

"Now I'm curious. What was he doing out there?" asked Ida.

"Studying trees," responded Martha. "That's his field of study. He's some kind of a biologist who studies trees, specifically old growth trees."

"Really?" asked Ida. "Are people allowed to just wander off the trail?"

"Not usually. He looked kind of embarrassed when we saw him and he started apologizing and explaining he was just gathering data for his field notes. But you know Dan. They began talking and soon discovered they both liked old-time music. Dan invited him to a band practice and well, the rest is history as they say."

"And how long has the band been together?"

"Eleven, twelve years, right Annie?" Martha asked. "What would you say?"

"They were together before my divorce ten years ago so, yes, I'd say about twelve years," Annie said.

"And you said Moses and Landis are in A.A. together," Ida chattered on nonchalantly. "I'm just trying to construct a time line here."

Annie moved a little closer to Ida and picked up a knife to help slice the cucumbers. "Landis was a heavy drinker when he joined the band. Free booze and unhappiness don't mix well."

"Is his wife still around?"

"Lord, no. He was divorced several years before we met him," said Martha. "They weren't married long. Fortunately, there were no kids, no contentiousness."

Annie continued, "The guys in the band gave him an ultimatum; join A.A. or he was out."

"Speaking of alcohol, I'm going to go the basement for some wine. Cabernet and Sauvignon?" Martha asked.

"Is it okay to have wine with both men in A.A?" asked Ida. "Shouldn't we be sensitive?"

"Moses told me it makes him uncomfortable when folks go out of their way not to drink around him. He has no desire for alcohol anymore, and he doesn't like others to change their ways for him," explained Martha. "I know Landis would feel the same." She unlatched the door to the basement to retrieve the bottles.

"What do *you* think of Landis?" asked Annie.

Ida flushed. She turned on the tap for a glass of water. "I'm just curious about the locals here, that's all."

"All the locals?" laughed Annie. "Or just the professor types?"

"He doesn't quite look like the professor type," Ida said, "although that bushy beard does kind of propel him into a unique category."

"Well, he's a great guy now that he no longer drinks. And single!" Annie teased.

"Okay, stop it right now," Ida stated emphatically.

"Really Ida," Elsa intervened. "I think Mom's onto something here. It's possible. You and Landis."

Ida said nothing. She mixed up the salad greens with a fork and began chopping tomatoes. "I'm not even going to dignify this conversation with a remark."

"Okay," Annie replied, "but what if there's a spark?"

"I'm too old for that nonsense."

"Oh bull," Annie said. "I call your bluff and raise you one."

"And once more, he's not my type! I bet he even has a tattoo. So that's that!"

"Oh no it's not," responded Annie. "This calls for a bet. I'll wager you ten bucks that Landis doesn't have a tattoo."

Ida turned and held out her hand. "You're on, missy. But as part of this bargain you're not allowed to come right out and ask him."

Annie laughed. "Elsa, will you be indiscreet and ask Landis if he has a tattoo?"

"It has to be a natural part of the conversation," Ida added. "I don't know how you'll manage that."

"I have my ways," Elsa replied playfully, her eyebrows cocked.

Martha returned with a large bottle of red wine and a sparkling non-alcoholic cider. "Do you hear the birds up here?" she asked. "There were barn swallows in the basement."

"Swallows in our basement?" Annie was astonished. "Mom, what are you talking about?"

"I saw barn swallows in our basement," said Martha.

The other three women descended into the basement to check on these sightings. They neither heard nor saw any birds.

"Maybe she heard noises and imagined them. The lighting isn't great down here," reasoned Ida.

"She did have a glass of wine earlier today," said Annie.

"Or she's playing us," speculated Elsa. "I bet that's what it is."

When they'd traipsed back upstairs Martha was busy setting the table with plates and silverware. No one said anything about her joke. Elsa placed green and red candles on the long table before stoking the fire with more wood. They heard the jeep as they quickly carried the appetizers to the living room.

"Timing is everything," Martha announced.

"So I've heard," said Ida.

"Hope you have cash for that bet," Annie said to Ida.

"Back at ya."

The men came bundling into the warmth carting boxes and spreading good cheer with greetings. The women rose to welcome them. Ida took their coats and Western hats. The other women peeked into the boxes. Presents. Wine. Club soda. Pies. A ukulele!

"What's all this?" Martha pointed to some small red and green boxes.

"Well let's see, these are called presents. This one is for you," Beaming, Moses lifted a small box and handed it to her. He followed suit with all the other women. "And for you and you and you. From both of us. Landis and me. Just a Christmas token!" He seemed self conscious then, picking up the large box to place it near the door.

Landis unpacked the drinks. "Pinot noir and Sauvignon, okay? Club soda for us big guys."

Annie hugged both men, pulling them to the living area. "Come in and sit down."

"I'll get drinks for everyone," said Elsa. "What will you have?"

They talked of the weather, their dinner menu, a Christmas Eve service Moses had attended at Karen's church, and the visit Landis had with his sister's family in Missoula. He had driven back the night before.

"Were there any places open Christmas Eve?" asked Ida.

"The usual," replied Landis. "Gas and Coffee. Those places are open 24/7, 365 days a year. I was up for most of the week. I don't really do Christmas. My sister has five grand-kids – five *noisy* grand-kids, so I'd rather let them have the time for themselves."

"So now – you go ahead and open those presents. We didn't bring these boxes for you to look at." Moses was elated about his gifts. The women dutifully opened their presents: hand-made silver necklaces by a local artist, each one unique.

Elsa squealed, "I love it! Thank you!" She bounced up from the sofa to give each one a hug.

"This is lovely," Ida agreed, keeping her distance. "Thank you both."

"These even go with flannel shirts," said Martha.

"Did you get these at the Bozeman Arts fair?" asked Annie.

Landis glanced at Moses. "Actually, a friend of mine made them but they're from both of us."

Later at the dinner table, Ida asked Landis about his academic studies; a safe topic.

"I taught at Montana State for years but now I'm seg-ueing into retirement, working part-time with Montana Conservation Corps. I'm teaching one night-class at State. I may do some international work this summer." He answered succinctly. "So enough about me. What about you, Ida? Were you connected with the university in Boulder?"

"Just for a degree. Social work."

"And what did you do in the war – as the expression goes? What did you do with your degree?" he asked.

She looked to Martha and then back to Landis and the others. She hesitated in how to talk about her career. "I worked the oncology ward in a hospital and later helped develop the hospice program. Working with dying patients and their families was my lifework."

He went on respectfully. "I assume it was meaningful but it must have been hard personally?"

"I learned a lot from people. Each situation was so different – some harder than others." She sighed and shifted in her chair, looking around the table. "I think…really… this is not an ideal conversational topic – especially on Christmas Day."

"We learned a lot from Grandpa when he was dying," said Elsa. "His silliness was there – even near the end."

"Like what?" asked Annie.

"Remember near the end when he was sleeping most of the time and all three of us sat vigil beside his bed? One day he woke up and asked why we were all there. Grand-mom said we were there because he was dying. He looked at us, shook his head, and said, "Well, I've changed my mind. You can go home now.""

"Oh Dad," Annie sighed. "He'd be happy that you guys are here with us today."

"Yes, he would," Martha agreed, "and he'd be happy that Ida was here."

"Why is that?" asked Landis. "How did you two friends reconnect after all these years?"

Martha responded, "Again – Dan's death. Ida read about it in our college newsletter – online, right? She wrote me a note. Then I asked her to come visit."

"Everything happened pretty fast. I came for a short visit, extended my stay, and then extended my extended stay, and then Martha and I began imagining what we might do to live together again. The guest house idea was in the works, I had some inheritance money, she had some money, so we invested in this business for Annie as well."

"That's pretty amazing. But you two would have gotten together again regardless of this venture, don't you think? Just your longtime connection and affection for one another? Wouldn't you have tried to be together?" Landis asked Martha pointedly.

She stared fixedly at him as if an idea just popped into her head. "Uh, Landis, you know Ida and I are not lesbians. We're just old friends!"

Moses hooted. "You owe me some money, buddy." He looked around the table at the perplexed faces. "I wasn't about to say anything. Landis thought you two were...well together...you know – together."

Martha looked at Landis and stated coolly, "I was married to Dan close to forty years."

He looked directly back at her. "And your point is?"

Martha smiled. "All right, it's conceivable."

"Wait a minute, you guys bet on this?" asked Annie. "Whether Mom and Ida were lesbians?"

Landis looked sheepishly down at his plate. "I'm a little embarrassed now. This might be considered over the line."

"It's a bit creepy, Landis," said Martha. "Why would you care?"

Ida thought the same thing but wasn't about to say it. *What was it about deep-rooted friendships between women?*

"I personally think it's kind of funny," responded Annie. She elbowed Elsa.

"That reminds me of another bet," said Elsa. "We also have some money riding on a friendly bet."

"What's this?" asked Martha.

"I think you were in the basement getting wine when Annie and Ida made a bet," explained Elsa. "Can I ask him please? Please?"

Now Ida looked sheepish but Annie said, "Let's get this out in the open."

"Landis, do you have a tattoo?" Elsa blurted out.

"That's it?" asked Martha. "That's what you bet on?"

Moses chuckled. "Making bets for entertainment?"

"Or to make a little cash. I'm on a fixed income." Ida responded gamely. "And you haven't fessed up. Can you show us your tattoo?"

"Before I reveal all, I'd like to know who bet what." He regarded Ida evenly.

She lifted her glass of wine. "My bet is that you have *some* kind of tattoo."

"And I bet you don't!" exclaimed Annie.

Landis stood up and began removing his sweater. "It's pretty warm in here," he said.

"Oh stop teasing!" Annie said. "Do you or don't you?"

"I don't!" he declared a little too enthusiastically. He was enjoying this. "I hope this doesn't mean you'll be eating lentils the next few months."

"I love lentils, thank you," Ida replied. "It could, however, put a dent in my wine budget."

It was then that Moses pushed his chair back from the table and cleared his throat. "Anyone object if I take a little time to read the nativity story from Luke?"

The others appeared bemused at the abrupt change in conversation but Ida was happy to shift the focus. "I'd like that. Should I get my Bible from the cottage?"

"I have one here." He reached down into his backpack on the floor. "I just don't feel like it's Christmas unless we have a little scripture on how this whole thing started."

No one could argue with that. The others sat back, settling in to listen.

"In those days Caesar Augustus issued a decree that a census should be taken of the entire Roman world, and everyone went to their own town to register...And there were in those days shepherds abiding in the fields, keeping watch over their flocks by night. And lo, the angel of the Lord came upon them and the glory of the Lord shone around them and they were afraid..."

His deep resonant voice ushered in a sense of the solemnity for the night. The birth and sojourn story – whether a myth or a historical accounting – carried with it the years of oral tradition. Candles on the table burned low as he finished reading the passage from the Gospel of Luke. Ida was glad he ended with Mary pondering the mystery that was about to happen to her and the world. It was one of her favorite verses. *And Mary treasured all these things and pondered them in her heart.*

They cleaned up together after the dinner and carried the pies to the living room for dessert. Ida pulled Moses aside and asked quietly how he was doing. All the events and recent updates about Miriam were still swirling in his head. He thought he'd go visit the morgue in Bozeman to see about the body. He wanted to do more.

Relaxing into the soft cushions of the sofas and chairs, contentment set in. Their stomachs were full and conversation was easy. When Elsa entered with a stack of board games, Moses abruptly rose and announced it was time for him to take care of the horses. Landis suspiciously leaped up, volunteering to help, saying he needed some fresh air too.

"Is it me or does the timing seem pretty coincidental?" asked Ida.

"Moses always finds the nearest escape route when we bring out the games," said Martha. "He always skedaddles – even when we say we'll play teams."

Rusty arrived on cue to represent the male gender in a rowdy game of charades. When the men returned from chores, Martha sat down at the piano. "I can only play carols without sharps and flats so I'll start with those."

They sang the more familiar ones, crowding around the piano to see the words for second verses. Ida attempted the alto but gave up when she realized Martha could only do one thing at a time and could not join her in the harmony..

"We need to get a piano for the lodge," Rusty whispered to Annie.

"What lodge?" Elsa perked up. "I heard you say lodge,"

119

"Rusty and I are going into business together," said Annie. "We're going to build a lodge in the aspen grove across the lane."

"We're thinking later in the spring." Rusty glanced at Annie. "There's a demand for places like that for reunions and weddings."

"But that's a huge change for this place," said Elsa. "Weren't you going to discuss this with the rest of us?"

Martha stopped flipping through the hymnal and rose from the piano bench. She sighed. "They did discuss this with me. This is Annie's decision."

"But it will affect all of us," said Elsa. "Really, Mom, you should have talked this one out with all of us."

"Rusty and I want to maintain it a small operation, but to keep our rooms at maximum capacity we need to have a larger venue for gatherings."

Elsa flopped into a chair and hugged a pillow, obviously miffed at her mother for not consulting her on this major change.

Annie continued, "Suffice it to say there will be construction going on this spring. We don't need to go into the details tonight."

Landis unzipped his ukulele case and asked Elsa, "What holiday tunes do you know?"

"Deck the Halls" and "Jingle Bells" are my standards, but I'm game to try anything you are," she said. When he had strummed a few chords, Elsa picked up her flute and joined him to accent the melodies. They worked their way through a medley of spirited wassailing tunes.

Finally Landis lay down his ukulele after their rendition of "The Holly and the Ivy."

"I hate to break this evening up," said Martha standing up "but it's way past my bedtime and I rise early."

Ida sprung up to join her. Martha was not going to leave her behind. Landis stretched before putting on his coat, a gesture that communicated he felt at ease, *at home* with them all. He turned to face Ida directly. "Thank you again for including me. The food was great and thanks for not making me play charades."

"You missed a great chance to be a kid again," Ida said, zipping up her parka.

"I like being a kid when I can," he said, "and I appreciate you permitting me to crash the family dinner."

"I'm glad Moses remembered you," Ida straightened up as tall as she could. "We trust his judgment."

"On most things Moses hits the mark,but I'm sorry you lost your bet. If I get a tattoo next week, will your bet be good retroactively?"

Annie overheard and gave him a friendly shove. "Nice try old man! Too late for that."

Peabody rose from his place by the fire to lead the group outside. Ida and Martha walked the two men to the jeep and waved as it disappeared down the lane into the dark winter air. They turned to watch Rusty and Annie playfully banter through the kitchen window of the guest house. Upstairs, Elsa's bedroom light flipped on. Peabody emerged from a nearby bush and hurried to leave his night time markings in his favorite spots.

"Why is our friendship so hard for people to accept? A friendship that isn't sexual, isn't a romance?" asked Ida scanning the blanket of stars above them.

"People like those stories where high school sweethearts find one another years later and get something going. And isn't it mostly men who have a hard time understanding friendships between women?"

"Like women wanting to live together – it's just assumed they must be lesbians?"

"Lesbians. Us, huh?" asked Martha.

"I'm kind of flattered really," remarked Ida.

"It's not the first time someone thought that," Martha said. "Remember Dan asking us that years ago? He was trying to figure out why we were so close."

"Oh, he was asking because he was interested in you. And you played it coy because you weren't sure about him," recalled Ida.

"Landis may have been inquiring for the same reason Dan did way back when," Martha said, looking sideways at her friend. "He's interested in you."

"Yeah, sure. I've seen the way he looks at you," Ida remarked to the open sky.

Martha fisted her hand and knocked Ida squarely on her arm. "Don't you do it! "Don't you use me to protect your scared little heart. Don't you hide away, and don't you hurt Landis either! You know you felt that spark with him." She whistled to Peabody then, following him inside without another word.

Ida lingered in the winter-white darkness in a still-point of awareness. An inner yearning for something intangible pulled at her sacred core. She had no name for the aching. She opened her eyes and her ears, listening, as if there might be a specter on an ethereal plane. She wished she knew how to pray. She felt fullness, contentment but not contentment, restlessness but not restlessness, and she wanted to go walking and walking in one direction and not have to stop. She thought fleetingly of Buddhist practices that had helped her find the middle way between the extremes of living. She thought of Christian admonitions that cautioned against too much focus on individual wants and needs. Sometimes there was no help for it all but just to experience the given, live through it. She prayed the only way she knew how, to the God of good intentions, love and compassion, for the awful terrible things in this world and then in gratitude and astonishment for things past and for things yet to come.

JANUARY

ONE

The second Saturday of January brought a lovely snow-fall but not enough to keep them from going to town. Snowfields blanketed the world around them as Martha drove Old Gus on the crusty road. She would attend the second WoCA meeting with Ida with the agreement that afterwards, she could go to the hardware store while Ida picked up groceries.

The Elk House coffee shop was quiet at this hour. Martha and Ida ordered coffee and scones and spread out at the two tables protectively, as if other customers were ready to nab their corner. The names of the women were scribbled in Ida's notebook so she wouldn't forget: Madeleine, Josephine, Karen, Sadie, and Millie. They arrived and spent the first half hour catching up on news about each other,. Then Ida cleared her throat. "I think we'd better get started. Our topic today is *Best Friends*. Would anyone volunteer to start?"

Josephine was not one to hold back. "All of you are probably going to talk about best friends as women but I'll say straight up, my husband is my best friend. We didn't really find each other till we were in our fifties. Both married to other people. Both divorced. But I got to tell you, he's the one who knows me inside and out and loves me anyway. I can tell him off when he's getting on my nerves, and I know he's not going to go away in a huff. He doesn't let me get away with stuff either. He gives as good as he gets."

"What makes him a best friend?" asked Ida.

"It's knowing him so well. He's my best friend because we're so honest with each other. We'd never think of deceiving the other. We're straight up all the time, even if we know the other person may not like what we're saying. He's my soul mate."

"A soul mate seems like a fantasy," replied Martha.

Josephine turned to her. "He's my best friend and soul mate."

"Okay," Martha said, "but I'm just saying soul mates seem unrealistic. Like something in a country-western love song."

"Well maybe my marriage is like a country and western love song," said Josephine.

"So would your soul mate love you if you didn't get your face tightened? Is that in the country-western song?" Martha dunked her scone in her coffee, took a bite, and acted as if she wasn't the least bit confrontational.

Josephine appeared ready to pack up and leave. She pushed her half-eaten bagel away and slung her purse over her shoulder.

Ida leaned forward with her elbows on the table and said, "We probably need to establish some ground rules in our discussions. We all want to feel safe to share with each other. Let's try and be supportive of one another."

Martha looked up as if she just noticed Josephine's discomfort. She managed to mutter, "Sorry about that Josephine. I was out of line. You and I go back aways so we may have some unresolved feelings."

Josephine clung to her purse and said, "I can get defensive at times. I know Martha always speaks her mind – regardless of how it affects others."

Martha glanced at the others. "I said I was sorry." She turned specifically to Josephine. "I know your feelings were hurt."

"Yes, they were, but I don't need your insincere apologies either."

"Well, when you try to pass yourself off as something you're not…"

Karen, the pastor, intervened, "It might be helpful if we accept that we have differences and that we'll support each other without being critical. Or at least try."

"Yes, I agree," said Ida. "Let's try to respond with positive comments."

Martha and Josephine regarded one another warily. Both were opinionated women. Neither one budged.

Karen continued, "Is it okay if I share now?"

Everyone nodded. "My best friend is my sister. She lives in North Carolina so I don't see her often, but we talk every Sunday evening. As a minister I have to keep my personal boundaries with people in my daily life. It's been good to have my phone connection with my sister.. My family moved around a lot so we always had each other's backs. I wouldn't use the word soul mate either...just the best sister and best friend I could have." She leaned back in her chair and said, "I'm done."

"I think it's great that your sister is your best friend," said Madeleine.

"Yes, sounds like you've always been there for each other," agreed Sadie.

"I always wanted a sister," added Millie.

"Well, I'll go next," said Sadie. "You know Millie and I are best friends and partners. I don't know about soul mates. I'm just happy to be around Millie, even when she makes me fighting mad I still like, well, love her...and yes, she's my best friend."

"Sadie and me, well, it's not like we went out of our way to love each other," responded Millie. "We just knew we were different from other women; never cared for men or at least not to marry one of them. So, when we became friends way back in our twenties, well, it just seemed like we found the other parts of ourselves."

"But I had a best friend when I was a child long before I met Millie," confessed Sadie. "We'd laugh for hours over silly things. I suppose we can have best friends at different times in our lives – with different people."

They all agreed on that point. Best friends could come and go. One didn't have to just have one best friend for life.

Ida and Martha looked at one another. Who would tell their story? Martha nodded to Ida.

"My best friend is Martha here. As you know, I moved from Colorado to live with her. What you don't know is that we hadn't seen each other for close to forty years, until I visited about three years ago. Long story short – we knew each other in our twenties and just clicked. We seemed to understand one another without having to work at it like some relationships. We were in a commune together and after that, lived near each other a few more years."

"Then Dan and I had a harebrained idea to marry and travel around the country to look for a place to live. We wanted to strike out on our own far away from family. I'd been raised in Kansas on a farm. I knew I wanted to live in a rural area. Dan too. We tried some other parts of the country, but we ended up here in Montana – closer to Ellis originally. I lost touch with Ida. Once or twice we tried letters but just lost touch."

"It's a *gift* when you find that best friend – her – or him," Ida said to include Josephine. "I sometimes think of a best friend, or even a good friend, like a favorite book. You connect with it and it stays with you, even if you don't pick it up and read it again. You may even forget about it for a spell. But it's there. Your friend was there. Does this make sense?"

"I like that idea," Madeleine commented. "A good book stays with you – or some part of it does…like a good friend."

"So we may have several favorite books and each one influences us in a different way," added Josephine.

"Hey, that's a good one," agreed Martha. "Even Josephine and I might be books to remember."

Good friends. The threads of one's life intertwine with others, separate, and a pattern may form or it may not. How we stitch our friendships, our meanings, is not just our doing, but what is given to us, who comes our way. The women were philosophically in agreement by the end of the morning's talk. They agreed readily to meet the second Saturday in February to discuss the next topic: *Home*.

***

Martha dropped Ida off at the grocery store, agreeing to be back to pick her up in a half hour. "Thirty minutes. Keep an eye on the time," she admonished before gunning the motor.

"Always do," replied Ida. She found a cart and began her rounds, arranging the list of items in the order that she would find them in the store.

"Whoa there, you about hit a pedestrian," laughed Landis as Ida swung around a corner aisle.

"Sorry. I got caught up in my list," she held up her paper fragment. "Is this your shopping day?"

A woman dressed in a brown suede coat and long flowered skirt appeared beside Landis carrying a basket. "Hello," she said to Ida.

"Hi," Ida replied reflexively, her eyes taking in the full measure of the woman's proximity to Landis. She had to be around sixty, with a full head of blond hair and no navigational wrinkles on her face.

"Ida, this is my professor friend, Shelby. Shelby – this is Ida…" said Landis.

Shelby rested her hand on his arm. "Landis, your *professor* friend?" She turned to Ida with a raised eyebrow. "We're friends first and professors second. I'm glad to meet you."

"Oh yes. Nice to meet you too," Ida replied. *Shelby. Definitely a sixty-year-old's name.*

Landis elaborated. "Moses and I went to Christmas dinner at Ida and Martha's place and would you believe it, Ida made a bet on me – on whether I had a tattoo or not. Pretty funny, huh?"

Shelby laughed but eyed Ida respectfully. "He does look a little like someone who'd have one."

Ida smiled. "Yes, well, it was just for fun. We were just having a bit of fun."

Landis felt a need to go on. "And then I confessed that we'd made a bet whether Ida and Martha were gay."

"Guess we look like we could be," Ida responded, "Lesbian wannabes."

"No, no," Landis said, "I wanted to apologize for that. It was a stupid cultural assumption. Not funny – not like the tattoo. It's been bothering me and I'm sorry."

"It's okay, really, it's fine. It's pretty funny that we both made bets." She turned to Shelby. "Really I'm not the betting kind."

"No, neither am I," said Landis. His eyes focused on Ida.

"Okay you two, I think you've been forgiven." Shelby shifted her basket to the other hand and asked, "Are you coming to hear the band tonight?"

"Sure, you should," said Landis. "At the ski lodge; it's not quite the down-home place as Jack's but still could be fun. You should try and make it."

"Okay maybe…yes…I'll tell the others." Ida began moving away. "We'll maybe see you then. Nice to meet you, Shelby."

She pushed forward, easing her cart down another aisle. Thoughts fluttered by without tethers. Shelby, *sixtyish? A professor? Friends first, professors second.* Yes, that made sense. *It stands to reason Landis would be with someone younger, active, energetic.* She focused on her list of items. *Peanut butter. Shelby, probably a skier. Cheese. Yogurt.* What was her field? She didn't look like a scientist unless it was some psycho-social science. Probably something like Human Sexuality. She'd read that was a popular course these days.

She crouched over, inspecting the lower shelves for a can of almonds, the lightly salted ones, and then stood up to see Landis behind her.

"Sorry to startle you," he said. "I just wanted to reiterate that you should come tonight to hear the band. It's not far for you to drive."

"Okay, that's good to know," she stalled. "I'll talk it over with Martha."

"You can come alone you know. You're not attached at the hips, right?"

Ida was flustered. *Why is he being so pushy?* "Yeah okay. I'll think about it."

"It's right off the highway. We start at eight." Landis was explaining when Shelby appeared behind him. He turned to her. "I was telling Ida the directions to get there tonight."

"I'll save you a seat!" declared Shelby.

What was that, a whiff of possessiveness? "Thanks," Ida said. "Maybe I'll see you tonight."

Somehow she got through the list and managed to avoid checking out until after Landis and Shelby left. She was ten minutes past her meeting time with Martha, who sat idling Old Gus in front of the store. Ida placed the bags in the back and hopped up to the cab. "Did you see Landis?" she asked.

"Yep, I saw Landis."

"Did he see you?

"Yep, he saw me."

"Did you talk to them?"

"Nope!" Martha concentrated on getting Old Gus out of the parking lot onto the highway where a constant stream prevented her from moving.

"Do you know her? Do you know Shelby?"

"Shell -bee is her name?" asked Martha pulling out of the lot, accelerating to fifty.

"Yes, Shelby. Do you know her? Why are you smiling?"

"I'm smiling because I know you. And I know you're probably thinking that anyone named *Shelby* probably has mystical wiles to lock up old Landis's heart."

"It's not his heart I'm thinking she has locked up, but you're right, Shelby probably has mystical wiles."

"Sexual wiles?" asked Martha.

"Do you know her? You didn't answer my question."

"No, I'm sorry. Never saw her before. Did you talk with them?"

"Yes, I practically rammed into Landis. He introduced us and then went on and on about the Christmas betting as if it was some inside joke. He apologized though, for assuming we were lesbians. I don't know. It was weird. I mean lesbians don't apologize for being lesbians...why should he apologize for assuming we might be?"

"Sounds like he just felt awkward."

"Not a wrinkle on her face," Ida continued. "Sixty probably with some help from a surgical tool."

Martha looked at her friend. "You might be reading something into their relationship."

"Shelby specifically made a point to say they were friends first, professors second."

"Well friends, okay, she didn't say *special* friends."

"It's okay. I'm fine. It was just a surprise, that's all," Ida said. "He did ask me to come hear his band tonight, but I'm not too interested if Shelby is saving a seat for me."

They drove in silence for the next few miles. Ida brought up the WoCA meeting so they shared thoughts on that. By the time they arrived back home and unpacked the things from the truck, Ida was ready for a late lunch. "I'll make a salad and heat up the leftover soup," she said.

"Sounds good to me," responded Martha. "You okay?"

"Never better. I'm relieved to be out of that picture. I'm moving on."

Martha said, "So neither one of us is interested in going to hear the band tonight, right? I have a full day tomorrow. Moses doesn't come and Annie could use some help with a full house of guests."

"I'll pass. Maybe we could go up to Jack's again sometime. I enjoyed hearing them there. But tonight, I'm good with a hot bath and a good book."

Ida was moving on. She had no time for jealousy. So petty at her age. He wasn't interested in her. Any trifling fantasies of love she'd had were now wisps of nothingness, floating into the uppermost regions of this earthly world. Let them go. Lines from a Sylvia Plath poem came to her: *I let her go, I let her go/ Diminished and flat/ As after radical surgery.* Yes, sometimes we just have to cut out the offending piece, what perhaps should not have entered us in the first place. Let it go.

FEBRUARY

ONE

"It's hard to believe but February is starting off as one of our busiest months!" Annie exclaimed. "It's a great month for skiing but our older travelers on the Verdant Pathways tours, they like coming out here just for winter changes in the scenery and wildlife."

"And the sleigh rides too?" Ida asked.

"Special only for our VP groups – only Thursday evenings."

It was during one of these Thursday afternoons that Ida was engaged with an older Swedish gentleman, listening to his tales of visiting the far northern city of Kiruna. He was expounding on the nomadic traditions of Laplanders and how things were changing as the northern cities became more developed. A sociologist by training, he had the gifted eye of someone skilled in observing patterns of social behavior.

Ida was fascinated by the old Swede's descriptions of an ice hotel built just for tourists. She was ready to ask him about the heating in the hotel rooms when she heard a noise at the kitchen door and a stomping of boots.

Landis was in the kitchen peering into the living area. "Sorry. Sorry to interrupt. I was…uh…looking for Moses. Sorry."

Ida jumped up to greet him. "Don't be silly. You're not interrupting. We're just talking about Lapland – and ice hotels. Come in!"

He unlaced his boots and kicked them off. "If it's okay, I'll just stay a little bit. I really am looking for Moses."

"He's out in the stables if he's still here. But I'll call out there and tell him you're here. Come in." Ida went to the office to phone. Yes, Moses was there. Yes, he'd stop by the house.

When she returned, Landis was dialoguing with the old Swede, asking about a boreal forest in northern Europe. She listened as they discussed something called the "taiga," apparently a forest located near the top of the world. Landis was curious about the other man's travels there.

Other guests filtered into the room with coats and bags ready for the dinner hour. The old Swede realized the time and had to cut off conversation to wash up for dinner, so Ida and Landis moved to the kitchen.

"Moses will come by the house on his way out. Would you like some hot tea?" She pointed to the kettle.

"Sure, that'd be nice. I have A.A. tonight. I thought I'd find Moses first." Landis pulled out a chair to sit at the massive table. "Glad I found you though. I haven't seen you for a while."

"It's good to see you too," she remarked cheerfully. "Didn't you say you were teaching this semester?"

"You have a good memory. Yes, but only one evening course. Basic biology. Mostly freshmen getting a science credit."

"Still, it's good to interact with students, isn't it?"

"I give lectures to a room of fifty or more students. The TAs do all the grading. I don't really get to know students."

"I forget that you're at a state college."

"I think I'm just tired of academics. I'm happy doing my conservation work, but I'm ready for a break into real life."

"Real life? Retirement?"

"I want time to do things I like to do. I want to get up in the morning and ask myself, 'Landis, what do you want to do with your life today?'"

"That's my life!" she exclaimed. "Only I think I need to cut back on this socializing with guests." She nodded toward the living room.

"You had quite an interested party there today. He seems to like you."

"He likes anyone who will listen to his tales, but he's had a fascinating life."

Landis accepted the mug of hot water with a tea bag on the side. He added a spoonful of honey and stirred it silently.

"Want some cheese and crackers? We've got those too." She pointed to the buffet.

"No thanks. Might spoil my dinner. With Moses." Landis looked out the kitchen window.

"So…" Ida sat across from him with her own cup of tea. "How did your gig go a few weeks ago? I'm sorry again that I missed it."

"It was a different kind of crowd. The skiers were there to drink and hit on each other. Our music is irrelevant in places like that," Landis said with a twisted smile. "So, it probably wasn't your kind of scene."

"I've kind of enjoyed hibernating this winter." Ida was trying to be kind but all she could see was Shelby standing behind Landis. It was silly she knew. She might as well have been talking about a high school dance.

"Well, I know you go out to the grocery store," he said, stirring his tea intently. "I know you drive to town."

Was he trying to be funny? She was thinking fast about a retort. Something about him and Shelby, but she knew it wouldn't come out right. She sipped her tea slowly. "I do try to get out of the house occasionally."

The guests were leaving by the front door waving goodbye. The old Swede stopped by the table to acknowledge Landis and to give Ida a pat on her shoulder. He was an affectionate man. Moses appeared at the back door simultaneously. Landis finished his tea and stood up to greet his friend. Plans for dinner were bantered about as Landis put on his boots. The sudden commotion from both ends of the house left Ida feeling misplaced, in a state of overstimulation. She became preoccupied with her tea. Someone was talking.

"Ida, nice to chat. Thank you for the tea," Landis's tone was formal.

She could be that way too. "You're welcome."

"Maybe I'll catch you at the grocery store the next time you go out," he said.

Something snapped. "There's no need for you to be snippy about my comings and goings. I'm not a gadabout like some." With that she stood up, picking up the spoons and mugs to turn her back on him. He was mocking her. He wasn't interested in her.

Martha came in then and the men said their good-byes. Ida turned to nod, to acknowledge their departure. In that momentary glance back at him, in that nanosecond of an eternity, she saw in his eyes, disappointment. *Was it?* He moved away from her then, preoccupied with getting out the door. Had he been trying to reach out to her? Was he...?

She had just meant to keep herself from hurting, but she thought perhaps this time she had hurt someone else. It was the coldest she'd felt in a long time.

TWO

Ida could not shake the weary melancholy that came upon her after the shaky interaction with Landis. She was nearing the sixth-month mark in her move to Montana and had fits of fear it might not be enough to hold her here.

Underneath all the positives; Martha, the cottage, a new community, and friends – was the weight of a sadness that she could not dismantle. Scolding herself for self-pity, she pushed herself to interact more with guests, to make international friendships. But these were not friends who took up residence in her heart. They were connections. Associations. She felt the tiredness of it all.

She missed friends in Boulder, going to concerts or plays at the university, hiking the Rockies or just driving the Rockies, and she missed her little church. She'd thought about calling a friend or two in Boulder, but she really didn't want to complain or rehash what was going on. She knew she could talk to Martha, who'd say just go to work, get out of yourself. So she sat in the dusk of evening under a lamp casting a blue shadow, writing protest letters to her representatives in government. It helped her feel her voice in the world was still important. Before bed she'd read a novel; a fictional account of a life far removed from hers, and yet, in actuality, quite similar.

It was just the winter blues. She would get out more in spring. She'd buy her own car. She'd get more involved in Karen's church. This was just a bad funk.

Where was that copy of the poem she'd read after Miriam died? She leafed through her journal.

A New Thing is Creating
The bleak landscape surrounds me like a womb.
I never loved the winter fields,
brown and dead they stretch to the horizon as I pass,
dry stubble, sad vestiges of life and hope.
Bare branches like the gnarled hands
of ancient crones
beseech the brooding sky,
are met with icy silence.

Yes, that's how she felt. Winter holding her - like a womb. She didn't just have to age. She could be birthing too, birthing into something new; new that was creating. She just needed to learn patience. Delayed gratification, her father always said, was a spiritual discipline well worth learning. It was what nature did all of the time.

She'd get on the task of buying a new car. She'd do her research. Who could she ask to drive her to Bozeman? Martha would get bored there and didn't like driving. Maybe Moses. He might know something about cars too.

What about Karen? The pastor. Maybe she would be willing to have coffee, just to chat. She'd understand some of this winter blues, this aging blues. Because that's what it was too. Time was going faster all the time and she felt somehow something was still missing. She'd had a good life. If she died, well, she'd lived well and given much to others. Still, something in her core was rattling. And sad.

Well, life could be sad. It was misery and famine and poverty and loneliness. She would never have survived as a refugee. They had inner strength to keep going, to keep moving, to find new life somewhere. Mary and Joseph, refugees living on the road, bearing a son who turned the tables on what was expected. "I have come to fulfill the law"…but not with hate and distrust and a God-is-on-my-side mentality. Love yourself. Reach out to the least of these. Love others as you love yourself. And do for others as you would have them do. So simple. So profound. So, so difficult.

These rambling thoughts were leading to nowhere, but they somehow lifted her feelings. She would call Karen. She would share these blues. Karen was a pastor and a pastor has to listen, whether she's a friend or not. There was no shame in her loneliness in reaching out to a pastor.

And she could admit to some loneliness. It had come and gone, come and gone, many times in her lifetime. Perhaps she was more resilient than she gave herself credit for.

It was different from aloneness or solitude, which gave her inner spirit a voice. This loneliness sprung from a sense that she was walking beside something she could not see and would not be able to understand; something beyond her. Time itself taking on an ethereal shape to move with her, inside her, around her. Yes, something quite different rattling around in her inner core, in her soul.

THREE

The February WoCA topic was "The Meaning of Home and Place," something Ida had been contemplating during this dark season as she settled into living on a Montana ranch. The old adage that "home is where the heart is" rang true for all of the women, although they agreed that hearts can up and move to many different places. Josephine shared about her family moving every few years in her childhood, and thus, she had no favorite place or concept of home beyond what she had now. For Ida, home had connotations of a rootedness, where one felt a sense of belonging and a measure of safety. She thought again of refugees on the move to find a new home, a place of security, and she knew she had lived a sheltered life, a very privileged life.

Following the meeting, Ida pulled Karen aside and asked if they could meet for lunch sometime. "I'd like that," answered Karen "Where?"

"Would you want to come out to the ranch? I don't have my own car yet so that would be convenient – and you'd get to see the place."

"Sure, that'd be great." They agreed that she'd come the following Tuesday morning.

On the drive home Martha asked Ida point blank, "So are you thinking you made the wrong move coming out here?"

"What makes you ask that?"

"You just seem kind of moody. Not into that old happiness/gratitude stuff you kept spouting off the first few months you were here."

"I think I'm just in a winter funk. I have to figure out what I'm needing and figure out a way to meet that need."

"God, that sounds so clinical. What kind of need?"

"Oh, just simple things. Like last week I realized I need to go buy that car I've been talking about. I think if I had my own car, I'd feel more independent."

"You know you can use Old Gus anytime."

"And I appreciate it, but this thing isn't all that reliable. My plan was to buy a new car from the beginning, but I just keep procrastinating. I'm going to do something about that."

"Okay, but that's not what's making you all sad. Why don't you give old Landis a call?"

Ida's heart flipped. Had she been that obvious? "Landis? We've hardly had anything to do with each other. I'm going to have Karen out for lunch this week."

"Karen? As in Pastor Karen? To our place?"

"Yes, I asked her. I thought about the friends I used to meet for coffee and I thought maybe Karen could fill that void. I'm thinking of getting more involved in her church too."

"Yeah, that sounds good. I think you should do stuff with other friends. I've got my life outside of the ranch. You need to find your thing. But why not Landis?"

"Don't push him on me. That's not happening!" Ida turned away. *And he has his Shelby anyway.*

"Okay. I'm just concerned about you. It was a huge thing to move out here after years in a city where there's always stuff to do. I remember you saying your community was a hard thing to give up, but you were ready to let go. I don't want you to feel you have to stay here."

"I'm not leaving! I miss city life sometimes, but when it comes down to it, I was ready for a quieter pace. I love the ranch — meeting the guests that come through — and your family. This is just the winter blues. Really, that's all."

"I just want you to tell me if it's something more."

"You will be the first to know. I'm allowed to be sad and melancholy sometimes."

"This can be a hard and lonely life, but you've got the inner grit for sure."

"I guess that means something coming from you."

"Now don't say you're grateful or something like that."

Ida smiled. "What have I got to be thankful for?"

"There you go. Just get out there and get on with it."

***

Pastor Karen arrived promptly for their coffee date. Ida showed her around the cottage. Karen was impressed that they'd planned so many details that architects were just beginning to incorporate in building for the aging:, pastel painted walls, brighter reading lamps, motion detection lights in hallways and bathrooms, plug-ins at mid-wall, bathtubs with bars, and many windows for natural light. Ida showed her the plans for the additional room off the laundry area.

"It seems that you've given a lot of thought to how you hope to age," commented Karen as Ida poured her a cup of coffee.

"I started thinking about it a lot around my sixtieth birthday, but I suspect working in hospice with a lot of dementia patients affected my thinking. I just hope to live into my later years with a continuing love of life." Ida sat down at the counter and motioned to the other stool.

"I know what you mean. I get a little scared thinking about the reality, but I'm planning to move to a retirement community with my sister in a few years. I want to move before I need full-time nursing care!"

"Fortunately, we're of a generation where there are options. Too bad we don't have more pastors and social workers running our country. We might have single-payer health care and community-based homes for our elders."

Karen laughed. "That would be utopia. Or maybe just a clone of Finland - the happiest country!"

"I am an optimist most of the time," Ida replied. "but I did ask you here because of a personal need for reassurance."

Karen turned and said, "I'm listening."

"I told Martha I was just experiencing the winter blues, but I know I will likely feel the spring blues and the summer blues as well. I don't regret the move here, but I am feeling a need for more – something."

"It's not a weakness to express need."

Ida nodded. "Yes, you probably detected my delusion in thinking I don't need others. I draw strength from being alone, but I also appreciate learning from others, being with others with common connections. I think I miss my church in Boulder as well."

"And friends there?"

"Somewhat. I didn't have the closeness I have with Martha, but there was always someone to do things with. And if there wasn't, well, it's a city and there are people around. I'm convinced that's why there are so many coffeehouses."

"And bars," added Karen.

"And bars," agreed Ida. "Public spaces where people can sit with others, even if they're mesmerized by their phones."

"One can be very lonely with a lot of people around."

"Existential angst?" Ida asked.

"I think of Paul Tillich, the theologian, who said something like 'language has created the word loneliness to express the pain of being alone, and it has created the word solitude to express the glory of being alone.'"

"Yes, that's the dualism I feel for sure. And I sense that some of this melancholy is a spiritual need, that it's part of the God-spirit knocking at my soul's gate."

"Wow," stated Karen. "Do you mind if I quote you?"

"Back when I was working full-time, I was overly busy and that busy ness made me feel important. I don't want to go back to that, but I'm very aware that one gets a sense of self-importance by being busy."

"Self-importance or self-fulfillment?" Karen had a way of targeting word choice.

"Maybe a little of both. Now, out here, I am aware of time and not wanting to fill it up - just to be busy."

"Sounds like you are practicing mindfulness. Isn't that meaningful too?"

"The thing is – I know having a sense of purpose and being open-hearted is what gives my life meaning.

Sometimes I just don't feel that way though." There, she'd done it. She'd admitted to feeling not good enough.

"You know, I think Jesus was a pretty melancholy guy. He went off by himself an awful lot; praying, wandering in the wilderness, and who knows what else? Then he'd come back to the squabbling disciples or crowds either cheering or jeering him. He probably wondered about his sense of purpose too."

"But he just kept doing what he did well – tell those parables and try to unlock the conundrums of the kingdom of God?"

"Why aren't you a minister? You're knocking this stuff out of the ballpark here."

Ida smiled. "I'd never make it to first base, to use your analogy. The language, the dogma, the congregational expectations! But I admire you for being a minister. It's one of the toughest jobs. So many critics feeling entitled to share their opinions of everything you do."

"Why do you think I ended up out here in a small, non-denominational congregation?" Karen asked. "And you did say you missed your church."

"I did say that, didn't I?" Ida reflected. "So perhaps I will show up again soon."

"It would mean a lot to me personally, but really, no pressure," Karen replied. "But getting back to your feeling a little adrift, well, you don't seem anxious about that. You'd just like not to feel it, is that it?"

"Once I name it, I don't feel it quite so intensely. I think just articulating it with you has lifted some of the dismalness of those feelings."

"It can be therapeutic to talk, and I'm always open to that."

"I'd like that. Maybe we can talk about you more next time."

"This was nice. I appreciate you initiating this coffee time. I don't get too many offers like this."

"Really? People don't invite you out so they can talk about themselves for hours?"

Karen laughed. "You have not done that by any means. I appreciate your willingness to delve into matters of the heart."

"Well, good, maybe we can delve together then!"

"I take it you're not one for praying?" Karen asked tentatively. "Having conversations with God?"

Ida thought about this for a bit. "I probably do pray and I probably talk with God a lot. I'm just not intentional. I don't address the deity by name."

"There are many forms of prayer. I suspect God knows what's truly in our hearts even before we do."

"I imagine God – whatever - as being very magnanimous and forgiving beyond our human comprehension," said Ida.

"But the mystery to me is why the first commandment is to love God with all of one's heart and soul and mind. The most important purpose we have is to love an unexplainable, mysterious, historical presence called God."

"Subtle, wasn't he, that Jesus?" asked Ida. "It's about giving, not receiving. Emptying out, not filling up."

"I think so yes." Karen reflected quietly.

"Well, that surely is a prayer."

"Or a spiritual aspiration?" As Karen got up to leave, she added, "Did you know Moses attends our church once in a while? He would be a welcome face for you."

"Like he attends regularly?"

"I wouldn't say regularly. Maybe once a month. He's an interesting man."

"Yes, yes, he is. He's a mystery of his own," agreed Ida. "And thank you again, for coming here today. And for listening."

"It was a gift for me too. A pastor's life can be lonely too. So…thank you."

FOUR

Another snowy blizzard blew its way through the state. Fresh layers atop the February snowpack added dimensional depths to the landscape. Tree and fence shadows playfully zigzagged gray designs across the whiteness. The sleepy silence of a snowy winter was jarred awake by whistling winds forcing contact with anything that moved.

Ida lay awake in the darkness of the early morning, basking in this feeling of being held in a warm place between flannel sheets under the down comforter. As a blustering wind roiled around outside, the little cottage held its own against the increasing belligerence of this storm. Overhead lights from the kitchen flickered on. A crash had her leaping from the bed. She grabbed her sweater off a hook by the door.

Martha lay on the floor, a barstool toppled beside her. "I'm okay!" she snapped. "Are those damn birds out now?"

"What birds?" asked Ida. She helped Martha to her feet.

"They're probably gone now. Soon as I turn on the lights, they're gone."

"I didn't hear anything except this crazy wind," said Ida. "Did you see something?"

"Those barn swallows were in my room again and they flew in here. Soon as I turned on the lights, they disappeared!"

"Barn swallows – like the ones you saw on Christmas?" Ida asked.

"Christmas? What are you talking about? They were in my room tonight! Swooping up and down. I'd know them anywhere."

Ida walked into the living room to switch on a lamp. Martha turned on the hall lights leading to the laundry.

"I hope they're not bats," said Ida shivering.

"I told you they're barn swallows! Blue barn swallows! Come look in my room."

Ida followed her, switching on lights in Martha's bedroom and bathroom. "Okay," she said calmly. "They're not here now."

Martha walked about peering up into the corners. "They always go away when I turn on the lights. They don't like light."

"That's good. But we're not sleeping with the lights on," replied Ida. She was convinced Martha was dreaming or hallucinating but wasn't about to start that conversation.

"Nobody said we would," replied Martha, emphatically flicking off switches one by one. "I'm going back to bed. If you hear them, you'll know I'm right."

Ida sat for a few minutes by a lamp in the living room. The wind continued to blow through the trees and even the roof of the little cottage trembled slightly. She didn't want to bother Annie with this incident. It was just a fright in the night, a trick of the mind on a cold winter's night. Barn swallows.

***

The next morning Ida ran outside to nab Moses when he pulled up in his pick-up, his truck bed brimming with fire-wood. He backed up to the woodshed intending to spend some time unloading and stacking.

"How are the roads this morning?" Ida called.

He stepped down from his truck and pulled out gloves from the front seat. He tipped his hat towards her in his usual polite manner. "Mostly passable. Plows are working."

She approached him directly, not wanting to yell across the yard. "I have a favor to ask you. I need to buy a car. I know what I want and I know which dealer in Bozeman, but I was wondering if you'd drive me up there."

He appeared surprised but pleased. "I'd be happy to do that. I don't know a whole lot about car-buying, but I'd sure help you get there and kick a few tires for you."

"That'd be great. I've been wanting to get my own 'wheels,' as they say. I think if I did I'd feel freer to just get out and about."

Moses nodded. "Is this coming Monday the first Monday in March? I'm heading to Bozeman for lunch that day. Do you think this Monday would work for you?"

"Sure, perfect."

"Let's plan on that."

Before he could turn away, Ida continued, "Martha woke me up early this morning by turning on the lights and falling over a stool. She said she saw barn swallows."

Moses scratched his head. "That's a little strange, don't you think? A little early for nesting birds. Was she dreaming?"

"I hope that's all it was, but this is the second time she's claimed to see them. Last time was on Christmas – in the basement of the guest house. The rest of us checked and didn't see anything."

He shut his front passenger door and put on his hat. "I'll keep an eye on her today if that's what you're asking."

"I don't know what I'm asking. Just thought you might have seen something similar. She said they go away when the lights are on."

He thought about that for a moment. "Well, that could explain why she has a sudden inclination to keep the lights on in the barn. I did think that was a bit odd, but it's winter, it's darker. Always something isn't it?"

"I'm not worried, just curious." Ida was already backing towards the house. "I'll let you get on with your day. It's probably nothing."

"I'll keep an eye out," he said as he began throwing wood into a pile on the crusted snow.

It's probably nothing. Hopefully nothing.

SPRINGING

MARCH

ONE

They arrived at the Subaru dealer late that Monday morning. A gaggle of salesmen grouped around the coffeemaker, chatting and checking their phones. One exuberant young man broke from the pack and headed toward the pair, his eyes moving from one to the other, uncertain which one to address. "Hi, how are you? My name's Zach. How can I help you?"

Ida held a print-out in front of her. "Well, Zach, this is the car I'm interested in test driving. I might also look at a Forester, but I'm pretty sure I'm set on this Outback."

"Great! Sure, let me show you what we've got." He threw his arm out towards the massive parking lot of cars.

She pointed to a dark, wine-colored Outback like what she'd found online. "This is it, Moses. What do you think?"

He walked around the vehicle a few times and sat in the front seat inspecting all the knobs and buttons. "Looks like a cockpit, but I think you can handle it."

They took it out for a spin. It felt familiar, akin to Annie's model. It would do the trick in all kinds of weather. And there were even fancy heated seat cushions. She was an easy sell.

Moses stuck his head into the office several times as Ida read and signed papers, getting credit approval on the four-year loan. He held up his wristwatch.

"What's wrong, Moses? You seem antsy," she asked.

"I'm just wondering if you're about done. I like to get to the diner by twelve before it fills up for lunch."

"I'll try and get through this." She turned to the mid-level salesman Zach had passed her off to. "You heard the man. Could we speed this up a bit?"

In her new Subaru, Ida followed Moses to the diner on the same side of town. She was feeling giddy and a bit nervous after making such a major purchase. Her lifelong frugality kicked in whenever there was a major financial outlay. She dickered with herself about need versus want. Still it had not been impulsive. She had researched well and she rationalized that a reliable set of wheels was a necessity now. Just let it be, Ida, and be happy you did this.

She sat across from Moses in a corner booth and beamed as she scanned the menu. "Now this is my treat today, so you get whatever you want. I'm celebrating!"

"I might just have to get some pie then," he smiled. His eyes circled the room behind her and he nodded to someone. "Hey Landis."

Ida turned to see Landis beside their booth. She glanced from one to the other to determine if this had been arranged.

In semi-bewilderment she blurted out, "I just bought a car. We're celebrating."

"How about that? Congratulations!" said Landis. "And I'm glad you picked our meeting hole for your celebration. May I join you?" He sat down beside her without waiting for a reply, scooting her over by force of will.

"I meet Landis here the first Monday of every month," Moses confessed sheepishly. "I didn't tell you because I knew you'd think you were intruding, but he and I..." he pointed to Landis and himself, "we do like other company once in a while."

"Did you know about this?" she asked Landis.

"Nope, this is his doing. It's a surprise. But a good surprise!"

"Well then," she said, "I'll treat you too. I'm just full of the celebratory spirit today."

"I told her I'm getting pie – if she's paying," winked Moses.

Her exuberance about the new car swept her along through the lunch conversation. She didn't have time to ponder the serendipitous encounter. She didn't have time to feel ambushed. "Did you know about heated car seats? I never, in my lifetime, thought that such a wonderful thing could be in a car I owned. I've marveled at electric blankets but now heated car seats!" They talked about many things, none of which mattered. She liked sitting beside Landis in the booth. He didn't make her feel nervous today.

When she was paying at the cashier, Landis thanked her for lunch and said, "I'd like to officially invite you to join us next month for our first Monday lunch. Moses, what do you think?"

"You're putting him on the spot," Ida interjected. "This is your time together."

"Wait a minute, give me a moment to speak for myself," said Moses. "If I didn't want you here, I wouldn't have gotten you here today under false premises. Is that the word? Premises?"

"See." Landis looked almost smug. "You are welcome to join us. We might talk about you if you don't come."

"That's a real enticement," Ida replied. She tapped her hand playfully on Landis's arm. "I wouldn't treat every time…if I do decide to join you."

Both men responded with exaggerated shrugs and "Oh well, then…" comments.

She thought at the time her uplifted emotions were sourced in the anticipation of driving a new car. Later, she reflected that quite possibly sitting with Landis and Moses, talking about nothing in particular, that this friendly conversation had sent that rippled charge of energy through her. She still felt the muscle in Landis's arm. *Oh my.*

And once back home in her cottage she couldn't sit still. It was Monday so there was no guest house social hour. Restlessness drove her to cleaning and vacuuming the cottage with a vigorous kinesis. Then she took to making soup, a vegetable soup that required chopping and slicing, simmering and spicing at specific timed intervals. The mindfulness of soup-making.

What is this? she admonished herself. *A little interaction with a couple of friends and you're a flurry of energy gone haywire.*

By the end of the evening, after the soup had been consumed and the dishes washed and put away, and she finally was able to sit quietly with Martha watching some innocuous program on the screen, she acknowledged that perhaps she did have a little crush on Landis. Maybe that was okay. Maybe she could just keep it her little silent crush. That would lighten her mood, and she wouldn't tell anyone. It would just be her secret resource – kind of how she regarded her memory bank of stories and poems. He could just nestle in there – in her mind. It was superficial, but if it did the trick, she thought herself quite clever.

"What are you smiling at?" Martha asked her. "Or is this documentary amusing you?"

Ida shook her head. "I was just thinking about something that made me smile."

"Something or someone?"

"Just a little daydream. That's all." She tried to concentrate on the film but for the life of her, she couldn't seem to focus. She'd discovered a key to partially escape her winter blues and she'd use it, but only in small chunks. Like anything pleasurable it could become addictive and she was only going to keep it as her little "stash," her private clandestine resource.

TWO

Ida had never cared for spring. Something about everything sprouting up all cheery and colorful was an act of artifice. These diversions were devised by nature so she wouldn't pay attention to what was happening underneath, within the hidden world. Spring in Montana meant snow cover keeping those diversions out of her range longer than usual.

On the first two Sundays in March, Ida attended Karen's church, though Karen would be the first to say it was not *her* church but the congregants'. People welcomed Ida after the service. They knew a guest when they saw one. Moses had not been in attendance either one of the Sundays she had. Hit or miss for both of them.

She perused the bulletin for weekly events. There were numerous opportunities to volunteer in the area – a healthy sign for a small congregation. A "Scriptures Unleashed" coffee klatch sounded promising, although it was likely just a catchy name for Bible study. Not that there was anything wrong with that. But there were reasons why she called herself a marginal Mennonite.

"I'm so glad you came back this second Sunday," Karen said shaking her hand after the service. "We didn't scare you off."

"I don't want to get your expectations up about my attending, but I do appreciate your sermons," Ida replied graciously. "I admire you tackling some of those Old Testament texts."

Karen leaned in and murmured, "I'm off the third Sunday of every month, just in case you wanted to know that."

Ida nodded and said her thanks as she moved along, aware of others behind her waiting to exchange words with the minister. *That's good to know.* Put it on her calendar at home. On the drive home she became aware of that loneliness that often came upon her after a religious service. What was it about church that brought on this weariness of the soul? The sermon had been thoughtful and a reminder about the needs in this world. But greeting others and passing the peace had left her feeling hollow.

Loneliness. She had walked with it plenty and had chosen it at times over relationships that wore her out. Plenty of her married friends experienced loneliness, despite partners, children, and grandchildren. She had expected the move to Montana to carry with it aspects of loneliness. But this surprise this morning – without so much as a ready or not, here I come – had landed her in a sorrowful solitude.

At a pull-off along the highway, she parked her car and regarded the barren snow-covered vista of the hills. Curtains of slate-colored clouds scudded by to inadvertently reveal a bashful sun. It really was a marvelous day to be alive. She inhaled the vast beauty before her. A painting of these landscapes could never touch the depth in the masterpieces created by the chaos and intentionality of Life. And now she had loneliness to thank for bringing her to this place of overflowing appreciation and wonder. Such irony would never be fully understood in the ways of this world.

***

On March 21, the first official day of spring, Ida found two envelopes addressed to Moses in their mailbox at the end of the lane. She sought him out to hand-deliver the letters, both with return addresses of Kansas City. She found him in the barn with Martha, tidying up the tack room. Old prescription bottles and hardened ointments were finally being discarded.

The first envelope he opened was professional. It had a cover letter and then attached legal materials with the appearance of a financial prospectus. "This doesn't seem right," he said. "It appears to be saying I am the recipient of half of Miriam's inheritance."

Both Martha and Ida moved closer to peer at the document. "That's what it states clearly," said Martha pointing to the sentence on the paper.

Ida skimmed over the words quickly. Yes, Moses was identified as one of the heirs to Miriam's financial estate.

He carefully folded up the materials and replaced them into the first envelope. In the second one was a hand-written letter from Miriam. He glanced over it and returned it to the envelope saying he'd read it later.

Later that evening, he visited them in the cottage. At the door he held up the letter. "I need to tell you something or I think I could burst."

"Something about Miriam?" asked Martha.

"Remember when you said the police told you Miriam had a son who she gave up for adoption?"

Ida gasped. "No really? Was it your son?"

"It seems so. Miriam wrote about it quite matter of factly. She knew she had to give him up. There was no way she could raise a son by herself, let alone one who was bi-racial, and she hadn't intended to let me know at all, but he came back into her life. He's the one who helped her find me."

"Wow," was all Martha could say.

"So, is there a way to find him? Or more to the point, do you want to find him?" asked Ida.

Moses shook his head. "I don't know what I want. What I should do. What's right. I just don't know."

"Well, apparently he knows where you are – if he helped Miriam find you," said Ida.

"But what is expected of me?" asked Moses.

"Wow," reiterated Martha. "This is a tough one."

"I think I'll sit on it," replied Moses. "I guess I could write a letter and send it through this bank. I don't know what I'd say though. I think I'll just leave it be."

"If he wants to find you, he will," replied Ida.

Moses nodded. "The other thing I need to ask you is about scattering Miriam's ashes in the aspen grove across the road. I've got the documentation now to claim her remains."

"That's a good idea," replied Martha, "but probably up higher – away from where they're planning weddings." "I looked around here at all the different trees. The pines and firs are nice but they shed needles. I asked Landis what trees. He suggested aspen for lots of reasons. I like the idea of a single root system, being one big family and connected. Landis also said it's a strong wood that doesn't splinter or split easily."

"It seems appropriate for lots of reasons," Ida remarked.

"I'd like to have a little service too. Maybe on Memorial Day?"

"Check with Annie but sounds good," Martha said.

The ranch lost money during March. Annie needed to figure out how to bring in more regular income during the off seasons of spring and fall. Meanwhile, Rusty was moving more of his belongings into the house. He was the one to initiate the idea of holding events at the guest house, and that they needed a reception hall of some sort. He proposed the Dusky Grouse could advertise itself as a venue for small celebrations, intimate weddings, and family reunions. Food preparation could be done through several catering services.

So with the help of an architect friend, Rusty and Annie designed a new building with solar panels on a low, gabled roof. Oak beams and a massive fireplace set up a country ambience. Dimmer lighting and portable furniture allowed for flexibility at different events. Three public bathrooms were added and a large kitchen. Wooden hooks zigzagged across one wall and an open closet lined the small mudroom entrance. Narrow windows brought in the southern exposure. They called this new space with capacity for a hundred, the Tamarack Lodge.

Fifty feet towards the southwest range, the Madison Mountains, a grove of aspens provided an idyllic setting for outdoor wedding or anniversary ceremonies. Rustic pine benches and a vine arbor provided an intimate gathering space.

When Moses heard about their plans, he approached Annie with the idea of using the inheritance money to help. He thought Miriam would want that. He wanted to do something useful with the money.

Martha was having none of it. "What would *you* like to do?" Martha asked him. "How about traveling? Don't you want to go see the world?"

He swatted his hand at her. "That's not me! I got all I want right here. I spend my days with these beautiful creatures – the horses, not you ladies – although I suppose one could say you're beautiful too."

Ida asked mischievously, "Hey Martha, what about the room we're going to build on our cottage? What about Moses coming to live with us?"

"Now there's an idea!" Martha exclaimed.

An explanation was in order. "To tell the truth, Moses, we have plans to build another room already. We want to be able to stay in the cottage as long as we are able. We'd planned on another room for a future caregiver for us. So, we're going to build it regardless of what you choose to do."

"You wouldn't want me living there with you," Moses scoffed. "I can't see it. You two would be hovering over me interfering in my business."

"What business would that be?" snorted Martha. "And besides, you're going to need a caregiver before long and do you want some stranger all about your business?"

He was silent. "I'm not keen on a nursing home. I'm hoping I just keel over."

"We all hope for that," agreed Ida.

"And you'd have to take this money Miriam left me. You'd have to let me use it for that," Moses insisted.

Martha nodded. "We could use the financial help, but just part of it."

"Well…" He was wavering. He scratched behind his ear. "If you don't mind my lousy company."

"We'll show you the plans. The space is there – right off the laundry room. You'd have your own bathroom," said Ida.

Then Martha added the final enticement. "And you'd be only steps from the barn."

Moses leaned toward the two women. "Let me see those so-called plans. Would the bathroom have a tub? I always wanted a tub."

"We could even do a walk-in tub," said Ida. "I hear they're all the rage."

"What's that?" Moses asked. "There really is such a thing?"

"But you'll have to keep out of our business," Martha winked. "No listening in on our conversations."

"I'd listen if there was something worth listening to."

"Well, you give it some thought," Martha said. "It would be nice to have you with us."

"I agree wholeheartedly," stated Ida. "You think about it – seriously."

He put up a fuss for a few more days but eventually warmed to the idea, especially if they allowed him to put Miriam's monetary gift towards that. Construction on his room addition would begin after the Tamarack was completed, maybe in June. It would give them time for all three to get used to the idea.

APRIL

ONE

Changes were indeed coming.

For one thing, Ida and Martha instituted weekly dinners every Monday with Annie and Rusty and whoever else would be living at the ranch. Ida confessed this idea evolved from her need for community, but everyone agreed it was important to have a weekly meal together. Duties were divided into meal preparation and clean-up.

Annie was hiring more staff, hoping to have four wranglers and three housekeepers by the third week in May. Lily, one of their first guests, would be helping with horses and housekeeping. The bunkhouse cabins were cleaned up and refurnished, providing living space for a total of twelve workers. And in another week, Annie's old friend, Sidonnia, and her daughter would be arriving to work.

"I remember her," said Martha. "You were good friends in high school."

"We were," agreed Annie, "and we've kept in touch. She and her daughter have been living in Missoula. I asked if she'd have any interest in coming back to this area, living in the Dusky Grouse, and she said, 'Big Sky. Heck yeah!'"

"Sidonnia is an unusual name," commented Ida.

"I always thought it was a lovely name. She's Native American but I don't know the origin of the name," said Martha. "Do you feel okay about sharing Sid's adoption story with Ida?"

"It's a bit complicated," explained Annie. "Child welfare took her from her home when her mother attempted suicide. Her mother's depression was enough for the state to place her into the welfare system. Her adopted parents were good folks – kind and all that, but she had a hard time. Anyway, moving back here puts her closer geographically to the Crow Nation if she wants to connect."

"Which is where exactly?" asked Ida.

"South of Billings, near the border of Wyoming."

"When I told her about this place, she said she'd love to work here with all the other 'misfits'." Annie babbled happily. "And she's raised Romona as a single mom. Romona's older than Elsa – I think she said twenty-five."

"Will they stay in one of the bunkhouse cabins?" Martha asked.

"That's what I was thinking. With the common living area and bath, it's more like an apartment," said Annie. "Rusty wants to hire four wranglers and four housekeepers this summer and they can stay in the other cabin. They both will be retrofitted for four bedrooms."

"I remember Sidonnia riding in competitions with you. Do you think she'd want to work with the horses?" Martha asked.

"Absolutely! I asked her and she said yes, she'd like that."
Annie grinned. "Rusty will be happy to have Sid around
too. Anyway, he's busy getting ready for overnight trail trips
and finishing the construction projects.

"Romona can help in the house. Maybe she and Elsa can
change off on breakfast duty," said Martha. "And both of
them could give Ida a break on those social hours."

"Since they're so burdensome," Ida deadpanned. "Those
three hours a week are killing me."

"It can get exhausting doing the hospitality thing," said
Annie. "I get that. Just mixing it up will help everyone."

***

Siddonia and her daughter moved in the following Saturday.
Romona drove their pick-up while Siddonia managed the
U-Haul van. A couple of high school boys were hired to
unload and move the heavier things into their cabin.

"I didn't know I had so many possessions; I think
someone else packed their stuff in my truck," laughed
Siddonia when Ida and Martha came out to greet her.

"I found out the same thing when I moved here," said
Ida. "It's a good culling process – at least for me it was."

"Oh most definitely," agreed Siddonia with a sideways glance at her daughter. "And then there are all
Romona's things."

"I'm the minimalist! You're the hoarder," her daughter
responded. "You can see we have different points of view."

"As all mothers and daughters do," responded Martha.
"Sid, could you spare a few minutes to see the horses?"

"I'd love to right now. I need a break." Siddonia laced up her shoes and headed to the barn with Martha. Romona returned to the job of unpacking as Ida turned toward the sound of an engine, spotting Moses rambling up in his old truck.

"I see our new ranch-hands have arrived." He gestured toward the moving van as he hobbled towards her. "Do they need help?"

"They hired some guys from town to unload. Sidonnia is getting the royal tour from Martha. You can meet her."

He started toward the barn, then abruptly turned back to face her. "I just remembered. Landis asked me to remind you about our lunch on Monday. I'd hear it from him if I didn't say anything to you about it."

"That's sweet of you, really. I enjoyed lunch with you both, but I'd feel kind of funny about coming again."

"If you want to hear me say how much we'd like you to join us, I can do that too. Truth is, Landis has been asking about you. A lot." Moses squinted at her as if she should be receiving a telekinetic message.

"You can tell Landis he can ask me any questions he wants, he doesn't have to bother you." It was on the tip of her tongue to say maybe Shelby would be available, but even in her mind it was too snippy. "I think I will have to decline, but thanks for asking."

"You know Landis is going to give me what for. He's going to be disappointed."

"Oh please," she turned back toward him, not sure what would come out of her mouth. "You can tell Landis if he has something on his mind to say it to me, to say it directly.

And if he has questions he wants to ask me, he should ask me directly. He knows where I live." And with that, she spun around and headed to the cottage.

He called after her. "I hope I can remember all that. I think I got the gist."

She waved without looking back.

So Landis wanted to see her. Landis liked her company. Not enough to initiate on his own. Did he just want her to hang out with them as friends? That didn't seem to be what Moses was implying. And what about Shelby? What was that?

She reached the door and threw up her hands. "Who cares?"

She'd rather keep him in her little mental fantasy anyway. Sex was never an issue and he was much sweeter and kinder to her in her thoughts than he'd ever be in person. That's how men were in her experience. Much sweeter and kinder in one's mind than in reality.

TWO

The night of the third ranch dinner there was a light frosting of April snow showers. The ground had warmed up, but the air temperature was cold enough to keep the snow from melting. They gathered in the farmhouse in the big kitchen again. There were nine tonight, what with the two new housekeepers in the refurnished bunkhouse; Sidonnia, Romona, Rusty, Moses, Annie, Ida, and Martha.

Rusty was holding off on bringing in the four wranglers; two women and two men. Martha told him she'd be okay with Rusty doing the hiring as long as he hired women. She'd found women to be more focused and less driven by ego than the men. If a male wrangler wouldn't work for a woman, well, that told you just about all you needed to know about his work ethic.

At the Monday dinner, without much fanfare, Annie and Rusty announced their engagement to be married.

"We want to be the first couple to be married in the new Tamarack Lodge," announced Annie. "Well, technically, in the aspen grove, but the reception will be in the lodge."

"Let's raise our glasses in celebration!" exclaimed Ida.

"Congratulations you two," said Moses. "This is a great reason for a party."

"Will there be dancing?" asked Romona.

"Oh yeah," said Rusty. "We've got a band lined up. They play all kinds of music, not just country swing, so we'll get everyone out on the dance floor."

"When is it?" asked Sidonnia.

"First weekend in June," stated Rusty.

"It just seemed like the right time," added Annie, "and Elsa will be home then."

Even Martha was smiling. "Congratulations. I can't wait."

Rusty hustled over to her, "I know you haven't always approved of me, Martha, but I do intend to be the best husband I can be to Annie."

"You're all right. You've kind of grown on me," she said. "But don't give me a hug yet. We'll save that till you're really part of the family."

Rusty laughed and held up his free hand. "I'll always respect your boundaries, Martha."

"You and Annie have big plans for this place it seems," she stated noncommittally.

"Yeah, we have the place booked for the summer. We've got weddings, family reunions, sisterhood trail rides." Rusty took a swig of beer. "But you and Ida, you can do what you want to do. We've got the work covered."

Martha looked intently at him. "You're going to bring in your own horses for most of the rides, right? I don't mind you using mine in a pinch, but I'm counting on you having your own."

"I wouldn't dream of touching your horses without your permission. We can keep them separate if you want."

"Heck no. It's good for them to mix it up. But I will say it's best if we put all them together in the largest pasture for a few weeks, till they sort out their pecking order. Old Black Hawk thinks he rules the roost, and Cimarron can be downright bossy."

"That's a good idea. I know horses can beat up on each other but the more space they have, the more room they tend to give each other." Rusty went on. "I got a large draft called Apache, who actually swaggers when he meets new horses."

It's always kind of fun to see what cliques they get themselves into."

"You notice that too?" Rusty asked. "The way sometimes they find buddies."

"Oh yeah, like old friends or something," added Martha. "I think it'll be just fine.

"I have six mules that are good for packing trips. My horses stay away from them since they know mules bite and kick if harassed. You okay with your horses around mules?"

"I heard mules get attached to horses they work with. Is that fact or fiction?"

"The teams I put together are a mix of mules and horses and I expect them to be team players, or they're not working. Mules really do much better on the rocky terrain. They carry game better."

"I never have heard a mule sing," commented Martha. "Maybe I'll get to hear that some morning."

"The Rocky Mountain canary – that's a mule crooning."

"Well, let's just keep an eye on the lot of them," said Martha. "There's room for all."

"Thanks Martha," Rusty smiled. "That's mighty generous of you."

"You're part of the family now." She stood up. "Might as well welcome you aboard."

THREE

Tour groups were clamoring to reserve space at the Dusky Grouse. There was a market for smaller groups, with maximum numbers of fifteen, who traveled together during the tour and who preferred "family-run lodging." It was in one such group that a distinctive, middle-aged man arrived, inquiring about Moses.

Ida was preparing the drinks and hot water for the social hour when she noticed someone in the room resembling a younger version of Moses, sans Western hat and pants. Tall and gaunt with a stilted gait, he inspected the farmhouse interior with a tight-lipped demeanor. He gazed intently at the décor, the rustic furniture, the paintings on the wall, and the moose-head over the fireplace. She almost called out, "We've been expecting you," but she bided her time, waiting for him to approach the buffet.

"Quite a spread you have here." He gestured toward the plates of cheese and crackers, but there was no warmth in his voice.

"I enjoy meeting the guests," said Ida. "This is my favorite job."

"I know you met my biological mother. She went by the name of Miriam – well, Gretel. She passed away here." He gazed at her with a non-committal expression.

"Yes, I remember. She was a very kind lady," replied Ida congenially. "She told us her son sent her on the tour. Was that you?"

"I didn't send her. She did this on her own. I just helped her find the information she needed," he said flatly.

"As in the missing pieces from her past?"

"Her past *and* mine." He leveled his eyes to hers." I understand my biological father is still living… still working here at the ranch?"

Ida let out a breath. "Yes. Moses. He just learned that he had a son about a month ago. Your mother wrote him a long letter, which was with her will."

"Moses?" The man gazed keenly at her. "That's him."

"He was in a state of shock to discover he had a son, to say the least."

"Yeah, well, he might be in more of a state of shock after he meets me."

His cockiness unnerved Ida. She focused on sounding upbeat. "And he – you. He took some of the working horses to another ranch today, but he should be back around suppertime. Do you want to see him this evening?"

"The sooner the better," he said. Other guests were nudging their way into the drinks. "I'm not planning to go out to dinner. He can meet me here." He pointed to the living room.

Ida didn't know what to think. He did not exhibit the openhearted gentleness of his father. There was no genetic programming for kindness. It was a learned trait. She continued serving drinks and making conversation while keeping a watchful eye for Moses and Martha to return home. Finally, as the guests were departing for dinners, the truck and trailer appeared in the lane.

Ida ran outside to flag them down. "Moses, he's here! Your son is here. He's waiting to meet you inside." She was breathless.

Moses turned to Martha in the driver's seat. "Guess this is it. Can you manage?"

"Go," said Martha. "Sidonnia will help me."

Moses entered through the backdoor and went straight to the kitchen sink to wash his hands. Ida followed, pretending the busy work of cleaning up. She watched him take a deep breath and exhale before moving with long strides into the living room. Her busy work continued as she moved back and forth between the two rooms, her ears perked up.

"Good evening," he announced, holding his hand out in greeting. "I might be a little clumsy here, but my name is Moses."

The man stood up but did not shake the extended hand of his father. The two took the measure of one another in a few brief seconds of silence. Moses dropped his arm.

"I've come a long way to meet you," the man said without inflection.

"I wasn't sure you'd want to but I'm glad you did. Your name is...?"

"The name's Trent."

"And where's home for you?"

"St. Louis. But I found my mother, my biological mother, in Kansas City. She was happy to see me. A little happier than you appear to be anyway."

"I apologize if I come across that way; I'm not one for showing emotion. I can assure you I'm happy you've come."

"You don't know why I've come." The tenor of Trent's voice was just mean-spirited. There was no way around it. "You won't be happy to know why I've come."

"How's that?" Moses asked innocently

"I'm not really interested in you or your part in my life, but I am, let me say this clearly, I am *invested* in you giving me what is mine."

"Whoa," said Moses. "I think we'd better sit down."

Ida appeared with two glasses of ice tea. "I thought you'd like something to drink," she said placing drinks on the coffee table. Romona entered the kitchen looking to make something for supper but was shushed by Ida. They stood by the door, unabashedly eavesdropping.

"So, do you want to know anything about me?" asked Moses.

"I'm not really here to be all buddy-buddy."

"I can understand that. The news that I even had a son is still a shock to me."

"A shock? You ditched my mother and ran off to the wilds of Montana where she couldn't find you!"

"Hold up there. It wasn't like that."

"You ditched a pregnant white woman, all alone with a baby on the way," he added scornfully.

"At the time I had no idea she was pregnant. Believe me."

"If you loved her why didn't you stay?"

"It's complicated. I loved her in a different way." Moses sounded uncomfortable with the conversation. "To be truthful, I'm gay...I *was* gay before it became acceptable."

"Acceptable? It's not acceptable now – where I come from."

"Maybe acceptable is not the right word."

"It's still not *acceptable* to be black – where I come from." A deeper bitterness had entered Trent's voice.

Moses cleared his throat. "What is it you want from me?"

"Not any fatherly advice, that's for sure."

Moses must have been thinking. There was silence. Then he asked, "Money?"

"You're getting warmer, *Dad*." He emphasized the familiar term with a cruel edginess.

"Miriam's inheritance?" Moses asked softly.

"Now you're talking."

"The half she left me?"

"She meant to leave it to me." Trent's voice was louder now. "I was the one who helped her find you. The money was coming to me, before she found out about you."

"You seem to know a lot of the details."

"It's in my interest to know the details."

"And you seem to be speaking for Miriam when it's not clear that's what she wanted." Moses spoke slowly as if to allow time for the consequences of their words to sink in.

"And you know what she wanted?"

"I know she probably thought about this fairly," said Moses. "Knowing who Miriam was, she wanted to do right by you."

"Then why would she want to do right by you? You — who never did anything but abandon her!"

Moses sat back in his chair and folded his arms. He either could not or would not speak.

Trent continued in an accusatory tone. "You're old. Your life's over. Why would she give an old man so much money? Did you blackmail her? Ha. *Black*mail!"

Moses still didn't respond. Ida wanted desperately to intervene and defend him. She wanted to confront this bully.

She heard Moses push back his chair and stand up. "Were you this rude and disrespectful to Miriam, to your mother?"

"You can't shame me."

"I'm just surprised she left you anything."

"I was her only son. She loved me."

"You may have conned Miriam, sweet as she was, but you're not going to threaten me."

"You abandoned my mother!" Trent burst out. "And really – you know it – you abandoned me!"

"You don't know me and I don't know you, so neither one of us knows the truth. But I have to say you are one disappointing human being." Moses spun around and strode out past the two women standing silently in the kitchen, out to the darkening evening.

Trent stomped past the two women in the kitchen to follow Moses outside where he yelled into the windy dusk. "See you in court!" He returned through the kitchen, stopping short beside the two women.

"I think it's time you cleared out your room and left," Ida stated. "You are no longer welcome under this roof."

Trent's lips tightened, "I wouldn't stay here another night if you paid me. What a dump. Call the tour guide and call me a ride to the airport."

"Gladly," Ida said. Beside her, Romona crossed her arms, a bulwark of steely resolve.

"Tell the old black faggot he'll be hearing from my lawyer." He spun around to go to his room, then re-entered and faced them both. "You can also tell him he will never get within an inch of his grandson. Yeah, that's right! Tell him that he has a grandson – who will never know about his weasely grandfather."

"What a prick!" Romona declared loudly as he left the room.

"Probably has a bully lawyer," replied Ida. "I just feel sad that it's come to this. Miriam would be devastated."

Trent departed the ranch that evening and his brutish threats were diminished by distance. Moses hired a lawyer and he secured rights to the inheritance. If Trent had never showed up and badgered him, it was likely Moses would have complacently given up his rights to the money Miriam left him. But the confrontation had shown Moses that evil and malice are alive and well in the hearts of some men, and Miriam had been deceived by her own son. It was for Miriam more than for himself that Moses found himself defending the gift she had left him.

MAY

ONE

Life's mysteries slip into our days disguised as ordinary events and people. Who could've predicted Martha striking up a kinship with a simple man just doing his job installing walk-in tubs? Ida stumbled upon the two of them sitting on the bathroom floor in the afternoon when he was installing the plumbing lines. A stocky, diminutive man with a gnomish face glanced up at her, with Martha nearby ready to hand him whatever tool he requested.

"Oh sorry," Ida said, "I didn't know you were here."

"Excuse me for not standing up, but it takes me a day and a half just to get up. I'm Tom." He stretched out his hand towards her. "Tommy – to my real friends."

Martha gazed up at Ida too. "I inquired if he needed help and he asked if I was a psychiatrist. I said I probably could be, and so here I am, helping him with his troubles."

Tommy kept on working with the plumbing lines in the wall, but he chuckled. "I think she wants to get out of paying me by pretending to care about my silly life."

"Maybe I just want to learn something about plumbing. I might pick up the trade."

They talked for the next few hours while Tom finished his work. Both had lost spouses. Neither one was interested in getting involved with another partner. Still, when Tom invited Martha to watch his crew install another bathtub, she was very keen on learning all about it.. Apparently, Tom was just as curious about horses and the tack room, about boot-jack pullers, and hoof picks and how packed manure in hooves can cause thrush fungus.

So it was that Martha found herself in some kind of emotional entanglement with a little man with a head of white, curly hair and a handlebar mustache that sprouted full bloom. She even talked about him at the WoCA meeting. Their topic that Saturday was, "Things we think about when we wake up at night." Martha had love for everyone at this meeting. Even for Josephine. She was a merry soul these days.

Following the WoCA group they headed to the Farmers' Market in the square. Fruits and vegetables of the season had arrived from farther south. Vendors with displays of woodworking, watercolors, jewelry, and textiles lined the street.

This was happiness they said, sauntering along, taking in the whimsy and cleanness of the spring air. Suddenly Martha pulled Ida toward a booth where a woman with long blondish hair huddled over her display of silver jewelry. Martha blurted out bluntly, "I think I've seen you before!"

Ida's graciousness kicked in. "You're Shelby. Hi. I met you a few months ago."

Shelby looked up at both women with no apparent sign of recognition. "You look familiar, but I don't know where I would have met you. Sorry I can't recall."

"My name is Ida. You were with Landis in the grocery store last January. I just met you briefly."

"Oh yes, the lesbians. Or the bet about the lesbians," Shelby said.

"This is my friend Martha. The one I live with – where the rumor started," said Ida.

"How is Landis?" asked Martha. "We haven't seen him in a while."

"He's supposed to be here today," Shelby said. "He's been doing some study. You know – his *research*."

She said research as if it was a haranguing weight. Ida looked over the silver jewelry on display, spotting a necklace which resembled the one given to her at Christmas. "I recall you were a professor friend of Landis's. Do you teach?"

"I taught a night art class at the high school, you know, Adult ED, but I'm not really a professor. That was his little joke." She threw back her long hair and gave them a wink. "You know, his little nickname for me."

"Lovely pieces," Ida remarked.

"Nice to make your acquaintance," Martha said to Shelby, tugging Ida away.

"We'll be seeing you." Ida waved towards the booth, then whispered to Martha, "*Nice to make your acquaintance?*"

"I can be polite. I had to get us out of there."

"I appreciate you extricating us from the situation but who the heck are you? *Nice to make your acquaintance?* You are a new Martha these days."

"I'm hungry. Let's get some veggie tacos over there." They strolled to a booth at the end of the street and reviewed the chalkboard menu. Picnic tables lined the street so Ida gave Martha her order and went to sit. She put down her bags and stretched holding her arms high above her. That felt good. She turned her head to the left and then to the right, her neck muscles tight.

"Ida?" She pirouetted to see Landis behind her with a baseball cap and sunglasses.

"Hi," she said. She froze. She could not think of one single thing to say. He was a fantasy and in a fantasy she could control him and the conversation. *Not here, not now.*

He gestured towards her head, "New haircut? Looks nice on you."

She pointed at his baseball cap. "New hat? Looks nice on you."

"Our summer looks?"

"A little change is always good," she answered solemnly and sat down at the table.

He stepped forward and plopped beside her on the bench. "So, at the risk of enraging you, I'm going to say again I hope you come to hear our band, or don't you like bluegrass?"

"I like the old-time bluegrass. I'm glad it's not B*ro-grass* though," she recalled a phrase Annie had used.

He chuckled. "Bro-grass, huh? You don't wanna hear songs about pick-up trucks? Beer...the flag?"

"And guns," she looked quickly down at the ground. She'd said it reflexively. She didn't know where he stood on the issue, but she might as well be clear where she stood.

He was still smiling. "Bro-grass. We're not about that I guess."

"I got that from Annie. I was asking her more about the band."

"Just about the band or about certain players in the band?" He was definitely flirting. There was a smile on his lips.

"Oh, I'm learning lots of new things since I moved up here," she replied in a non-committal tone. "I try to be open to new ideas, new people."

"But without leaving the ranch?" he asked and then added, "Sorry, I apologize. I'm giving you a hard time. I'm just teasing."

"It's just been my first winter here and I'm getting acclimated to everything; the ranch, the town, the cold, Martha."

He chuckled. "Just how exactly do you acclimate yourself to Martha?"

"Very cautiously."

"And with a good sense of humor?"

"Yes, that too," she said, "but I have taken a lot of long walks around the place. I've probably blazed some new trails for the horses."

"Sometimes we all need something to get us out. The band – it gets me out of the house…and myself."

"Winter is over. I can't use that excuse anymore, not that I need an excuse. And I have my new car now. I just…yeah okay, I'll try and make it to one of your gigs this summer," she stuttered.

Martha called for her to help carry the drinks over.

Lands rose quickly. "Don't get up. I'll get them." He carried the drinks to the table.

"Can you join us?" Ida asked.

"Sorry I can't, I'm meeting someone," he replied.

"Shelby, perhaps?" blurted Martha.

He looked surprised. "We agreed to meet here. Did you see her this morning?"

"We saw her jewelry. Quite nice," Ida said.

Landis just nodded. He took off his cap and ran his hand over his smooth head. "Sun feels pretty damn good. Moses mentioned you all went out riding a few times."

"We try and ride once a week," Martha replied, "You're welcome to come join us."

"That sounds alright," he said. "I've been out hiking a lot lately."

"Work or play?" asked Ida.

"My work is my play," he replied, his eyes turning towards the mountains. "I can't imagine living anywhere else."

Martha had devoured her taco. "I'm going to look for some ice cream. Landis, can you keep Ida company till I get back – or do you have to get to your date with Shelby?"

"It's not a date. She's just a friend," he said emphatically. "I'd be happy to fill in for you." He made a big deal of sitting down and facing Ida across the table. "So…" His eyes met hers. "What's going on in your life?"

"I always hate that question," Ida said. "It's like when someone asks 'what's new' and you feel compelled to come up with something juicy to hold their attention."

"Fair enough," he said. "Okay, let's see. What's happening at the ranch? Moses told me there's some construction going on?"

"Some pretty major construction. Annie and Rusty are expanding. Martha and I are out of the business end now. We get to enjoy the guests without doing a lot of the work."

"I suppose you meet a lot of interesting people," he remarked, stroking his long beard. "Any returning guests?"

"Yes a few. I think we'll have more regulars as we go on in the next few years."

"Any more Swedes?" he asked impishly.

"Not quite as engaging as the old Swede. He was quite sweet – the old Swede."

"But you get lots of interesting folks staying there."

"And I do like that part of the hospitality business," she replied. "It keeps me from getting too insulated in my own little world."

"So you must have some stimulating conversations."

Ida couldn't read the intent behind his remarks. "Well, we only interact with guests at breakfast and during the social hour in the late afternoon. There's not a lot of time for deep discussions."

"But attractive looking older guys, right?" He gave her a half-smile.

"A few," she responded and rested her chin on her palms, elbows on the table. "But I'm not really interested in the guests in that way."

"In what way is that?" He twisted the band of his wristwatch.

"In the way I think you're asking me," she eyed him with a slight twinkle.

He looked a bit sheepish but he said calmly, "I think you know why I'm asking."

"I'm not entirely sure." She hesitated and then thought *what the heck.* "But none of them plays a ukulele. So there's that." She turned away suddenly toward the crowds, appearing to search for Martha.

Out of the corner of her eye she saw that he, too,was surveying the square as he asked, "What do you think of our farmers' market?"

"It's got a small-town feel. Friendly! Festive."

"And the local art talent?" She swore his head tilted towards Shelby's booth.

"Ah well, there's a smorgasbord of local talent."

"Hmm," he said, "I appreciate your diplomatic spirit." His eyes lifted towards the mountains again. "Do you ever go hiking?"

"We just took Peabody out last week. To Drinking Horse Trail, I think it was called, on the north side of Bozeman? It was a bit slushy in points but we had a great time."

"Would you come hiking with me?" he asked.

"Just you?" she asked.

"Just me – unless there's someone you want me to invite."

She smiled. "I think I'd like to go hiking just with you."

"Nothing too strenuous."

"I can handle a hill or two."

"Next week?" he asked. "How about Monday?"

"Monday?" It seemed soon, then not soon enough. "That'll work fine."

Martha sauntered back, ice-cream cone in hand. Landis rose to his feet, placed his cap on his head, and said directly to Ida, "I'll pick you up around eight then; maybe we can get breakfast on the way?"

"I'll be ready." She nodded. "I look forward to it."

Martha's eyes followed him as he walked towards Shelby's booth, then she turned to gaze at Ida. She said nothing.

"Thank you for your having an ice cream craving," Ida said calmly.

"Timing is everything," Martha replied.

"Yep, I've heard you say that."

TWO

Ida laid out a pair of hiking pants on the chair by her bed, and socks and boots on the floor by the door. It was fortuitous she'd kept that quick-drying shirt worn white-water rafting three years ago. She assembled other necessities: water bottle, sunglasses, sunscreen, bug repellent, and hat. Finally, she turned on her lamp to read in bed when Martha stuck her head in the door.

"I'm going to check on Rhiannon. It's time."

"At this hour?"

"A baby waits for no one. But you need your sleep for tomorrow."

"I really wanted to see this birth."

"Bernice is coming over. You go to sleep."

Ida tossed in bed, checking the time every so often. Her sporadic dozing could not be called sleep. When it was midnight and Martha hadn't returned, Ida pulled on her rubber boots and threw a sweater over her pajamas. A white truck was parked near the barn. Ida assumed it belonged to Martha's old friend. She found the two women leaning against a stall wall.

"We're just trying to recall about the foal Rhiannon delivered two years ago. We think it was a pretty fast birth," explained Bernice. "Usually if one is easy the next one is too, but I'd wager we're several hours away from the delivery."

The horse huffed in a way that reminded Ida of the Lamaze panting she'd been taught so many years ago. She imagined the horse's lament: "Just get this baby out of me!"

"Can I do anything to help?" asked Ida.

"Could you bring out a thermos of coffee? I'm not leaving until this foal is born." Martha pulled down some old blankets from another stall and grabbed a handful of rags to place near-by on the hay. Bernice was wrapping Rhiannon's tail with tape to prevent it from getting drenched. Ida hustled back to the cottage and made a strong pot of coffee. She found a few apples and a hunk of cheese, slicing it into edible bites.

They sat on the concrete floor with horse blankets beneath them to buffet the cold. Bernice was a born conversationalist. "Have you heard about the one-armed, pregnant raccoon that's taken up residence with Sadie and Millie?"

"Oh Lord, they've got their hands full with sheep and cats and even trained squirrels," exclaimed Martha. "What the hell are they doing with a wild raccoon?"

"They felt sorry for it. I did mention it was one-armed and pregnant," responded Bernice. "They probably feed the raccoon so it doesn't go after their sheep – all five of them."

Bernice regaled them with a few more tales of strange human and animal interactions. It didn't seem like gossip with her common-sense expertise involved. She asked Martha to tell the story again about the two horses who were reunited after several years apart.

"That would be Seneca and Sundown. I bought them the same year: Seneca was mine and Sundown I bought for Annie. They became fast friends always keeping track of each other. Then, a couple years later, Annie moved away from the ranch and took Sundown. I didn't notice right away but Seneca became kind of a loner, keeping her distance from the others. A few years later when Annie came back home, she brought Sundown into the corral and – just like that – Seneca ran over to her nickering and nuzzling. It was closest thing I'd ever seen to a horse embrace another."

"That's amazing," Ida said.

"Yep," Martha agreed. "Horses form bonds and they remember one another for years."

Around two a.m., Rhiannon emitted a gush of amniotic fluid. She struggled to remain standing up and gave out three heaving attempts. Bernice entered the stall, stroking her side and soothing her with a calm voice. She gave the horse wide berth. Better to stay out of the way. After several contracted pushes, the amniotic sac appeared with one tiny front hoof. Several minutes later, the second foot with a diminutive head tucked between the two legs nudged itself out, then stalled. Bernice put her hand through the fluid, grasped the first leg tightly and pulled. Seconds passed. Rhiannon snorted and huffed. Suddenly an oceanic ripple moved through her body. Oozing out of the birth canal was a perfectly shaped tiny horse. It was a colt.

They set to work scooping away placental material. Rhiannon twisted her head around to eye her baby. She lay down on her side on the straw when the umbilical cord snapped off. Blood pooled. Rhiannon put her long legs under her and stood up again, sniffing at her newborn. The little one had only a few more minutes of rest and then he also lifted himself up.

Tentatively taking a few wobbly steps, bumping into the stall wall, he toddled toward his mother's attentions.

Bernice said her good-byes and slipped away quietly. She hadn't needed to come but what birth isn't miraculous? A time to reflect on how life gives and life takes away.

Ida brought a pail of warm water to clean up the messy fluids. Martha gave both mom and colt fresh water. The women watched the colt searching for the mother's teats in an instinctive attempt to nurse, the two horses affectionately nudging one another.

Rhiannon was wary and vigilant. She kept turning to look at Martha, then back at her baby. *Stand clear, give me space, this is my time.*

"They'll be okay," Martha stated. "We can go now."

Ida glanced at her watch as they switched off the barn lights and headed to the cottage. "It's almost 3:45. I'm not going to be in any shape to hike tomorrow. I can't cancel even if I wanted to."

"Are you sleepy now? Do you think you'll fall asleep?"

"I'm exhausted," Ida responded. "Even if I only sleep four hours, it's better than nothing."

"Text him. Tell him and maybe he'll come later," Martha suggested.

"Text him? I don't have his number." Martha didn't own a phone so she was no help.

"Write a note. Tell Landis to go see the new colt. Buy some sleep time." Martha was already headed to her room.

"I'll tape a note to our porch door. That's what I'll do." Ida searched for a notepad and pen and scratched off a quick note.

Dear Landis,

We are just now going to bed at 4 am. Rhiannon had a colt in the wee hours. Amazing! I'll set my alarm for 8:30. I know I can't hike unless I get a few hours of sleep. Please check on the new colt. I hope we won't get off too late!

- Ida

Ida was so tired she fell asleep within minutes of climbing into her bed. She woke to sunlight. *What day is it? What happened last night?* She looked at the clock. 10:40 *Damn.* She checked the alarm and saw she'd set the p.m. light. *Double damn.*

She got up quickly, shuffling to her bathroom for a wash-up and a brush of the hair. Throwing an old sweatshirt over her pajamas, she padded into the kitchen. *No Martha. No Landis. No note. No coffee. Damn.* She looked out the front window, saw the old jeep belonging to Landis, and quickly dressed in the clothes she had so meticulously laid out yesterday. *Damn. Damn. Damn.*

A quietness pervaded the interior of the barn. "Martha?" she called. "Landis? Moses?" She went outside to count the horses in the north pasture. Five. The others must have gone for a ride. Standing by the corral gate, she watched Rhiannon and her colt. How quickly they adapted, formed a new attachment.

Make yourself useful, Ida. She had enough things to do. She always did, though she couldn't think of one at the moment. The sound of voices wafted from the trees beyond the north pasture. Three riders were headed her way. She waved and walked across the yard between the corral and the pasture.

"Have you been up for hours?" she inquired of Martha as her horse sauntered by.

"I'll pay for it," Martha replied. "Just couldn't sleep."

Moses continued behind her. Landis stopped and dismounted from old Grayson, leading the horse by the reins toward her.

"I'm so sorry," Ida said, "I really did mean to get up earlier."

"It's not a big deal. You got to witness something pretty spectacular."

"Did you see him? Did you see the new colt?" she asked.

"He's quite frisky."

"It was amazing!" Ida couldn't seem to keep from talking. "So, what do you think? Can we still go hiking? Is it too late?"

"I'd rather save it for another day if that's all right with you."

"Okay, sure, that's fine," she answered. Disappointment was not something she hid well.

"But I do have a lunch that needs to be eaten, and I'd still like to share it with you if you're up for that?" he asked. "Just let me get Grayson's saddle off and brush him down."

Moses and Martha met them at the barn door. Moses reached out and took Grayson's reins and Martha handed Ida a pile of blankets.

"Okay you kids, go have your picnic. We've got it covered from here," Martha said.

THREE

They found a spot in the grove of aspens behind the barn past the north pasture. Ida spread the blankets over the tufts of pasture grasses. Landis threw his hat on the blanket and opened his cooler. "I made avocado, tomato, and cheese sandwiches. Vegetarian."

"On what kind of bread?" she asked to be difficult.

"Wheat. Oh no," he said dejectedly.

"It's fine. I love wheat bread!" she enthused. "Any water by chance?"

"I do have water but I also brought you this." He held up a miniature bottle of red wine.

"Okay, that's a nice thing to do, but really, I don't normally drink wine this early in the day."

"I'd never assume you did, but I thought it was pretty charming of me to think about it, don't you think?"

"Charming. Absolutely."

He handed her the water and the wine and the sandwich after she settled herself into a seated position on the blanket. She wanted to ask about his work. "Tell me why these trees are called 'quaking' aspens."

"Aspens are called quaking because of the loose way the leaves hang and flutter from each branch. See that. They're unusual because the leaves turn upside down when they quake so both sides get sunlight and absorb photosynthesis. Do you remember that word from science class?"

"I do, yes. And plants need it to survive."

"Right, and chlorophyll is the process that turns the light into sugars, nutrients for the trees, and greens up the leaves."

"Chlorophyll, yes, another term from biology class. And all of these aspens are connected by the root system, right?" she asked.

"That's right. Sometimes the trees are regarded as clones of each other because they develop from a single root system, which can grow for miles underground. Family groups from one parent so to speak." He looked up at the silvery leaves above them. "Aspens are susceptible to diseases and kinds of mildew but they regenerate quickly."

"So what exactly are you studying when you are out doing research? What are old-growth forests?" she asked.

He'd taken a bite of sandwich and held up his finger as if to say wait. Chewing slowly, he finally swallowed and launched into an explanation. "Well, long story short. Old trees actually grow faster the older they get. They hold more carbon. I study specific trees to assess growth rate in different years and the amount of carbon collected. Old-growth forests are actually full of young and old trees, living and dead trees."

Ida had never thought about the life of trees before. She felt very ignorant on the subject. "Is there such a thing as an old-growth tree?"

"Yes," he nodded. "Usually any tree over a hundred fifty years old is considered old growth, but there are some that are thousands of years old."

"Is it hard to get funding for your research?"

"Well, generally politicians don't care about these old-growth forests, but they do care about saving money. Healthy tree growth in cities means more shade, which saves utility costs and removes pollutants from the air. So…

yes, there is interest in trees if there is an economics angle. The more carbon dioxide collected by trees, less ozone loss, and thus – money saved."

He stroked his long, silvery-peppered beard and looked at her sideways. "You know why I have this bushy growth don't you?" He paused and waited till she looked at him directly. "Because it's collecting carbon every minute I'm alive. I have the equivalent of an acre of Brazilian rain forest here."

She laughed. "I bet you've been working on that one for a while."

"An old Letterman joke," he replied.

"So does that mean you're putting out a lot of oxygen then?"

"That's right. I might be good for you to be around." It wasn't cockiness really; he was just being playful.

"I feel healthier already." She hugged her knees close to her chest and looked at the purple and yellow grasses in the pasture. "We are stardust, a billion year-old carbon."

"How's that?"

"Joni Mitchell. Woodstock."

"Were you there? I could see you at Woodstock."

"Nope, not me. Neither was Joni, but she wrote a great song about it though." Ida wanted to return to his research. "What's causing the demise of so many of our forests?"

"There's a lot of controversy about the bark beetle and how to handle it. Those little buggers decimate trees – any tree is fair game, but they usually take over unhealthy ones first. We have more diseased trees because of droughts

– climate change, so many people think culling the forests is the way to go."

"What do you think?"

"I think logging has its place and taking out dead trees helps prevent fires. But I work with some entomologists – you know, the ones studying insects, who believe we combat them by building up our forests, with more water, more nutrients in the soil. Healthy trees resist the beetles by emitting a natural chemical. But I'm not opposed to cutting down the infested trees."

"Martha told me about a fire nearby that started in a farmer's field. He got out his tractor and disked circles to create a fire line. He had it under control until the wind carried some sparks onto the Nature Conservancy land. Because it was then on federal land, he wasn't allowed to contain it and the fire took over 100,000 acres." She stretched her legs out in front of her again. "Martha says if the locals had more control, many of the fires wouldn't grow so fast and become so widespread."

"She's probably right." He stood up suddenly and pointed to a higher ridge on the mountains to the east. "See up there – that swath of dead trees. The standing dead timber from the beetles and bud worms on the firs is actually dryer than what you'd get at the lumber yard, so it's great kindling for a rampant fire."

He bent over and foraged in his bag. "I brought some granola bars. Homemade ones but now I can't find them."

"Home-made? I'm impressed."

"Oh, not by me. My sister stocks me with all of her loot." He held up a bar wrapped in cellophane. "Want to split it?"

"Sure, I'm game to try it."

He unwrapped the clear wrapping and carefully divided the bar in half, heedful of keeping his fingers off the edible part.

Before taking a bite, she asked, "What are you looking for when you're out tromping around in the woods?"

"These days I've been looking for signs of the bark beetle."

"Like how? What do you look for?"

"First of all, if you're walking among pines and you don't smell the pine scent, that's the first clue. Walk close to the trunk and you'll observe teeny, tiny holes, I mean holes the size of a pin. Sometimes you'll see wads of sawdust clumped on the bark. If you cut the bark away, you'll find round little pests. Some say they look like mouse droppings but they remind me more of chia seeds."

"And those teeny, tiny, little creatures are wreaking havoc among these forests?" She pointed to the mountains behind them.

"And in forests all over the world. Some call it Beetlemania."

"That's clever. But it's a scary thing, isn't it?"

"Lots of things going on around us, beneath us, inside of things we can't see."

"Invisible forces. Things unseen," she said. "The micro-biome."

"Micro-biome? What do you know about that?"

"Not much, but I like the word." She smiled at him. "I just find it fascinating that micro-life is happening everywhere around us."

He lay down on his side, facing her, resting on his elbow. "Micro-life. Can you tell me something about your *micro-life?* Something I wouldn't know from just looking at you."

Her micro-life was full of hormones flinging emotions all over the place. *Talk about something safe.* "Okay. One thing you wouldn't know from looking at me is that I was born and raised Mennonite - which has impacted me my entire life, even though I'd be considered a lapsed Mennonite by many."

"Menno-night? Is that like a Hutterite? There are Hutterites here in Montana."

"We have the same Anabaptist roots. I think they believe in similar things as Mennonites, like non-violence and not participating in war. But Hutteriites live in tight communal groups. Mennonites don't."

"Anabaptists? Against baptism?"

"Sorry, not anti-baptists. Ana-baptism. Technically re-baptism as adults but it's mostly about being old enough to know what you're doing when you get baptized. My fore-mothers and fathers were burned at the stake for believing this when Catholicism was dictating the rules back in the sixteenth century."

"And non-violence. Are you a pacifist?" He was sincerely interested.

"Hmm, well, here's the official line. Mennonite theology is grounded in the teachings of Jesus so, historically, we've been opposed to war and violence. Jesus was pretty clear about turning the other cheek. Am I a pacifist? I've never been in a war, or been without food, or had family members shot. Truthfully, I'm not sure how I'd react if I lived in the Gaza Strip or someplace where violence is the norm."

Landis turned and lay on his back, his hands cradling his head. Gazing up at the clouds he asked, "And so your social work degree led you to work with the dying?"

Ida reflected on this question. What to share? "When I was thirty years old, I gave birth to a baby girl who was stillborn. The only way for me to live with my grief was to dig deeper. And studying about it and then working directly with those facing death, well, it gave meaning to my loss."

Landis sat up giving her his full attention. "I'm sorry. That's got to be one of the hardest things to go through."

"I'm telling you this now only because there's never a good time to share it in a friendship. I thought you ought to know. It's part of who I am." She held up the mini-bottle of wine that had been tossed on the blanket beside her. "I think I will have this wine now, if you don't mind."

"Appropriate, I'd say. Hey, I have a cup." He rummaged through his cooler and handed her a blue plastic one that reminded her of a sippy-cup.

In exchange, she held out the wine. "This is embarrassing, but could you open it? With my arthritic hands, I just can't maneuver those caps anymore."

"Okay, as long as you're not playing up to my masculine strength," he kidded, accepting the challenge. "I don't know why they make these things so hard to open."

"Exactly," she said. "Like medicine bottles where you have to squeeze and hold and turn?"

"Or pills in plastic that you have to use a shears to cut open?"

"Or toilet bowl cleaners! Those are the hardest things for me to squeeze and turn!"

He opened the wine and handed it back with a devious grin. "I'm happy to open your wine or toilet bowl cleaners anytime."

Ida poured the merlot into her cup, a bit disconcerted at the shift in the conversation. Maybe the talk of the still-birth had made them both uneasy. She felt cheated. She had shared some deep stuff and he remained a mystery.

But he continued. "The closest I've come to death is Vietnam. I lost a couple of good buddies. Death was different there. Talk about violence being the norm."

"Vietnam. God. There were so many painful things about that war and that time period. Our country so divided. Were you drafted?" Ida asked.

"I enlisted when I turned eighteen. My mom died when I was fifteen and I needed to get out, and 'experience life' as they say. Ironically, I experienced death more than life." Landis fidgeted with his wristwatch. "It was a terrible time. Sometimes I still think about Vietnam – but mostly I'd rather let that chapter stay closed."

Ida was without words. She sat very still, looking down at the wine in her cup. Then she heard Landis sigh and say, "And now my father's dying at age ninety-six. Congestive heart failure that's become acute. He lives with my sister in Missoula. I try to visit them about once a month."

"The family you visited before Christmas?"

"Yes, my sister is the saint. He's receiving hospice services now."

" Ninety-six years old. Is your father lucid?"

"Amazingly so. He told me last week he didn't know dying could be such hard work."

Ida smiled. "It is hard work. Your dad sounds at peace with his life – and his death. Did he re-marry or raise you kids by himself?"

"Never remarried. He did a pretty good job with us as teenagers. My sister is younger and closer to him." Landis looked up again at the cumulus clouds overhead. "I didn't anticipate covering such heavy topics today."

"You asked me about my job. Always seems to bring down a conversation." She poured the remaining wine into her cup. "How did you start playing guitar?"

"How? Or why? The usual reasons. I began playing guitar to impress girls. I took lessons in high school and joined a band. I played the hard rock stuff. Pretty crazy times." He took out an apple and an orange and held them up. "Want one?"

"Not with my wine, thanks. And did it? Did it impress the girls?"

He squinted over at her. "One or two."

"How about the ukulele?"

"That's just a recent thing. It's so portable. I bought it for fun but it works well with the bluegrass stuff." He hesitated and looked away. "Don't know yet if it impresses the girls."

He placed the fruit between them on the blanket and lay down again stretching out his legs. "Do you mind if I take a nap? I just need ten or fifteen minutes to shut my eyes." Landis didn't wait for a response but slung his right arm over his eyes. She didn't trust herself to stretch out beside him. Finishing the wine, she threw out the last sip and stood up to stretch. She bent to touch her toes, then stiffly hobbled towards a trail leading into the woods.

Why had she shared so much so soon? Why did she think he'd care about her past? She walked farther, following the trail, trying to recall the names of the trees and birds. There was the two-mile loop beginning about fifty yards ahead. She hiked a bit farther and then turned back. Perhaps she'd given him enough time.

He was sitting up munching an apple when she returned. "So you didn't leave me."

"I get stiff sitting, and walking always helps." She sat down beside him. "I guess we ought to get back pretty soon."

Landis nodded and threw his apple core into the deeper grass. "Ida, you may have figured out I'm kind of interested in getting to know you, and not just in a friendship kind of way. I can't quite tell if you feel the same way."

Ida took a swig of water. She wasn't sure what she'd say. "I know I like you. There's something here that I'm not used to feeling, and I don't know…I like talking with you."

Landis squinted at her. "I'm not sure what that means. I've been thinking a lot about you. I just want to get to know you better. If talking is all you and I do, then that's fine. I might be disappointed, but that's okay."

"I just don't know if I trust myself – or you. I'd like to spend more time with you." She flipped her hand over to tap his arm. "I'm a pretty serious person sometimes. Not always fun to be around."

Landis seemed to contemplate what to say next. He swayed towards her ever so slightly. "Well, I figure there's a few things you need to know about me. One, I'm a veteran, so to me pacifism seems just plain silly. Two, I'm an atheist and have a hard time with any religion, although it's kind of fun saying the word Men-no-night. And three, I own a gun and I carry it in my car. Now from what you told me about yourself today, that puts me at odds with you on at least three accounts."

She liked his bluntness. "Only three, huh? And are these three open for debate?"

"I'm open to further sparring, especially with you." In his eyes was the flicker of a playful spark.

Ida shook her head and bit her lip. "Humor is always with you isn't it? You don't take life too seriously, do you?"

"I take lots of things seriously," he replied. "Ask me something serious. I can be serious."

"So, I know you're a scientist, but what do I call you? A botanist? A biologist?"

"Actually, I'm called a dendrochronologist."

A tad bit of smugness there. "Okay," she replied. "Chrono – time. What is the dendro root?"

"Trees."

"Ah, hence the study of old growth trees. Chronology of trees? How long they live?"

"And why or how they die."

"Wow," she replied. "I just never imagined such a job." She ran her fingers through her hair and pointed to her face. "Can you determine the age of this old tree by her wrinkles?"

Impulsively he reached out and brushed her cheek. "Hmm, I'd say approximately seventy-two years – give or take."

"*That* is impressive!" she stated, his fingers' warmth imprinted on her face.

"Sometimes I use historical context and relative events to make determinations. And I happen to know Martha turned seventy-two last December." He smiled and continued in a self-congratulatory tone, "I just turned seventy. There. That's out of the way. What else would you like to know about me?"

"Well, word is that you were married and that you attend A.A. Should I know more about these things?"

"Those are two very separate things. I do attend A.A. and I've been sober six years. Moses helped me through some rough spots. Plus - getting old helps."

"But you just told me you're an atheist. Doesn't A.A. hold a tenet about believing in a higher power?"

With his right hand, he reached over and plucked a blade of grass. Holding it between his thumb and forefinger he blew on it ever so slightly. "See anything?"

"Your breath," she said, "or rather, the grass moving from the *effects* of your breath."

"That's my higher power. The give and take of all this." His arms swept the air before them. "The interactions of the natural world – with or without us humans here. Some of it can be explained scientifically and some of it is just a mystery."

"Some people might call that 'God'" she said. His simple analogy moved her.

"Some people might." He threw the blade of grass into the wind. "As for my marriage, well, it was another lifetime."

"Is she still in your life?"

"We divorced over twenty years ago, and we were married *two long* years. It wasn't love that drove us together. More like the love of drinking."

"Does she still live around here?"

"Nope, she's long gone. Moved to Texas."

"Okay," she replied. "You should know I decided a long time ago that I need lots of quiet time by myself."

"And you never married. I doubt that's from lack of opportunity."

She held her hands out, clasping them tightly in front of her. "I've never been married, never wanted to marry, never intend to marry."

"Never, never, never?"

She gave him a look of dismissal. "If you're going to tease me about these things, I will seriously reconsider whether you're worth my time."

He held up his hands. "Sorry. Old habit, this teasing business. So, what do you think? Can we keep meeting like this – just the two of us?"

"What if we just be – buddies?"

He leaned back on his hands, a roguish smile on his lips. "Friends, huh? I suspect you're a little afraid of me."

She stood up suddenly and began picking up discarded baggies and bottles. "I think we need to go back."

He pushed himself to a standing position shaking out the blanket they'd been lying on. He held out one end to her to help fold it up. They did it silently. She knew he was watching her even though she could not look at him.

"I'll carry the blankets," she said and turned away. He picked up the cooler and followed. Why had she let herself get into this thing with him? What had happened here? *Wake up Ida.*

She spun around to confront him. "Look, nobody likes to feel vulnerable, and I don't like it one bit, but here I am, and I've said some things that I probably shouldn't have said. You come into my life and start stirring things up. What's this supposed to be between us – at our ages?"

"You think you're the only one who's scared here?" he asked slowly. "I don't know what I'm doing!"

"So we're both miserable." She hugged the blankets tighter, shaking her head. "Jesus!"

"Yeah, but miserable in a good way?" he said with a mischievous twinkle.

"I suppose it's in a good way, but sometimes it doesn't feel very good." She smiled up at him. "Please, can we slow this down? Take a little time here?"

He put up his free hand as if to signify a truce. "Got it," he replied.

She walked him to the jeep and leaned against the vehicle, holding the blankets with both arms. Peabody suddenly appeared underfoot, nudging and sniffing the masculine interloper.

Landis placed the cooler in the back seat and knelt down to meet the dog at eye level, rubbing his hands behind Peabody's ears and through the soft fur. Standing again, he turned to face her, his eyes playful. "You know you still owe me a day of hiking."

"I think I owe you for wimping out this morning," she said. "Could I make you a dinner sometime?"

"I'll take you up on that, but I have to go see my dad this weekend."

"When do you leave?"

"I'll drive up Friday and come back Sunday. How about Sunday evening?"

"Perfect. I'll even cook a veggie meal for you."

"Good for me. I'll try and get here by five or so."

"But Landis," she said, "I think we need a little compromising here."

He gazed at her guardedly.

"Maybe you could leave your gun at home when you come?"

He threw up his hands and grinned. "Already you're making deals with me?"

"Just checking out wiggle room," she replied. "Possible negotiable issues."

"It's a good thing I like you," he replied as he opened the driver door. "I'll see you Sunday."

"Without your gun?"

"We'll see. I like to leave my audience guessing," he said, turning on the motor.

"Good-bye Landis," Ida said. "Thanks for lunch. I did have a good time."

"Me too," he said.

***

Martha was chopping carrots and cucumbers to add to a tossed salad as Ida entered the cottage. They looked at one another without any commentary. Ida went to wash up and put on jeans and slippers. When she returned, Martha was sitting at the table with two cups.

"You look like you have something you want to say to me," Ida said, spooning honey into the hot tea.

"When's the last time you had sex?" asked Martha as she raised her cup.

"Don't beat around the bush, Martha. If you have something to ask me…"

"I just did. When's the last time you had sex?"

Ida rubbed her forehead. "You mean with someone else?"

Martha shook her head. "Not funny."

Ida thought for a bit. "I'd say quite a while ago…I think I've averaged about one relationship per decade, except for in my sixties. Then I just lost interest."

"You know about post-menopausal dryness, right?" Martha asked. "You know your vagina has aged."

Ida laughed. "Okay, Mom. Tell me what I need to do."

"I'm telling you this for your own good. When you see Dr. T in a couple of weeks, you need to ask about estrogen creams, or you're going to regret it. Once I had the cream, I felt like a new woman."

"Okay, I get that. Sex at our ages is a different set of issues, but sex is sex."

"So, you also need to be sure Landis has been tested for STDs too."

"Really? You think Landis sleeps around?"

"Isn't that what you thought he was doing with Shelby? It's not outside the realm of possibilities. I'm just saying men are men, and you'd better be sure before you get yourself into something."

"Mostly I don't want to think about sex. Now, thanks to you, I will be thinking about it."

"Maybe that was my intention," grinned Martha.

"I wish it was the other way around. I wish it was you going gaga over someone."

"No you don't," replied Martha. "This is a good thing for you, Ida. It is. But I have to tell you that sex was much more for me as I got older. We may not have had that intense, explosive stuff like when we were young, but it was slower and more powerful."

"More soulful?"

"You could say that. The glow was more satisfying."

"The *glow*. Oh I like that."

"I don't have your gift for words. I'm sure there's some Buddhist word for that enlightened sexual act."

"I think glow just about sums it up."

"You wait," Martha continued. "If this thing you have going for Landis lands you in a bed, you may surprise yourself in your old age."

"And what about you and Tommy? What's going on there?"

"I'm talking about you, not me. I'm worried you'll work yourself out of this one."

Ida closed her eyes. "I wish, but I think it's too late for that."

"Are you a goner?"

"Well, just to be clear, and just to get things out in the open, you'd be okay if Landis spent the night here sometime?"

"If he stays in your room, yeah, I'm fine with that."

"Martha," Ida's voice turned serious, "I'm really not cut out for this. I didn't want this kind of love again. I'm kind of pissed it happened and I'm pissed I can't make these feelings stop. I'm too old for this."

"What are you afraid is going to happen?"

"It's like I'm twenty years old. Tumbling emotions and weird physical urges – and thoughts that have no logical framework. I want to be with him all the time, and then when I'm with him, I want to run. It's awful."

Martha finished her tea, sat back and smiled. "Sounds like you've got it bad."

"Yes," Ida agreed. "Yes, I think I do."

FOUR

Ida drove to town that Saturday to pick up some fresh produce for the dinner with Landis. She'd invited Martha and Moses too; human buffers so she wouldn't be alone with him. She stopped by the grocery store and picked up fresh salmon, or at least unfrozen salmon, and the few other items in her narrow repertoire of menu options.

Sunday afternoon she put on clean jeans, not too tight, not too baggy, and a dressier tunic. She thought *Why should I care?* But she did. She tied a long apron over her clean top knowing full well she'd dribble something on it before the night was over. She'd been buying multi-colored tops the last few years, the better to camouflage stains from food or drink that landed below her neck.

Spinach dip, chips, and cut-up vegetables were appetizers. A green salad and the couscous was prepared and refrigerated. Salmon would wait till everyone was here. Should she bring out the opened bottle of wine? She'd wait. She'd made iced mint tea for the men.

Martha came in smelling of the barn. Ida regarded her coolly. "I hope you're going to shower."

"Really? It's just Landis and Moses."

"And me. Please shower before dinner today."

"Are you going to ask Moses to do the same thing 'cause he's not using my shower. He can use yours."

"No, he's okay. I'm just asking you."

"I sense a little sexism going on here," said Martha. "I really think it's all about the women smelling good."

"Okay Martha, then don't shower."

"No, I was planning to anyway. I'm going."

Ida shook her head and finished arranging the appetizer plate. Through the front window she saw the white jeep pull up. She might as well go out to greet him.

"Hi Landis," she called. "You're right on time."

"I brought you some home-made wine from a friend in Missoula and some chocolate chip cookies from my sister," he said, lifting a basket from the backseat of the jeep.

"Wow. Very nice. Thanks." Ida accepted the basket. "Forewarning. I've invited Martha and Moses to join us for dinner. I hope that's okay?"

If he was disappointed it didn't show. "It's always great to see them both." Peabody sniffed around Landis, nudged into him for a pat, and then trotted obsequiously behind him, ready to be his new best friend.

In the kitchen, Landis found the corkscrew in a drawer and opened the wine himself.

Ida placed two wine glasses on the counter. "I have ice tea or water or…"

"Ice tea sounds great," he said pouring the wine into her glass. Moses entered as she put out the glasses of mint tea.

"Let's sit." She nodded toward the living room. The men made themselves comfortable with the appetizers and their usual topics of conversation: fishing, work, the band, rodeos, the last A.A. meeting. When Martha joined them, Ida jumped up.

"I'm frying up salmon tonight. We're eating fish!" she said much too excitedly and trotted off briskly.

"She appears to be a little hyped up tonight, boys," said Martha, a hint of amusement in her voice.

"Looks like Ida might need a little assistance in there." Ida overheard Moses and imagined him tilting his head in the direction of the kitchen.

Landis stood tentatively by her side as she applied pats of butter on the salmon and squeezed half a lemon onto the pinkish flesh. He reached for the salt and pepper and handed them to her. "Thanks," she said. "Do you put anything else on it?"

"Keep it simple I say." He leaned against the counter watching as she flipped the salmon onto the frying skillet and turned up the heat. "You seem a little out of sorts. Are you okay?"

"Yep, fine. Yep." she responded, eyes on her prize dish. "How was your visit with your father?"

"He's pretty talkative these days. It's almost as if he wants to get out all his memories before he leaves us. Physically I see him getting weaker. He's not much interested in eating."

She looked up at him then. "Is he talking a lot about his childhood?"

"Yeah, as a matter of fact, he does. Is that significant?"

"My personal theory is that it happens more when folks had happy childhoods. I never heard unhappy stories – so I always figured the ones who talked had good memories. I think someone should do a comparative study."

"I think you might have a reasonable theory there. And those pleasant memories often don't get recognized till we get old and have time to remember them." He picked up her wine glass on the counter and handed it to her. "Did you have a happy childhood?"

"Oh my, yes!" she enthused. "I had free range in a small town. My friends and I rode our bikes all over creation, making up mysteries, spying on poor souls in their old houses. We even had a detective club, though we had to make up crimes to solve."

"I had a pretty good childhood too – at least till middle school. My parents didn't know where I was all day, but as long as I came home for dinner, it was all cool."

Ida flipped the salmon over. It had lovely crusty brown ribbons across it. "Yes, exactly. And then all the neighborhood kids would gather in the evening, playing games in the dark until our parents called us home."

Landis took the spatula from her and lifted the bottom of the fish to check for doneness. "I'd give it another two minutes. Well done!!"

Table conversation centered on horses. One was going lame and they wondered what to do about it. Martha wasn't ready to put him down, but Moses thought it needed to be done. How to take care of the horse's injuries and medical needs was an on-going topic of discussions between the two. Then there was Molly. Martha knew she couldn't put that death off much longer.

"And what about names for the new colt?" asked Ida, switching to something more pleasant.

"I'm thinking of the name Harrison – after our neighbor," announced Martha.

"Now, that's just plain silly," Moses said. "You don't name a horse after a dearly departed friend."

"Oh really? I'm thinking Moses is a great name for a horse – if and when you ever kick off," she declared.

"Allow for a respectable mourning time. Harrison died two days ago."

"You have a name, do you?" Landis asked Moses.

"Yep," he said, folding his arms across his chest.

"So don't make us badger you, Moses," said Ida. "Tell us!"

"Music. I wanna' name the foal Music."

Landis chuckled. "Like the Willie Nelson song?"

"Exactly," said Moses. "A horse called Music."

"I guess that'll do," replied Martha. "Harrison might seek retribution in his afterlife anyway."

"You know he sold me his backhoe before he died," said Moses. "I'll take it out to the northwest site and dig a couple of graves." He helped himself to another slice of salmon.

Martha stared at her empty plate. "What day?"

He glanced at her face. "We'll give it a couple more days. I may play around with the thing and get to digging next weekend."

"I'd appreciate that. It might take me a few days to say goodbye to my Molly."

"Done deal," said Moses.

The remainder of the conversation centered on a community theater production and upcoming festivals in the region.

Summer notably brought new bands to the area for weekend celebrations. There were numerous weddings scheduled at the guest house throughout July. When it came time for dessert, Moses and Martha coincidentally excused themselves at the same time, each headed off in different directions of the house. Landis and Ida were left with a plate of Louise's homemade chocolate chip cookies

"So…" Landis hesitated and smiled, "alone at last."

"I don't know why I'm so nervous this evening."

"Why don't we just ask each other questions like we did last week? That seemed to work pretty well."

"That I can probably do. Let's go to the living room."

Once settled into places opposite one another, Ida slipped off her shoes and curled her legs beneath her. Peabody curled into a space on the floor at Landis' feet.

"Did you bring your gun tonight?"

"Whoa, pretty blunt there," Landis replied. "You don't take any time to warm up your audience do you?"

"It doesn't require a thoughtful response. Yes or no?"

"No, I did not. I'm counting on you to protect me."

"Is that why you carry it? Seriously. For self-protection? Do you think you could actually shoot someone?"

"There are lots of crazies out here. I could be attacked by a human or an animal."

"A bear?"

"A bear or a moose. Sometimes elk start ramming people. I don't think I'd shoot a human being, but if somebody came in here and attacked you, sure, I'd use it."

"Very low odds for something like that to happen, but it seems like a common fear that gun owners bring up. I just think if you own a weapon you're more likely to use it."

"Still…" he said. "This is NRA country, Ida."

"Yes, I know. I just don't buy into all of their propaganda." She looked down at her lap and then up at Landis. "You don't have to answer this, but you probably shot people in Vietnam?"

His hand rubbed his forehead as if he was suddenly very tired. "I don't have words for the hell that war was. We were trained to think they were the enemy. It wasn't like I ever came face to face with another man." He paused. "But yes, I killed. And I have to live with that."

She didn't respond.

"I was shot at too. That's when adrenaline sets in."

She was trying to think of how to get through this difficult conversation and the questions that had nagged at her. She couldn't let it drop.

He looked at her seriously. "Do I regret my time there? Yes, every day. War is just the worst part of being human – and fighting for an idea – well, it's hard to justify loss of life for an idea. I guess I've forgiven myself for that part of my life. I have to. It was a long time ago."

"And what about our wars in Afghanistan, other Mideast countries? Do you think we should be there as a country?"

"I don't know. I think our military is doing some good in these places. Loss of life is minimal."

"Loss of *American* life," she pushed.

"Yes, loss of American lives. War is hell. And I have a bullet wound to always remind me."

"I'm sorry," she said. "You were wounded?"

"In my thigh. Small price considering the suffering others did."

"There are so many places of suffering in this world."

"What about you, Little Ms. Buddha? You have any Vietnams in your closet? Anything you regret?"

Ida tugged at a loose thread on her tunic. If she pulled on it more, the fabric might start to unravel. She was thinking back over her life, and not able to look Landis in the eye. "I suppose of all the hard choices in my life, I'd probably say I regret getting an abortion. It's something I don't talk about. Something I felt I had to do at the time."

He was slow to respond. He appeared to be thinking what to say. "You know I figure there are some things that are just meant to be between us and God."

"Like your Vietnam?" she asked.

"If I believed in God, yes."

"I think you're right," she said thoughtfully. "I don't need to be asking you about that time in your life."

"I can handle it." He paused, reflecting on a thought. "You know, if we had met thirty years ago, we probably wouldn't have given each other the time of day. I know I was pretty rigid."

She nodded. "I think you're right. I still have pretty strong beliefs. I'm trying to learn forgiveness – of myself and others." She glanced at him. "I still like a good debate. A healthy argument."

"So…you got any more ammo for me?"

"Okay here's one," she said leaning forward in her chair. "Are you a Democrat or Republican?"

"Oh no. Didn't take long to get here," he smiled. "I'm an Independent."

"Ha!" she exploded. "That means you're a Republican. Just hiding behind the guise of an Independent."

He chuckled. "So, you're probably a Democrat. Always right!"

"Well yes, on the issues that matter," she responded smugly.

"You know I've never been asked so many interrogating questions by a woman before," he stated flatly.

"Maybe it's because you haven't been with a Mennonite woman before," she grinned. "I think we're opposites in many ways. Do we have *anything* in common?"

"Martha. Moses."

"Yes, they can vouch for our characters," she laughed. "I do like your sense of humor."

"I like that you think I have a sense of humor." He put his arm up to rest on the back of the couch, seemingly reflective. "I also like that you're deep. You think about things."

"Deep? Me?" She shook her head. "Or is this an example of your humor?"

"No, I'm quite serious. You think things out for yourself."

"I think I have you fooled."

"No, you don't. You don't spout off someone else's ideas as if they're your own." He was thoughtful about his words. "You know stuff in your soul, and it shows in who you are."

She knew she was flustered now. This was a compliment to her. More than if he had told her she was the most beautiful woman in the world. "I really don't know how to respond to that."

"You don't have to. I guess I just wanted you to know I've thought about you." He fumbled with his hands then and looked at his watch. She liked that he wore a watch with an old-fashioned wristband. "So, can I take it that since you're asking me all these questions – you're kind of interested in me?"

"Kind of," she replied with a twitch of a smile.

He stood up and stretched, "Well okay then. I think this went pretty well. But I think I'd better get going."

She stood up too and felt a muscle spasm in her hip. "Oh Jesus, that hurts!" she exclaimed as her hand went to her back. "Sorry, it's my bad hip!"

He nodded. "As opposed to your good one?"

"I'm fine really. It just happens when I sit too long."

"Me too. We get to this age, we're going to be dealing with something."

"Come on, I'll walk you out. We will *not* begin talking about our health!"

Once she opened the front door, Peabody was underfoot and ready to bolt. He took off for his favorite bushes, sniffing for nocturnal life. Landis and Ida stopped to take in the panorama of the night sky. Looking upwards they witnessed countless pinprick speckles on the indigo ink canvas.

"Beautiful," she remarked.

"Fantastic," he agreed.

"We really are insignificant in the grand scheme of things."

"Speak for yourself," he teased. He took her hand then and turned to face her. "Thank you for the great dinner and a great evening. Really."

"Thanks for indulging me with all my questions."

"It's all right. I like the attention." He spoke to the heavens above him then. "And I take it as a sign that you like me as maybe more than a friend."

"Yeah, I think I do." She peered at the sky too.

He dropped her hand and leaned in to kiss her forehead. "Good-night Ida."

He was in his jeep before she knew it. That was it? He hadn't said he felt the same about her. What had she been hoping for?

She cleaned up the kitchen, berating herself for being so inquisitive, so nosy. It was too soon. He'd been put off. And she had come across as so sanctimonious, holier than thou. She was such a fool. If he didn't feel the same, well, all right. She didn't like feeling all gaga anyway.

She saw the forgotten basket on the counter at the same time she heard barking. "Dammit, I'd leave Peabody out for the night if he didn't remind me." Opening the door, she saw the jeep backing up the driveway. She picked up his basket and called, "You forgot something."

"Yes, I did," he replied, stepping out from the front of the jeep. He took the basket from her and leaned over to kiss her gently on the lips. "I think I forgot to say I really like you too."

This time his exit was clean and smooth. It was mutual. He might be trusted. How could this be at such a late stage in her life? She had ceased expecting love such a long time ago. Apparently she wasn't done with feeling gaga after all.

FIVE

Elsa arrived home the third week in May, sulky and reserved, paradoxically unlike the young woman she'd been at Christmas. During spring break she'd done a service project in Haiti, so they had not seen her all those months. Annie had wanted to grant her daughter space and honor her growing independence. Phone calls and emails had not disclosed this changing personality. On her second night home, Elsa announced she was not returning to the university in the fall.

"What?" Annie exclaimed. "Why? What happened that you'd come up with this?"

"I hate it. I hate the academic competition! I hate the cliques! I hate the stupid social scene! I just don't want to go back there!"

"Where is this coming from? You never said anything!" Annie went to her daughter and hesitantly reached out to embrace her.

"Please don't make me go back there," sobbed Elsa.

"Nobody is going to make you do anything you don't want to do," Martha said reassuringly.

"It's just that I felt so out of place there," Elsa cried, "I just don't belong."

The older women glanced at each other. Annie put her arms around her daughter and allowed her time to cry. "Maybe you can go to state next year, not so far away," she suggested.

"Dad will be so disappointed in me," Elsa said. "He really wanted me to do well at the U."

"He wants you to be happy. We'll figure out something. But you don't have to go back to something that makes you miserable," Annie comforted her. "We'll work it out. Dad will understand."

"I mean I liked being closer to Dad and I saw him more, but I didn't belong there."

"It's his Alma Mater, but it doesn't have to be yours. Let's give it some time, okay?" Annie was pushing the hair back from Elsa's face.

"I want to stay home next year and figure out what I really want to do with my life."

"That's what Ida and I say too," laughed Martha. "For one thing, we decided we don't need to be doing so much work around here. We pull our weight, but we just don't need to be involved in the daily operation of this place."

"I never thought I'd hear you say that," Elsa said, "but you seem really happy, Gram."

"Yep, I am. I couldn't be much more content than I am these days," confessed Martha.

"What about the social hour?" Elsa asked Ida. "Are you still doing that in the late afternoons?"

"Only on Tuesday and Thursdays. On Wednesday afternoons, Sidonnia holds a yoga class in the Tamarack room. And I need my yoga!"

"Is the yoga for anyone – guests and staff?"

"Yes, for anyone. Sometimes I'm the only other one there," Ida replied, "but it's for anyone. Free."

"Maybe I could cover the Wednesday social hour then."

"You and Romona could do the social hour. She's over twenty-one and we need to have someone older since wine is served." Annie went on musing about her plans. "Sid helps with the administrative stuff and we trade off breakfasts. You can help with that too. We'll work out a schedule for everyone."

"And you're not mad at me for not wanting to go back to school?" asked Elsa.

"I'm concerned, but not mad," replied Annie. "We'll talk about it once you've been home for a few weeks."

"I'm glad to be home," said Elsa. "It feels like home."

IDA AND MARTHA
A Montana Story

SIX

Martha and Ida drove to Bozeman to the larger farmers market on Memorial Day weekend. The square was bustling with people with arts and crafts tables, jewelry, Western wear. They were on a mission to pick up fresh produce for Miriam's service on Monday. They'd spent the morning intermittently stopping among the booths selecting ripe berries and vegetables that hadn't appeared yet in Ida's garden.

"Okay, I have everything on my list," Ida stated. "I'm ready to go."

"Let me get some tomatoes here, and I'll be on your tail."

Ida waited while Martha inspected and selected the ones she deemed perfect. She turned out of curiosity towards Shelby's booth across the square. *Is it? Is it Landis?* She couldn't be sure from this distance but from the physical height it would appear so.

"Martha, I think I see Landis. I'm just going to stroll over and say hi."

Martha finished paying. "I'll come with you."

Ida stopped short. Martha followed with her eyes. Landis was animated, obviously engaged in a repartee of some sort. The two women watched as Shelby maneuvered around her jewelry table and put her hands up to cup his face.

Ida froze. It was an intimate act.

Martha said, "Hell no," and began walking toward them.

"Don't Martha," Ida mumbled, her voice cracking.

Martha was upon them. "Damn it, Landis!"

He jerked backwards, first aware of Martha and behind her, Ida. Martha started to say more, but he brushed past her. Ida turned sharply and scudded towards their truck as fast as her little legs could carry her.

"Ida," he called out. "Wait!"

She spun around and said coldly, "You know, I really don't want to hear it right now." She was off, scampering quickly, away from the conflict. She heard his footsteps. Again, she turned around, "I think you need to leave me alone right now."

His hands were open in front of him, palms up. "It's just Shelby. It's nothing. It's just the way she is."

"Okay," she nodded. "Now I'm saying, you need to leave me alone right now." She turned abruptly and walked away.

She heard Martha pass him, saying, "Nope, Landis, sure doesn't look good."

Martha got in and turned the keys. A grinding sound indicated the engine was not about to turn over. They couldn't make a clean getaway. She tried a few more times. "I'll see if I can get somebody to jump the battery. That's probably it."

Ida lay her head on the backrest. She slunk further down and eventually curled up with her head on the seat near the steering wheel. *Please no one see me.* A knock on the window indicated otherwise. She opened her eyes. *Shelby.*

"Hey look, Landis and I are just friends." *That confident smile, such self-assuredness.*

Ida rolled down her window and said, "Shelby, this is not about you."

Shelby snapped, "Well maybe it's not about you either." And she was gone.

That's probably right, Ida thought. *It's not about me either. It's about Landis.*

Martha was directing Sadie to hook her truck up to old Gus. They connected the charged wires and Martha started the engine. "That'll get us home anyway. Thanks Sadie!"

"You'll return the favor sometime I'm sure," said Sadie. She went around the truck and opened the passenger door so Ida had to listen to her. "Ida, you know I think men are generally pigs, and if you're messing with a dirty pig, you're going get dirty too. You should know better. That's all I'm sayin'… I like Landis but he's still a man, so that's that." She slammed the door of the truck and shouted, "You take care of yourselves."

They drove home in silence. When the truck was parked up by the barn where it would be left to die, Ida spoke, "Maybe it wasn't like what it looked like."

Martha turned to her and said, "Yes, it was what it looked like."

"Maybe it was just a simple affectionate gesture of sorts."

"Of sorts?"

"Is Landis a dirty pig like Sadie said?"

Martha shook her head. "For as long as I've known Landis, I've known him to be a kind and honest man. I can't reconcile what I saw today with who I think he is."

"It could be something silly. This is stupid. It just hurts, that's all."

"Landis has always been a bit of a flirt. But if he's serious about you, he needs to get his priorities in line. Too bad you have to see him Monday, at the service for Miriam."

"Two days to let the heavy stuff sink to the bottom and the clarity rise to the top."

"Like worms after a rainstorm?"

"I'd forgotten that one. Truth tends to rise to the surface like worms after a rainstorm."

"Or lies." Martha said. "Lies tend to rise to the surface."

"Either way – more clarity."

"I'll make dinner tonight. We'll open a bottle of zin, sit on the porch, tell old stories. How does that sound?"

"If you're volunteering to make dinner, you're really feeling sorry for me," Ida said.

"You better believe it. Poor pitiful you. I wouldn't do this for just anybody."

When they arrived back at the ranch, a rumbling motor could he heard coming from the northwest. Martha stamped toward the house, a look of distress on her face.

"You okay?" asked Ida.

Martha turned back. "It's Moses. He's digging the graves. I have to take Molly out there around sundown."

"Do you want me to come?"

Martha shook her head.. "I'll just walk her out there. I never stay. Moses will do the deed."

"Will you be okay?"

"Probably not, but what can I do? It's time to let go." The slow steps Martha took towards the barn to spend her last hour with Molly were ones heavy with love.

How parallel were the feelings of grief with heartsickness. Ida struggled to find words to understand why she felt so betrayed, why it hurt to think of Landis being so attentive to another woman, how she had allowed herself to get to this vulnerability. She was angry and despairing, but she knew time would get her through to the other side.

And now having to put Molly down. Well, come on into this heart, there's plenty of room in here for more hurt.

Disappointment. Hurt. Came from having expectations. *Why haven't I learned that? Hope leads to risks, which build on expectations, which almost always result in disappointment. So maybe it's for the best that this awakening happened now, before I fall any deeper into this attraction, this spellbound love, this craving as Buddhism might say. Maybe for the best,* she thought. *Maybe for the best.*

SEVEN

A semi-circle of chairs inside the new Tamarack lodge created a crescent space for Miriam's memorial service. The space could hold a hundred people but once tables were set up, it divided itself into cozier corners. A woodsy ambience was derived from the massive oak beams and pine siding. Outside, strings of white lights lined the branches on the newly planted saplings.

Moses had worked on the service with heartfelt diligence, approaching friends shyly to ask for their participation. Guests would gather for the service inside, walk to the aspen grove for the scattering of ashes, and return for a light supper. Romona and Elsa volunteered to serve the light meal.

The somberness of the occasion called for more attention to dress. Martha told Ida that Montana men don't wear suits unless they're going to a courtroom for a crime. For this they'd wear long-sleeved, dark-colored shirts. Ida dug out a dark-green sundress from an unpacked box of summer clothes. Martha wore her black pants with a mauve linen top.

They counted twenty people, all friends of Moses, clustered in groups. She hardly recognized Landis in a navy sports jacket, or Hank and Tipp in their handsome shirts without their hats. They were playing softly in a corner. Elsa's flute joined them for a slow rendition of "Will the Circle Be Unbroken."

Moses stood up and spoke in his deep resonant voice. "First off, thank you all for coming today. I want to say this matter of love has been on my mind a lot lately. Love is something that often seems to come and go, but looking back on my life I realize it was kind of there all along, underneath it all."

He shuffled through some note cards in his hand and continued. "We're here today to honor the life of Miriam Mailer. She was a kind soul who had a pretty hard go of it. She came into my life a long time ago. Her step-father abused her and her husband bullied her, but she, herself, was never bitter or mean-spirited. We were good friends and we helped each other out the best we could at the time."

He cleared his throat looking down at the floor and then continued, "A few years ago, she came into a little money – from that same husband, so I suppose there is some justice here. Anyway, she came up here looking for me, but in-cognito, as they say, so I didn't recognize her. This was just last December. She died in this guest house. I suppose you could say she died looking for me. That might be a bit dramatic. I like to think she was happy in her later years. Now, in her death, I want to give some peace to the hurtfulness she had in her life."

He waved to the musicians as a grand marshal might signal to his courtiers. Ida glanced at Landis playing his guitar. She shifted uncomfortably in her chair. When the music ended, Moses resumed his air of authority.

"Martha, Annie, will you join me?" He began reading carefully: "*First Corinthians 13: If I speak in the tongues of mortals and of angels, but do not have love, I am a noisy gong or a clanging cymbal. And if I have prophetic powers, and understand all mysteries, and if I have faith, so as to move mountains, but don't have love, I am nothing."*

He handed the Bible to Annie, who read with solemn intention: *"Love is patient; love is kind; love is not envious or boastful or arrogant or rude. It does not insist on its own way; it is not irritable or resentful. It does not rejoice in wrongdoing, but rejoices in the truth. It bears all things, believes all things, hopes all things, endures all things."*

Martha put on her glasses and accepted the book from her daughter. *"When I was a child, I spoke like a child, I thought like a child, I reasoned like a child; when I became an adult I put away my childish ways, for now we see in a mirror dimly, but then we will see face to face. Now I know only in part; then I will know fully, even as I have been fully known. For faith, hope, and love abide, and of these three, the greatest is love."*

The words on the transforming power of love moved Ida deeply. Sometimes Scripture could do that. The words of Jesus were the most powerful. Paul, she suspected, might have had help from a good editor.

The musicians began the old gospel tune "Down to the River to Pray." Elsa began singing, throwing out her arms, gesturing for all to join in. The banjo and guitar maintained the melody:

> *When I went down to the river to pray, studying about that good old way, and who should wear the starry crown, good Lord, show me the way…
> …Oh brother, let's go down, let's go down, come on down,
> …Oh sister, let's go down, down to the river to pray.*

When they had sung themselves down, Moses again stood up inviting everyone to follow him to the grove of trees off to the west, past the wedding site. A disarrayed queue of folks trailed him to where the aspens fluttered and shushed in the evening breeze. He lifted the small canister and dispersed the ashes into the air.

Ida recalled lines of Emily Dickerson. *"She slipped from our fingers, like a flake gathered by the wind, and is now part of the drift called the infinite."* There was more to the quote questioning where the loved one went, but she couldn't recollect how it went. Some of the ashes blew back onto those standing close. Farther up amongst the trees was a stone remembrance.

Walking back down the path, Ida turned to wait for Landis, who lingered beside Moses. She watched them speak softly to one another and could not turn her eyes away when Landis patted Moses gently on his back. He saw her waiting then and came toward her, hands in his pockets, eyes on the ground. She stood still, wondering what she would say, but feeling she had been foolish, impulsive, quick to judgment.

He stopped beside her and asked gently, "Ida, how are you?"

She touched his upper arm and, even in that moment, acknowledged the palpable twinge deep inside her. "I don't know what to say, but I need to say something."

He nodded. "Well I need to say I'm sorry. I've been going over it and over it in my head and if I had seen you doing what I was doing, yeah, I would've lost it too. I'm so sorry."

"I just don't know where I stand with you," she said. "I thought we'd come to a mutual understanding of this relationship, new as it was, but then you – with Shelby – it just shattered that. I'm seventy-two years old. I can't do this."

"Look I know it's hard to trust me, but I have to tell you I can't seem to concentrate on anything right now. I really do want to be in this thing with you –– whatever it is."

She looked into his eyes and said, "I'm just not free and easy. I don't compete with other women. If I'm in this thing, it's got to be monogamous. So you've got to figure out what Shelby means to you."

"Shelby is…Shelby was…just a diversion," he answered calmly. "That relationship is over. It wasn't even much of a relationship. It was just that, a diversion."

"And am I just a *diversion*?" she asked.

He shook his head in that slow, stilted way someone does when they don't believe something they're hearing. He sighed and muttered, "Incredible."

"Landis, answer me."

He reached out and held her shoulders clenched in both his hands. "She was a diversion so I wouldn't have to think about you! I'm a mess, Ida, and I'm sorry. I'm truly sorry if I hurt you by some stupid thing I did." His hands dropped back down to his sides. He didn't seem to know what to do with them.

"It did hurt. I didn't want it to matter, but it did."

"I'll tell you straight out. I want to do things right with you. I don't want to mess this up."

"Just be honest with me." She looked intently at him.

"That I can do. I do honesty pretty well," he said with a smile.

240

"Because as scared as I am to get close to you, I know now I want to, I want to get to know who you are." Her voice softened.

She saw him swallow. "I've been thinking a lot about this too. I want to know you before time gets going any faster."

She reached out and pulled him close to her. Standing on her tiptoes to reach his lips, she felt the pressure in her chest puncture. Mercy. She hadn't known how very deep her soul had been holding pain. HIs arms tightened around her.

"I need some of that oxygen you put off," she whispered to him. "I can barely breathe."

"Don't let go," he murmured into her hair.

There was a certain solace in finally touching one another. A calmness in just their arms around one another. Ida eventually spoke, "What strange old creatures we are."

"Kind of evolutionary wonders, aren't we?" he asked.

"I just want to be here with you, listening to your beating heart," she said.

"Can you really hear something in there?"

Ida breathed deeply and took a step back with her hand on his chest saying mischievously, "I think this is the point in the movie where they start ripping off one another's clothes."

"Don't think I haven't thought about it." He said with that winsome smile.

"What am I going to do with you?" Awkward and clumsy, she still clung to his hand. "We've got to start acting our age."

"You mean me, I need to be more mature."

"I'm guilty too. I'm acting like such a stupid, silly girl."

241

Landis stepped towards her and whispered, "You don't have to be afraid of me. Really."

Her little body nestled against his mountainous frame. She could not move.

"I guess we have to go back, don't we?" he said finally.

"Yes, I think we do."

"But if we didn't we'd sure give them something to talk about."

"Slow down, mister. We've got to slow this down."

"It feels like I've known you a long time, but there's so much I don't know about you."

"It's only been a couple of weeks."

"I've thought about this. Part of it is that I've known Martha and Moses a long time, and a friend of theirs had to be okay. But you were more than okay."

"Smitten by association?" she teased. "But I know what you mean. Your friendship with Moses maybe perked up my interest."

He raised his index finger to make a point. "And the old Swede. That guy showing up definitely changed up the game. I didn't know jealousy could whack me in the face." He paused and then continued in a serious tone. "I have to tell you something and it might as well be now."

"Oh oh," she said. She let go of his hands and crossed her arms in front of her.

"No, it's not about us – though I suppose it could affect us. It's just that I've agreed to do a study in Poland during July and August. I've been torn about it because of…well, with my dad dying, and now…well…you."

"What is it? Did you know about this for a while?"

"I agreed to it six months ago. It's in Poland, in the Bialowieza National Park, one of the best preserved old-growth forests. I'd be part of a team."

"A team of scientists?"

"Apparently there are some parts of the world that still regard the work of scientists in determining policies."

"You need to go. I know leaving your father at this time will be the most difficult. Leaving me now? It'll be okay."

"I agreed to do it thinking it would be a great transition into retirement."

"And it is. What a tremendous opportunity."

"The timing couldn't be worse."

"If we hadn't talked today, if we hadn't cleared up this… misunderstanding, then it would have been awful for you to go."

"It's actually only for six weeks. I'll be back for Moses' birthday."

"When is that?"

"August eighteenth. His eighty-fifth."

"We've got to celebrate that one – though he's bound to put up a fuss."

"And we still have June. I leave the first Saturday in July."

"Maybe I could visit your father with you? Maybe in the next week or so? Would that be okay?"

Landis thought about it. "Yeah that would be nice. I think that would work."

They held onto one another, treading carefully through the weeds and wildflowers in the grassy pasture till they reached the gravel drive. The lights strung out on the trees led them back to the gathered community, to safeness, level-headedness, common sense. How could she subdue the effervescence within her? She squeezed his hand and let go, entering the room a few feet ahead of Landis and nearly colliding with Moses.

"Ida, dear Ida," Moses said as he hugged her close.

Landis came up beside him and nudged him gently. "You'll be happy to know we made peace with each other. She trusts me again…I think."

Moses looked at Ida and back at Landis. "You two better not mess this up. You may not have as much time as you think. Life is short."

"Spoken like a true sage," Ida said. "The wisdom of Moses."

"I'm a lot smarter than I look," responded Moses.

"We won't argue about that," grinned Landis. "We'll let you have that one."

SUMMERING

JUNE

ONE

"So, you're going to have to learn the two-step for Rusty and Annie's wedding," Landis chided Ida.

"I'm not musical. I'll fall over myself. And over you too."

"You can learn this one. I'll teach you."

"Wear steel-toed boots because I'll be stepping on your feet more than any two-step."

"Stand up," he ordered. "Let's just try this. Here – quick, quick, slow, slow."

She got up and faced him. He placed her left hand on his upper arm, one of her favorite spots on his body. HIs left arm swung around her and his strong hand pressed on her back. "There, isn't this nice?" he said.

"But we have to move, right?" she asked.

"You're going to move backwards. Start with your left foot. Quick. Now the right. Quick. Repeat left slow. Right slow. See…you did it." They moved through a series of repetitions but when he tried to turn her, she kicked him in the knee.

"I warned you," she said. "You didn't tell me the woman has to move backwards."

Landis chuckled. "You did great. It's your first time with country dancing. You'll get it when you hear the music."

"We'll see," she replied.

The Saturday afternoon of the wedding was breezy and cool. Martha appeared as radiant as her daughter in a new dress she had purchased for the occasion. Moses walked Annie down the path with a solemnity only he could dignify. Elsa, the ring-bearer, deposited the treasures in a pocket on her dress for safe keeping and enthusiastically tossed posies as she pranced to her designated spot. When it came time for the exchange of rings, on-lookers heard her exclaim an expletive, and watched in suspense as she fervently searched the grass near her shoes. Within seconds Rusty took two steps toward her, retrieving the band on the ground and holding it aloft for all to see. Applause spontaneously broke out as a chagrined Elsa hugged Rusty, and then her mother Neither Rusty or Annie had been schooled in any semblance of Bible-reading growing up, but they had both been moved by those passages read at the memorial service for Miriam, and asked if these could be used at their wedding. Little did they know 1st Corinthians 13 was the most popular scripture read at weddings. Pastor Karen took liberties in framing the scripture into the context of romantic love. She read the verses clearly; love is patient, love is kind, love is not boastful or arrogant, and then called Annie and Rusty forward to share their vows. They'd known each other a long time as friends. They knew love was hard work and not just an intoxication. Being rural folks, they were not afraid of hard work.

Ida regarded Martha's face as her daughter stated her vows. Was she ruminating perhaps on wistful thoughts of Dan? Times like these were when one felt the absences of lost friends. Martha had become fond of Rusty in the past few months, mostly for his care and attention in the handling of horses. If he was gentle around the horses, she figured he would treat Annie with respect and tenderness.

Josephine, decked out in a slinky lowcut dress, clung to a massive man under a Stetson hat attired in what might be called a western tuxedo. His swagger emitted the self-confident brashness of a wealthy rancher who was used to getting his way. Together the pair comported themselves with a gravitational certainty that they were to be seen as vitally front and center in this event as the newlyweds. At the reception Josephine pulled her man over to face Martha and Ida.

"Seb, this is Ida, the woman I've talked about who started our little women's group."

Martha intervened. "Seb! Now there's an authentic nickname. Has a ring to it that all those actor types will warm to."

Sebastian remained unfazed with barely a nod in her direction. "Always a pleasure to see you too, Martha. And Ida, I've heard only good things about you."

"You're Rusty's father, correct?" asked Ida. "I've seen your picture on a billboard."

"Thought I might as well get my mugshot out there in case I run for political office someday. Right now I have my hands full with some new projects."

"He just bought another resort closer to Yellowstone," added Josephine conspiratorially. "There are just so many stars who want to come up here to Big Sky to learn how to ride. You wouldn't believe who we've taken out on the trails. Some big names!"

"I'm not sure I'd know who they were if I ran into them," said Martha. "Your place always was a Hollywood to dude-ranch pipeline."

Sebastian perked up. His massive body swiveled around to survey the surrounding area outside the tall windows. "You've got yourself a nice little place, Martha. If Rusty wants to put all his eggs into your basket here, well, I say more power to him."

"Some of us work hard to get where we are," replied Martha cooly. "You don't have to worry. We're not in competition for your clientele."

Josephine patted Sebastian's arm and gave a little wave toward the buffet line. "I think we're supposed to go through the line next - as parents. Martha and Ida, do you want to go first?"

The women excused themselves, claiming they wanted to find their place settings on the tables before queuing up for the food. Ida pretended to be scrutinizing the name cards in a secluded corner of the room when she whispered to Martha, "What was all that about with Josephine's husband?"

Martha scoffed. "Agh. My first wrangling job was on his ranch. I worked for him three long years. He hired a guy to be the head wrangler who was a real jerk, an incompetent fool who made up for his inadequacies by being a brute."

"Towards you?"

"No, towards the horses—which, in my book, is worse than if he'd tried something with me. But he also thought he was God's gift to women."

"Did you ever report him?"

Martha stopped the pretense of looking at name cards, straighting up and turning to face Ida. "I documented everything I saw. Including his off-color remarks to me and the other women. Seb did nothing. *Nothing.* I left, and went to work on a ranch with Moses and thought I'd forget Sebastian. But turns out he's one of the ranchers buying up a lot of the land around here. Corporate farming and tourist dude ranches. That's their idea of Montana life."

"Is this the reason for your animosity towards Josephine?"

"Maybe it has something to do with it. Sebastian doesn't value the family-run businesses. Josephine, she's just oblivious. Which also makes me mad. Why does a woman have to act clueless?"

"And why it took you awhile to warm to Rusty?"

Martha nodded. "I sure didn't trust him, but now I know Rusty really doesn't like his dad's way of doing business. You watch him with his dad. Sets his teeth on edge."

"Hopefully you won't have to encounter his parents more than necessary," said Ida, "but this sure does explain a few things."

After dinner when the music started, Annie and Rusty moved to the center of the floor for the traditional first dance. Soon the band picked up the tempo with tunes for country swing and two-step.

Landis pulled Ida out on the dance floor. "Let's go," he said, "I've been waiting for this."

She went reluctantly and tried to follow his lead. He was right about the music. The beat helped her pick up her heels and move a little more gracefully. The music changed suddenly. The band played some popular music and golden oldies. The younger folks thronged the dance floor as groups, dancing in a kind of call and response. Ida and Landis returned to Moses tapping his fingers on the table. Elsa and Romona came over to invite him out to dance with them. He obliged in his good-natured way, shuffling out as if he was the center of attention.

Martha whispered to Ida, "Hey, let's go use our bathrooms in the cottage." They excused themselves and hurried across the lane up to their home. "I just wanted my privacy. Are you thinking Landis might spend the night?"

Ida bit her lip. "No, I don't feel ready for that. He'd like that, but I just don't feel ready."

Martha nodded. "I'm not ready for Tommy to stay over either. I just wanted to be clear."

"You'd think at our ages, we'd be ready to get going on this sex stuff, but I'm kind of scared."

"Yep. Not quite ready to get back in the saddle as they say."

Returning to the reception, they had no sooner sat down than the band played a slow tune. Landis nudged Ida. "Are you ready?"

"Can't keep me down, but don't try any fancy footwork."

She followed his steady lead, mainly just stepping side to side in a slow shuffle, mainly just hugging. It was the closest physically she'd been to him in any sustained way.

"Is this okay?" he asked. He put his hand on her hair and held her head against his chest.

"I'm just taking in that oxygen," she said.

Later, at the table again, she leaned over to him and whispered, "I'm sorry, but I can't invite you to stay with me tonight. I just wanted to get that out in the open."

He nodded with a smidgen of a smile. "Too soon," he said. "Anyway, Annie gave me family rates at the guest house. I've already got a room-mate with Tommy."

"I didn't think you'd make assumptions, but I just thought I'd be honest," she stumbled. "Not that you'd be presumptuous."

He shook his head slightly. "It's fine, Ida. We're doing fine just the way we are. At least I think so." He looked at her quizzically.

She reached out for his hand and gave it a squeeze. "You're a pretty smart man. I think I need to trust you just a little more."

"I don't know about that," he said, "but I'm happy to hear you say it. I think everything you say is pretty darn wise."

"Okay, okay," responded Ida. "Maybe we should stop this jabbering and dance again."

"Ready to two-step, are you?" he asked, standing up. This time she pulled him out on the dance floor and this time she truly let him take the lead.

TWO

Landis and Ida began a routine of exchanging daily texts and emails in the early weeks of June, sagacious and sensitive to the other's sense of privacy and space. Tentative and restrained, each tested out invitations and ideas for spending time together. Ida felt caught in some kind of emotional snare, ready to snap. Sleep was not something she enjoyed anymore. What was she to do with this restlessness?

Then in the middle of the third week, Landis phoned to say his father had been taken by ambulance to the hospital. Louise heard him fall in the bathroom, his head striking the edge of the tub, and was frantic when he didn't respond. By the time the paramedics arrived, he was lying on the tiled floor, eyes open but unable to move, confused and weak.

Landis and Ida left early Friday driving the two hundred miles to Missoula, stopping only once. Louise came out on the front porch when they drove up.

"About time you showed up," she said walking out to the curb to greet them. "Just in time for lunch. I'm Louise, and you must be Ida."

"Yes, that's me. Good to meet you," Ida shook Louise's hand and pulled out her small bag from the car.

Landis hugged his sister. "Any word today? Any changes?"

"I went to see him this morning and he talked a blue streak. He kept telling me stuff about his childhood, lots of stories, and oh, yeah, how much he loved me. He didn't mention you, Landis."

"Well of course," Landis said, "Dad always liked you best."

254

They went inside for a quick lunch before heading to the hospital. It was unsettling to pass through the vacant living room which had become Henry's hospice bedroom. His books and spare belongings were strewn about. Landis showed Ida to the guest room, which, he pointed out with a twinkle in his eye, was directly across the hall from his room.

"Is there a lock on my door?" she teased.

At the hospital Landis and Ida found his father sitting up in the reclining bed. Mashed potatoes, meatloaf, and green beans sat untouched on a tray.

"Hey Dad, how are you?" Landis reached out to hold the older man's hand. "It's me, Landis, and this is a new friend of mine, a special friend. Her name is Ida."

"Mr. Reid, Henry. Hello. I'm so happy to meet you." She went to the other side of the bed so they both were near him. "Is this a good time to talk?"

Henry nodded at her. "Always have time to talk to the ladies. I want to make sure you know what you're getting into with this fella' here."

"He's a handful, isn't he?" Ida asked.

The older man held tight to her hand. "He's a good son. He just needs someone to keep him on the straight and narrow."

"I think I already know that," she said bemused. "He's a bit of a tease."

"You're onto him, that's good," Henry said. He turned back to Landis and gave him a thumbs-up.

"So you had to have a little drama? Take a fall?" asked Landis.

"I'm fine. I want to go home."

"Still think you're dying, old man?"

"Dying? Hell yes, we all are. Some of us a little sooner than others." Henry turned back to Ida. "Dying is the hardest thing I've ever done, but it'll get done."

Landis blustered on. "Dad, my friend, Ida here, is a Men-no-night. I just like saying that word! A Men-no-night. What do you think of that?"

Henry eyes sparked. He perked up and stared at Ida. "A Mennonite? I know something about Mennonites! You ever hear of something called CPS?"

She smiled, surprised by the question but well versed in this aspect of her church history. "Civilian Public Service. Yes, I do, sure. It was a program for conscientious objectors during WWII. I know there were lots of camps for these men as an alternative to serving in the military. How do you know about that?"

"CPS! Those Mennonite boys came up here to fight fires! They were smokejumpers!"

Landis explained to Ida, "Dad worked for the Forest Service all of his life. Early on he did his share of fighting fires, jumping from planes as well as digging trenches on the ground."

Henry was off and running. "We thought they'd be worthless little cowards, but they were farm boys, used to working hard all day long, from dawn to dusk. There was a water-tower we used for training. Put an old harness on them and made them jump. Those boys weren't cowards. They were the real deal!"

"Fighting fires has always seemed dangerous to me," Ida remarked. "Did you lose any lives?"

"We never lost a soul, but a lot of men got hurt." Henry rambled on. "We had to untangle parachutes after landing. And try not to land in trees! If you avoided the trees you'd still hit rocks and logs, sometimes a barbed-wire fence. As soon as you landed you had to take apart everything, deflate your chute, get your gear out…and then walk miles to fight the fire!"

"So, you trained the CPS men?" asked Ida. "And some of them were Mennonites?"

"Most of them were. They wanted to do something of importance for their country if they didn't fight. That's what they said. They wanted to do something of national importance. They loved their country, but their religion kept them from fighting and killing."

"Yes, their faith beliefs. CPS was a place for men to be of service to the country without forcing them to do something against their conscience." She bit her lip, and continued, "My father, actually, did Civilian Public Service."

"Really? Where did he serve?" asked Landis.

"I'm not sure. I think he was in a camp somewhere out here for a few months until he got transferred to a state psychiatric hospital in Pennsylvania - because he was pre-med in college. He never talked about that time too much but he had said he wanted to do something for the country during the war."

"Yep! And they were still patriotic in their own way. Damn good workers!"

"Dad worked up by Seeley Lake. There were thousands of acres without roads so they had to hike everywhere. They built trails there as well as in The Bob."

"The Bob?" inquired Ida.

"The Bob Marshall Wilderness."

"And young lady," Henry gestured for her to come closer, "he doesn't know this, but Landis was named after one of those Mennonite smokejumpers."

"What?" She couldn't help laughing.

"Yep. A fellow by the name of Landis carried me out of a fire on his back. Must have been five miles he carried me! I told him I'd name my firstborn after him and I did. And he was Mennonite!" Henry looked gleefully over at Landis and back at Ida.

"What?" Landis asked. "You never told me this. You're making this up."

"How else would you get a name like Landis?" his father asked.

"Do you remember where he was from?" she asked.

"Oh, somewhere in Pennsylvania! There was a slew of Landis boys from Pennsylvania." Henry recalled. "Why I remember that, I don't know." He suddenly appeared weary, lying his head back on the pillow.

Landis was astonished. He had not heard this part before. "And five miles? That's embellishment! The distance gets longer every time you tell it!"

"It's my story and I'll tell it like I want to," his father said as he closed his eyes.

Landis leaned in close to him. "Dad, we'd like to take you home if we can break you out of here."

Henry nodded with his eyes shut. "I'd like that. Nothing quite like home."

They tiptoed from the room and Landis went to talk to the nurses at the station. Henry wasn't eating and barely drinking. He had moments of alertness and clarity and then would fall into deep states of sleep. He complained of pain most of the time.

"I know he'd rather be at home," declared Landis. "Please let the doctor know we'd like to have him be at home in his final days. Can we request that the doctor sign release forms?"

"You'll need to speak with the doctor," said one of the nurses. "I can page her for you."

"Yes, thanks, I'd appreciate that," said Landis. He turned back to Ida. "I think I need to stay here and talk to her. Do you want to hang around or go get coffee or something?"

"I'll go get coffee. Sounds like something to do at a time like this." She gave his arm a squeeze and went searching for a coffee hub.

When she returned twenty minutes later, it was evident he was disappointed. He slumped back in those upright industrial chairs so common in waiting rooms. She landed him a latte and sat down. "What's the word?"

"They need to keep him overnight. He really shouldn't be moved at this point. Maybe with the morphine drip, he'll just stay here."

"Landis, have you told your dad you're going to Poland for six weeks?"

"I knew you'd bring that up. No, nope, I haven't." He sighed with a tone of irritation. "When would you suggest I do that?"

She didn't respond to the bait. "I just asked if you'd told him."

"I know I need to tell him. It's just a stressful time to do that."

"He was very alert this afternoon."

"This is the best I've seen him in weeks," said Landis. "Maybe it's not the end."

"Maybe," said Ida. She didn't have the heart to tell him how often she'd seen patients rally near the end. Sometimes they'd manage to keep going, surprise everyone with another few days, even weeks. But like Henry said, dying is hard work. It's hard on everyone.

"How about if I drive you around this fair city? Want to see my old high school? Where I ran track?"

"Don't you need your power nap?"

"I think I could use a short one."

As they passed his father's room, they peeked in one more time to see Henry sleeping soundly. Landis said, 'I'll tell him tonight. I will. I know I need to say good-bye."

***

When they arrived that evening, Henry was sitting up, staring out the window.

"Hi Dad," said Landis, "How are you this evening?"

"Oh, I'm pretty tired." Henry looked at all three visitors. "I just get tired remembering."

He lay back and closed his eyes. He faded in and out of their conversations. Louise and Landis sat by the bed sharing childhood stories hoping their father would be roused enough to add his commentary. His eyes flickered open sporadically and closed, the weight of it all just too much.

Finally, visiting time was over. Louise bent over her father and kissed him. "Good-night Daddy. I'll see you in the morning."

Henry asked sleepily, "Did you get some of your mother's bread? She was baking all afternoon."

"Mom's not here, Daddy. You're dreaming things," Louise said.

"Take some with you. She wants you to take some with you," he mumbled softly.

"Okay Daddy, I'll get some. I love you." She walked out of the room with her eyebrows raised, leaving the two of them alone with Henry.

Landis sat on the edge of the bed, leaning close to his father's face. "Dad I have to tell you something important. I may not see you for a while. I'm going to be taking a long trip. I'm going to Poland for two months."

Henry nodded at his son and whispered, "I'm going on a long trip too. You be a good boy."

Landis put his head on his father's chest and wept with his eyelids shut tight. Ida went to him, placing her hand on his back, rubbing it gently. He stood up and turned, struggling, wiping his eyes with the back of his hands.

She too leaned over the dying man and kissed his forehead, saying, "Henry, it was so nice to get to know you – even for a short time. You're a good man. Your children love you very much. Good-bye Henry."

She left Landis alone with his father. He didn't need spectators. Saying "I love you" to someone dying feels like you're giving permission to them to die, as if the words themselves are an acknowledgement that the time has come. It comes blurted out like a blessing. *Here, my final offering to you. I love you. Good-bye.*

***

Sunday morning, they found Henry in a non-responsive state. He no longer opened his eyes. He might live another week, possibly more, but the end was imminent. He would not be going home. They sat in his hospital room talking quietly and Landis played some familiar old folks songs on his ukulele. Henry gave no indication of hearing. It was as if he just wanted to rest in the presence of his children, to hang out with them one more time. When it came time for good-byes, Ida again gave Henry a little kiss and left Landis standing beside his father's bed.

Leaving Missoula at noon, they stopped several times along the highway for the views. Landis showed her a map of western Montana and pointed out Seeley Lake. "We should go camping there sometime."

"Thank you for sharing your family and your hometown with me," Ida said.

"I think I'm at peace with Dad now. I'm especially happy you met him, or he met you. That means a lot."

"Did you feel like you wanted to stay with him this week?"

He didn't respond right away. His eyes were on the road. "Dad told me several times in the past few months he feels saturated with life and is ready to die. Those were his words;

'saturated with life.' I suppose he was saying it's okay to let him go."

"Once a person has accepted the end, they sometimes keep themselves alive for their loved ones. It's the ones who are still here who have a hard time letting go."

Landis looked out his window onto the green terrain they were passing. She thought he was fighting back tears. She allowed silence to take up the space. They drove beside lush forests and rocky mountainous areas. After many more miles and minutes had passed, she spoke again. "It was absolutely amazing to me that your father worked with Mennonites in CPS. What were the odds?"

"I had no idea he had that connection. And absolutely no clue that I was named after a farm boy from Pennsylvania! Just stunned." He glanced at her. "A twist of fate perhaps, and that I would find and fall in love with a Mennonite girl."

"Hardly a girl," she responded. *Had he said love?* "And that your father trained all those smoke jumpers! My head is spinning. I have to do more research."

"Your father didn't change his name, did he?" he asked playfully.

"No, he was *not* a Landis. That would take the cake! I'm really not sure what he did in the camp out here."

"Dad never told me much about his early years. It sure seems those smokejumpers had a hefty influence on him." Checking the rearview mirrors, he pulled into the passing lane. "What happened during Vietnam? Were there CPS camps?"

"CPS camps existed only during World War II. With the draft during Vietnam, men had to declare their CO status when they turned eighteen and find alternative service that would be approved. Mennonites had their own voluntary service programs."

"I knew medics who were Quakers and Jehovah Witnesses. They served in a non-military capacity alongside us in Vietnam."

"Do you think your buddies saw them as cowards?"

"Some might have. They proved themselves though. They were right there with us, getting out the wounded and the dead. I'm sure they were shot too. Kind of like my dad said about those Mennonite farm-boys working harder than anyone else."

"Mennonites generally have a positive reputation of being hardworking people. I like to think that it's mostly positive, but I know many who are narrow-minded and holier than thou. They can be clannish too."

"What about God?" he asked.

"What about God?"

"You never said whether you believe. You didn't bat an eye when I said I was an atheist."

She thought about it. "I don't know. Truly I don't. I believe in a life-force and I believe in the power of love. They could be one and the same. Maybe calling that entanglement God solves the problem." She opened her bag to find a mint. She unwrapped the paper and offered one to Landis.

He shook his head to decline, his right hand adjusting the rear-view mirror, his eyes constantly, checking the road behind them.. "You remember I told you I was an atheist?" He glanced over at her and she nodded. "I guess I just don't believe in an omniscient being looking over every single one of our little lives. I like the idea of a life-force. That's definitely a concept I could embrace. A life-force is evident in nature, in trees, plants – they reach out to each other in community too."

"Microscopically?"

"Well, lots of ways. Trees share nutrients and sugars with each other through their roots and filaments underground. And some studies indicate scents emitted from trees are a form of communication. That's a life force to me."

"Many paths to the truth," commented Ida. "Do you think more about God with your father in his final days?"

"Maybe," he said. "I'd like to believe there's something more."

They drove in companionable silence on the journey, the quietness between them a part of the courtship. The sign for Bozeman was up ahead. Their time together would be ending. Ida squeezed her hands together and faced him. "May I, could I, spend the night at your house tonight?"

He glanced at her, then back at the road. "You know I'd like that. You haven't been to my place yet. I didn't clean up. It might be a mess."

"Like that would be a deal-breaker?"

"Well, at least you'd know I wasn't planning for you to come. I wasn't expecting it."

"Oh Landis, you're just too funny," she said looking out her window. "I think I'd like to see your place – and spend the night with you. I mean I have my overnight bag and everything. One would think I was planning it, I was expecting it."

He pulled off the highway onto an exit ramp, and into a gas station. Before he got out of the car, he turned towards her and said, "You know you're catching me at a vulnerable time, don't you? You can come to my place and I'll fix you dinner. Then we'll see. You're not holding all the cards here."

She scrambled out of the jeep to run to the bathroom at the truck stop while he pumped the gas. The women's room was spacious Looking around to dry her hands, she spotted what looked like an antique condom machine. Someone had scribbled with a magic marker above it, "Don't buy this gum…It tastes like rubber!" *Humor. It goes a long way.*

South of Bozeman, Landis took a winding road west where homes were set back in the deep woods. He spun into a lane that curved around a few boulders before leading to a one-story log cabin.

"This is it," he said. "An old skiers' cabin." They unpacked the car and carried their things up the porch steps. Landis unlocked the front door with the caveat, "It's usually a bit musty when I come back after several days."

She stepped through the doorway into a mud entrance. To her right was the kitchen, updated but small. A countertop bar with high stools divided that area from where an overstuffed couch and chair occupied space in a living room. A hallway led to a bathroom with two rooms on either side. In the corner was a winding stairway to a loft above the bedrooms. She put down her things and began climbing upwards.

"Make yourself at home," Landis said.

"I've always been fascinated with lofts," she replied. At the top, she surveyed the desk with lamp and computer and papers strewn about. A lazy boy chair was in one corner. When she came back down she said, "I see you haven't gone paperless."

"I warned you I didn't clean up." He was in the kitchen, running water to get rust out of the pipes. "I have some frozen soup. I'll defrost that for supper."

"Where's your bedroom?" she asked.

He turned the water off and walked to where she stood, took one hand, and led her to the room behind the living area. She didn't wait for him to make the next move. She took off her jacket, then her blouse, and loosened her jeans. He helped her with the rest. They were under the covers together in his bed – as curious about one another's bodies as they'd been curious about each other's character.

And it wasn't hard to remember what to do. Not hard at all.

THREE

Discriminating between a weed and a sprouted seedling was not Ida's forte. She identified a few weeds: lambs quarters, thistle, but clearly she was allowing far more foreigners into the garden causing an imbalance to the order of things. Weeds were not interested in co-existing; weeds dominated and strangled the seedlings working hard to survive. She didn't want to think about analogies of plants to people.

Standing to stretch out her stiffness, she looked towards the willows ever watchful for moose. Martha said that was where they came to have their babies every June.. Peabody rolled around on his back in the grass, oblivious to everything but the joy of his self-massage.

Down on the ground again, she scooted on her fanny between rows of peas and carrots, potatoes, and peppers, thinking the earth was surely getting harder. She looked up. Elsa was coming towards her with a large cup of water.

"I thought you might need replenishment," Elsa said. "You've been out here all morning."

"That's thoughtful. Thank you."

Elsa plopped down beside her, crossing her knees. "I need to share this with someone and I think you're the one I want to tell first."

Ida searched Elsa's face. Her eyes were red, her cheeks flushed.

"I think I'm pregnant," she blurted out. "I feel nauseated all of time and smells – like horses – they make me feel like I could puke."

Ida reached out and put her hand over Elsa's. "Can you tell me what happened?"

"It's one of the reasons I don't want to ever go back to school. I was stupid. It was a party where I drank too much. Yeah, I slept with a guy who I hardly knew. I was so stupid." The tears welled up and she was sobbing into her hands.

Ida pushed up on her knees and put her arms around Elsa's shoulders. She murmured whatever came into her head: "It's okay. It will be okay. You are so precious. This is not your fault. You will be okay."

Eventually Elsa calmed down and relayed more of the story, but the bare bones were that it had been a hook-up at a party where everyone was stoned or drunk. She claimed she hadn't gone to anything like it all year. She had attended thinking she might feel more a part of things.

"You'll need to tell your mom and grand-mom very soon, you know," Ida said. "They will support whatever decision you make about this."

"I'd like to make sure I really am pregnant first. I don't want to tell them unless it really is a thing. Can you go with me to the clinic?"

"Yes, of course. Should I make an appointment with Dr. T?"

"No, I want to go to the women's clinic. We don't need an appointment. We can just go."

"All right, I can go any day this week."

"Tomorrow? Tuesday? Romona will cover for me. She knows. She's been great."

"Let's do that. We can say I need a new outfit. You're my personal shopper." Ida stood up and felt her hips adjust. "How about late morning? We can do lunch too."

"Yep, thank you." Elsa gave Ida a hug and walked slowly back to the house.

All the seeds beneath this ground sprouting up to find the sun, and now Elsa may have her own new life growing. What would she tell Elsa about her decision to have an abortion? It was a different time, when single moms were still regarded as negligent sinners, and she had no job prospects and had been living in poverty really. She had no financial means or any support system to raise a child. Her mother would not have approved. Her father, well, he would have rather not talked about difficult situational ethics. Elsa had a community of women here. A baby would be welcomed by her mom, grandmother, and auntie. Still, it was Elsa's body and her decision. She didn't have to share her story with Elsa. No, she didn't need to share everything.

***

That evening, Ida searched the Internet for Bialowieza National Park, a thousand miles of old growth forest on the border between Poland and Belarus. She learned about its biodiversity, its long history, and the current social/political arguments taking place in Poland. She suddenly understood Landis would be walking a fine line between conservationists and the government who stood with the logging industry. The arguments made by the anti-environmentalists were for culling the forest to fight the bark beetle outbreak. The conservationists had the backing of UNESCO with the belief that logging would be breaking international forestry rules and destroying natural bio-diversity. Landis was funded by a private group: arbiters between the two forces. He was being commissioned to walk into an environmental war zone. Greenpeace activists had camped out in the forests. Meanwhile logging cranes were advancing, chaffing at a confrontation.

She sent him an email saying she'd been doing a little research and included the link to the article. "Worried? A little – now that I have an idea where you'll be and what you'll be doing."

He responded, "I'm not there to take sides, but rather to report on what I observe. I'm aware of the heated rhetoric. I'll try to be like a Mennonite peacemaker."

Henry died that night. Landis called the next morning to let her know they'd have a service Thursday in the late afternoon and a family gravesite visit Friday morning. Landis was booked to fly out Saturday afternoon. Would she accompany him to Missoula for the service? She offered to drive her car and pick him up, then bring him back to his cabin Friday for their last night together.

***

Elsa and Ida arrived promptly on time for the scheduled appointment.

Within twenty minutes it was confirmed Elsa was about seven weeks pregnant. A nurse practitioner examined her and answered Elsa's questions. She still had time to decide if she wanted to proceed with the pregnancy. If she decided to terminate, she would be required to receive counseling and a referral. "You will tell your mom and Martha today won't you?" asked Ida on the drive home. "Really there's no reason to put it off, don't you think?"

Elsa looked out the car window. "Yeah, I guess so. I'm still just a bit numb about it."

"Sometimes talking out a problem helps make the options clearer."

"Sometimes." Elsa replied, and lapsed into a silence. Several minutes later, she turned to Ida, and said, "I also think I'm gay. Romona has sparked something in me."

"Oh my, Elsa, you do keep me guessing. I didn't see that one coming," said Ida, her eyes intent on the highway. "Do you think Romona feels similarly?"

"She wrote me a love poem and left it in my room. I haven't talked with her about it. We've only discussed this." She pointed to her abdomen. "But I can't stop thinking about her. I've wondered about myself in the past, but with Romona, it just seems different."

"You haven't known each other very long."

"I know you think I'm flighty and I am more emotional lately. I feel so different around Romona. Turned on – but safe. Excited – but secure."

"I don't think your mom and your grand-mom will have an issue with you and Romona, but I do think you need to share one piece of information at a time."

"Did you know Romona's mom was a foster kid?"

"I think I recall Annie telling me this."

"People from the state came and basically kidnapped her from her birth mother and put Sid in foster care when she was little. They claimed it was for her safety because her mom attempted suicide!" Elsa was ruled up. "The State of Montana stole a lot of Native American children and put them in foster care, up for adoption to white families, for lots of stupid reasons."

"Did Romona tell you this? Maybe it's confidential."

Elsa was going full steam. "She was in foster care and then adopted by white parents in Helena. Romona says her mother grew up always feeling like she didn't belong. I mean, her white parents weren't abusive or anything. Their intentions were okay, but that's not the point. She was taken away. Not even her grandparents were allowed to raise her. Ripped from her culture! So sick."

Elsa's diatribes these days were infused with cultural commentaries with a sliding scale of moral fury. Introductory Sociology and Psychology classes had opened doors not only to examining the world in new ways, but to a new thesaurus of words to legitimize her attitudes.

"I thought there were laws protecting tribal families," Ida said tentatively. "Children of the tribe would be returned to the community rather than be put up for adoption. In my social work classes, I recall the Child Welfare Act – sometime in the 1970s – enacted to keep this from happening."

"But I bet it still does." Elsa said indignantly. "The shit our white culture has done!"

"I don't disagree with you. It's easy to despair," Ida said calmly. "But Sidonnia seems to have found a way to move forward. She's so open-hearted."

"It just stinks. Sometimes I hate being white!"

Ida was taken back. Elsa's declarations were often for shock value, but beneath the words were real feelings. Not shame. Not really anger. What was it?

"You hate what has been done, the *injustice*," Ida tried articulating.

"Well yeah," Elsa's tone implied the obvious, "but I hate being associated with the oppressors."

"Hmm, yes. It's more liberating to be part of the oppressed than the oppressors." Ida had no idea where that 1960's cliché had been residing.

Elsa regarded her companion with surprise. "Karl Marx?"

"I don't really know," Ida said. "Maybe from Women's Lib 101."

"Maybe that's why men who harass women make themselves into victims. The oppressed groper! Ha!" Elsa had a long list of social ills she was ready to take on.

As they neared the ranch, the Subaru bounced and jolted them around. The lane was ridged with mud holes from winter snows and runoff.

"I'm abandoning you for the next few days," Ida stated as she parked the car in the lane. "I'm driving Landis to Missoula for his father's service and burial, and then he leaves for Poland on Saturday."

Elsa leaned over the gear shift to give a hug. "I'm happy you and Landis found each other. He better know how lucky he is."

"Yes, well, we'll see how it goes."

"Thanks again for going with me today."

"I was happy you asked me."

"And thanks for listening to me."

"I'm glad you could talk to me. You may not want to hear this, but you're so much like your grandmother back when she was your age. But you remember always, you are your own person. Your own woman! Very much so!"

It was mid-afternoon and Ida felt the urge to lie down for a nap. Why fight it? She changed into old jeans and a t-shirt before collapsing on her bed. She thought she heard Martha come in, rattle around in the kitchen, and close her own bedroom door. Two old souls taking afternoon naps. Could be the start of a poem. Something quite right about that, something that made all the other sorrows of the world fade, at least for an hour or so.

THREE

Louise's son and daughter and the five grandchildren gathered at her house. Two young boys came running full-speed out to the car when Landis and Ida arrived.

"Uncle Landis! Uncle Landis!" They jumped up and down on the sidewalk, squealing in delight. He ran around the back of his jeep and pulled them both towards him in a bear hug. They giggled and tried to get away. It was a game they'd played before. *Bet you can't catch me.*

"Hey guys, this is Ida. She's a very special friend of mine, so you'd better be very nice to her! This is Ross and this is Rick!" He said pointing to each boy, tickling them as he did so.

"HI guys," she said. She intentionally reversed their names. "You're Rick and you're Ross?"

"No. No," they responded in an exasperated tone. It was clear grown-ups were a bit dense. They scurried up the steps expecting the others to follow.

Once inside the house, family members and friends gathered round to introduce themselves. Louise led them to the guest room and said with a straight face, "I'm sorry, but you're going to have to share the bed tonight since we're a bit cramped on space."

"Okay, Louise, thanks, I think we can manage,' replied Landis. He closed the door, buffeting the noise from both children and grown-ups. Landis turned to her. "It's going to be a bit chaotic the next few hours. I'm sorry I didn't warn you about the family. Now you understand why I only stay a couple of days when I come here."

Ida patted his arm. "It'll be fine. I can handle a few hours of chaos."

"You can excuse yourself anytime. Just come back here if you need to," he said.

"Let's go do this," she replied. "It's important to be with family."

***

Henry had attended the same Presbyterian church all of his life so the congregants were well acquainted with his life story. He'd requested no formal eulogy. Two friends shared impressions about him from decades of his life. Louise spoke of his playful personality and how he had stoically raised the two kids as a single father, and of course included a few anecdotes about how much trouble they caused him, *especially Landis*. The oldest grandchild read a silly poem about her grandfather's delight in taking them fishing and teaching them to skin a fish. Interspersed among the readings and scripture was a cellist playing Bach.

Landis held Ida's hand as they walked to the fellowship hall for the reception. He asked her to stay beside him in the receiving line, but she whispered no, it was family time. People wanted to express their sorrow in the loss, and the family needed to hear it. She stopped to talk with Hank, Jon, and Tipp standing in line to pay their respects, appearing lonely and ill at ease without their musical instruments as social partners. Their fathers were no longer living and this day marked the end of not just Henry's life, but the end of an era for all four men.. She sidled to the coffee and helped herself, then found a solitary space at one of the long tables. An older gentleman around Henry's age approached her with his plate shaking in his hands.

"May I join you?" he asked courteously.

"Please," she said jumping up and pulling out a chair. "May I fetch a drink for you?"

"Coffee. Black. That would be grand," said the man plopping into the folding chair.

When she returned, a couple of older women had moved to occupy the chairs facing him. Ida introduced herself to all four.

"I'm Burt," said the man. The women stated their names which Ida promptly forgot.

"Did you all know Henry from this church?" Ida asked.

The women nodded affirmatively, but Burt shook his head. "We were friends and we were rivals. He worked for the forestry service and I worked for the National Parks. So we had our disagreements over the years."

"Really? Were they contentious disagreements?" asked Ida. She sipped the percolated bitter coffee. *Church coffee.*

The man chewed his ham and cheese sandwich slowly. "Do you know what the term 'ramification' means? It's kind of like that. We're from the same tree root, tree trunk, but our branches just took us in different directions."

"Both searching for the sun," Ida asked smiling.

He shook his index finger at her and said, "Yep, that's right, always competing for the same resources. We'd still go fishing together. Still buddies."

She let him eat his food while she finished the last dregs of coffee. "Are you going to eat?" he asked her. "Go get something to eat."

"There are lots of casseroles back at Louise's house," she said. "I'll save room for those."

"And how do you know Henry?" he asked.

"I just met him recently. I came with Landis."

"Ah," Burt exclaimed, slapping his forehead. "You're the girlfriend."

"I guess you could call me that. We're good friends."

"You know, Landis was kind of wild in his younger days. Henry had a rough time with him after Betty died."

"I imagine it was hard for Henry raising two teenagers." She was about to say more when Landis pulled up a chair beside her.

"Hello Burt," he said. "Telling tall tales to my sweetheart here, are you?"

"Landis!" the old man smiled. "Only the truth, son, only the truth."

"Burt and Dad used to take me fishing back when they thought they could reform me," Landis said to Ida but loud enough for Burt to hear. "They never gave up on me, but Burt, he's a good man!"

"If you're trying to flatter me, you can keep it up," chuckled the old man.

"Burt tried to get me to hike the Pacific Coast Trail with him, but I was too lazy. Thanks for trying, though," Landis said with sincerity. "Did you end up hiking it by yourself?"

"Yep, sure did, but I was much younger then. I could've used your company."

"Are you still hiking?" asked Landis.

"Why sure. We call ourselves the Over-Eighty Amblers."

"That's so great," said Ida. "Is it a club?"

"It's part of the activities at the home where I live now. They keep us busy with lots of things going on. Someone always goes out with us."

"You probably know the trails by heart. You've done them all, haven't you?" asked Landis.

"Funny thing about that," Burt paused to wipe his chin with a napkin. "I may have walked them before, but now each one path seems new to me. Sometimes I remember a specific turn in a path, but it doesn't matter. It's just a joy to get out whenever I can." He stared into the air, encompassed in a nimbus of memories.

Landis stood up and motioned for her to join him. "We've got to get going but it was good to see you again."

Burt was dignified and stately in his old age, but he had a look of bemusement in his eyes when he turned towards them. "Landis, you've made your old man proud. I know he was proud of you."

Landis took the old man's hand in both of his and said gently, "Thank you, Burt. That's kind of you to say. It means a lot coming from you."

Burt waved them away and commenced talking to the ladies across the table who appeared all abubble to have his attention at last.

Back at the house several casseroles were heated and put out for family. Everyone ate for lack of knowing what to do. Fatigue set in. A pull-out bed in an old couch was extended from its hiding place. Air mattresses were pumped and thrown down in various corners void of furniture. Soon the house was dark and silent.

The next morning Landis and Ida departed after the graveside gathering, his trip abroad their excuse to slip away early. He still needed to pack and make final arrangements. Ida would drive him to the airport the following morning.

***

Afternoon naps were in order when they arrived at the cabin. Landis was somber, understandably entangled in the blues of losing his father, his rock, his only parent for so many years. Numbness was the initial tranquilizer, but deep sadness would come.

Ida couldn't sleep. Once she heard his rhythmic breathing, she tiptoed out and shut the door. Wanting to research more about the Bialowieza Forest, she climbed the stairs to the loft and logged onto the computer. Skimming through several articles, it was evident there were massive political disputes in Poland over the use of the forest resources. Only seventeen percent of the old growth forest was designated a virgin park reserve, virtually untouched by humans for thousands of years. The only way in and out was by horseback or on foot. Polish politicians on the right asserted that environmental experts, *serious scientists who had been studying the problem for years*, should be jailed. She had to trust that he would be safe.

The front door stuck. She had to push hard before stepping out into the cool forest air. The pines emitted a strong wood fragrance. Landis had said this scent was a sign of healthy trees. These were simple gifts of the tall, solid giants rising toward the sun. She walked the path in the woods around his cabin several times, creating her own labyrinth of serenity. Calmness settled slowly into her heart.

When she re-entered the cabin, sounds of knocking and tapping and the splashing of water emanated from the bathroom. Still in her sundress from the morning service, she attempted a few standing yoga stretches to release the knot in her neck. She really didn't feel like doing much of anything.

Landis opened the bathroom door and padded down the hallway. His blue towel was wrapped around his lower body, but her eyes were drawn upward to his naked, beardless face.

"Oh my, what happened?" She went to him, fingering his soft hairless face. "Who is this stranger?"

"I'm laying myself bare for you, so to speak."

"Did you just impulsively decide to shave it?"

"You don't like me this way?" He raised his eyebrows.

"That's not it. You just have to give me a few minutes to adjust."

"I thought I'd better shave it in case I'm mistaken for a terrorist."

Ida pulled his head down. "I think I could like this stranger."

"It'll grow back this summer."

Ida kissed him and slyly unwound the towel around his waist. He leaned down and attempted to lift her into his arms.

"No, Landis! No! We'll both end up on the floor!" she babbled. "Put me down."

They collapsed onto the braided rug, arms clumsily entwined, her skirt bunching up as they stretched out beside one another. Landis adeptly removed what was underneath. She kept fingering his face, unable to reconcile this with the bearded man she had come to love; but when he began touching her elsewhere she knew this was definitely Landis.

Afterwards, flushed and suddenly cognizant of their Eden-like state, they helped one another up and shuffled quickly to the bedroom. Embarrassed by their own lust, they dressed silently into old jeans. Ida went to the bathroom to wash up and brush her hair. Catching a glimpse of herself in the mirror she shook her head. *Who are you? What have you become?"* She splashed cold water on her face. *As if that will help.*

Landis was frying onions and green peppers on the stove. "How about some black beans over rice?"

"Perfect. Anything I can do?"

"I think there's spinach if you want to make a salad. You'll have to take whatever's left. I can't have this stuff sitting around for six weeks."

She opened the fridge and shuffled around milk, carbonated water and orange juice. At the back of the top shelf was a six pack of beer. *Four bottles were missing. Was it non-alcoholic beer?* She scrutinized the carton to read: 7.5 alcohol content. *Quite high for beer.* She lifted out the carton and placed it on the counter.

"I couldn't help seeing this," she said. "I'm not assuming anything, but I'm curious."

He looked at the bottles and back at his frying pan.

"Landis?"

"Yep, I had those the night Dad died."

Ida was stunned. Didn't that mean he was drinking again? Didn't that mean there was a problem here?

She went to sit in the living room, switching on a lamp with darkness falling. She heard him mix rice and water in a pan. He puttered in the kitchen for several more minutes and then came to sit beside her on the couch. "I was going to throw the rest out before you got here. Maybe I wanted you to see it. Yes, I drank it. Yes, I regret it."

"Has this happened before? Have you relapsed before?"

"I haven't had any alcohol in six years - until the other night."

"I'm speechless."

"I called Moses."

"And what did he say?"

"He was pretty upset with me. But he was glad I'd called." Landis sank back into the other corner of the couch. "Not telling anyone is when the real trouble starts. So now I can no longer say I've been sober six years. I have to start over in the count."

She sighed. She was tired. Things had been so good between them. Now there were little niggling worries slyly creeping into her mind, upsetting the cart of euphoria she'd been experiencing. "You know I'm going to worry about you now, drinking. It would be so easy on this trip. You will be so tempted."

"I know," he said. "And I know it's hard to trust me. I'm not sure I trust myself, but I've got to start over." He got up to check the boiling rice. She followed him into the kitchen. "Look." He took the church key, opened the remaining bottles and dumped beer into the sink, then carried them to the outside porch. She heard the crash of the bottles in the recycling bin.

Ida picked up the dish soap and squeezed liquid over the bottom and sides of the sink. She turned on the faucet full-force and splashed water around. Her hand moved round and round over the soapy surface until she could no longer smell any lingering fermented spirits. From the refrigerator she retrieved spinach and tomatoes for a tossed salad. Landis set plates and silverware on the middle aisle counter. She poured water into two tall glasses and sat down on a stool waiting for the rice and beans.

They ate side by side. Neither one had the energy to start a conversation that would lead back to the painful disappointment of broken trust. When they'd both finished, Landis spoke.

"I could have been drinking something much stronger, whisky or something."

"Yes, you could have," she replied. "Still…"

"Look, I'm sorry."

She rubbed her eyes with her hands. "I just don't know what to say."

"I don't want to lose you over this."

"You haven't lost me. I'm disappointed in you, but you have not lost me. I just don't want you to fall back into that place that took you years to crawl out of."

"Me neither."

"And nothing is going to fill that hole of your father leaving you. Not alcohol. Not absorption in your work. Not sex."

He looked dubious. "Not even sex with you?"

"I'm serious. I want to have faith in you. I hope you can find some ways to deal with your grieving because you're going to feel it."

"Okay," he said as he cleared the plates and silverware from the counter. He opened a drawer and took out several plastic twist ties used on ends of bread bags. He carried them to where she was sitting and dumped them in a heap. He selected different colors, one by one, twisting them together to fashion a bricolage that circled his wrist.

"What's this for?" she asked.

"To remind me of you – and to hold me to the straight and narrow. It'll be with me everywhere I go."

"And if it breaks?"

"They have to be melted down to break," he said. "But if it does, I'll look for a tattoo parlor and get a tattoo. Then you won't lose any more bets on me."

He struggled to wrap it around his left wrist. Ida helped him fasten it tightly. They attached three more wires around the single bracelet for reinforcement.

"I'm going to worry about you on this trip, there's no way around it. The Polish government is hostile to scientists. One guy said you should be sent to Putin's gulag."

"We have scientists coming from all over the world. Biologists, entomologists, toxicologists…I suspect the data analysts will be the most threatened because the statistics will tell the truth. They may make disgusting accusations, but they won't harm us. It will be covered by the BBC."

"Well then! The BBC!" she exclaimed, "That's reassuring."

"I'll email you every night. I probably could text you, but I may have too much to say."

"What's the time difference? About ten hours?

"Sounds about right."

"Okay, that alleviates some of my concern, I suppose, but it'll be hard to tell if you've been drinking."

"I will not drink alcohol. It will become my mantra." He held up his left wrist with the multi-colored twists and shook it." I will not drink…I will not drink."

"You'd better finish packing. I'll leave you to that." She hopped off the stool and went to the sink to clean up the dishes and pans. "I'll finish here."

Later that evening as she was curled up reading in the living room, he came out with his guitar and started fingering chords. She put her book aside. He played a few simple tunes then said, "I've been saving this Dylan one for the right time. You probably know it."

He ended his mournful version of "You're Gonna Make Me Lonesome When You Go" with a sigh. She bit her lip and asked, "Who are Verlaine and Rambo?"

"Verlaine and *Rimbaud*. Two French poets who had a tumultuous relationship. One shot the other in his passion. Can't recall which. One left his wife."

"Yikes," she said.

"That's putting it mildly."

"It's a sad song but I like it. I will be lonesome for you when you go." She pulled her knees up and wrapped her arms around them. She wanted contentment to be there, but some thread had broken. She knew he was trying to connect.

"Will you?" he asked, setting his guitar in its case and sitting down beside her.

"A little bit."

"I'm lonesome already for you," he said.

She nodded but held her arms tight around her legs. She closed her eyes and said, "I can't be close to you tonight. I want to, but I can't."

Landis clasped his hands together and looked down at his interlocking fingers. "I can't do much more than say I'm sorry. I'm sorry. I'm sorry. I'm sorry."

"I know, Landis," she said. "I want it all to be behind us. We'll just have to see how we feel when you come back."

"I know how I'll feel, Ida," he replied.

"I want to believe it. I'm just feeling a bit lost right now."

They slept restlessly. What were they doing together in this seventh decade? Her mind was agitated by life's circumstantial fastballs. Henry's death. The newness of their love. Global distances. A fall from grace. They both tossed and turned. One time she'd awakened to feel him rubbing her back softly, tracing her spine. She opened her eyes and contemplated what she'd say to him at the airport. Her stomach was a visceral knot. *I've let myself get too tangled up in his life. I need to go back to my quiet cottage with Martha. It's too disturbing out here.*

When she heard his distinct, bear-like breathing, she slipped out to the living room to sit in the darkness. *Three a.m. existential questions came fast and hard no matter how old she became. She was not equipped to deal with these profound feelings that pushed and pulled. Neither one of them was a spring chicken. They didn't have years and years to be together. She wasn't ready to let go of his love. He was in pain too. His father was dead.*

She crept back into bed and he reached out for her hand. He squeezed it gently. She lay on her back, feeling the warmth of his hand. *This is nice. Just breathe here beside him.*

Then like any rush of the spirit, it wasn't enough. She rolled over to lie on top of him, her ear pressed to his beating heart. He held her snugly. She heard it clearly, his beating heart.

***

They agreed to say good-bye outside the airport. The Subaru edged in next to the concrete sidewalk. Ida turned off the key and hopped out, scurrying around to where he was unloading his suitcase and computer bag. She impulsively wanted to come with him, just walk with him until he went through security. But they'd agreed to get the good-byes over with at the curb.

She gave him a quick peck on the cheek, but he pulled her in close for a hug. When he let go, he held up his left wrist and jangled his new bracelet.

"Six weeks," she said.

He nodded, moved away from her, through the sliding doors, pulling his black, wheeled suitcase. That was it.

She drove away from the curb barely looking in her mirror for any rearview calamity. *Somehow the time would go by. She wanted to get back to the Dusky Grouse ranch, to her cottage, to Martha and Moses, to Annie and Elsa. She wanted to meet new guests. She wanted to be weeding the garden and pulling tiny carrots from their plot. She wanted to go to yoga and meet with her women friends. She wanted oh so very much to escape the intensity of her need for his presence, to burnish the jagged way the ache in her heart hurt.*

JULY

ONE

July brought in more revenue than the ranch could have anticipated. Weddings were booked every weekend and the VP tours were at full capacity. Annie breathed sighs of relief that construction loans would be paid off in the next year.

At the Monday dinner hour, Elsa called everyone together for a "family meeting" barbecue in the patio garden behind the guest house. The black flies of July were not invited but showed up anyway.

As they enjoyed their postprandial drinks in the cool evening, Elsa stood up on a stone planter, clapping her hands, calling for attention as if delivering an expected oratory for the evening.

"I have something I need to share with you all and I need to do it as quickly as possible."

Annie looked from Elsa to Romona and then to Sidonnia. She smiled and leaned forward, not knowing what to expect next from her daughter. Ida pulled her chair off to the side. Did Elsa intend to share her news with this extended group?

"Okay, friends and family. I have some difficult news to share with you, but because I love and trust each of you, I wanted you to be here." She looked about at the bewildered faces, then down at the ground in front of her. With a gust of courage, she turned for a full-on frontal interaction with her mother. "I'm eight weeks pregnant!"

"What?" exclaimed Annie. *"What?"*

"I'm pregnant, Mom. With child. With fetus."

Annie was stunned.

"Are you sure?" asked Martha. "Have you done any tests?"

"I went to the clinic for an official test. Ida went with me, and don't get mad at her for keeping it secret! I had to tell someone. She's the one who said I needed to tell you all."

Ida had not said she needed to tell everyone. She specifically said her mother and grandmother needed to know. Here she was announcing it to the world for some social cushioning.

"Is this the reason you don't want to go back?" asked Annie. She rose to stand near her daughter, not quite ready to embrace her but there for proximity. "I wish you could have told me this personally."

Without saying a word, Moses, Tommy, and Rusty vanished into the night darkness. The five women were left alone. Elsa sat down and began weeping, sobbing really. Romona took her hand and held it.

"Does the boy...*the sperm donor*...know about this?" asked Martha.

Elsa shook her head. "No, and if I have this baby, I don't want him to! In fact, I'm not sure who the father might be. I went to five frat parties the last week of school and yes, I slept with different guys. So…" she threw out open hands. "I'm a slut. But I'm not going to go looking for one of those guys to be responsible. I was stupid. I got drunk. I slept around."

Ida was perplexed. She spoke up. "Elsa, I thought you told me it was just one party, one stupid night, one man – one mistake?"

Elsa eyes shifted to the ground as she heard Ida's words. "I told you that because I was so embarrassed I slept around. Somehow it didn't seem so bad to say it was a one-time thing. I was stupid. I was just depressed and kept going to these booze parties."

Romona cleared her throat and spoke. "Elsa confided everything to me and we agreed, both of us together, that it was best to come clean. She wants to make this decision on her own – without any male involvement."

Sidonnia had been quietly listening but now sat up straight, shaking her head at Romona as if to silence her.

Annie sat down beside Elsa and began tapping her bare foot against her flip-flop restlessly, like an animal rapping its tail on the ground. "Okay, so what are you thinking? You've obviously been talking this through with Romona." There was irritation in her voice. The mother had passed from sympathy over into anger and disapproval. "You didn't use birth control and now…What is your inclination now? Abortion? Options? Do you actually think you can raise a child at your age?"

Elsa turned to Romona, throwing her arms around her friend. Elsa cast a defiant look at her mother and around the circle of women, and spoke. "We've decided, the two of us, that we can raise up this child together."

Both mothers stared at their daughters in disbelief.

Martha had pulled herself up to pour another half-glass of wine. She overheard Romona and sauntered back to the circle of women. "So...Is this a declaration of love here, between you two?"

Elsa and Romona nodded. "We thought our relationship was pretty obvious."

"Also, still very new," replied Martha. "You've only known each other a few weeks."

Elsa regarded her grandmother. "You told me many times you fell in love with Granddad only after knowing him a couple of weeks. How is my love for Romona any different?"

"Touché," said Martha. "I'm happy for the two of you. But a baby? A child is a huge commitment on top of a relationship."

"We'll deal with it," Elsa replied, still clinging to Romona's hand.

"So let me see if I've got this right," said Annie. "You're planning to have this baby. You're planning to drop out of college. You're planning to live and work here?"

"That's the plan for now," responded Elsa.

"And the two of you think you're going to do this as partners?" asked Sidonnia.

"We'll see where our love takes us," answered Romona. "Just let us be happy."

"You sound like you don't trust us!" said Elsa. "Like we won't be fit mothers." No one seemed to know what to say, but their muteness was bonding. A cricket chirped nearby and locusts buzzed intermittently from the west pasture. Ida heard a deep-throated staccato tone in the taller prairie grasses.

"Was that…was that a bullfrog?" she asked, pointing towards the peculiar sound.

"That deep little hoot? That's the male grouse," Martha whispered in response.

"The dusky grouse?" Ida asked.

"A blue or a sage. Same."

"With all the oil drilling, I'm amazed there are any left," said Ida.

Three deep notes emanated from the grasses. "It's like Tom Waits grunting," Annie observed. "That is one odd bird."

"It's too late for mating," said Martha. "Maybe he just wants company."

"Maybe he's your grouse," said Ida, "the one who was sending those signals to you at three in the morning."

"Are you all just going to go on talking mating calls or do you have anything else to say to me?" asked Elsa.

"Now that the initial shock is over, I think we might all be okay," Martha conjectured, turning back towards Elsa. "We just might survive this."

Ida added, "You have all of us here. You know we won't desert you."

"You and me, Sid, we're going to be grandmothers – at forty-five!" observed Annie, still stunned. "I'm just going to need a few days to wrap my head around all this. It's just a bit much."

"I'm going to need more than a few days," said Sidonnia dryly. "I'm not sure I know my daughter anymore."

Martha finished her wine and held up the empty glass. "To Elsa and Romona! Annie, Sid, Ida, and me. We're not going anywhere. We'll be here for each other."

"A tribal community of women!" exclaimed Romona. "How cool is that?"

Elsa stood and raised her arms as if to encircle the others. "You're all I have – all of you. I know we can do this because we have all of you."

Sidonnia began gathering up the plates and bowls quietly, without looking at the others. Romona rose to help her, collecting glasses on a tray which she carried gingerly. Mother and daughter would talk privately in the kitchen.

"You'll have to tell your father at some point," Annie admonished. "He deserves to know this."

"I've started my speech to him in my head. I was waiting to first share this tonight," explained Elsa. She walked to Annie and threw her arms around her. "Mom, I know this is not the news you expected, but thank you for being here for me."

Annie hugged her in return. Elsa let go of her mother and walked towards her grandmother.

"Grandma-ma," Elsa addressed Martha. "You know I love you too even though you never like to get mushy. You might be disappointed in me, but I never want to hurt you."

Martha did not get up. She looked up at Elsa standing proud and strong in front of her chair. "If anything, you've brought out the best in yourself tonight. Honesty will carry you a long way, and you did the right thing being honest with yourself and your family."

Elsa leaned over and kissed her grandmother on the forehead. Martha just waved her hand in front of her face. "Okay, okay, you've done your duty." Elsa patted Ida's hand before carrying the remaining dishes into the house, leaving the two friends alone.

"So you knew about this little surprise, huh?" Martha turned to Ida.

"Seems only partially."

"You don't think it's the whole truth?"

"Not sure. She was awfully quick with the rationale for her behavior. I know these things happen, but it doesn't all square with how I see Elsa," reflected Ida. "

"Me neither," said Martha. "Something's not quite right."

"Five fraternities?"

"I'd think she'd be traumatized. She doesn't put herself into any victim role, that's for sure."

"If she did sleep around while heavily intoxicated, she sure is stepping up to take responsibility for her actions."

"Yep. Something's not quite right," Martha repeated.

"Still…It's her body, her decision."

"Yep. Agreed."

"Still…she needs our love and support."

"That she does," Martha stated, and then solidified. "That she has. Always."

TWO

"I've learned to write down my passwords but then I forget my username." Martha was struggling to access online forms on her laptop computer. "Why don't they just let me use my email address?"

"Don't you use the same password every time?" Ida asked.

"Sometimes it says you need a number or a capital letter, even in the username. I've forgotten which one I use. Even plain old Martha doesn't work anymore."

"What irks me is when I call customer service for help and get an automatic voice and they connect me to three or four different automatic responses until I finally get to speak to a real person."

"You know why they do that don't you?" Martha asked.

"So they don't have to talk to an irritated old woman?"

"They know we get angry. We can yell as much as we want if it's just a robotic response."

"Press one for this, two for that." Ida mimicked an automated voice. "Your call is important to us, please stay on the line. Oh, and then the voice says you can have your choice of music – press one for jazz, two for classical… it's infuriating."

"And they wonder why you're being such a…well… bitch by the time someone talks to you."

A clattering from the back door brought Peabody darting into the kitchen. Siddonia followed, carrying a plastic container. "Hi. Good morning. Brought you some fresh granola baked this morning."

"Thanks Sidonnia!" said Ida. "What a treat."

"Did you miss me this morning?" Martha asked her.

"I did. I wondered why you didn't make it out to the barn. So out of character." Siddonia pulled up another stool to join them. "Are you okay?"

"I'm just testing you. Seeing what happens if I don't show up."

Ida looked at Martha. "*Are* you okay?"

Martha closed her laptop and took a swig of her coffee. "Yuck, this is not even lukewarm." She got up to place the cup in the microwave.

"Martha, what's up? You never miss a day," stated Ida.

Martha took her time taking the coffee out, stirring and sipping. She returned to the counter. "I felt a little sluggish this morning. That's all. I'm entitled once in a while."

"More than once in a while – if you want," said Siddonia. "You've put in your time. But I missed you."

"Well, that's good to know," Martha nodded. "But do you *need* me?"

Siddonia responded emphatically, "Martha, I need you, Moses needs you, and most of all – the horses need you. I'm here this morning on their behalf."

A twist of a smile appeared on Martha's lips. "Thank you Sid, for your little endorsement. I appreciate it."

Siddonia climbed down from her stool and walked to where Martha was sitting. Throwing her arms around the older woman she said, "It's the truth. Old Grayson, Lulu, they wanted nothing to do with me. They wouldn't come when *I* called them. Acted like they were ready to stage a hunger strike."

"Okay, now, enough of this. You don't have to make it more than it was."

"Well then, are you coming out? I'll wait for you."

"I guess I can mess with these health forms later." Martha padded off to her room to finish up.

Once Martha was out of earshot, Siddonia whispered to Ida. "Does she seem okay to you?"

"She hasn't said anything more about seeing barn swallows. That was a couple of months ago. Sometimes I think she gets up at night. But I do that. I get up and read."

Siddonia nodded. "Has she complained about being fatigued more often?"

"Now that you mention it, she does admit to being tired lately. She usually takes a nap too."

"The other day Moses and I watched as she walked in the pasture. She'd take a few steps and stop, take another couple and stop. She was looking up in the sky occasionally shaking her fist, not yelling just talking, but of course we were too far away to hear anything."

"Did you ask her about it?"

"We did, but of course she belittled us for watching her – as if we didn't have enough to do. It was just odd behavior for Martha."

"I thought she'd been out to the barn and back this morning. I had no idea she'd been here the whole time."

"I'm thinking maybe I'll come by in the morning if she's not out there. If she wants to come in later, that's fine, but it's so unlike her."

They curtailed their talking when Martha reappeared. "I'll get my boots. I'm fine. Really. Both of you stop worrying just because I decided to take a day off."

"Okay," Ida replied, "but like Sid said, it's so out of character for you."

"Maybe it's time I start being somebody else. Out with the old, in with the new."

THREE

Summer vacations were interfering with WoCA dates, so the group decided to meet the third Saturday in July. Martha grumbled to Ida all the way to town about this month's topic which Josephine had selected and would lead: "*Our Aging Bodies.*" *Earlier* that morning, Martha had first feigned an upset stomach, then a headache, and finally tried to claim conjuntivitis by rubbing soap in her eyes, but Ida didn't give her an inch.

"This group is one of the few times you interact socially. If you can't spare a couple of hours a month, just talking with other women your age, then there's no stopping your mental decline. You're nothing but a recluse, and a lousy one at that." Ida wasn't sure what she meant by that last accusation but it felt good to say it.

Martha muttered, "Nothing wrong with being a recluse, though I somehow take offense at being called a lousy one."

My point exactly!" said Ida. "And besides, admit it, you get something out of ruffling Josephine's feathers. Nobody gets under her skin like you do."

"Really, do you think I piss her off?" Martha asked.

"For sure."

"She's a user!" Martha exclaimed.

"What?"

"A user! She uses people. Sucks their ideas up and claims they're hers."

"She's got her own opinions."

"You watch her over the next few months. She doesn't think for herself. She takes someone else's ideas and spouts them off like she thought them up herself. You watch!"

"So, she doesn't give someone else credit? Lots of folks do that. They read it somewhere and they appropriate the idea as if it was their own original thought. I'm not sure there are any new ideas really, we keep recycling them…like Ecclesiastes. Nothing is new under the sun."

"Stop being such a goody goody. Just agree with me for once!"

"Maybe she's just a borrower. You know – just borrowing your ideas."

"Oh for pity sakes, you know I'm right. And there's always that one-upmanship she's got going too. Everything in her life is the most wonderful and greatest and best – as if she's the only one who experiences anything!"

Ida knew what Martha meant, but she felt Martha was being overly critical. "This is Rusty's stepmom you're ranting about."

"Plus her entire demeanor is a facade." Martha wasn't finished berating her nemesis. "Fake face! Plastic surgery! Fake. Fake. Fake."

"Why are you angry?" Ida asked.

"I'm angry because she's so damn self-righteous, so right all the time." Martha was definitely in a huff.

"Not like others we might know." Ida glanced sideways. "Let's hear her out on this topic. We can share our aches and pains and wrinkles and hair loss. And you can bring up your perverse obsession with vaginal cream!"

Martha was downright gleeful at the idea. "I might bring that up. See if she appropriates that!"

The Elk House was busier with a music festival inundating the village with out-of-towners. Sadie and Millie placed dibs on an outside table, appropriating six chairs from various tables. Warm breezes under a cloudy gray sky made it quite pleasant.

Josephine pulled her writing journal from her purse and began skimming her notes. Handing out paper and pens to everyone, she said, "I'm going to ask you a couple of questions and then I'll give you a little time to write down your thoughts. Okay, are you ready? Question number one - *What are some physical limitations you feel with the body you have now?*"

The women asked her to repeat the question several times as they scribbled it down. "I'll give you all a few minutes to jot down your responses, and then I have a second question."

The five women began writing their physical complaints, the pens scratching frantically on the papers. One by one they laid down their pens as they finished.

"Okay ladies, you may have more to write, but let me ask you to write down one more question. Here it is: *What do you like about your physical body?*"

There was a notable absence of furious scribbling after this question. Ida was stymied. It struck a nerve. Women never liked their bodies. At any age. There were always too many imperfections. She felt it was a trick question. We may learn to be content with our bodies, but we never really like our bodies.

"Do you mean what we like about our bodies now, at our ages now?" asked Madeleine.

"Yes, consider at least one thing you can say you like about your body – at the age you are now."

There was the sound of scratching on paper with intermittent slurps from their cups. A few more minutes of penciled thoughts, then she said, "Time's up! What are some of the physical limitations you feel now?"

The women called out their litany of physical woes: Sore hips. Creaky joints. Arthritis. Incontinence. Back pain. Sore feet.

Josephine nodded sympathetically. "Vaginal dryness!" added Martha.

There was a disparaging tightness of Josephine's lips, but she carried on, judiciously avoiding a confrontation. "Do these limitations affect your everyday moods? Does the pain prevent you from doing things you like to do?"

The women listened to each other. They mostly agreed these ailments, these "complaints," did not hold them back from most things they enjoyed doing. The reality that more limitations may be coming down the pike sobered them.

"We know we're getting older and weaker," said Sadie, "but just not right now please."

"If we can keep shuffling and moving, we're still doing all right," agreed Millie.

"Some of us a little easier than others," added Madeleine, "but I'm still here, and that's more than I can say about the friends I've lost."

The second question, identifying something they liked about their bodies, was a stumper. No one was willing to say straight out they liked some feature about themselves.

Finally Martha spoke up. "I guess I appreciate my muscles. I still have strength from working around the horses."

"There you go!" said Josephine. "Your body is strong and muscled, built for heavy work."

Martha looked askance at her, but she held her tongue. Madeleine liked that her body was still flexible and that she could still do most yoga stretches. Sadie scratched her head but eventually said she supposed she liked her good teeth, blessed with only one cavity her entire life. Ida liked that she was short. She felt compact and closer to the ground.

"I just can't think of anything I like about my body," replied Karen. "It makes me uncomfortable even discussing it."

"Do you appreciate feeling healthy most days?" asked Ida. "Maybe it's enough to like that you're able to move around freely without a lot of pain?"

"Yes, I can definitely affirm that. I am grateful that, with insulin, my diabetes is under control," answered Karen.

"Diabetes?" Madeleine exclaimed.

"You never said a word," replied Josephine.

"Managing that is a huge affirmation," said Ida. Everyone agreed.

"I've had it since I was a teenager. I just watch what I eat," Karen replied.

"And exercise, isn't that important?" asked Martha.

"So maybe I can even say I appreciate my diabetes, in a way," said Karen. "It's not a physical attribute, but it is a part of who I am and affects my physical health."

"Well maybe just liking that you have a healthy body. You don't have to like your diabetes," said Madeleine.

"I don't have to like it but I can appreciate how it has made me more aware of how I live my life." Karen waved the air. "But enough about me. Josephine, I'm interested in your answers to these questions."

The other women turned attentively. "Let's hear it. What do you like most about your physical self?"

"Well…I have to say I like my bone structure. I've been blessed with good bones," said Josephine.

"What a hoot!" blurted Martha. "Seriously? You have the gall to say you like what's been medically enhanced? I thought we were being honest here."

"I have never had surgery." sniffed Josephine.

"Botox?" asked Madeleine.

"That's not surgery!" replied Jacqueline. "It's a drug treatment. I have chronic migraines!"

Martha was not about to give her this one. "You mean to tell me you're getting Botox for chronic pain and the only side effect is a wrinkle-free face?"

Josephine looked trapped. "Oh Martha, I have wrinkles."

Martha looked around at all the other women. She opened her mouth to say something but thought better of it. "I won't state the obvious. It just bothers me that a lot of women feel they have to iron out all the little crevices on their faces!" Martha sat back regarding the others, apparently letting the jury rest. "Okay, I'm done."

Sadie and Millie eyed each other and nervously drank the rest of their cups of tea.

Madeleine laughed, "Martha, are you welcoming your wrinkles?"

"Or do we just make peace with these life lines?" Ida pointed to her own face.

"I've learned to appreciate wrinkles," commented Karen. "Didn't somebody famous say they're laugh lines?"

Josephine stated to no one in particular, "I like to keep myself up. If others want to let themselves go and don't care what they look like, it's a free country."

Martha leaned forward and was ready to launch into another tirade when Ida kicked her under the table and spoke up, "Josephine, these questions were excellent prompts to get us thinking today! Thanks for taking this on."

"I don't give a damn if women want to spend money on body restorations," said Sadie.

"It's just not our business," added Millie.

"Thank you, Josephine, for your questions and guidance today," said Karen.

"This was a good session," confirmed Madeleine.

Martha wasn't quite finished, "We're still victims of a profit-making industry that targets our self-image."

Ida stood up. "Okay. We need to end our time together. Thanks everyone. And remember we're not meeting in August because of our vacation schedules. Have a great end of summer!"

"I'm still holding yoga classes through August. Everyone is welcome to come," reminded Madeleine. "Monday and Saturday mornings."

Martha was the last to get up from the table. She followed begrudgingly.

"Let it go, Martha. What is your thing with Josephine anyway?" Ida asked as they returned to the car.

"Why is our culture so obsessed with wrinkle-free faces? That's the point. It's not Josephine, but the fact that she feels like she has to alter her face to be attractive. Why aren't wrinkles attractive? They tell the world where we've been!" Martha sat back sullenly in her seat, folding her arms across her chest.

Ida started the engine and backed out. "For what it's worth, I agree with you. God forbid someone looks old.

"We're the only species to think about how we look."

"How do you know that? What about extra fluffy plumage of birds in mating, eh? Or let's see, baboons and gorillas. They preen and groom."

"The friends I've had always just seemed like genuine farm folk with more on their minds than how they look."

"I have to confess I've thought about my looks more now that I'm with Landis," admitted Ida. "What does that say about me?"

'It says you're moon-eyed. It can happen to the best of us."

"I'm glad you take me as I am."

Martha smiled at her. "Will you? Will you take me as I am?"

"We are old Martha. Is that okay to say? That we're old?"

Martha slapped her hand across her heart. "Yep, we're old and getting older. But we're still here."

"I'm happy you're here and that I'm here and we are *old* friends."

Martha appeared to finally have calmed down. "*Old* old friends."

FOUR

Ida awakened to hear voices in the living room. The clock on her side table read 6:05. "What in the world?" She put on her robe and ventured forth. Martha sat on a chair in front of the couch, her arms on her knees, rambling away to a body reclined before her.

"So I'm trying to get into the bathroom and Dan is there blocking my way," Martha said. "He told to go somewhere else. This one was taken."

There were mumbles from the form on the couch and Martha continued, "I know, it was strange. But then I tried again a few minutes later, because it's my bathroom. But Moses is there guarding it, and he tells me it's not my time, to go somewhere else." Martha glanced up to see Ida. "I'm just telling Tommy about my dream this morning."

Ida pointed to the couch. "Why is he out here?"

"Tommy didn't want to disturb me with his snoring, so he came out here. More than likely I was the one snoring." She regarded the life-blob with affection. "But I thought he was dead. I didn't hear him and he was still as a clam out here."

Tommy threw back the cover. "Here I am – alive and kicking."

"But I thought you were dead, Frodo. You scared me!" Martha confided. She leaned over and gave him a peck on his forehead.

"Thanks for checking!" said Tommy. He did look like a hobbit with his round, ruddy face and chubby cheeks.

Martha regarded Ida again. "So, I was talking about my dream. Both Dan and Moses were telling me I couldn't use my bathroom."

"Weird one," responded Ida. "I wouldn't read too much into it."

"But they both told me it was already occupied and I had to find my own bathroom." Martha shook her head. "Maybe it's about finding my own path."

"Or maybe they want you to share more?" asked Tommy.

"I think there's room for you and me in that bathroom, old man," Martha smiled at him. "You can go back to my bed. I've got work to do." She waved at Ida as she headed to the door. "Could you make some coffee for my little man there?"

Ida puttered about the kitchen shushing herself when a pot clattered. She ran the water and poured it into the coffeemaker, turning it on before heading back to her room, and calling out, "Coffee will be ready in a few minutes, Tom. Help yourself."

He sat up. "Ida, can I ask you something?"

She came and stood near-by. "What's up?"

He scratched his head. "Is Martha okay? Does she seem okay to you?"

"I've seen some changes, yes," answered Ida slowly.

"She often gets out of bed during the night. Sometimes I hear her talking to someone. She's acting out dreams or she's seeing things."

"Does she respond to you? Does she come back to bed?"

"I usually say, 'Martha, come back to bed' and she comes right away. This dream she was talking about – she was at the bathroom door arguing with someone. Saying stuff like 'What do you mean it's not my time?' I was a little spooked."

"Is that why you're out here?"

"Ah, no, I really do snore – and she does too, so it's just to catch a few winks. I won't desert her, but I'd like to know if you're seeing changes in her."

"Yes," Ida replied. "I think Martha is even aware of it. She does see things – birds mostly and hears them. She tires easily and she forgets things. I do too, but she forgets where things are."

"Well, okay then," Tom said.

"I hope to bring up the idea of seeing a doctor."

"Keep me posted. And let me know how I can help. She's a good woman."

"Will do," said Ida. "And yes, no arguments there. She can be ornery but she's a very good woman."

A door opened from down the hall and Moses shuffled towards them. "Did we wake you with our gabbing out here?" Ida asked.

Moses sneezed in a boisterous outburst. He wiped his nose with the sleeve of his elbow.

"Gesundheit!" responded Ida. "Bless you."

"Got a little something going on in here," Moses said thumping his chest. "Good morning Tom. Is Martha out already?"

"Up and at 'em!" responded Tom. "She's a creature of habit."

"I'll make some hot tea with lemon." Ida was already heating water and banging pans. "You can take a day off, you know."

"And let Martha know that? No, I'm fine." Moses turned around. "I'll have that tea and then I'll head out to the corral."

Tommy and Ida regarded one another idly. "I'll have coffee with you, Ida. And I'll even make some bacon and eggs."

"That's kind of you. I'll take the eggs but you can have my bacon."

Tom slapped his forehead. "I keep forgetting you don't eat meat. But do you know what Martha had last week when we went out to dinner? Elk tenderloin!"

Ida spun around and gave him a quizzical look. "Hmm, okay. Sometimes she may be a creature of habit and other times, she'll keep us guessing."

Tommy laughed. "She'll keep things interesting, that's for sure."

AUGUST

ONE

"So you're the six sisters I've heard so much about?" Martha asked, approaching a group of women sitting together during an afternoon social hour. Ida had talked of little else but the five phenomenal sisters on a Verdant Pathways tour and insisted Martha had to meet them.

Ida led her friend over to a spunky woman, who leaped up to shake Martha's hand. "This is Eva, the youngest. I think you told me you were eighty, is that correct?"

"Yes, I'm the baby of the family. They'll tell you I was spoiled rotten but they made me this way," she chuckled. The other women, with a little exerted effort, rose to their feet forming a semi-circle.

"I'm Gladys. I'm eighty-three," giggled the second woman., "There's going to be a little test at the end of our introductions so pay attention!"

"Nice to meet you, Gladys," replied Martha. "But I was never very good at tests."

Next in line was a taller woman, very hardy looking, a little heavier than the others. "I'm Mabel. I'm eighty-six. Do you see a mathematical pattern here?"

"I see your mother liked old fashioned names." She pointed at each identified guest. "Mabel. Gladys. Eva!"

"Okay, and I'm Ethel. Do you want to guess how old I am?" She eyed her sisters with delight. They'd played this game before.

Martha held up a finger, directing it toward the women who'd been introduced. "Let's see… Eva, eighty. Next was Gladys, eighty-three. Mabel, eighty-six, and Ethel, now, let me take a wild stab at say, eighty-nine?"

"Bingo!" said Ethel and Gladys together.

Martha swung around to the two remaining women, one with white curly hair and the other with a short, gray, spiked cut. "I'm Alice. Yes, I am ninety-two. And this is…" she held out her hands as if bringing someone on stage.

"Beulah. *Beau*, as in Beautiful, Lah as in La la la." The last lady clapped her hands.

"Beulah? That's wonderful! "Martha beamed. "And are you really ninety-five years old?"

"That's correct! A-plus for you," responded the woman with a twinkle in her eye. "Nothing slips past you."

"Do you live near each other?" Martha inquired.

Beulah responded, "All of us live in the same retirement community in Pennsylvania. Only Alice and I live together in an apartment."

"Close enough to walk to see each other," added Eva.

"And do you often travel together?"

"Once a year for the past ten years," announced Gladys.

"Always together?" Ida inquired.

"So far, we have," chimed in Beulah.

"The hardest part is agreeing where we all want to go," explained Eva. "None of us like to fly."

"And my daughter doesn't want any of us driving ourselves," added Mabel. "So usually we take the train, join a tour group or hire a driver of a van."

"None of us care for those big bus tours," confided Ethel.

"I know," agreed Ida, "too many people getting on and off the bus everywhere you go."

"Oh, it's not that," said Ethel, "it's the single men."

"Don't get us started," laughed Gladys again, the merriest of the five. "We have nothing against men – and most are charming, but we just want to have a good time as sisters and not have men hitting on us."

At that point two older gentlemen wandered into the great room. One put up his hands in mock dismay when he spotted the group, "Oh we apologize,we didn't mean to intrude!"

"We're here for the social hour," stated the other. "We won't bother you. We'll just get our drinks."

Ida hurried to help the men at the buffet but she heard Martha whisper, "You've got them trained already." The six women nodded in their merriment and sat back down, sensing the fun was over.

Gladys eyed her sisters and then, as if she'd received their silent consent, called out to the men, "Oh come join us. We'd like some company."

"I have to excuse myself," said Martha, "but I am glad to have met you."

"Test time!" challenged Beulah. "Names again?"

"Okay." Martha rubbed her hands together. "Oldest to youngest this time. Alice. Beulah, Oh I'm terrible with names. Eva?" She looked at Ida for help.

Ida stepped in. "Ethel, Mabel, Gladys, and...Eva!"

"Well done!" The sisters applauded. They waved to her as the men joined their circle.

"What a hoot!" mumbled Martha to Ida as they walked through the kitchen. "What's with the three years' difference in their ages?"

"Their parents were on a three-year fertility cycle," mused Ida. "But aren't they a delight?"

"If only we're that happy in our eighties."

"They're happy and this makes others happy."

"A lesson for this sourpuss?" asked Martha, amused.

Ida patted her on the arm. "Something to aspire to. Let's remember they have their health, and they have money to do these things."

"Luck again!"

"Well, good genes and a savings account. Almost makes you want to feel grateful for a few things, doesn't it?" teased Ida.

Martha waved her away. "Who are you preaching to?"

"I love you too, Martha."

T W O

They'd kept in communication the past six weeks through emails. Landis sent her links to read about Białowieża and she was both disturbed and comforted by the protesters who wanted to save the forests from logging. The bark beetle was wreaking havoc with the forests in Poland just as it was in Montana – and she found herself somehow reassured that the same controversies here also raged across the ocean. In his last email, Landis had teased that she would be particularly gratified to know about the microbiome. Over a thousand kinds of macofungi thrive on the plentiful dead wood littering the forest floor. Birds, bison, and lynx were important to the biodiversity of the forest as well. He was enheartened about the Polish government being open to expanding the boundaries of the park if it meant profit. Eco-tourism was a huge incentive to preserving the old growth forests. After his discouraging first few weeks with the study group, this was positive news and he was returning feeling elated and hopeful.

Ida didn't sleep the night before he was expected home. She didn't think she'd been that excited. Her body said otherwise. Just when she was in that twilight space of consciousness and sleep she heard a thump from the living room. She turned on her back and listened. A creak in the floor, then a startling thud. She sat up. Someone was definitely in the living room.

She crept to her door, turned the handle silently and peered into the darkness. Grabbing a book from a shelf, she rounded the corner into the living room and flipped the light switch. Martha froze in the middle of the living room, fear in her eyes.

"What are you doing walking around in the dark?" Ida demanded.

"I could ask you the same thing!" retorted Martha. "I got up to go the bathroom and lost my way back to bed." "But your bathroom is off your bedroom. It's not out here." Ida stated the obvious.

"I don't know. Maybe I was sleepwalking. Just help me get back to my bed."

Ida took Martha's arm and walked her through the kitchen and back to her bedroom. "Do you need to use the bathroom?" she asked.

"Not anymore," said Martha. Then after she had laid down under her covers she said, "You might want to check the living room floor." She sighed and Ida thought she heard her say "I'm sorry."

Ida returned to the living room and turned on some lights. She smelled urine. Peabody remained asleep on his mat. By the front door on the hard-back chair (which they normally used for sitting while tying boots and shoes) was a little puddle. Oh my. Ida went to get old rags and some paper towels. She grabbed a spray all-purpose cleaner from under the sink.

Better get Martha up to change her pajamas. Upon opening the bedroom door and seeing Martha asleep, she thought otherwise. Ida could launder everything in the morning.

Maybe Martha had been sleepwalking. It happened. Only a few days ago Martha had lost her way inside the grocery store. They'd agreed to get specific items and meet back at the cashier. Ida had waited and waited. Finally going in search of her friend, she found her perusing the red meat section. They didn't eat meat. Oh well, Martha had said. You're here now.

The next morning, Ida asked if Martha remembered losing her way to the bathroom. "What are you talking about? I know where my bathroom is!" Martha stormed. "You must have been dreaming."

"I didn't dream you urinating on the chair by the door," said Ida. "We'll have to warn Moses to lock his door, or he may find you in his bed!"

Martha turned her head away. She finished her cereal and headed out the door. Maybe it was nothing. Just a one-off episode. Tommy was coming to spend the day with Martha. This was reassuring since Ida was picking up Landis this afternoon and she just might not make it back to the cottage tonight.

***

Ida checked the arrivals. The plane from Dulles was on time. She texted him, "I'm standing in front of the geese." It would be hard to miss the airport's sculptured birds in flight.

There was a bald head and a silver-speckled beard on someone in a tweed sports jacket coming through the doors. *Landis.* His beard was back, though not to where it could collect mass amounts of carbon dioxide. This well-trimmed face might be suitable on an academic professor but not the unconventional dendro-chrono-biologist she had come to know – and about whom she wanted to know so much more. She leaned against the railing, waiting shyly for him to spot her. He bent over slightly, straining to see her if it was her. She moved to meet him.

He rested his computer bag on the floor and opened his arms wide. She'd forgotten how small she'd felt with him but she managed to wrap her arms tightly around his frame. He picked her up and swung her back and forth before setting her down. Then, lifting his right arm to display the tattered remains of his homemade wire bracelet, he declared, "It's a bit worn, but it did the trick. I did not drink any alcohol."

She bit her lip. "I think you can remove it now. It served its purpose."

"No way," he replied. "It's a great conversation piece and I might go into the jewelry making business."

Both were chatty while waiting at the baggage claim: The flight. The time change. What he'd eaten on the plane. Moses. How long it took for the bags to arrive. Martha. Tommy. The ranch. Białowieża. Elsa and Romona. New friends he'd made. New foods he'd tried.

In Bozeman, they stopped at their favorite restaurant for Landis to order a bison burger to verify he was back in Montana. She said she didn't think she could eat, but he cut several bites of salad for her and shared his fries. They had so many questions for each other. The man she'd just begun to know was here again.

On the way to the airport she had stopped at the cabin to ensure the cleaning crew had come. The place did not smell musty. No dust or countertop film. The beds were freshly made and the floors dry mopped. She unlocked the front door for him to carry his luggage through to the bedroom. *What to do next? Maybe a glass of water?* She opened the refrigerator reflexively. *Empty. Bare. Of course.*

"We should have stopped to pick up some groceries for you," she said when he joined her. He was rolling up his shirt sleeves. She thought *that is one of the sexiest things I've seen in a long time,* but she said, "Martha and Moses are making dinner for you tonight. They want to see you."

He held up his watch. "It's only 4:35." His kind eyes twinkled at her. "What should we do until then?"

She gazed at the floor. "Maybe we need a little time to just get reacquainted. Maybe we should take a walk or something."

He nodded toward the couch. "We could talk here?"

But sitting beside him did not mitigate the yearning. This was not the time to be sedate or proper or coy. She pulled him down beside her and began the age-old ritual of touching, removing, unbuttoning, skin on skin, slowly this way, that. It was an ancient human interaction between any two lovers. It was giving and receiving communication, a synaptic congruity. It just seemed like so much more between two old souls, aging neurotransmitters be damned.

THREE

Moses probably had an idea there was a party brewing for him but he pretended his eighty-fifth birthday was just another ordinary day. That afternoon, Rusty kept him occupied in the barn shoeing horses. Moses would, by necessity, have to take a shower after such work..

He had not moved all his worldly possessions, limited as they were, into the cottage, but was transferring things in his truck day by day. His entrance was off the mudroom in the back, wheelchair accessible, in case it was needed. Moses said it was better to plan for physical challenges now. He was the one to install an adjustable medical bed. He wanted things in place if he ever needed those "bells and whistles."

The band set up in a corner of the Tamarack room, arriving mid-afternoon to practice. Moses wouldn't hear them from that distance. Vehicles were parked and hidden on the western side of the house. Romona baked a cake in the shape of a cowboy hat, and Elsa found a plastic horse and cowboy in her stash of toys to place on top. Two candles prominently displayed the numbers eight and five. Barbecued pork, corn-on-the-cob, potato salad – all the favorite Moses fixings were ready to go.

Elsa was designated to retrieve Moses from the cottage. Peabody trotted happily beside them, the merry canine escort. Moses expected his "family" to be there to welcome him but not thirty extra friends as well.

"Damn!" he said when he saw the crowd. "You pulled this one off pretty darn well."

"So, we did surprise you?" exclaimed Martha.

"Where did you get these folks to impersonate friends of mine?"

"We're still getting paid, aren't we?" someone shouted.

"Somebody told me we were extras for a movie," said another.

Moses simply nodded and worked his way around the room greeting each person by name and thanking them for coming. The band members filled their plates to eat first so they could begin playing. Others followed through the buffet.

"Nice job," Moses said when he reached Ida. "I know you had a hand in this."

"We've been planning for months and months," she replied. "How are you doing?"

"If I was any better I couldn't stand it!" He stated this as if it was a new revelation though she heard him say it every day.

"We couldn't stand it if *you* were any better!" she replied raising her voice above the timbre of the music.

"I know you didn't have anything else to do when Landis was gone – but now?" He looked over to where the band was setting up to play. "Now, I probably won't see you anymore."

"He only got home two days ago. That's not fair."

Moses crinkled his face and leaned in close to her. "You take as much time with him as you need to. I wouldn't wish it any different."

The band began by playing "Happy Birthday" and then launched into several Willie Nelson favorites – "just for Moses!" Soon the music turned to the familiar two-step and country swing beats. Folks partnered up and followed the familiar turning and stepping. They all seemed to know the quick-quick, slow-slow steps and so many twists and turns. As the evening wore on Moses got out on the dance floor to shuffle around with his friends.

"He looks happy, doesn't he?" asked Martha with Tommy in tow.

"Yep, he does," Ida agreed. "Moving like he's twenty-five out there."

"That's because he thinks he is." She turned to her paramour. "Hey, Frodo, dance?" Tommy grabbed her hand, spun her round, oblivious that he was spinning from below.

Elsa and Romona sashayed back and forth, making up dances, shoulders moving to the rhythms. Not even touching, they were creating erotic storms within the radius of their two bodies. *Young love*, Ida thought. Then she regarded Landis playing his guitar and experienced an odd electric shiver in her body. *Okay – old love too.* She acquiesced to her own logic, but it was new to her.

Moses plopped down beside Ida after several dances, winded and hot. She handed him a paper plate to fan himself. Peabody lay at their feet. They heard Elsa announce the band would attempt a special tribute to the guest of honor. Moses approved with a thumbs up as they slowed down the tempo and sang the words clearly for him to hear.

Singing together galvanized the guests into newfound affection and chumminess. The band attempted to draw the evening to a close but dancers jumped up and down yelling, "More, more, more." Landis looked at the other guys and they broke into the old John Denver song "Wide Montana Skies." Everyone but Ida knew the words.

Tipp stepped to the mike and said, "Well, folks, we're going to end this evening the only way we know how – by cranking it down. This one's a slow-dancin' melancholy tune. Hey, thank you all for coming!" Moses stood up and swayed side to side. Ida threw out her arms to him and they waltzed slowly. One, two, three. One, two, three.

The music eventually stopped, people clapped for a spell, and then lingered to file by Moses to wish him well. The musicians packed up their gear and joined the circle of family and friends seated around the guest of honor. Annie had offered them guest rooms so they didn't have to drive. Half of the hat of the cowboy cake remained.

"Not bad, Moses," replied Martha.

"Hell of a party, old man," said Landis, shaking the man's hands.

Moses agreed. "Not bad at all for an old black, gay cowboy. I guess I turned out okay. I am grateful to you all." He held up his glass of ginger ale.

"Cheers!" called Tipp.

And others responded in kind. "Cheers!"

"Got anything you want to get off your chest?" asked Landis. "Any stories we haven't heard?"

"Or even stories we have heard," Ida said.

"Any regrets?" asked Martha. "Anything you wished you might have done, but didn't?"

Moses thought about this. "Well damn, yes, there's always something we could've done differently. I don't live my life thinking about regrets. I got no complaints."

"Where did you grow up?" asked Rusty.

"That's assuming I ever did grow up!" Moses chuckled. "I was born on a farm in Missouri, but we moved north to Chicago when I was around twelve. We were poor but rich in family like they say. My father was a janitor at the University of Chicago. My younger brother actually ended up going to school there.

"So how old were you when you left home?" asked Hank.

"Let's see...I dropped out of high school after tenth grade and got a job loading freight cars. Pretty soon, one of my buddies got a job as a porter and he got me hooked up in the dining car. I liked that – traveling across the country with free room and board on the move. I did that for about two years, waiting on white folks in my fancy suit. Then I wandered into that place in Kansas, and Martha's dad hired me. I never looked back once I got myself around horses."

"So, you were pretty young when Dad hired you," said Martha. "As a little kid looking up to you, I thought you were old!"

"You know I probably felt old. When I was working on the trains, I noticed I was different from other men. It took me awhile to accept it. I guess that was another reason I took the job on your dad's farm. I thought I could hide there, maybe not have to deal with who I was." He shook his head. "It doesn't work that way. I heard about places in Wichita – bars for people like me. Didn't take me long to find those. Funny – finding my own kind of people in bars. They're kind of like churches that way."

Landis said, "You don't have to tell us everything. It's not our business."

"Do you want to hear my story or not?" Moses asked smiling. "Especially while I still remember some of these things. I felt safe up here on the ranch. People just let me be and I appreciate that. And yes, I've been in love. Why'd do you think I went to the gay rodeo for several years in a row? He was a really nice guy, but…well, I wasn't going to move to Nevada for anybody. And he wasn't going to leave his mother."

"His mother?" asked Martha.

"Yeah he lived with his mother," Moses stated matter of factly. "Nothing else you need to know about that. There's lots of kinds of love you know. I loved Miriam too. I love all of you. I think I am happiest living vicariously through the lives of others. Yep, lots of different kinds of love. Any more questions?"

"Have you been back to Chicago? To see your family?" asked Ida.

"I went back for my mother's funeral…let's see…must be over thirty years ago. Yes Ida, to answer your question, I saw my brother then. Let's just say he's the kind of Christian that doesn't want to be seen with someone like me."

Moses stood up and held onto the back of a chair for balance. "Well ladies and gentlemen, this has been a lovely evening. I thank you – one and all. If you don't mind, I'm going to excuse myself and head for bed – in my new home. Good-night all."

Martha and Ida both struggled to get up quickly to accompany him, but Elsa was there by his side. "Moses, mind if I walk you over to the cottage? I feel kind of like you're my grandpa now – so is that okay? Can I call you Grandpa?"

"That's quite okay with me Elsa. I'd be privileged."

Tommy and Martha followed close behind. The others stacked their chairs and deposited cans and bottles for recycling. Landis turned to Ida. "Care to walk me to my door?"

"Where are you staying?"

"Room number 4. You can only walk me to the door, but that's all. My roommate would be scandalized if you came inside."

"We have rules about fraternizing with the guests. You won't get any hanky-panky from me," she said.

"Really? No hanky-panky whatsoever?" he grinned.

"It's perfectly acceptable for me to invite you to my room."

"Is that an invitation?"

"Do you want to spend the night in my room?"

"With you? In your room? In your cottage?"

She let out a sigh of exasperation. "Yes, Landis. With me – in my room – in my cottage."

"You've never invited me before. I'm in shock. I don't know the rules of etiquette here. Like…do I get my overnight bag from the room, or am I expected to sneak out of your room later tonight?"

"Go get your bag with your toothbrush and all that stuff. You can stay with me tonight. We'll see what happens in the morning. I'll wait for you in the kitchen."

Annie and Rusty were turning off lights and cleaning up. "Thank you for all of your help," Ida replied. "Annie, it was especially nice to offer rooms for the band members."

"I figured for events like these, it's good to have folks feel they can stay the night."

When Landis returned, Ida opened the outside door. They strolled across the yard to the cottage where a single lamp shone in the darkness. Only a few stars were visible on this cool summer night.

Her bedroom felt crowded with Landis there. She let him use the bathroom first and quickly put on her summer pajamas. Could it just be a sleepover without their usual amorous entanglements? *How do we get to that place?*

"This is the first time I've seen you in pajamas," Landis commented. "It's kind of exciting."

"Oh stop it," she said, "you're incorrigible."

"Sounds like something a teacher once said to me."

"Probably more than once," she replied. She turned out the light and lay down beside him. "We need rain."

"Yes, yes, we do," Landis agreed sleepily.

"Rain makes some people melancholy and moody but I think I'm just the opposite."

"We need rain badly," he murmured. He lay on his back, eyes closed.

So they could just lie together and not get all charged up? Would he let her alone to sleep? Could she leave him be?

She turned on her side facing him and placed her hand on his chest. "What do you think Moses meant when he said there's lots of kinds of love?"

Landis sighed, "I suppose he meant more than just erotic love."

"He and Miriam loved each other in a strong but different kind of way. He's so kind with everyone he meets. He loves the horses too. I just think it was kind of intriguing."

"Hmmm "

"And that he said he enjoyed life vicariously through the lives of others. I suppose there are many, many souls who do that in this life. They don't get the chance, the luck, to find personal love. And it is luck so many times."

She waited for a response but there was just the hum of his sleeping breath. She took her hand away and turned over on her other side. He wasn't rebuffing her. They could just lie together without expectations. Couldn't they? This was good.

She had thinking to do. There were forms of love she knew she didn't understand. Loneliness often convinced people they were in love with someone else when, really, it was just a fear of being alone. She had resisted that notion most of her life. She was happy he was here now. That was all. And what was their love? Was it love? Would she be able to go back to her singleness, her self-containment? She was already too far out on the hanging branch – over a raging river.

Thank you to the life-force. Thank you to the God of her childhood, a simple loving presence that had something to do with her will to love – like the commandment – with all her heart, and soul, and mind. That commandment had more to do with having the courage to love in the face of hate, in the front lines of cultural justice. She hadn't really had to deal with that. Still, it was important to cultivate heart-fullness, soulfulness, and mindfulness with respect to oneself if one was ever called upon to put it out to the world.

She suddenly felt very small in the world, small and insignificant. She understood it didn't matter. She was just a pinprick of cellular life passing through on its way to somewhere else. *Kind of comforting really.*

FOUR

Ida encountered Martha sitting on the front porch one afternoon staring into her hands. She pulled one of the rockers closer to her friend. "May I join you?"

She was met with a gesture towards the other rocker.

"Watching the sun set?"

"Yep, and listening to the trains," replied Martha.

"Trains?"

"You don't hear them?"

Ida sighed. "Can't say that I do, but maybe my hearing is going."

Martha nodded and again stared at her hands. "I know there aren't trains out here. I heard them though. And I heard a train whistle."

Ida's eyes focused on the high ranges of the Rocky Mountains off in the distance.

Martha continued, "Once when I was around five years old, my dad woke me up in the middle of the night to go pick up my mother at the train depot. She'd gone on a trip to see my aunt in Indiana. I still get a whiff of that engine and see her getting off the train with a baby in her arms. I thought she'd gone away to get me a sister or brother. But no, she was just holding the baby for someone."

"Did your dad take you to the station in your pajamas?"

"That's how I remember it. It was special like that."

"Did you ever ride in a train?"

"Mom and I took a train to Ohio to see my grandparents when I was little. We couldn't afford the sleepers, but we had those big seats that pushed back. And the dining care was fun for a kid."

"And to travel with just your mom. That was pretty special."

Martha sat back in the rocker, kicking the floorboards to get momentum. "Isn't that something to think about? That we were once so young. And here we are, getting old, moving along on a train called time."

"That's a good one. A train called time. I read once that trains in literature are symbols of being carried somewhere else, a journey I guess."

"Or that a train is like a church – you get on and stay on, or you get off and get lost."

Ida was amused. "I never heard that one. A train is like a church."

"But right now, the train is just a train…connecting to a memory I guess," said Martha. "I always liked the sound of those whistles – especially at night."

"I remember them from Kansas. Lonely and mournful. *Lugubrious* I think is the word."

"I kind of liked hearing that train out here. Hope it comes back. Maybe I'll hop a ride." Martha was done talking. She rocked silently, gazing off towards the mountains. Ida wished she could hear that train too.

***

The next morning Ida ran out to stop Annie on her way to do errands,. There was no more putting off the peculiar sightings and hearings and accidents.

Annie rolled down her car window. "I didn't see any eggs this morning? Is Mom out somewhere?"

"She was up and out early like usual. But I'm concerned about her."

Annie looked quizzical. "What's going on? Is she seeing birds again?"

"I haven't told you. I've had to clean up messes she's made during the night. Twice now. She gets up and urinates somewhere – in the kitchen, the living room.

"Oh no, Ida, that's not right. Something's going on." At first I thought it was just sleepwalking - and she forgot about her own bathroom. But not after two times in the last two weeks."

"And then yesterday we were sitting on the porch. She said she heard trains."

"Where is she now?"

"I don't know, but I'll go check the barn."

"I'll go with you."

They didn't find her in the stables. Moses was cleaning the hooves on a couple of horses and when they asked him if he'd seen Martha, he waved the pick toward the north pasture. There she was, close to one of the three spruce trees a half mile away. When she saw them coming towards her, she headed back with long measured strides. Walking appeared to be an arduous task.

Ida pointed to the horses in the pasture. "Do you know you have an audience?"

Martha looked behind to see two of the geldings following in her wake. "They love me. What can I say?"

"We were worried since we hadn't seen you all morning," Annie said. "We didn't see any fresh eggs in the kitchen."

"I've been busy," Martha stated. "I'll get the eggs now." She brushed past them, trudging sluggishly in her high rubber boots. Martha usually considered herself groomed if she pulled her long hair back out of her face. Today it hung down, tangled and knotted.

"I'll help you," Ida followed her friend through the barn.

The gate bolt to the chicken yard stuck stubbornly in its metal frame. Martha jammed her hand against it, then spun around quickly, confronting Ida. "Why are you following me? I can do this!"

"I just offered to help. You don't have to bite my head off."

"You don't have to spy on me."

They gathered eggs silently and placed them in an extra crate by the fence. "I'll take them to the house and then I'll lie down for a nap," said Martha with a careworn expression. "You can stop following me."

"I'll be at the cottage. And I'm not following you."

Later that afternoon Ida picked green beans in the garden to put up bags for freezing. She brought in a large basketful, turned on the stove for boiling water and sat down to begin snapping the green ends. Martha appeared from her bedroom, face washed and hair brushed neatly back, with a renewed spirit. "What do you have going on here?" she asked pleasantly.

"Thought I'd blanch and freeze several bags of beans. Want to help?"

"What do you need?"

"Probably some quart-size freezer bags?"

Martha looked confused. "I don't know what you're talking about. What are *freezer* bags?"

"Like zip-lock baggies."

Martha opened several drawers. "Where do we keep them?"

"Look in the bottom drawer by the refrigerator."

Martha pulled out several boxes of baggies and aluminum foil and waxed paper. "You choose." She went to the stove to put the kettle on for tea. It made Ida nervous the way Martha turned the flames up high on gas range. She might forget to turn it back down sometime. They stood at the counter attentive to their tasks – Ida blanching the green beans and Martha waiting for the water in the tea kettle.

"Ida, something is very wrong with me."

Ida finished the beans and turned toward Martha. "What's happening? Can you tell me?"

"I'm just not right. I know I'm forgetting all kinds of things that used to be right here with me. I feel stiff and tired and just plain old."

"We all feel that way from time to time."

"And then there are those episodes at night. I know you've cleaned up more than one."

"There were a couple of accidents."

"I'm just scared. I don't feel like myself. And I'm scared it's something really serious."

"These symptoms – and I'm calling them *symptoms* because that's all they are – could be due to many things. What about seeing Dr. T for a start? Can you call her for an appointment or would you like me to do that?"

"I'll call her. I don't think I can ignore this anymore."

"No, I don't think we can. And I do mean "we." We're in this together."

"I know you and Annie were talking about me today."

"Just today."

"It's just scary. I hear things and see things – and I don't trust myself. I don't want to get dementia, Ida. I'm so scared I'm losing it."

"We'll get to the bottom of this. You call Dr. T's office and try to get in as soon as possible. There are lots of reasons this could be happening."

Moses opened the mudroom door and they heard him kick off his boots before opening and closing the door to his bedroom. Soon he'd come join them in the living room. He liked to have a cup of tea and watch the evening news.

"I'll finish these beans another time. Let me see what I can find for dinner tonight." Ida looked in the refrigerator and pantry. She would make up a casserole of garden acquisitions - zucchini, tomatoes, potatoes.

Martha helped herself to a glass of wine while Moses took out a mug. "Is that hot water in the kettle for anybody?"

"It's for you," Martha replied. "Glad you've joined us."

"Now that you mention it, I'm glad to be here. Feels like home."

After their dinner Moses rinsed off the dishes and silverware in the sink. Martha stood at his side placing them delicately in the dishwasher. She helped him scour the casserole pan and wash the salad bowl. They had adapted readily to their togetherness. Their daily routines were comforting, solidifying the newfound ways of being family. And they were a family.

FALLING

SEPTEMBER

ONE

Martha endured a battery of tests in search of answers; some semblance of a diagnosis for the symptoms that came and went. She had body tremors and hallucinations and stiffness in walking. Sometimes she couldn't concentrate. She'd force hereslf to get up and walk, even if it meant just going from one side of the house to the other. Her frustration in not finding a word or forgetting what she'd wanted to say made her choose silence over attempted conversation.

"Did you brush your teeth?" Ida appeared at Martha's bedroom door. They were preparing for a drive to Bozeman for an MRI that morning.

"Yes, yes, and I combed my hair. See the brush and comb are on the counter. I put them there after I use them so I know I'm done."

"Okay great," Ida said. She returned them to the drawers labeled: *Teeth* and *Hair*. "I'll go start the car."

Ida sat idling the Subaru for a few minutes then shut it off. She checked her phone for emails and read the *New*

York Times headlines. After ten minutes she went inside to find Martha sitting at the table eating a bowl of cereal.

"We need to get going. Can you finish up quickly?"

Martha looked at her inquisitively. "Where are we going?"

"We're driving to a hospital in Bozeman. You're getting a test called an MRI – where you'll be lying on your back and going through a scanning machine."

"I know what an MRI is! You don't have to talk down to me."

"Okay sorry. We need to get going. The appointment is for ten."

"Why didn't you tell me?" She picked up her bowl and carried it to the sink. "I'll go brush my teeth and I'll be ready to go."

Ida shook herself. She waited until Martha completed her grooming and walked out to the car with her.

At the hospital, Martha was whisked away by a vivacious young nurse. Ida found a seat in the waiting area and combed the numerous pamphlets addressing dementia-related diseases. One had bullet points for what to expect in behavior changes while another articulated helpful tips in responding to loved ones. At the bottom of this, with pen in hand, Ida scribbled: *Learn patience!*

Martha had been given a prescription for Lorazapan to take during her trip into the tubular MRI, to calm her anxiety in a tight and noisy space. Dr. T had told her it would not be euphoric, not to expect elation, just a general feeling of well-being. When the nurse guided Martha back to the reading room, it was obvious the woozy peacefulness was ever present.

"It wasn't so bad," Martha said, "there was a wonderful white hue within the machine that felt comforting."

Ida chuckled. "It sounds a little too much like that white light people claim to see in near death experiences. Did you see that?"

"Don't be silly," chided Martha. "I wasn't near death. I do think they could enhance the experience by using colors though, maybe rippling across the top of the tube."

"Like the Aurora Borealis?" asked Ida. "Northern lights?"

"Exactly!" exclaimed Martha. "Although making the experience too pleasant might create a high demand."

"I can see it now," said Ida as she directed Martha towards the door. "The latest trendy step to enlightenment - have yourself an MRI with Icelandic colored lights."

For lunch they stopped at a family restaurant where the plastic menu had touched-up glossy photographs of their favorite offerings. Martha pointed to a hamburger and fries. "This looks delicious. We never have these anymore."

"A hamburger?" Martha hadn't eaten meat in years; well, not until Tommy had informed her about the elk tenderloin. "Martha you've been vegetarian for a while. You haven't eaten meat. Are you sure you want a hamburger?"

"Yes, I want a hamburger! And French fries! If I only have a few months to live, I want to enjoy the last few months."

"No one has given you a terminal diagnosis. You're not dying!" Ida exclaimed. "What you have is not terminal."

Martha eyed her friend. "We're all terminal. We're all going to die."

"Yeah okay, but you're not leaving me as soon as you might like to!" Ida declared. "I already got cheated out of forty years."

Martha dusted off some salt crystals from the table. "I know. It seems so silly how we left each other… I was pissed you were with *him*!"

"You were angry? Do you remember that?"

"So I ran off with Dan. So romantic," she said wryly.

Lately Ida was amazed at the clarity with which Martha remembered things from long ago but had no recollection of what she'd just said. The past seemed to always be with her.

"I gave up a lot moving here," Martha said now.

"You love Montana!"

"Yes, but I still gave up a lot. I left Dad and you."

"But not Moses!" Ida added. "What a fortuitous thing that he came up here to help you."

"Yep – good old Moses!" Martha took a sip of her tea. "Oh, that's cold. Too much ice. What did we order again?"

"You ordered a hamburger. Do you still want that?"

"I ordered meat?" Martha asked. "Oh well, what the heck. I might like it."

***

The following week Annie drove Martha and Ida to Bozeman for the results of all the blood-work, the MRI, and a psychological evaluation. Dr. T entered her office and shook each woman's hand. She opened up the computer on her desk and clicked till she located what she needed, and then swiveled in her chair to face them.

"This is a difficult diagnosis, but I want you to understand what it is Martha is dealing with. We think she has something called Lewy Body Dementia. It's a disease that is a result of protein deposits disrupting normal brain function. The hard news is – there is no cure. The better news is – there are treatments to alleviate symptoms and side effects. Symptoms can be treated to slow down the progression of the dementia, and we can manage sleep and bladder abnormalities." She paused to allow time for them to absorb the information.

Martha responded first. "Okay, good. Looks like I have more than a few months to live then."

"You may outlive me," said Dr. T.

"But I might be more of a pain in the ass to live with?"

Dr. T. smiled but continued in her professional manner. "You may forget words and where you're going, and you might experience tremors or shaking. You may have difficulty walking sometimes. But we can begin medications immediately and these will inhibit some physical symptoms."

"The dementia is here to stay though, is that right?" Annie inquired.

"In all likelihood the dementia will become more noticeable over time. I can't say how long Martha may have already had this but I'd say not too recently or you would have noticed it."

"Do you know what causes this?" asked Annie "Is it genetic?"

"There's not a strong genetic correlation – at least not that's been researched," explained Dr. T. "If you search the

Internet you'll likely find some environmental factors, but nothing has been determined to actually cause this."

"Environmental factors like where one lives?" Annie pushed.

"I really can't say. I'm not a toxicologist. I'd caution you not to believe everything you read on the Internet either. Let's do what we can for Martha."

"So other than taking the medication, are there other things we can do?" asked Ida.

"Keep to a daily routine. Label things she uses frequently – comb, toothbrush, even things in the refrigerator. Take walks and exercise. Martha, you need to let the others know if you're not sleeping well, if you have hallucinations, or if you get depressed. Don't make them rat on you. You need to be honest with them!"

The doctor wrote a prescription and handed it to Annie. "Have her take these twice a day with her meals. I'm also prescribing melatonin if and when she has trouble sleeping. Let's check in once a week via Tele-Health. The assistants at the desk can set up a weekly time for that. I hope things go relatively smoothly. We'll try and deal with this the best we can." She stood up to indicate the end of their time together.

Ida rose and asked, "What about riding horses? That's Martha's life. Can she still continue doing what she loves to do?"

"I don't see why not but it would be prudent to know someone else is around if there is an emergency of sorts." Dr. T gathered up her things and headed towards the door.

Annie and Martha went into the hallway while Ida stopped beside Dr. T. "One last thing – Martha has gotten up at 5:45 am every day for the past forty years to start her chores. Is this still okay?"

Dr. T lowered her voice and advised, "Turn her alarm clock back one hour. She'll get the extra hour of sleep but still have her schedule. Is there someone who might be willing to get up then too?"

"Wise counsel, Dr. T," responded Ida. "One of us can be up with her by that time."

"She will get more fatigued with LBD."

Ida had to think. "LBD - Lewy Body Dementia. Ok. Got it."

***

On the third Thursday in September, Landis and Ida were serving guests during the social hour with the VP group of fourteen individuals, ages seventy-five to ninety, from Peru, Argentina, Portugal, and Germany. The eclectic dynamics of the group resulted in lively discussions and arguments. The guests treated their hosts like wait staff – there to pick up glasses and serve appetizers. Guests freely helped themselves to the wine. Ida pushed the tip jar front and center with this group.

Landis left early with Moses for their A.A. meeting, so Ida was cleaning up when she saw Martha walking alone towards the stable. She threw the dishrag over the sink faucet, grabbed her jacket, and followed. From behind the back barn door, Ida watched the two foals trot up to Martha, nudging her without fear.

She listened. Martha was definitely singing to them: *"When peace like a river attendeth my way, When sorrows like sea billows roll / Whatever my lot, thou hast taught me to say, It is well, it is well, with my soul.*

It was a familiar hymn from their Mennonite past, the deep four-part harmony filtering through in unforeseen ways. Martha's voice was soft: *"It is well (it is well) With my soul (with my soul)/ It is well, it is well, with my soul."*

Ida backed up abruptly. She turned and headed to her weedy garden where she regarded the expanding lushness. Savage ferocity overtook her as she began rapaciously pulling out green things. She didn't care if she pulled up flowers or vegetable roots. Bend over. Pull. Uproot. The brown earth revealed slimy worms oozing through the soil, here, then gone, into the depths. Martha's footsteps stopped behind her. Pull. Uproot. The plants were blurred to her as she plundered the lot, kneeling now on the ground, collections of dead weeds stacking high by her side. She couldn't look up.

Martha whistled to Peabody pestering the wild turkeys in the north pasture. She put her hand softly on Ida's head and tousled her hair, cleared her throat, and said, "I'll make supper tonight. I'll use the tomatoes and zucchini."

Ida barely nodded. When she was sure Martha was inside the cottage, she fell forward over her knees, head cupped in her hands in the dirt. "Whatever my lot, thou has taught me to say, It is well, it is well with my soul."

***

Conversation lagged at supper. News of the world seemed removed from them. Ida's taciturnity affected them all. Martha and Moses finished quickly, excusing themselves for a PBS special. Landis finished his coffee and Ida sipped the last of her wine. He reached over and with his thumb swiped under her eye. "You've been crying."

She swallowed and eyed the ceiling. "My heart is heavy. I'm feeling sad."

"About Martha?" he asked.

"Yes." Rising slowly, she carried the glass to the sink to rinse it. She turned slightly, extending her hand for him to pass his bowl and spoon. He rose to move near her, standing side by side at the sink. Ida leaned her body into his; he held firm and let her push.

"I can't let her see me like this," she whispered. "Please just tell them I'm not feeling well."

Ida retreated to her bedroom and sat on the edge of her bed. She wondered what to do next. She wanted to be strong but tonight she was weak. Landis entered and asked, "How about if I run some water for a bath? You can just relax. I don't need to stay tonight."

"No, please stay," she said. "A bath would be nice, yes. But please stay."

He ran the water in the tub and said he'd go visit with Martha and Moses for a while.

The hot water immersed her in her own fatigue. Breathe in, breathe out. It seemed that pesky little thoughts eddied around the grander serenity Ida was attempting to bask in. Despair wanted in. People were always getting sick and dying. People always were leaving.

Ida dried off quickly in the coldness of the evening and put on her flannel pajamas. The bedside lamp was still on as she closed her eyes. Opening them a few hours later there was only darkness. Her hand reached for Landis, solidly secure beside her. A sequoia if there ever was one.

"Will you just hold me?"

The guilt of her self-absorption spiraled away into a state of aching grace. This was comforting. She drew strength from this connection. She could do this for Martha. Hold her in her metaphorical arms, in the strength of the old growth, still rooted in the deep past, still receiving sustenance from the undergrowth, the community. She had not abandoned her friend. She had not forsaken her. She was still there. She would be there.

It is well, with my soul. It is well. It is well. With my soul.

TWO

Around sundown on Saturday, a young man drove up in a white compact car. Ida and Martha watched from their front porch as he got out and walked the perimeter of the farmhouse, holding his phone in one hand and gesturing with the other. Elsa bounded out the backdoor, confronting him, hands on her hips.

"Okay, I'm nosy enough to want to hear this." Martha stepped off the steps and strode out to the lane with Ida on her heels. The appearance of the young man could be summed up in one word: hipster. He wore the skinny jeans and the black rimmed glasses of the clones she'd seen in Boulder coffee shops.

"What are you doing here?" Elsa demanded.

"I came to see if you were okay. You didn't show at school. You weren't answering my texts. Are you okay?" He put his phone in his pocket and took a few steps towards Elsa.

"Stay right where you are." Elsa's tone was calm and firm. "I'm fine."

"So… are you pregnant? You look pregnant. What's going on, Elsa?"

"I might be. It's not your concern."

The young man shook his head in disbelief. "A baby. It's mine, isn't it? That's why you weren't returning my texts."

Elsa just regarded him coolly. She folded her arms in front of her chest. "Look, we decided it was over between us. And it is. You need help and I'm not the one to give it to you."

"I need help?" he asked incredulously. "Like you don't?"

"I'm not the one with anger issues. You're the one who exploded."

"But you're the one with lying issues. And here you are again...lying about having a baby."

"Who's the one who gets all abusive and out of control?" Elsa said.

He looked away. He shoved his phone into a back pocket. "I'm getting help. I've got it under control. But Jeez, Elsa...a baby! You didn't have the decency..."

"You don't need to get involved. I'm having this baby on my own. You don't owe me anything." Her eyes glared at him.

"We need to talk. This is crazy."

"You're crazy. I didn't ask you to come."

"But I love you. You know that. I can be there for you – and the kid. My kid!"

"Look, Corey, I don't want you in my life anymore. I told you I don't love you – and I don't want your love. Please, please just go away!" she pleaded, her voice rising.

"No! I'm not going anywhere till we talk!" he shouted back. "This is stupid!"

Romona came swinging out the backdoor, walking with deliberation to stand tall beside Elsa. She glared at Corey asking in an even tone, "Everything okay here?"

Elsa replied, "This is Corey. Remember I told you about him. He thinks he's the father."

Corey looked at her bewildered. "You're saying I'm not the father?"

Elsa sighed. "Look, Corey. I can't handle you being in my life. I've moved on. If you don't leave on your own, I'm calling the police."

Romona held out her phone. "I'm dialing now. You heard Elsa."

"Who are you, anyway?" He addressed Romona.

Elsa grabbed Romona's hand as if to subdue her. "She's my friend and anyway, it's not your business who my friends are."

Romona repeated, "I'm dialing. It's ringing."

Corey threw up his hands. "I'm just the father. Guess a father doesn't have any rights anymore?" Romona was speaking into the phone. "We've got a serious dispute out here at the Dusky Grouse ranch. A stalker."

"A stalker? Because I came to visit you?" He looked from one to the other.

"Just go now and leave us alone! Don't you come back here either." Elsa's voice hardened.

"Okay, I'm leaving, but you still owe me the chance to at least talk." He hurried to his car and got in.

Elsa walked up to the driver's side. "This borders on stalking, Corey. I saw your car here yesterday. I'm serious. Stay the hell away from this place."

"I still love you Elsa," was all he said as he turned on the motor and pulled down the lane spinning wheels in the dust.

Elsa acknowledged Ida and Martha observing the situation, and called to them, "So you witnessed that, right? That's Corey."

"And why is he here now?" asked Martha.

"*He thinks* he's the father." Elsa said matter of fact as if it explained everything.

"Is he?" asked Ida. "Is he the father?" She couldn't stop herself. Elsa had told several different accounts about this pregnancy and nothing seemed beyond reason.

"Yes," she replied defiantly. "Yes, he is."

"And the other young men?" Martha left it hanging.

Elsa stood her ground, arms crossed, her feet firmly planted. "I made them up. Corey's the father. He's the only one I slept with. But he has anger issues. *And he threatened me.*"

"That's a whole lot of stuff right there," Martha stated. "I don't know what to believe anymore. He may be trouble but it's troubling how many lies you've been telling. I know it's not my dementia this time."

"She just wants to have this baby on her own and raise it without him around. She knew he'd cause trouble if she told him," interjected Romona.

"Well maybe he should cause trouble if you're keeping him away from his baby. Seriously, Elsa, where is your heart?" asked Martha.

"You haven't seen him get angry. He's irrational." Elsa shook her head. "I mean, I'm scared of him when he's off his meds."

"We need to tell your mom and Moses and Rusty and anyone else who might be here if he returns." Martha was visibly shaken. "We don't want him threatening you, but there ought to be a way to sit down rationally with him."

"I don't want him to have any say in this." Elsa was not ready for conciliation. "I'll tell Mom about him but no one else needs to get involved. This doesn't concern the two of you. Come on, Romona." The two huffed away into the farmhouse letting the screen door slam behind them.

Martha turned to Ida. "Montana fires. They flare up in all seasons."

"This is not going to be an easy one to put out," responded Ida.

THREE

Martha was right. Montana fires flare up in all seasons.

The drought of the summer hoisted itself into the last weeks of September and with no rain in sight, the governor declared a state of emergency with high danger levels for fires throughout the state. Roads were re-routed. Firefighters worked day and night. Smoke clouds filled the horizons. The end of September normally signaled cooler nights but with the drought had come unusual warmth.

The four older friends sat on the porch of the cottage one evening, attempting to watch a sunset amidst the smoky skies. Four rocking chairs faced the southwest pasturelands with the Madison mountains as the backdrop.

"Look at the sun descending behind that mountain," said Ida.

"Yep," said Martha. "Like a dirty egg going down."

"It's disgusting. Nothing but brown dust," said Landis. "It's like those old photos of the dustbowl during the Great Depression."

Moses struggled to stand upright from his rocker. Once on his feet he shuffled over the wide plank boards, hobbling down to where the lane divided to get a good look at the southwest pasture. He stood still, his eyes scanning the horizon. Landis joined him, gazing intently past the edge of the field. They appeared to be conferring with one other when Landis turned abruptly and shouted, "Call 911. There's a prairie fire!"

Ida ran to the guest house where Annie and Rusty were at the door. "Call the fire department! There's fire in the southwest pasture."

Panic broke. Everyone scattered. Annie and Rusty pulled a hose from the side of Tamarack Lodge and sprayed down the walls south and west. Moses and Martha rounded up the horses, moving them quickly to the north pasture, far away from the potential flames. Landis grabbed the garden hose from the side of the farmhouse forcing jets of water onto the bunkhouse cabins. The farmhouse was stone but the cabins were pine. Ida pulled Peabody into the cottage before returning to help with a bucket brigade.

An unbroken linear fire worked its way across the pasture grass, ravenously taking in the dry prairie. Sparks went airborne but with no wind, they'd float briefly and waft back down. Meadow birds flew up, scattering to the woods.

It was possibly fifteen minutes but it seemed an hour when the fire truck rambled up the lane to park between the lodge and the old house. Burly workers scrambled off the truck with tanks attached to their backs, running into the field. They spread out, warriors advancing in a line, spraying and beating back the reddish orange flames.

A police car appeared as containment was at hand. Black smoke hovered over the ranch. The fire was out but the smell lingered, along with a haze that melded into darkness. They walked the field to see it for themselves. Two policemen scoured the edge of the woods. They traced the fence line back towards the guest house, stopping here and there to examine the ground.

The firefighters packed all the equipment back in the truck, grabbed bottles of water, and stood waiting for instructions. The ranch crew gathered around wondering what had happened, and in their state of shock, asked what to do next. The uniformed officers approached the group wearily.

"You have any idea about the cause?" asked one.

"We're hoping you tell us," said Rusty.

"Well, it was set by someone. Did you see anybody out there?"

They looked to Moses since he'd been the first out to notice the fire. "I couldn't say for sure. I saw something sparking up. Landis was the one who called it. My reaction time's kind of slow."

"I saw the line of smoke first, then flames," added Landis. "I couldn't say for sure I saw somebody out there."

The fire chief nodded. "We walked the perimeter. There's evidence. Probably a lighter he carried with him. This was intended to do damage for sure."

"Whoever did this meant for us to feel fear," replied Moses.

"What do you mean?" asked Martha.

"I mean somebody did this to create fear, for us to be afraid, set us on edge," said Moses.

"Corey!" declared Elsa. They looked at her.

"What?" asked Annie. "You really think Corey is capable of this?"

"If he was angry enough," said Elsa. "I told you – he's got issues."

"I'll need to get this individual's name and any way we might reach him," said the older policeman, whipping out his pad and pen. "Do the rest of you know this young man? Would you agree?"

"It's plausible," said Annie. "He could have done this."

Moses cleared his throat and spoke, "I believe this was done by someone with more malice in his heart. I suspect this was intended as a message to me." He turned to the sheriff. "Perhaps you could track down the whereabouts of someone who had a motive to scare me. First name's Trent. I'll give you more information."

The two policemen stepped aside to confer with Moses.

"Who's this Trent guy?" asked Annie.

"The son Moses didn't know about. Miriam's son she gave up for adoption."

"He's the guest I asked to leave. He bullied Moses," explained Ida.

"He was a jerk!" added Romona. "That greedy s.o.b. threatened Moses!"

"He was definitely mean enough to have a motive," said Ida.

"But I wouldn't put it past Corey in a certain state of mind," said Elsa. "He's capable of being nasty and vindictive."

"Tell the sheriff. They'll check it out." Annie was ready to call it a night. "I'm going to make dinner. Anyone else want to join us?" The others agreed, forgoing their supper menu for a dinner with the group. Thanking the firefighters one by one, they trooped to the farmhouse together to sort through the frightening event.

The fire chief nodded to the police and signaled to the brigade to get ready to pull out. It had been a long evening.

***

Both suspects were found within the next few days and both denied anything to do with setting a fire. Corey had the alibi of being back on the university campus at the time with witnesses substantiating his story. He was still taking classes in Missoula. The man called Trent had no such alibi and was found with an empty kerosene can in his car. The police found two lighters in the glove compartment. Trent was ready with excuses. He'd used the kerosene in a lamp. The lighters were for a campfire (prohibited during this fire season), and he was a smoker. Not a crime to smoke, he said, if I'm smoking in my own car. He was taken in for further questioning. Before the night was over he was charged with arson. A history of previous arrests indicated a long pattern of abusive threats and possibly other incidents of arson. Moses was right. The person who did this meant to bring fear. There would be a trial but the police were confident with his history he would be found guilty. He could no longer harass Moses and he would no longer threaten the ranch.

FOUR

It rained on Ida's birthday.

During the night she'd awakened to thunder and lightning. She heard wind blowing through the trees and raindrops falling heavily on the roof. This was too exciting to stay in bed. She opened the front door to feel and hear the fresh storm air. Temperatures were dropping but it felt good. She eventually returned to bed, lying awake and listening to the pounding sounds. She thought the storm one of the best birthday presents she could ever have.

Awakening in the morning, she didn't feel a year older. Still when she threw back her comforter, shivered, and said, "I feel *chilled*," there was a vision of her mother in her later years saying the exact same thing. "Aren't you *chilled*? I'm *chilled*."

She padded into the kitchen in her pajamas and slippers to be welcomed by a dozen red roses in the middle of the kitchen table with a card propped against the vase. *"Someone told me women like roses on their birthday so here you go. Love, Landis."*

She hadn't told him. She hadn't told anyone. How had Martha remembered – of all people? But it had to have been

Martha. No one else knew. Had he left these roses with Moses to put out? It was too early for the florist to deliver.

Pouring herself a cup of coffee she sat down to ponder the mini-mystery. How had these roses gotten here on her kitchen table so early in the morning?

Then she saw him coming from the guest house. What was he carrying? Was it a basket? Opening the front door, he bustled in with Peabody, exclaiming, "You're not supposed to be up yet!"

"Nobody told me that," she retorted. "What are you doing here?" Whatever he was carrying held the aroma of melted cheese and eggs.

"I'm bringing you breakfast! Happy Birthday!" And he leaned over to give her a quick peck. Unpacking became a dramatic scene: he rolled out three blue placemats, pulled silverware from the kitchen drawers, arranged plates and mugs just so, set up the small glasses of orange juice. He proceeded to lift the quiche from the basket with one hand, waving its exquisite flavors into the air with his other. A basket of baklava appeared. Last was a bowl of sautéed mushrooms, broccoli, and onions.

"I knew you couldn't consume a decadent breakfast unless there was some kind of veggie offset."

She beamed at him. "You're kind of sweet, do you know that?"

"Did I surprise you?"

"Absolutely. Well done!"

"Seventy-three is it?" he asked.

"Looks like I'm three years older than you now."

He looked chagrined. "Sorry to disappoint, but I snuck in my birthday when I was in Poland. The ratio of our years remains the same."

"When was it? What date?"

"August 1."

"Rats! I missed your birthday! Can I share mine with you today?"

"That's just silly," he said. "but if it makes you happy, I'm in."

"Yes, that would make me happy. But I'm happy you're here this morning. I'm happy it rained like the dickens last night. Just brimming over with happiness!"

"Okay, enough of that," he said, sitting down to eat with her. "Where's Martha? Should we wait for her?"

"She's out for her morning chores. We'll save her some."

"There's plenty. Let me get a serving spoon." He jumped up and opened a drawer as if he knew his way around this kitchen.

"Where did the baklava come from?" She eyed him with a smile. "I know you have many talents but baking something like this is not one of them."

"They're from a bakery in Missoula. I think it's owned and run by refugees."

"Really? Where are they from?"

"I don't know. Syria? Afghanistan."

"I'd like to go to that bakery sometime."

"I'm sure you would. You'd be their number one supporter."

"What's that supposed to mean?"

He held up his hands. "Peace. I come in peace. But I know your views by now. You'll say something like Jesus would be hanging out in that bakery too."

She laughed. She couldn't help it. "I might say Jesus would be the one advocating for free bread for the homeless outside the bakery, to break bread *with them*."

"See?" he said. "Your Jesus was such an activist."

"It was because he was such an outspoken activist that he got himself killed."

"And in your world there isn't any evil intent. If everyone would just be kind, there'd be no social problems."

"That's just not true. I'm not that naive," she responded. "But just because someone looks different or practices a different religion doesn't mean I have to be afraid of them or distrust them. It takes a lot of courage to get here to make a living."

"But why come to our country if there are so many other more tolerant places?" he quizzed.

"*Our* country?"

"Yeah. Our country."

"Not the Iroquois or the Sioux or the Crow?

He just looked at her blankly. "Seriously? Yes, this country, that *we white males* stole from them."

She took a few bites of the egg dish. "This is excellent!" She put down her fork. "You fought in a war that made no sense and many Vietnamese and Cambodians came here. Did you feel this way about them?"

"I don't hate anyone. I know they're trying to earn a decent living and maybe save enough money to go back."

"If there is ever some semblance of peace for them to return to."

"I'm trying to learn tolerance too. Doesn't it bother you the way they treat women?"

"Ooh boy, okay. Most religions are oppressive. Let me tell you. Mennonite women historically were under the thumb of men - like all other faiths. The men dictated how much women could participate in worship. The men prescribed how they should dress. The men controlled the money. Marriage was for women to be submissive. They always claim it's Biblical."

Landis simply listened. She had to get this off her chest. He might not have meant to set off this firestorm, but there it was.

"Like all religions, we've had sex abusers and cover-ups up by men in authority. We've had the loud voices calling LGTBQ sinners, calling women who've had abortions murderers. Using scripture as a weapon. Pious men. Who decides who's in and who's out? Casting stones all over the place – without looking at the specks in their own eyes." She looked out the window, suddenly aware that she was pounding the podium.

Landis chewed on his food silently. When enough time had lapsed he said, "So yes, I agree sometimes people have to flee their own countries. I think our educational system would be a huge draw."

Ida was back. "May not be much to go home to," she said calmly.

"It took years but Thailand and Vietnam are now top tourist spots."

"Have you ever thought of going back?" she asked.

"I'm not sure I want to do that. I know lots of guys who have, and they said it's kind of redemptive." He caught her eye. "I suppose I could use some redemption don't you think?"

"Redemption?" she asked softly. "I'm not going there. That's entrapment!"

He just smiled at her. She picked up her fork. "This is really delicious, Landis."

"Happy Birthday, Ida," he said.

OCTOBER

ONE

One afternoon in early October, Ida encountered a group of strangers out in the west pasture, busily engaged in attracting and catching birds. They were from the Teton Raptor center, making their way through Montana, rescuing injured birds and tracking the flights of eagles.

Ida watched as they placed a helmet on the pigeon's head and dressed it in a protective vest as part of their concession to PETA (People for the Ethical Treatment of Animals). The pigeon was sent out as bait for eagles which, with their "eagle eyes," they could spot from miles away. Theoretically, the eagle would swoop in for the pigeon, and once netted would be banded with a GPS tracking device and released to see how far it might fly. They had recorded eagles as far away as Colorado within a twenty-four-hour period. Usually, an average daily flight was around a hundred miles, give or take wind conditions.

Guests like these folks gave her hope for the world. They were so earnest in their desire to help all winged creatures and excitedly dragged Ida to their van where three injured birds would be transported back for care before releasing them into the wild again. She peered into the cages of a Northern Goshawk, a Prairie Falcon, and a Great Horned Owl. "They're spectacular creatures. What causes them to get hurt?"

"Usually they fly into something – like a glass window or maybe barbed wire," said one of the women. "Look at this owl and you'll see it has a broken leg.."

"Sometimes we pick up sick birds that have eaten something poisonous or maybe human trash."

"Really?" asked Ida. "They eat litter from the side of the road?"

"Yes, frequently. Usually they recover on their own."

"And what do you do with all this information you collect?"

"It's entered into a national database," explained an older volunteer. "There are a lot of us wildlife re-habbers!"

"Well, I personally am very grateful you are," said Ida. "Thank you for this good work."

She needed a long walk. Calling for Peabody, they set off together through the north woods. Sunlight filtered through the autumn trees revealing palettes of leaf colors; masterpieces of spontaneous art – here and gone. The yellow leafed aspens with their ghostly white trunks contrasted sharply with the darker green hues of the Douglas firs and Lodgepole pines. Peabody was frantic in his quest for new smells. Squirrels skidded away from the marauding canine in playful hide and seek. Branches blown down from the recent storms scattered across the terrain, and several trees had uprooted and fallen across the trail. Maybe Landis could come out with his chain saw to take care of those.

Back at the cottage she found a bottle of Spanish wine someone had given them. She opened the refrigerator looking for leftovers. She was hungry for an autumn dish with root vegetables. Maybe there were sweet potatoes and red beets in the pantry.

Martha came through the house, passing by her without speaking, on her way to take a shower. When she returned, clean and groomed, she was in her flannel pajamas. Taking a glass from the shelf, she helped herself to the wine, sipping it silently while sniffing the hodgepodge curry on the stove.

"This smells good! Anything I can do?"

"You could set the table."

Martha looked at the labels on the cupboard and located "dishes." She took out two. "I think Moses will be eating with us tonight," Ida said. Martha nodded and added a plate and silverware for three.

At dinner Ida shared about the little pigeon with the helmet and talon-proof vest sent out as a decoy to attract eagles. The entire bird rescue operation was inspiring to her, although she admitted the wild birds scared her.

"Birds can be mean," said Martha. "I've been attacked by sand cranes before, especially when they're in their gangs."

"Well, I have to tell you about my afternoon," said Moses. "I have a bird story too. That old wild turkey came around by the corral again, the same one that laid her babies near the shed last year. I steered clear of her all right, but when I came round the front side there she was coming right at me."

"What'd you do?" Martha asked.

"I stopped and stood still as a mouse. She got all aggressive and starts coming at me with her whole back up, making those protective motherly noises. I stood my ground. So she struts toward me, backs away, then comes towards me again, then away. She did this little dance for a while till all of a sudden she comes two-stepping up to me and drops a feather at my feet. Just like that! Then does an about-face and struts away with her old fanny up. That darned old turkey gave me a feather!"

They were amazed. None of them were inclined to read much into it. Still it was a feather gift.

After the evening meal was cleared away, the three gathered in the living room to sit in their favorite chairs. They'd just read quietly until one of them had something to share with the others. It was a good half hour later when Moses closed his book and remarked philosophically, "I read something about how time goes fast both in the beginning and in the end of our lives. I think I can attest to the truthfulness of that observation."

Both women looked up, startled by his serious tone. Ida leaned toward him to speak to his musings. "I guess I never thought much about our beginning days on earth, but now that you mention it, a baby does a whole lot of learning and growing those first few weeks. Time must whiz by."

"That's right," Moses nodded, "and now here I am an old man and though my days sometimes seem long, they're going by me like a speeding train. Who would have thought I'd be a father *and* a grandfather at the age of eighty-five? It may be some kind of blessing but it's just tiresome. I don't mean to complain." He sat reflecting for a moment and then slowly began humming to himself.

"What's that you're singing?" Martha asked.

"Ah it's an old timey hymn. It just keeps playing in my head. 'And I can't feel at home in this world anymore.'" He hummed a few bars and repeated the line "And I can't feel at home in this world anymore."

His left hand encircled his right wrist as he often took his sitting pulse in the evening. Closing his eyes, he took a deep heaving breath, and laid his head to rest against the back of the soft sofa cushion. He stirred slightly. "Martha," he said in his matter-of-fact voice, "I think I'm dead."

"You think you put in enough work today, do you?" she teased. "You're lucky if I pay you for your slack ass."

"Moses!" Ida called out. She jumped up and stepped in front of him. *Was his chest moving?* She picked up his wrist and held it. "Martha, I think he's dead. Really!"

The two women tugged his body onto the floor where Ida began CPR with the flat of her palms pumping as she counted. "Call 911!" *Just pump, no more mouth to mouth,* she recalled. Ten. Twenty. Pump pump pump. Thirty.

Martha frantically dialed 911 and phoned the farm-house. Then she was back on her knees shoving Ida out of the way, her palms on Moses's chest. Pumping. Counting. Pumping. Martha put her lips on his and breathed.

Behind them Annie rushed in, leaned over the taut body and checked for a pulse. Martha continued to press and pump. Twenty-eight. Twenty-nine. Thirty. Breath. Breath.

Annie shook her head. Ida put her hand on Martha's shoulder.

Moses was gone. What had he said? *"Martha, I think I'm dead."* He had called it.

***

The body they called Moses was taken away.

Martha and Ida tied themselves to the living by sitting with others through the evening and the next few days. People deposited meals. Deaths in small communities brought out the best recipes for frozen casseroles.

No therapy, no medication, no humor, no booze eases the death of a friend in the ordinariness of our daily lives. Moses had been with them, then he was not. His body, his shell, had remained in the room but not Moses. He had fled the scene, into the drift, somewhere they couldn't follow.

They looked up the hymn that the mind of Moses chose to share with them in his last moments. "This world's not my home, I'm only passing through." They tried to make sense of the language of angels beckoning from Heaven's shore. The loneliness of his life was between the lines; he had only shown them serenity and solace. He had been their Moses, guiding them through the wilderness of this life by his gentle strength of character.

No matter how often Ida sat with the dying and with their families, there was no normalcy to the unraveling. Each loss tore a tangible, jagged piece from life's fabric, each so remarkably made. The threads that run this way and that, webbing through and beyond, were often not apparent until after death. And this was the true mystery. How it takes an ending of one's life to see, really see, through that glass darkly to the immense weaving, and to accept finally there is more to this life than just us.

TWO

The bedroom in the cottage where Moses had moved reflected the sparseness of his austere life. His few shirts and pants hung tidily on hangers. The bureau drawers were neatly organized with socks and under things. An old green trunk contained two quilts and a well-worn comforter. By his bed was the book *The Bartender's Tale* by Ivan Doig. A ragged, well-used Bible sat on his desk atop a stack of papers. A will, notarized and legal, indicated Moses had taken pains to ensure that half of the inheritance money from Miriam would be placed in an educational trust fund for his grandson, a grandson he had never met. Moses had found a way to bridge the anger and distrust from his own son to ensure his grandson had money for college.

The other half of the inheritance was designated to a market fund for easy withdrawel specifically for Martha's medical expenses. Annie, the executor, would use her discretion in paying the bills, but Moses must have had an inkling of the high cost of extended health care.

Moses had expressed wishes to be cremated. Ida researched online for biodegradable urns with pre-mixed soil and seedlings. The directions read like a recipe on a soup can for creating that special casserole. Spoon cremated remains into pre-mixed soil, mix lightly, pot the entire planter in the earth, then add water and sunlight. Let the dish cook in the ground over the winter and expect a sprouting of a hardy tree in the years ahead. Moses would have appreciated this rebooting of growth. Landis helped select a Douglas fir that would acclimate to the forests on the ranch.

"Let's take a ride into Bozeman this afternoon," Ida said to Martha one day during lunch. "I want to purchase some potted flowers for the Moses service. We can keep them as houseplants through the winter and plant them next spring."

"We also need a few things at the grocery store too. And I found a recipe of my mother's that I'd like to try."

"For the Moses meal? Is it a casserole?"

"It's potato salad. She used to make it with celery and some kind of seeds." Martha got up from the table to look in her recipe file on the counter. She returned with an index card. "Yep, here it is. It calls for celery seed. Do you think we can find that?"

"If your mom found celery seed in Kansas, I dare say we'll get lucky here in Montana. If not, I'll send away for it. There's nothing we can't find online nowadays."

"Okay, I'm putting this recipe back in the box. Help me remember that. I'll go get ready. When do you want to leave?"

"Let me finish making a grocery list. I'll brush my teeth and then we can go."

"Good! I don't want to hang around this empty old house too long today."

***

The hunt for celery seed was not successful. Martha was clearly irritated by the disappointing limited stock of spices in the store. Ida reassured her she could order it online. The Moses service was still a few days away.

They picked up the few remaining items and headed to the check-out. A line for the one open cashier meant they'd have to use the automated check-out. Ida swiped her store card and Martha placed their recycled bag on the counter. The robotic voice stated: *Please wait, help is on the way.*

"Oh Lord," Martha exclaimed. "I put the bag down before it told me to."

An attendant strolled over and swiped his manager's card to erase the damage. "Thank you for the help," said Ida.

They meticulously scanned each item before placing the product in the bag, not wanting to be called out by the automated cashier sentinel. Despite their attempts to be careful, something triggered the warning voice: *An unexpected item is in the bag. Please wait for assistance. An unexpected item is in the bag. Please wait for assistance.*

Ida looked at Martha. "Did we put something in there?" She checked the screen. "Nope."

An unexpected item is in the bag. Please wait for assistance.

Martha searched for the attendant. He was talking with another cashier, unaware and unconcerned. "I wish we could turn up the volume on this thing. Maybe if they'd hear it all over the store we'd get help." They waited a few minutes more. Ida walked over to him and pointed to their dilemma. He looked perturbed but came and swiped his magic card once again.

A bag of organic lemons really set the automatic scanner off. *Code not identified. Please set this item aside. Code not identified. Please set this item aside.* No lemons for you.

When they were nearing the end of their mission another glitch occurred. Again the voice rang out: *Please wait, help is on the way.*

The two women regarded the attendant now assisting a pretty young girl who'd apparently forgotten to put a shirt on over her bra.. Martha rolled her eyes at Ida. She called to the attendant, "Hey excuse us, but these old ladies over here need some help."

He said something to the girl who giggled. Another automated voice announced: *Unexpected item in the bag. Please remove the unexpected item from the bagging area.* The attendant swaggered to that checkout and pulled out an item, did his magic card swipe, punched a few numbers, and voila, it was fixed.

"He's a regular whiz with that card of his," remarked Martha.

He went back to chatting with the girl oblivious to the robotic drone at their checkout: *Please wait, help is on the way.*

"Oh, for God's sake! We don't need these things!" Martha picked up their recycled bag, turned it upside down and dumped the contents out on the belt. A grapefruit rolled across the floor. "Let's go. We don't need to be treated like this!"

Martha's civil disobedience, blunt and to the point, sent a charge of pluckiness up Ida's spine. The attendant hustled over to them before they exited the door, his voice urgent and apologetic. "Sorry ladies, let me help you pick these up."

Martha stopped and speechified to whoever was listening. "Look, I'm an old woman, but I'm not invisible! Don't treat me like you can't see me! I'm here. I'm alive, and dammit, I don't need to buy your crappy groceries in this one-horse store!" She turned on her heels for a grand finale, but abruptly pivoted back. *"And just for the record, you didn't even have celery seed!"*

Once safely ensconced in their car, but reeling from the audaciousness of the dramatic scene, Ida spoke. "I gotta say, Martha. You still have it. Nobody's going to make you go quietly."

"It just pissed me off." Martha said, staring glumly out the window. "I don't know where we're going to get groceries, but I am NOT going in that store again."

"I'll call Landis and ask him to pick up some stuff. He can do it on his way over tonight."

"Did I let out any obscenities?"

"I think the most offensive thing you said was something about a crappy one-horse store," confided Ida.

"A one-horse store?" Martha laughed. "What the heck is that?"

"I've heard the expression a 'one-horse town' but I think you invented a new insult."

"That was a pretty good scene, huh? Turning that bag upside down – dumping out all the groceries?"

"Improvisational genius!" Ida said.

"I'm blaming it on my Lewy Body stuff. And anyway, I probably won't remember any of this and you'll be left to mend the fences."

"You sure are getting mileage out of that diagnosis," Ida replied.

They stopped at the hardware store to select a few indoor plants and took pity on a ragged red geranium. Mums were plentiful and could be planted outside, so they stocked up on several of these for a variety of color.

"We have to clear space for all of our plants in the south window," Ida commented on the drive back. "Maybe we can bring in that small table from Moses's bedroom to put by the window."

Martha zipped up her coat and pulled the hood over her head. "I miss him."

"Dan?"

"Moses."

Ida nodded.

"He's been in my life longer than anyone else. I was closer to him than my own father."

"It does seem like that." The realness of his absence was here now.

"Dan's death feels like a splinter inside my heart that I can't get out, but Moses – his being gone feels like a logjam in there."

Ida drove on thinking. *Yes, that's grief, that's the pain all right.*

"I just took him for granted." Martha said. "I thought he'd outlive me…especially now with this stuff going on with me."

"You'll still hear his voice," Ida cautioned. "He'll be telling you what to do for a while yet."

"That's for sure. I can hear him right now telling me to buck up, stop feeling so sorry for myself. Get on with what needs doing."

"That's Moses."

Martha frowned and turned her body stiffly towards Ida. "And this may be hard to hear, but I know you wouldn't be here if Dan hadn't died. That sometimes really good things come from someone's death. I don't like to think it but you wouldn't be here with me if Dan hadn't died."

Dazed by this acknowledgement, Ida pulled the car off onto a side road and killed the engine. Martha continued. "Who knows what else? We might not have built the guest house or the cottage. Lots of good things have happened, and if Dan hadn't died we'd be doing the same old things."

"I suppose some of what you say is true. But if Dan had lived you'd be experiencing other things, good things too."

"Maybe, but you have to admit this has been a hell of a year. You coming back into my life at this stage of the game – who would've predicted? And Landis – you? Maybe we need to do that gratitude thing you like so much and maybe say, thanks Dan."

Ida lightly punched her friend's arm. "Not right, Martha. Even in jest. Not for someone who died."

"Oh you know Dan would get a kick out of it. In fact, I like to imagine God and Dan in cahoots with a gigantic board game in front of them, moving us little pieces around here and there."

Ida smiled. "So now Moses will be in the game as well. I'd be extra careful if I were you."

Martha finally laughed. "I know it. Moses *and* Dan *and* God. Yikes."

"They should focus their attentions on the Middle East instead of our puny little concerns, maybe even do something about income inequality?" Ida suggested.

"But we're much more fun to mess with. And now, with me forgetting things and losing control of my bladder and acting irrational – more irrational than usual – well, I say, bring it on!"

"That's the Martha I know and love!"

"We sure like to think there's a great spirit keeping watch over our lives, don't we?"

"Maybe watching's the wrong word, but yes, it's comforting. What does it all mean if we're not connected, if there isn't that mysterious interweaving?"

Both women fell into a contemplative mood sensing a change in themselves. And in the weather. Winds were picking up even as they sat in the car in the dusk of the day.

"Something's blowing in," said Ida.

"Yep. Better get on home."

"You okay now?"

"Yep. Let's go."

They made it home and into the house just before the storm broke. Thunder cracked directly above their cottage. As they scurried about shutting all the windows, Martha called out, "Now do you believe me about Dan and God?"

"And Moses!" Ida laughed.

"Moses most of all."

"What was your expression?"

"I said I'm ready to play. Bring it on."

***

THREE

The "Moses service" as they called it, was a gathering of his closest friends. His life had been celebrated on his birthday while he was alive. The "Moses meal" was one he would have enjoyed: barbecued chicken, potato salad (with celery seed!), baked beans, and all varieties of cookies.

Pastor Karen held a simple service with a few meditative words about death and holding onto the memories and replacing despair with hope. Her scripture reading was from Luke 6: 43-44. How you shall know someone by what comes from his or her heart – just as a tree is recognized by the kind of fruit it bears. A good person brings forth good things out of the goodness in his or her heart, just as evil comes from a closed heart.

Because he'd been asked Landis spoke a few prepared words about his old friend:

> "Moses, to me, was an old growth tree. In the midst of many storms – wind, fire, brimstone – he drew strength from his roots and stood taller, prouder. He sheltered others and looked for sustenance above, below, and all around him. Like old-growth trees, his later years were the ones which gave him deeper purpose and enriched his soul. He cared about all of you in a profound way. Think of the old-growth trees. Some become tall and wide and strong. Others are gnarly and twisted and short beauties. When they die they can remain upright a few years, still providing nourishment and shelter. When they do fall, finally lie down on the earth's floor, they

continue giving nutrients and homes to a diversity of life. And that's how I choose to see Moses. He had a hard-scrabble life in his earlier years, times when he was treated unfairly and with prejudice, but he weathered on. There were episodes when he would say he was at his worst. He called himself a sinner to me a number of times, and it was not to absolve himself of those deeds, but to become a better person by being honest with himself and others. He lived his life with dignity and integrity. So Moses, we'll think of you as that old-growth tree standing or falling, but still providing nourishment and shelter to us still living in the undergrowth. Because we are the undergrowth, privileged to have known this great giant.

An evening of shared stories about Moses followed, though he wouldn't have wanted the attention on him. Ida sought out Landis as everyone worked together stacking chairs and cleaning in the Tamarack lodge.

"That was really a beautiful tribute to Moses," she said gathering up empty cups and scattered plates. "Actually, it was quite deep."

"Okay, I'm going to stop you right there and ask you to repeat that 'cause I'm not sure I heard you correctly." He bent down to her ear. "Did you say you thought it was *deep*?"

She gave him a little push with her shoulder though her hands were full. "Yes! Deep! And even poetic! Where did that come from?"

He actually blushed and avoided her eyes. "I worked on that pretty hard."

She threw the trash in a receptacle and wiped her hands on a napkin before turning about to grasp both his upper arms in her hands. "It was beautiful, Landis. It was genuine and thoughtful and moving."

He looked at her then. "Do you think you can love me?"

"I do love you," she responded. "I thought it was obvious."

He nodded his head pensively. "It's okay if you don't, but I'd sure hate to lose you."

"But I do," she reiterated. "How can you think I don't?"

"It's nothing I suppose, just some old insecurities."

She took his hand in hers and squeezed it tight. "Please come stay with me tonight."

He smiled and put his arms around her, but something had shifted and she was unsettled. She did love him, didn't she? Why did he have to ask?

***

The bio-degradable pot with Moses's ashes and soil with the spruce seedling would nestle on the table near the sunny south window of the cottage along with the geranium and others keeping it company. In the spring when the earth was warmer, the planter could be potted near the aspen grove. His remains would mix with the earth and the seedling would, over time, sprout up to become another proud and tall Douglas fir.

FOUR

In late October, fickle temperatures had everyone wearing t-shirts one day and fleece the next. Landis wanted to take Ida north to the wheat and grasslands. He booked a cabin at a B and B ranch near Grassy Mountain, the last weekend before elk hunting season began.

They picked up groceries and supplies and headed north of Bozeman, past the "M" for Montana State blazed with white rocks into the side of a mountain, past the Drinking Horse Trail where Ida had gone with Martha and Peabody in the springtime. The highway opened up to wide-open spaces where fields of alfalfa and grasses stretched outwards for undulating miles before touching the far mountain ranges. The sense of space and earth and sky and lofty clouds were gathered into a balm, a geographic solace for their grief.

Their cabin was cozy with a kitchenette and a wood-burning stove. After dispensing with the bags, they bundled in coats, gloves, and hats and hiked out with the owner to call the horses in from the pasture. Landis knew the owners from his early days at the music festival held annually in July, in White Sulphur Springs.

"You'd like the music, Ida," he said. "We should come next year."

"How large is it?" she asked.

Landis looked to the owner of the B and B. "Got any estimates on crowd size at the last festival?"

"I think they said 16,000 last year, but those were totals over several days."

Landis glanced back at Ida. "Guess we won't come to that."

"I know I'd like the music. I just can't handle the crowds."

The horses galloped headlong towards them, the white gelding in the lead. Horses in motion were rhythmic expressions of fluidity and muscular strength. Ida had recently learned of the famed beloved Montana painter and sculpture, Charles Russell, who captured such beauty in his art. His attention to details, whether animals or people, illuminated the cultural times in which he'd lived. Russell depicted Western scenes with a realistic eye to all its peoples and didn't shy away from those of bloodshed or calamity.

That evening they scrubbed white potatoes and cooked them on the stove. Landis made a chili sauce. Ida steamed broccoli. Crusty rolls and sharp cheese made the meal complete. She had intentionally left wine behind but now she missed it. She found some apple cinnamon teabags in the cupboard. That would have to suffice.

A scratching sound had them thinking mice were sharing their space, but when Landis went outside for firewood, he spotted a thorny rose scraping the cabin logs. A fire was made in the little potbelly wood stove, warming the room quickly, and after dinner they put on pajamas to read on the bed with pillows bunched behind them.

"So I have a question for you," Ida said, tucking her legs under her.

"Okay, what's up?" Landis asked congenially. He bookmarked his place in the book with a finger.

She sipped her tea slowly. "I'm guessing you've been with many women."

"Oh oh," he sighed and closed his book, laying it on the bedside table. "Why do women always want to know that?"

"I thought it didn't matter but lately I'm curious. I'm thinking it's more than you can count on your two hands."

Landis studied the ceiling. She imagined he was wondering how much he should tell her. "I guess I went through two phases where yes, I did seem to find comfort in the arms of women, but not enough to get very involved."

"I'm listening," Ida replied. "Not judging, just listening."

"This is a two-way thing you know."

"What do you mean?"

"I can be just as curious about your past…what shall we call them? Relationships? Romances? Flings?"

"I don't have much to tell," she said, "but I think you might."

"I admit when I came back from Vietnam I slept around a lot. I told you I hitchhiked around the country. So you know that time period. Sex was pretty available. The other period of my life I'm not too proud of was after I divorced. I wasn't sober yet, just a bit crazy." He glanced at her. "It's your turn."

"You're leaving out all the details," she said.

"I'm not being evasive." He shrugged. "They're fuzzy memories."

She suddenly felt she was being nosy. Like a probing relative seeking family gossip. "I don't think I really need to know."

"And?" he asked stretching out on his back.

"What?"

"What about your previous…what should we call them? Exploits?"

"Exploits?" she laughed. She crinkled her face. "Sounds seedy."

"You started this."

"Okay," she said, I slept with a few guys. There was one really nice man but I just didn't feel that spark."

"Tell me. Why have you never married?"

"I knew this question would come up sometime." She plumped up the pillow behind her. "Psychoanalysis might reveal a deep scar, but let's just say I never found the right guy."

"Nothing to do with the patriarchal nature of the institution, then?"

"Well, there is that," she smiled. "But…well…it takes a lot of work to be intimate, and my work was intensely emotional. And I just got busy, in my routines. As I got older, more and more women joined me in my singleness."

"But you didn't marry the man you had the baby with?" he asked gently.

"He would never have married me," she said trembling.

Landis waited.

Tears welled in her eyes. "I was told a long time ago I wasn't good enough, pretty enough, and…I think that's the catch." She got out of bed to search for a tissue.

"Who told you that? Did he tell you that?"

She remained standing across the room. She'd shared too much. This still hurt after God knows how many years. She wasn't pretty enough. Good enough. He started to get out of bed but she said, "Please stay there. Please just give me a moment."

Her voice quivered. "I didn't think I'd still feel this self-pity. I know better, but how…why…do I still get that feeling of… unworthiness?"

He opened his arms to her. She walked slowly toward him and allowed him to pull her close. "Those old wounds will always be there. We can cover them up and make them look healed but they're cutting into us all of the time."

How could this hurt come bounding out of nowhere? Where has this bugbear been residing? She wept as he held her close.

"Ida, I've been with a few women, but they're not part of who I am now. They are lost memories – like some town I might have passed through in my life. What matters now to me is you and trying to find ways to bring you some happiness. Can we leave it at that?"

She thought she might as well get this out in the open now. She stepped away from him and asked bluntly, "What about that last town you passed through?"

"Shelby?" He sighed, dropping his arms. "One night. It was one night only. And it was the night I came to see you at the guest house and you were preoccupied with the old Swede."

"You said you were there to meet Moses."

"I said that, but I came into the house to find you. I knew you did the social hour. I tried to talk to you, but you seemed to think I was making fun of you."

"I remember that evening. I felt later like I had rebuffed you, but I just didn't believe you were really interested in me."

He looked down at his hands. "So, I'm ashamed to say I licked my wounds in that rejection by going to see Shelby."

"So it's my fault?"

"You know I'd never say that. I was inept in my attempts to get you to notice me. But I did try and you kept that door shut. I'm just being honest. That's the only time I was with Shelby. That was the first and last time."

She knew she was being adolescent. She had pushed him to tell her. "And Shelby was interesting and available and maybe even in pursuit of you?"

He sighed. "It's flattering yes. But like you said about you and your 'nice man,' I didn't get that spark." His eyes opened wider then. "Not like with you."

She went to stand in front of the fire. She had wanted to know and he had been truthful. Why had she wanted to know this? What difference did it make? He just wanted her to be happy with him now. She'd needed to know because she cared. That was her truth.

She padded back to the bed and hopped up beside him. "You're right. Those past relationships, past encounters – whatever – they are like some towns we drove through. I'm not sure I really like that metaphor. But it might have to do for now."

Landis took her hand and held it in his. "How about if I say you're more like home than a town? How about if you're that place I want to come back to?"

"I'd say you talk pretty sweet, cowboy."

"I'm trying," Landis replied. He lay down and raised the comforter, inviting her to join him. She got in quickly and lay on her back. His eyes were closed.

"I think I'm kind of grateful to all those towns in your past."

He was groggy. "How's that?"

"You learned from those towns." She smiled and flipped off the lamp switch. "They taught you a few things about women."

He reached over and pulled her close. She wanted Landis to understand her love for him without having to put it in words. She trusted him. This was a new vulnerability in a late stage of development because what the heck, she didn't have time left on earth to give a damn about keeping her emotions safe and tight. And she liked that the matter of age had not detracted them from exploring and appreciating the way they felt emotionally or physically with one another. She liked the sexual sensation of the softness of their bellies - like Buddhas lying in repose and the exploring of ridges and wrinkles. Just lying beside him sometimes seemed to create a molecular reaction in her. *Here I am after so many years alone, baffled by the tumbleweeds of time and space, here in this place, still emotional, still spiritual, still sexual.* How could it be that it was happiness that overwhelmed and left her shaking and not loss, not grief, not suffering?

The next morning, they took their time getting up and puttering about the cabin. They'd planned a drive to Martinsdale to the Bair Family Museum, a tourist destination for this rural part of the state. Charlie Bair, an entrepreneur from the turn of the century, had made a fortune by being in the right place at the right time not once, but twice. His wife and two daughters traveled the world collecting ornate and downright bizarre furnishings for their country home. Now the home was a museum with a gift shop and painting gallery where even some of the works of Charles Russell, the beloved Montana artist, were displayed.

By Sunday the temperatures had spiked up into the seventies to become a perfect Montana day. They took a meandering route, venturing west and south toward Townsend, through livestock grazing country. At Three Forks off of I-90 where the Gallatin, the Jefferson, and the Madison converge to form the Missouri River, they stopped for lunch. Ida had an impression of greening everywhere in this lush valley.

Later, as they approached the Dusky Grouse, the sun's rays intensified, shining through the passenger window of the jeep onto Ida's face. She was drowsy from the rhythmic ride and the warmth of the afternoon.

"This sun is really bright. One would never know it was October! Do you have an extra pair of sunglasses?" she asked, clicking open the glove compartment.

No sunglasses but a handgun bounced on top of car registration papers.

"It's not even locked?"

"This is Montana. It doesn't have to be locked, "answered Landis. "All you need is a permit – and that's only in town."

"Well, there's nothing like the sight of that thing to dampen my mood," she stated, slamming the compartment door shut. "I can't believe you still carry that thing around."

"That thing is a Glock 19 and it might save your life one day," Landis said matter of factly.

"Oh please, do not go there," Ida replied. "A gun is far more likely to kill or maim than to save a life."

"It's a protective device, much like a condom." Levity was his default gear.

"Oh my God," Ida rubbed her face with her hands. "That's not even funny."

"It's used in an emergency – to protect oneself…much like…well, you know."

"That analogy is so full of holes." She just kept shaking her head. "You're joking and I'm serious. I find it upsetting that you're still carting a gun around after all you know about me."

Landis obviously needed to be careful what he said. "What would you have me do with it?"

"They must have ways to dispose of them…or turn them into police departments.."

He didn't respond, his eyes focused on the potholed road. She squinted out the window; the sun still hot on her face. She opened the compartment again and lifted the cold object onto her open palm, not sure what to do. A sudden anger in her curdled and locked on the gun. She wanted to fling it out the window into a muddy ditch, into a deep swamp where it might sink into an abyss. There should be a black hole in the universe just for guns.

They drove up the lane to see Elsa and Romona on the front walk, arms folded, talking with Corey, his hands in his back pockets. The body language indicated civility.

"He's back. It looks like an interesting discussion," observed Ida. "I think you'd better pull up beside Corey's car so you don't block him in."

"Am I too close on your side?" Landis asked looking past her to the white car.

She opened her door and squeezed out between the two vehicles. She still had the gun in her hand. Landis hurriedly got out and met her at the front of the jeep.

"Ida, you can't just take my gun."

She held it in the palm of her hands, outstretched – *the holy sacrifice: a chiseled piece of freedom or an explosive delusion.* "Here," she said, holding the pistol flat. "*Take it!*"

Landis lifted the gun from her hand, grasping it firmly. He walked resolutely around her back to the passenger side where he opened the jeep and deposited his gun back where it had come from. He refused to look at her.

She pointed to the jeep. "I won't ride in it anymore as long as that thing is in there."

He unpacked the back silently, lifting out the bags belonging to her. Peabody came running to greet them, dancing between the two of them, giddy with delight that they'd returned. Ida surveyed the group by the porch. They were watching her. She didn't want to talk to Landis. Rubbing her palms on her jeans she approached them, still fuming.

Elsa called, "What the hell, Ida? A gun in your hands?"

"What's the world coming to?" teased Romona.

Ida tilted her head towards Landis. "I think he keeps it just for a visual aid – to get my goat." She wanted a change of topic. She strolled closer. "What's going on here?"

"Corey has returned." Romona understated. "We're engaged in peaceful dialogue."

Elsa added, "He still seems to think he has a say in my pregnancy."

"I'm definitely outnumbered now," Corey said. He sounded tired, eager to get the peace talks over with.

Ida extended her hand. "Corey, is it? I'm Ida." Her clinical social worker voice clicked on, an impersonation of someone in charge. "How about if we all sit down and talk this out?"

Corey looked to Elsa for a cue. When she pivoted and headed to the porch, Corey followed docilely but his eyes reflected uneasiness. Ida staked out a rocking chair while Elsa struggled to sit down on the top step. Romona edged in beside her, a hand resting on her knee. Corey continued to stand awkwardly, restlessly swaying, his hands now in the front pockets of his jeans.

"Let's get this all out," directed Ida, plunging ahead. "Elsa, maybe you could explain in your own words why Corey might be here and why he sounds so upset."

Elsa sighed. "Corey thinks he's the father. I did sleep with him and if I ever said I loved him it was way last year. I've changed. I don't know why he's here because I never contacted him. I don't need him. He's come every day the last three days bothering us, not leaving when we ask him to."

Ida looked to Corey. "Do you have anything to say?"

"I'm here because I never got any answers! Elsa and I were lovers and now she acts like I'm some kind of serial killer or something." His hands sunk deeper into his pockets.

Elsa looked away. "We slept together. We were hardly lovers."

"I have some problems, but it's not like you're so sane."

"I don't threaten people. I don't put wires up across roads to damage cars. I don't harass people because they don't do what I want!"

"She's not dangerous to herself or to others – like you are," added Romona.

Corey was silenced by their accusations. Everything they said was true.

Ida asked, "Did you put a wire across the lane, Corey?"

"It wouldn't have hurt anything. It's just that cheap jewelry wire."

"But why do that?" asked Elsa. "Who does that?"

"I was just mad. I just did it to get your attention." His hands were out now, on his hips.

"Well, you have our attention now, and it's not going to change anything. I can't make myself any clearer." Elsa picked up a broken stick and began stabbing the earth making random indentations.

"Look, I'm seeing a counselor," he said. "I'm getting help."

Elsa shook her head. "It doesn't matter. You and I are done."

"But why?" Corey whined. "You're not being reasonable."

"Oh, stop thinking it's about you!" Elsa blurted out. "I'm my own woman. I've moved on."

"I love you." Corey's hands were now out in front of him, palms open. "I still love you."

"Stop whining! I don't care! I don't want you around." Elsa heaved breathlessly as she pushed herself up to stand. "Look, you don't have to feel responsible! I can handle this on my own."

"But it's not right to shut me out." Corey's words were clear. He pounded his fist into his hand. "This isn't right. This is not right!"

"It's not your business." Elsa's face was flushed red. She threw the stick aside. "This is my body! My baby! You don't get to come here and tell me what to do."

"It's *my* baby too. I loved you. You loved me." His hands outstretched. "Please talk to me. Please, this is insane!"

Romona exploded, jumping up and yelling into Corey's face. "You're insane! She doesn't want you – or any man around here. I think it's time for you to get off this property!"

Corey narrowed his eyes at Romona and began taunting. "So what is this? A dyke ranch?" He looked past Romona. "What the hell Elsa?"

Elsa leaned into Romona and glared at Corey. "If I knew you were going to come around looking for me and getting all into this pregnancy, I would've had an abortion. You and I are no longer 'lovers' like you put it. We're not anything!"

Romona flung her arm around Elsa tightening the grip. She eyed Corey as if to say, *She's my lover now.*"

Corey stared from one to the other. Ida thought he might kick one of them, but he spun abruptly and tromped toward his car, his face flushed.

Romona giggled loudly, "Kind of melodramatic, don't you think?"

"He always wanted to be a drama major," added Elsa.

They watched as if in slow motion: Corey staring at the ground, thinking, not opening his car door. Suddenly he reached through the open jeep. He staggered back towards them waving the gun in his hand. It had taken less than ten seconds.

"What *are* you doing Corey?" Elsa yelled. Ida stood up and joined the younger women on the lawn.

"Just stop messing with me! You know you love me! Stop screwing around with me and this dyke girlfriend," he ranted, gesticulating with the gun in the air. "Stop this craziness! You know you love me. You know you do."

"Okay calm down, I'll talk with you. But put the gun down." Elsa tried to speak evenly but her voice shook.

"Put it down, Corey," Ida said as calmly as she could.

Corey cocked the gun. He knew how to use it.

Peabody, who never barked, never got excited, chose this time to exhibit his shadow self. Running full speed towards the object in Corey's hand, Peabody let loose a snarl, a long dormant, wolfish growl. Something snapped. Corey aimed the pistol at the dog and fired. The air chilled. Peabody collapsed. Not even a whimper.

They gaped at the unmoving dog, trying to fathom what had happened. Ida's hand went to her throat. Pounding resounded in her head. Martha and Landis came running from the stables. Annie and the ranch hands appeared, all staring in silence. Landis reacted first. He strode over and took the gun from the shaking hand of Corey.

"I'm sorry, I'm sorry, I'm sorry," Corey sobbed, falling to the ground next to Peabody. "I'm sorry, I'm sorry."

Ida knelt down by her old dog and touched his fur. He was dead. She crumbled over his body, embracing her old companion of so many years. *This was not happening. This could not be happening.* Landis carried the gun away and returned with a blanket from his jeep. He stood waiting until Ida sat back, then he bent down to help her tightly swath the old dog. The tears finally came as Landis lifted Peabody to carry him to the barn.

"Ida, he's gone. He's dead." Landis said as she followed meekly behind.

"I just want to be with him."

Landis led her to a stall where he laid the body in the straw. In pullng the blanket back, the bloody fur stuck to the wool cover. She patted the head of Peabody, feeling the coldness setting in. He was gone from her. Landis helped re-wrap the blanket and put out his hand to help her up. She disregarded it, standing up on her own.

"You *will* get rid of that gun," Ida commanded. "There is no place for that thing here – or in my life. If you want to remain in my life...Peabody, good old boy, is gone... and why?"

She turned abruptly to go back to the others, leaving him to ponder her words. It wasn't long before the jeep started up and she watched him drive away, *with his gun,* back to his cabin. She didn't even want to say good-bye to him tonight.

Martha was kneeling beside the young man curled on the ground, stroking his back much like she did her horses. There was a sing-song quality to her voice. "It's okay, it's over. It's okay." Soon she plopped down on the ground and Elsa came to sit beside her. Martha's hands patted the shoulders of the two young parents, one on either side of her. Eventually all three lay on their backs, the heads of

Elsa and Corey resting on Martha's legs – a three-pronged human star.

When the sheriff arrived, everyone bustled out to explain their point of view. Elsa leaned into Romona's arms as Corey was meekly led away.

"They're taking him to the hospital now," Martha said as she joined Ida. "Corey agreed to go and Elsa decided not to press charges at this point."

"How is Elsa?" asked Ida.

"Well, she seems calm now…She hasn't been honest with any of us. Surprise. Surprise."

"Old Peabody," Ida said to no one. They entered the darkened cottage, flipping on lights in the kitchen and living room.

"Yes, poor old Peabody. Just a good old soul. I know you loved that dog."

Martha opened the refrigerator and took out a tuna salad. Ida spread bread slices and they created sandwiches for themselves, eating while standing up by the counter.

"I just can't believe he's gone," Ida said. "Shot with a gun. What was wrong with that boy?"

"He's in love and he can't have that love. He's in agony," Martha mumbled with her mouth full. "Not much different from grief is it?"

Ida regarded Martha with bafflement. How did she come out with such astute observations? Martha, who let life slide over her and was now living with a syndrome that left her off kilter most of the time. Yet she'd been the one to arbitrate and console in the crisis.

"You were the saving grace today," Ida said. "You were the voice of calm when the rest of us were in shock."

"Well, maybe it's my Lewy Body Dementia kicking in. It's gotta' be good for something."

"It was you. It was purely you out there."

Martha stuffed the rest of her sandwich in her mouth. "I'm tired. I'm going to bed."

"Don't forget to brush your teeth," Ida called out as Martha waved her away.

She opened the front door and called for Peabody. *Damn habit.* Her entire body ached in the loss of him, his absence a sad presence.

She thought about Landis. An ultimatum in a relationship is never a good tactic. She had been furious and hurt and adamant about her high moral ground. What had she said? *You'll do this for me if you want to stay in my life.* Her world was spinning much too wildly lately what with the sudden death of Moses and the prognosis for Martha and now her old companion dog gone. The centrifugal force might be throwing her off. What were Martha's words? "He's in love. He can't have his love. He's in agony. Not much different from grief."

FIVE

Ida was eating breakfast by herself the next morning, wondering what the fallout might be from the previous day's confrontations. She texted Landis. "Are you coming over today?" When he hadn't responded sixty minutes later she texted "Are you okay?"

The cottage held the empty, lonely feeling that always took over when someone left. They were grieving the death of Moses and now Peabody's absence would expand that emptiness. Today was a good day to vacuum and clean. Martha returned from her morning chores as Ida finished mopping the kitchen floor. They wordlessly poured themselves cups of coffee to sit for a spell.

"Did Romona say anything to you about Corey and Elsa this morning?" Ida initiated.

"Who's Corey?" asked Martha.

"The young man who went off the handle yesterday and shot Peabody! He was quite agitated. Remember – you sat with him and calmed him down," explained Ida.

Martha squinted her eyes at Ida. "Don't tell me what to remember! It's easy for you to say!"

"Sorry. He came to see Elsa and was very angry. He took the gun from Landis's jeep and swung it around in a crazed way. It was scary."

"And Peabody is dead! Shot!" Martha stated. "I do remember that."

"I think I'll be in shock for a time."

Martha got up quickly and pivoted. "Where's the bathroom?"

Ida pointed to Martha's bedroom. She followed Martha, waiting outside the door. When she heard the flush she darted back to her chair in the kitchen and resumed sipping her coffee with an air of nonchalance. "Martha, come finish your coffee."

"Stop telling me what to do! Why don't you just mind your own business?"

"We were having coffee together. I'm just trying to be helpful."

Martha appeared vexed. "Your help may not be wanted. Sometimes you're just bossy!"

"Well, I apologize if I am," Ida said, "but I'm just trying to do the right thing."

"Yes, you always try to do the right thing. Sometimes that's downright annoying!"

Ida rose to rinse and wash her cup. She accidentally dropped it with a clatter into the sink, disturbing the silent animosity between them.

"Don't I take medicine?" asked Martha. "When am I supposed to get that?"

"You've been taking it at lunch and dinner since we don't always know if you eat breakfast in the morning."

Ida picked up her phone again to check for texts. Landis had not responded to either query. Scuffling noises on their front porch made her think Peabody wanted in. *Good old dog.* Elsa and Annie appeared, helping themselves to coffee and gesturing toward the table, indicating both women should join them there.. Ida stood at the sink. She felt she'd already inserted herself too much into a complicated situation.

"Elsa has some things she needs to say to you," Annie explained, "including you too, Ida."

Elsa began, "I want to say I'm sorry for lying to both of you – Grandmom and you, Ida. First of all, I made up the story about sleeping around at fraternities because I thought I wouldn't have to deal with the paternity issue that way. It does happen. Romona thought it was a good story too. But it was a lie. I'm sorry."

Elsa looked to her mother for confirmation. Had she said what she needed to say?

Annie cleared her throat. "So…Elsa and Romona have strong feelings about raising this baby up together as a couple and they didn't want a man, any man, even the biological father, to be involved. But Elsa was involved with Corey last year. Romantically. She was in a relationship with him that he was committed to. She felt like it was over. But it's never over that easily when there is a pregnancy."

"Corey has a history of letting his emotions take charge," Elsa explained. "I always felt he was too sensitive about things and finally, he told me about it. Medication helps, but when he goes off his meds, he often gets irrational and angry. And when he gets angry, he stays off his meds. It's a bad cycle. I didn't want to be a part of that." Elsa took a few sips of coffee. "Shooting Peabody was way over the line. He's going to be sick about that for years. But he did it and he needs help."

"I'm trying to remember things that happened yesterday," Martha admitted. "I do remember Peabody getting shot – and the young man crying. There seemed to be lots of pain all around."

403

"Oh Grandmum. I'm so sorry that he came here."

"But didn't he come because of your baby? Aren't you having a baby?" Martha asked.

Elsa took her grandmother's hand and placed it on her belly. "Pretty obvious now. And Romona is my partner, she'll help me raise the baby. We don't want a man involved in this."

"Radical feminists!" Martha said dryly.

Where did that come from? A term from forty years ago.

"Seems like a little forgiveness needs to happen here," Martha stated. "If this young man is the father, you need to forgive him his terrible actions and find a way to let him be the father."

"But Romona and I don't want him in our lives," Elsa stated belligerently.

"I agree with your grandmom," said Annie. "Corey has a right to see his child after it's born."

"I know I don't really have a say in this," said Ida, "but it seems if you withhold that right from Corey, it will hurt him and the child in the long-run."

Elsa didn't respond. She was thinking hard.

"We'll set up a mediation time after Corey has stabilized. He may be pretty depressed after all this. Hell, I'm depressed!" Annie announced, standing up. "We don't have to make any final decisions today."

"I need some time," said Elsa. "I feel so bad about Peabody. I'm so sorry Ida."

"Thank Landis for us when you see him," Annie said to Ida. "We appreciate him driving over to help Rusty dig the grave for Peabody. Not easy with the ground getting hard."

Ida picked up her phone again to check his texts but there was nothing. "Okay sure, when I see him," Ida replied. She'd fix an early lunch for Martha, give her the meds, and maybe get her down for a nap. She wanted to catch him when he came.

***

Ida put on her jacket and went out on their porch to wait for his arrival. The old jeep came barreling up the lane, past the cottage, up to the stable. He got out quickly and went into the barn, not even a backward glance her way.

She searched through her recall of yesterday's events. Something she might have done or said. The gun. She remembered being adamant about him getting rid of it. Well, she was right. She had told him numerous times how she felt about handguns and he still carried it around in his jeep. He was not being sensitive to her feelings. She had been hurt and angry.

The pet cemetery was on the ridge behind the barn, at the border where the north pasture met trees. Ida walked slowly toward the men digging near the fence line. As she neared them her eyes fell on the swaddled lump lying near their feet. The acknowledgment that it was Peabody lying there dead overcame her. She stopped for a few minutes to breathe.

The men stopped shoveling when they spotted her. Rusty called, "Morning!"

Landis looked at her before heaving a breath, then kicked at a clod of dirt. "Coming to supervise?" he asked.

"I just wanted to express appreciation to you both for doing this." She rubbed her hands together. "Kind of brisk this morning."

"Has to be done," remarked Landis. "Some things can't be put off." He picked up his shovel to resume the task. Rusty seemed oblivious to their coldness.

"I won't keep you then," called Ida. "Landis, could you stop by later?"

"I'll see if there's time," he said. He was focused on that digging.

***

He knocked on the front door and waited. He'd not done that since they first began their courtship. He was wearing a green flannel shirt she'd never seen before, with horses running wildly across the front. She couldn't take her eyes off it as she opened the door to motion him in. "Come in, Landis. You don't have to knock."

Stepping into the mudroom, he halted to remove his hat and turn sideways to face her, his eyes on the floor.

"Won't you sit?"

"I prefer to stand, thanks," he said.

"What did I do?" Ida asked. "Is this about the gun?"

Landis looked at the door, then back to his feet.. "I'm going to Missoula for a few days to go through Dad's things. Then I'm helping a buddy on a pack trip. Elk hunting. I think you and I can use the break."

Her throat constricted. She instinctively reached out to touch his arm but he tensed up. He appeared to be studying the fine needlework in the rug beneath them.

"I'm sorry about Peabody. I know he meant a lot to you."

She swallowed. "It's just hard coming so close after losing Moses."

He nodded and said again, "I just think you and I could use a little break."

Ida bit her lip. "I think I said some things yesterday I shouldn't have said."

He sighed. "Maybe I can't be who you want me to be." He opened the door and walked out. Just like that.

Ida couldn't think. Her heart was too heavy. She stood watching him go. How had this happened? What had she done? What was wrong with him? Where was the playful teasing Landis who never took anything too seriously?

She heard his jeep drive away and went to lie down on her bed. Crying used to help in times like these. Tears now seemed just a waste of time. This is what the other side of love feels like. This Is grieving. *There was that stone weight in her belly. Love and loss. Here I am again*, she thought. *Here I am again. Oh damn, here I am again.*

SIX

Sidonnia became a responsible companion to Martha. She showed up at 6:45 every morning to get Martha onto the daily routines, starting with dressing and grooming. It was Sid who accompanied Martha to the barn and out to the pasture to bring in the horses. And it was Sid or the wranglers who lifted and carried the saddles these days.

But all it took was one morning for Martha to forget to wait for Sid. She was out early in the barn heaving a fifty-pound saddle off the wood rack by herself when it crashed to the tack room floor. Collapsing to the ground, rolling onto one side, Martha lay groaning in despair and pain until Sidonnia found her. They suspected the rotator cuff, but to be sure, they packed ice in a towel for Martha's shoulder, and helped her into Ida's car for the long trek to the emergency room. Annie made lunches for them to eat at the hospital. After Ida deposited Martha with nurses at the Emergency Room entrance, she parked the car and hustled back only to be handed a packet of papers to read and sign. They searched through Martha's bag for her Medicare card and skimmed over the list of questions, checking yes, no, maybe. No option for "Don't remember". Was there an easier way? Surely there was.

They ate the lunch of sandwiches and fruit. "Any cookies or chocolate in there?" asked Martha.

"Are you kidding? Annie packed these. I'll go look for candy bars," said Ida. As she got up, a nurse brought a wheelchair to take Martha away for tests. Ida found the vending machines near the exit and selected crispy chocolate wafers. It was day four since Landis had left. She apologized in her mind for what she had said although she felt he was still wrong about the gun. He was being petty. As empty as she felt without him, there was a moral righteousness to her pain. She was a victim of his obstinate devotion to a toy that killed.

Ida picked up a magazine and paged through it. Who were these celebrities anyway? Who cared if their children ate only eggs from free-range chickens? Did we really need to know about all the many nips and tucks they'd undergone? And what concern is it that we know if someone is multi-orgasmic? What was more depressing? Reading these magazines or the news of the day?

She didn't want to think about Landis. She tried to focus on the silly articles. She even read the advertisements. But she missed him. He would help her find humor in these things. Now she just felt sadness – the whole world a pit of scum and pleasure-seeking hedonists.

A nurse came to get Ida and walked her to the room where Martha was attempting to put on her sweater by herself. A young physician entered the room, accompanied by an electronic chart on wheels.

"Looks like you have damaged tendons in the rotator cuff." He showed them a graphic picture of a shoulder sliced away to indicate various muscles and joints with arrows pointing to specific spots. "We just treat this type of injury with physical therapy and anti-inflammatories. I'll give you a prescription and also a referral for physical therapy."

"I'm on medication for something else," Martha said. "Ida, can you let him know the names of the other drugs?"

Ida dug around in her bag for the written information and shared this with the doctor.

"The anti-inflammatories won't interact with the other meds." He nodded at them both and was off. Off to his next patient and the busy-ness of life.

On the way home, Martha turned philosophical. "Just one more thing to adjust to in this old age." She munched on the chocolate wafer. "Now I can really order you around."

"What's that supposed to mean?" asked Ida. She was still sensitive from the remark about her bossiness.

"Just that I get to order you around," replied Martha. "It's about time."

"About time I do your bidding?" Ida grinned.

"Damn right!" Martha exclaimed. "And I don't want Frodo helping me anymore either."

"What do you mean?"

"I told him not to come by anymore."

"You're going to break his heart. Tommy adores you."

Martha viewed the scenery breezing by her window. "He doesn't need to be my care-taker. I don't want him to do that."

"I think we're going to need to hire someone – at least for the nights."

Martha nodded. "I think I'll move into Moses's old room. He had that bed with the gadgets. He had the walk-in tub. It's closer to your room too."

Ida wanted to be cautious in how she responded. "Maybe Sidonnia could move into your old room – to help us both. What do you think of that?"

"I like Sid."

"Well, we'd have to pay her more…maybe free room and board would be negotiable. We'll have to talk with both Annie and Sid."

"I like Sid." Martha seemed to have settled the matter.

They drove in silence for a few miles until Martha asked, "What happened between you and Landis?"

Ida's eyes were on the highway before her. She wanted to tell Martha it might be over but she couldn't form the words. "I don't know."

"I can't remember but I know something happened that night that boy came to the ranch. I know you were angry about something that night. I miss Landis." Martha unbuttoned her coat and fanned her face. "It's warm in here."

Ida turned down the heat and settled back. She didn't want to trouble Martha with her silly romantic troubles. Sometimes they seemed silly. Romantic? That wasn't the word for what she felt for Landis. She was pretty sure she loved him now. She felt the symptoms of grief when he left her. The numbness and hurt. She hadn't even begun the five stages yet.

After hobbling into the cottage, Martha sat down in her favorite chair and clapped her hands. She called out, "A drink! I demand a drink! Where are my servants?"

"Okay, okay, Your Highness," Ida responded as she brought her a glass of wine. "Will this do?"

Martha sipped it gently. "Ah, yes, quite nice! I could get used to this!"

***

Martha did not let her injury limit her mobility. She devised her own physical therapy. It was called *brushing the horses down*. In the beginning, she could just barely raise her arm to their bellies. By the third week she lifted her arm and shoulder to brush higher each day. She kicked herself for not making an ink mark on the horses to show her progress.

In the afternoon Martha napped and then held court in the living room. On Thursday when Ida was getting ready to go to the guest house for the social hour, there was a knock at their door. "Come in!" Martha called from her throne.

Ida opened the door to Josephine holding a covered casserole dish before her. "Rusty told me Martha was a little under the weather and I thought I'd bring something over for the two of you."

"That's very kind, Josephine, thank you!" Ida took the dish from her to refrigerate. "Come see Martha in the living room."

"I won't stay long. I just came to drop that dish off... vegetable lasagne. I looked high and low for a vegetarian recipe and I hope that one is okay. Well...Hello Martha. How are you?"

"You might as well come sit down," said Martha.

"It's Josephine. We missed you at the last WoCA meeting!"

Martha looked confused but she prattled on. "Ok. I know you. Josephine. We've had our little spats. What's WoCA again?"

Josephine glanced at Ida. "Our group – Women of a Certain Age! You gave me a hard time when we discussed the topic of our bodies. Do you remember that?"

"I gave you a hard time?" she asked. "Was it because of your pretty face?"

Josephine winced. "Something like that. It doesn't matter. You don't have to like me. I just wanted to bring something for the two of you."

Martha leaned over and spoke clearly to Josephine. "Oh, I like you, I just wish you'd like yourself without having to doll yourself up."

"I guess we just won't agree on some things," Josephine replied. "I like to doll myself up -as you say."

"You don't have to agree with me. But you'd be plenty pretty just being yourself."

"Okay Martha, let's leave it at that." Ida had come into the room with iced tea.

"Well okay," said Martha. "Have some iced tea."

"Oh no, I need to go, but I hope you take care of yourself and get back to normal soon." She edged towards the door.

"Too late for that," Martha chuckled. "Too late for me to get back to normal."

"Thank you so much," Ida said again, seeing her to the door. "It was kind of you Josephine."

"I just wanted to do something," Josephine repeated. "Even if we don't always agree."

NOVEMBER

ONE

Landis called two weeks after their last encounter. She'd texted him twice but there was no response. He asked if he could come over some evening.

"Why not tonight?" she asked. He said he'd be there by seven.

Where could they have a quiet place to talk? Martha would be in the living room of the cottage with the fire going. There was a cold wind kicking up from the west. Snow was expected within the next twenty-four hours.

She bundled into her heavy coat and walked out to the jeep when he arrived. She motioned toward the guest house, suggesting it might be more private. There was no one around. Once in the great room, she turned on another lamp and they threw their coats over a chair. Ida sank into the cushions in the far corner of the sofa while Landis took a hard-backed chair across from her. He sat straight and rigid.

Her voice shook but she wanted to get on with it. "So Landis, I can only think that you're pretty upset with me. I'm sorry."

"Why are you saying you're sorry when you don't even seem to know what for?" he asked.

His irritation was clear. She said nothing.

He bit his lip. "Okay that wasn't necessary. I apologize. I guess I have some pent-up emotions." He expelled a long breath. "Well, where do I start?"

There was another awkward moment. Ida was not about to make any attempt to speak. She folded her hands on her lap, looking hard at the blue veins and the age spots. She was old.

"First of all, I care about you – deeply. You've got to know that. But…well… it just got to me that you always have to be in control."

She opened her mouth but he interrupted, "Just let me get this out. You and I usually talk back and forth, but I have to get some things off my chest. Will you hear me out?"

She nodded.

"The day with the gun…well, that put me over the edge. You said something like - if you love me, you'll get rid of that gun. You gave me an ultimatum. You *scolded* me. I know you were hurt and you needed to blame me for the fact Peabody was dead. I take responsibility for putting it back in the jeep. It was my gun yes, but Corey was a disturbed young man. I was hurt too. And then you basically gave me an ultimatum. So I said to myself – get some space. Give yourself time to think. So I went away to get some distance."

He stood up and paced back and forth behind the chair. "The thing is…I love you. I know that. But I can live without you. You're always little Ms. Perfect. And I don't mean that in a mean way." He put his hands up to his face and rubbed them across his cheek. "I went on a pack trip last week, something I do every fall. You know what that is?"

"A hunting trip?" she asked.

"Yep, it's elk hunting season. And a big deal around here. We take pack horses and mules and go up pretty high in the Rockies to hunt elk for the week. I shoot with a rifle. I kill. We haul 'em back on horseback to get skinned and cut up for elk meat. I help out a buddy who does this for big spenders every year."

She was listening, wondering where he was going with this.

"I'm just telling you this because it's something I like to do. I like to hunt. I didn't share that because you get so righteous about guns. And maybe I should have taken the Glock out of my jeep but I didn't. I'm not sure why. I suppose I don't want to do everything you ask me to do. Maybe that's part of it."

She shifted, trying to sit forward on the couch so she wouldn't lose herself in the cushions. He continued, "I like to play my music with my band and I wish you'd come hear us more. I like to go off walking in deep woods, and I think you might too. I thought we had a pretty good thing going – but not without a little more give and take. Mostly give."

He paused and looked down at his hands. He seemed not to know what to do with them. He curled his fingers around the back of the rigid chair and looked into her eyes. "Okay, that's enough from me. Now, now you can talk."

She looked back down at her hands. "What you say is true. I know I can get a little self-righteous." She lifted both hands and pushed the hair away from her face. "Please sit down."

He stood with his hands on the back of the chair.

"Sorry," she said, "not a demand. Won't you please sit down?"

He lips curved ever so slightly but he remained standing, not moving from behind the chair.

"I've been berating myself for that ultimatum. And I've been thinking about that stupid gun."

He stared at her, but he was listening.

"It is stupid. It is a *stupid thing* but it's what it represents. To me, it's this weapon that hurts and maims and kills. To you, it's your freedom, it's a power. It's a right. I'm not going to take that away. Nobody is taking it away."

"That's absolutely true. This gun thing is a symbol to both of us."

"And it's your decision what you do with it," she said. "I apologize for my remarks about it but I was hurt. And mad and I needed someone to blame. Peabody…"

"I'm truly sorry about Peabody too," he said.

"But I know I sounded like I scolded you. I was out of line. I had no right. I crossed a boundary."

He was quiet for a spell as he studied the ceiling, but his words came out slowly. "I guess I'm kind of scolding you now. It's a loaded word. But it feels like you're the one in control, who gets to decide the boundaries – or whatever.

When you told me you never wanted to get married, never would, I thought it kind of endearing, but now I think you just want to be in control. You can keep me out. Never let someone else really share in your life, never have to compromise for anyone else."

"Wow," she said, "that's quite an accusation."

"It's not an accusation," he said. "See – even that word – accusation – keeps me at a distance. It's my *observation*. So yeah, it may not be true, it's subjective, but it's my truth, my perspective."

"What do you want to do?" she asked. "Does this mean we're done? Our relationship is over?" She hated this. She didn't want to hear his answer.

"Well," he paused and sighed, "I do like the fact that you're asking me."

"I'll turn everything I say into a question if it means you won't give up on me," she said.

He sat down again on the straight chair across from her. "Just don't scold me. When I don't meet your expectations, don't scold me."

She looked into those dark eyes and asked, "Do I get to tell you not to scold me too, or do I have to ask you not to scold me?"

He shook his head. "Okay, tit for tat. You have a point. You and I are so different, but we've been pretty good together."

"Yes, I think…" she stopped and reframed her remark. "Don't you think we're respectful of our differences most of the time?

"You don't have to have the high moral ground all of the time do you?"

"Martha told me I'm bossy. I thought it was her LBD talking, but she's right. And you are right. And I don't think I'm little Ms. Perfect!"

"Pretty near," he teased with a straight face.

"Do you really want me to stop arguing with you about things I believe?"

His smile twitched. "See – you asked me and now we can agree. I don't want you to ever stop arguing with me. Challenge me. You can cuss me out. Just don't give me ultimatums."

"Cussing's got to be more fun than scolding."

He leaned back in his chair and folded his arms. She sensed he wasn't through. He cleared his throat. "I was thinking about you on my pack trip. I had some time to think while we're riding for miles."

"And?"

"Remember the time you told me how at peace you felt sitting with someone who was near death. You described it as a sacred stillness. Do you remember that?"

She nodded. "And you told me you felt a kind of stillness when you were alone in the forest. That you felt a presence that almost embraced you?"

"You remembered." He was touched but he remained stiffly upright, his arms crossed over his chest. "But what I was thinking was how difficult it must have been to find the strength to sit with those who was dying, folks leaving you for good – and doing this time and again in your work. And then I thought about you moving here, to this wild country, and learning to adjust."

She took a breath and re-crossed her legs. "I don't know," she finally said. "I've had to throw myself open to a lot of unknowns since moving up here. It was scary but I'm learning. I'm trying to be open."

"Yeah," he said, "Me too. I want to be more open to learning too."

"Sometimes the weight of the world does seem awfully heavy," she sighed.

"The weight of the world or the weight of those closest to you?"

Now it was Ida who leaned back and folded her arms. "Yes, especially when they always seem to be leaving - even if it's to go off elk hunting."

He shook his head and spoke to the rug on the floor. "How can I stay angry with you?"

He slipped across to sit beside her on the couch, putting his old arms around her. He took her wrist and with thumb and index finger encircled it. "Look at your tiny wrist."

"What?" she asked. "What's wrong?"

"No, I'm in awe. Look at how tiny your wrist is between my fingers."

The physical dimensions of their slightly arthritic hands together; one large, rough and hairy, the other with short fingers and little wrist, momentarily held their attention. This quiet aloneness together assumed a new shape of intimacy for them, the shared silence of post-conversational intercourse. They were content to sit side by side, holding hands as darkness enveloped them. Light from the single lamp across the room cast the room in autumnal hues.

I want to show you something," Landis said suddenly, rising and pulling her up with him. He grabbed their coats.

"Right now?"

"Yes. Now. Follow me." It was dark and windy outside so he took her hand and led her with his flashlight illuminating the way to the jeep. He opened the glove compartment and handed her a shiny garden trough. He shone his flashlight on the object.

She fingered the heavy metal and knew instinctively it had been his Glock 19. The gray black was still there welded into the handle.

"I just can't blame Peabody's death on this thing being in the wrong hands at the wrong time," said Landis. "If this gun hadn't been there in the first place…"

"…and they shall turn their swords into plough shares," murmured Ida. She turned it over and over in her hands. "How did you do this?"

"I'm not a welder but a friend of mine helped do it. He thought I was nuts but I told him, you know…what we do for love."

"This, this is just so…I don't know…so powerful."

"I looked up it up online – what to do with a gun when you no longer want it. There are lots of creative options out there. But I thought you'd appreciate the Biblical metaphor, a lapsed Mennonite, and all that."

"Even a judgmental, self-righteous one."

"Only once in a while," he smiled.

"I appreciate this very much," she said humbly. "It's a lovely image."

"Remember when we kidded about being like trees and you wanted to be the cottonwood?"

"Seeing spirits of the dead wisping into the air?" Both turned their eyes skyward, as if to glimpse a remnant soul on a rapture voyage.

"Well there's that," he said taking the tool from her hands and placing it on the roof of his jeep. "but the cottonwood looks forward to its fullest growth the last years of its life."

Ida turned back towards Landis. "Are you making that up?"

He held up his hand. "Honest. I read it somewhere."

"Well, I like that idea. There's more to look forward to in the old growth, in the final years."

"Yep, it's a mystery to me," he nodded. "I can accept it in the science of trees, but with us, the regenerating of feelings and thoughts, well the physics of it is just a mystery."

"It's painful getting old. I feel like I've finally figured some things out and now I don't have much time left. Time – that robber baron!"

He refrained from touching her and leaned against the jeep, crossing his arms. "I wish I had more time with you. Be with you more. I do wish that."

'I won't leave Martha."

I wouldn't ask you to."

"Thank you for the garden tool, the plough share," she said reaching up with her index finger to trace his facial lineaments. It felt boldly intimate, in the dark, with the wind whispering overhead. "Maybe I will have to re-purpose my thinking about marriage. If you could turn a sword into a plowshare for me, then I suppose I can think about changing a never into a maybe."

He looked at her sideways. "Don't toy with me."

"I said maybe," she responded as she laid her head against his chest and put her arms around his waist. "I can hear that old ticker in there. It's picking up its pace."

His head rested upon her head. "You are toying with me."

She looked up and said, "Only because I love you. And if I ever would change my mind about marriage, I think you're the one to change it."

"But you need more time to decide?"

"I'll just have to wait to be asked," she replied. "I mean I don't want to be bossy."

Landis heaved a sigh. She couldn't tell if it was one of relief or exasperation or contentment, but he seemed satisfied to just hold her there, letting her listen to his old heart beat in a rhythm of its own odd syncopation.

THANKSGIVING

Ida pulled out heavy coats from the front hall closet. "How about a walk this afternoon?"

"Okay, but we'd better bundle up good." Martha dug through the basket of gloves and scarves. "Where is my red stocking cap? I'm not going if I can't find that one."

"Here it is – lodged inside a sleeve of your parka. You must've stuffed it in there yesterday so you could find it today. Pretty smart."

"Yeah, that's right," Martha said, taking the coat and hat from her. "Butter me up. Tell me how smart I am as I lose my mind piece by piece."

"Oh stop it. Your self-pity is getting very annoying."

It was Thanksgiving Eve, and the late afternoon held that ambiance of amorphous gray so prevalent in November. Any distillation of sunlight filtered sparsely down between the arms of the rooted firs and aspens reaching upward. The women moved instinctively closer together as one force, to take on the bluster of the wind, or the forest shadows meddling with them as they made their way. With no snowfall the past weeks the brown earth provided solid footing on a favorite trail, one they'd ridden on horses many times. .

Martha took Ida's arm as they trudged up a rocky ridge. "Sorry," she said, "I should have brought my walking stick."

"I keep them by the door to remind us, but here we are, out on a rocky trail without them."

"I need to get you up on the horses more often. You've slacked off," said Martha.

"It's been too cold.. I'm not as tough as you are."

"Think of it as therapy for me. Maybe then you'd give a little more of your time."

"You're so devious," said Ida. "Guilt – the old manipulator,"

"I'm sorry about all this though," Martha interjected. "I'm happy as hell you're here and living with me, but I'm sorry for putting you through this stupid illness thing."

Ida halted in her steps. "Look, I signed on to whatever was going to happen to either of us. It could be me next. And then what? Right now – I'm brimming over with happiness."

Martha's breathing was labored as she stopped for a few minutes. "You say that but who knows how fast I'm going to go down. I may have a personality change and become mean and cranky. Or should I say meaner and crankier?"

"Is that possible?" Ida squinted. "Whatever you do, just don't cut me out."

"There you go being bossy again." Martha dug in her pocket to retrieve an old-fashioned white handkerchief. She took her time refolding it before wiping her nose. "Sometimes I'm kind of scared of what's happening to me, but mostly I'm worried that you'll be dealing with a hyperized – is there such a word? A hyper-sized me?"

"Don't flatter yourself," said Ida. "You've been larger than life for years and we dealt with you. This is nothing. We love you anyway and that goes a long way."

"Ah love," responded Martha. "Well, we'll see. I'm glad Elsa's baby will be here soon to take some of this attention away from me."

"She looks ready to burst and January is still aways off."

A tree root caught Ida's boot, forcing her to the ground, released from Martha's grasp. "Damn, didn't see that one!"

"Why didn't I catch you?" Martha asked.. She stepped back, confused.

Ida sat on her rump, removing her mittens. Her palms were scraped and her dignity bruised. "I'm no worse for the wear." She glanced up. "Martha! It's okay! Just help me up!"

Martha paused before bending over to help Ida, a haze of fear visible in her eyes. "I just had a memory of when I was little and I'd fallen on the gravel in our lane.. My mother was there saying 'Get up! Stand up!' She wouldn't help me and I cried harder. But I finally got up and she hugged me. She didn't hug me until I got up by myself."

Ida brushed off the snow and dust from her pants. "Do you think your mom was trying to teach you something?"

Martha shook her head. "I don't think she could help me. She didn't have the strength. She was dying, but I didn't know that then. Why did I think of this now?"

"That seems like a good memory. It's one of kindness with your mother," said Ida holding Martha's hand in hers. "Were you very young?"

"I must have been only five or six. Mom was sick for several years. Dad put a hospital bed in our living room, a bed like I use now that goes up and down. Think of that!"

"Do you remember her in that room?"

"There was a big picture window. Dad rolled her bed next to it. She'd watch me out the window. I'd play in the front yard. I can see her now, watching me, clear as a bell."

"That's comforting isn't it?" asked Ida. "Isn't that a good memory?"

Martha pensively watched the trees swaying about them. "Dad hung a tire from the old oak in the front yard. I had all kinds of imaginary friends and I played around that tire swing. And Mom watched me."

"I'm going to write down your memories that you tell me. We'll keep a record." Ida swung her arm over Martha's shoulder for a strong sideways embrace. She turned her around for the return journey home, their eyes adjusting to the shifting dusky light.

"Look at that fat old moon trying to get itself up into the sky." Ida pointed. "Let's use it as a frame of reference on our way home." They made their way cautiously, still clinging firmly to one another.

"I'm never been one to talk about God but I feel like there's something with me these days," rambled Martha. "Something walking me through this...this thing."

"This thing being life?"

"Well, that too, but I was thinking more about this brain thing, this dementia."

"But feeling like something is leading you?"

"Well, no…more like with me, yes, *with me!*" She seemed pleased she'd nailed it. "If it is God, then that's fine. If it's a psychological crutch, that's alright too."

A flapping of frantic wings startled them as it whooshed from a tree, swooning above them towards higher ground.

"I saw it but I could hardly hear it," said Ida.

"A gray owl," whispered Martha. "It's so quiet when it flies because its feathers are so soft."

"Ah, an owl. That surely means something!"

"You can be sarcastic,but in Native American lore, owls come to those who need to let go of something that's no longer needed. It's a message to face our fears. Or maybe for me to face my fears."

"It's a message to face our fears. Or maybe for me to face my fears."

"You just said you felt like a presence was with you these days, and to me, it comes back to what I've called invisible threads."

"You always had a bit of the mystic in you," said Martha.

"Oh, I like that! A mystic!" Ida exclaimed. "I think, though, all of us have a bit of the mythical Mary in us, carrying around the possibility to bring something into this world to make it a better place."

"Birthing and re-birthing the divine?"

"Maybe just the possibility to see or feel the divine, the *something* beyond."

"Like an owl swooshing by?" asked Martha.

"Maybe. Or barn swallows." She stopped to smile. "But the older I become, the more I get this feeling – looking back – that there was more to it all than just us."

"Well barn swallows or owls, I've seen them. They may not be invisible threads but they seem to be pulling me through." Martha leaned against Ida's side. They stopped once again and regarded the view back over the valley through the wooded terrain. Darkness was falling earlier than they'd anticipated.

"I also think," Ida went on, "about our roots and the connectedness of those threads of faith. Some things are just beyond words."

"Well, God needs to pull us back through these dark woods," said Martha. "Before we end up a feast for wolves or bears."

"Okay, let's throw it out to the universe right now. God, can you help us measly mortals get back home?" Ida spoke as if she was addressing the United Nations. "Yes, you've got famine and war and injustice and cruelty to work on, but could you take a moment to help these old ladies find their way home?"

Martha punched her friend, as she had so many times before, her signature affectionate fist to the arm. "Don't overdo it.

"Oh look! See the lights of the ranch now! A sign if there ever was one."

"It does look peaceful down there."

"Breathe in the smell of these trees." They paused to take in the scents about them. "You know, when I worked in hospice, we often asked our patients to think about what a good day might look like. Like – if you could create the scenario of a good day, what would you be doing?"

"I don't have to think about that," replied Martha. "I'd be sitting on our porch or in our living room by the fire with you."

"All day?"

"If I had to." Martha smiled at Ida. "That's a social worker question. If I really had an entire day and I felt strong enough, I'd do what I' do every day — Get up and go out with the horses, come back to the cottage for lunch, take a nap, have a glass of wine in the late afternoon, have some soup for supper, then sit with you in the evening. There, that's a good day."

Ida couldn't dispute any of that. She'd have said the same thing - except for the horses and well, she'd have put Landis into the time frame sometime, preferably in the evening.

Martha began singing the familiar refrain,as they continued on their way. Their harmony may have been off, but the intentions were pure. "It is well, it is well, with my soul." Nearing the barn, Ida spotted the familiar mud-splattered jeep. She chided herself for noting how the thought of Landis created a visceral stirring in her body. *How can that still be?*

Lights in the barn led them to where he was sitting on a bale of hay with two white fur-balls prancing on all fours in a stall.

"Baby goats!" exclaimed Martha. She reached out, falling to her knees to wrap her arms around a little one. "Landis, what have you done?"

"Not sure what I've done," he said, "but I thought I'd see if you'd make room for these two."

"Don't tell me." Ida said. "They were homeless waifs and you thought of us."

"Something like that," he replied. "I got them from a kid in 4-II in Missoula who raises goats and sheep. Do you think you can manage to take care of these two? They're neutered males."

Martha scooped up one of the tiny things but soon put him down again where it ran on wobbly legs over to its friend. The two nudged one another, sniffing, butting around the humans. One circled about Martha again and again. Ida sat down beside Landis who handed her a bottle of milk. She held it out and the other goat waddled toward her, eyes on something familiar.

"These are called Nigerian Dwarf goats. They're pretty popular at the livestock shows with the white bodies and black heads," he explained.

"Looks like they'll eat anything." observed Martha, her little one nibbling some old hay.

"I brought some grain for the next few months. They'll eat fresh grass in the spring."

"They're plenty entertaining!" observed Ida. "We could watch them play for hours."

"So could lots of predators." Landis nodded toward the dark woods.

"They can have this stall," said Martha. "They're safe in here."

Landis stretched out his legs and rubbed his hands together. "I wanted to give you both something – especially after Peabody." He swallowed.

431

Ida's eyes were on her frolicking goats but she said, "You are just too cool, Landis. Isn't he cool Martha?"

Martha patted Landis's shoulder. "You're a pretty good guy."

"You know," Ida wasn't finished praising, "like in the movies. A sensitive Humphrey Bogart. Just so cool."

Landis put his arm around her and hugged her tight. "I'll get you a whole bunch of goats if I get this kind of respect."

"This is enough."

She cuddled up against him, retrieving images from the last year in her new Montana life. Happiness comes on so unexpectedly, but it comes to everyone at some time in life. And she was thankful. So much had taken place in this past year, so much old growth in this last part of her life. There would be sadness and grieving, and there would be anger and disappointment, but it was for these small moments in-between the connected dots that brought richness to this thing called life. She was open to the invisible threads and to the pulling of the presence that brought the mystery into focus. This is what is given for now; this is life in its simple gifts. This was more than enough.

ACKNOWLEDGEMENTS

I am thankful for Peter, my longtime rock, who supported me through this writing project even when I was in my "wob" (writing obsessed bubble). My sons and their respective "families" were often on my mind throughout this book for their intregrity in the choices they've made in their lives..

I owe much to my friend Joy, the real Martha Joy, who is so full of goodness, no one would believe her credibility as a character. Thank you for a rekindled friendship, your knowledge about Montana's people and geography, and your patience in my lack of horse sense. You are one of the invisible threads in my life.

I owe gratitude to my parents, J. Winfield and Marguerite Fretz, for the values they instilled in me. I wonder what they would've thought if they had lived to read this book of fiction.

My Mennonite heritage with its deep roots and world-wide branches has often left me conflicted. However, when I return to the basic tenets which focus on agape love, peace non-violence, and remembering "the least of these" - as Jesus so often taught through his simple and sometimes puzzling parables – I am humbled and inspired.

I am appreciative of Janet Umble Reedy's trusting willingness to have her beautiful poem, *A New Thing is Creating* shared in an early chapter. Hopefully, she will now go on to publish many of her other treasured poems.

A nod of affirmation must be directed to those who have passed on - my grandmothers Sarah Steiner Geiger and Ella Landis Fretz, as well as all of my aunts who made appearances in various ways through characters who happened by– Alice, Martha, Ida, Ethel, Millie, Gladys, Beulah, Mabel, and Eva. Other family names also appear without any discernable intention.

Thanks to the many friends whose eyes did not glaze over when I spoke about this project with single-minded focus. It meant a lot that you feigned interest.

A thank-you also to the folks at Friesen Press for your help in the self-publishing of this novel. My editor's feedback was the guidance I required at several important stages in my writing. The staff is always friendly and helpful – and you know who you are.

ABOUT THE AUTHOR

An English teacher in public schools for many years, Sara Fretz-Goering observed from her personal reading a dearth of books with likable, older women characters. She decided to write one, drawing inspiration from memories of friendships with women over the years. The themes explored in *Ida and Martha* overlap with experiences throughout her life. Sara's first book, *Simple Life Fretz: A Kitchen Table Memoir of the first Mennonite Sociologist,* was published in 2016 as a tribute to her father. She resides with her husband in a large house near a wooded trail outside of Washington DC where she walks daily with her golden retriever.